SMILE AND BE A VILLAIN

Yves Donlon

Copyright © 2024 by Yves Donlon

All rights reserved.

CONTENTS

Trigger Warnings — VII

Historical Note — IX

Dedication — XIII

ACT 1

1. scene one — #
2. scene two — #
3. scene three — #
4. scene four — #
5. scene five — #
6. scene six — #
7. scene seven — #
8. scene eight — #
9. scene nine — #
10. scene ten — #

ACT II

11. scene one   #
12. scene two   #
13. scene three   #
14. scene four   #
15. scene five   #
16. scene six   #
17. scene seven   #
18. scene viii   #
19. scene nine   #
20. scene ten   #

ACT III

21. scene one   #
22. scene two   #
23. scene three   #
24. scene four   #
25. scene five   #
26. scene six   #
27. scene seven   #
28. scene eight   #

29. scene nine #
30. scene ten #

ACT IV

31. scene one #
32. scene two #
33. scene three #
34. scene four #
35. scene five #
36. scene six #
37. scene seven #
38. scene eight #
39. scene nine #
40. scene ten #

ACT V

41. Chapter 41 #
42. scene two #
43. scene three #
44. scene four #
45. scene five #
46. scene six #

47.	scene seven	#
48.	scene eight	#
49.	scene nine	#
50.	scene ten	#
51.	finale	#
Acknowledgements		482
About the Author		485

Trigger Warnings

This is a work of historical fiction, which contains the following potentially triggering material:

- Period-typical queerphobia

- Off-page outing

- Emotional abuse

- Physical assault

- Death

- Substance abuse

- Mentions of slavery

- References to anti-semitism (specifically of the expulsion of Jewish people from European countries)

- Animal death

- On-page depiction of war.

Historical Note

First of all, this is a work of fiction. I have drop-kicked many important historical figures out of the way to make room for Hamlet and Ophelia to exist in 1530s Europe, and I have relentlessly bullied many more until they fit the shapes I needed them to.

I did a lot of research for this book over a period of three years. Almost all of these materials were accessed thanks to JSTOR's COVID research policies and the academic institutions I studied (and worked) at: Trinity College Dublin and the University of York. They probably would have preferred I use my library access for my actual degrees, not to write weird queer Hamlet books; regardless, they both let me graduate, and one of them even employed me, so who's winning now?

Kronborg Castle
In the 1530s, Kronborg Castle would have been known as Krogen Fortress. It was not turned into the castle

that stands today until the 1570s, when renovations were commissioned by Frederik II. I refer to the castle as 'Kronborg' throughout this book, and used the floor plan of Kronborg as the basis for my castle. There isn't a complex reason for doing this: it made sense, in terms of the research resources available, and also Kronborg read better to me than Krogen. I also think the castle Shakespeare imagined was probably closer to Kronborg than Krogen, and I thought I should probably give William *something* here.

12 Collegienstraße

Hamlet lives with Rosencrantz and Guildenstern at 12 Collegienstraße, Wittenberg. This is sometimes referred to as Hamlethaus, because according to popular legend he lived here. It is also meant to be the location of some law tutorials for University of Wittenberg students. It seemed like the right place for my Hamlet to live.

Historical Figures

There are some real people depicted in this book, but those depictions aren't meant to be unbiased or entirely true to life. Martin Luther was a divisive figure in his day, and I have depicted him as such; Philip Melancthanon *was* actually lecturing at Wittenberg, but his lectures might have been very interesting for all I know—I wasn't there.

War

In 'Hamlet', the war is about thirty years prior to the events of the play. I wanted to explore the play as a story about trauma, conflict, and nationhood, so I moved the war forward. I think there's a really interesting story somewhere in keeping the war where it was and looking at military fathers and 'impotent' sons, but that wasn't my story, so I changed it. I hope to read something like that soon.

Marginalised Communities in *Smile and Be a Villain*

The 1530s were a painful time for many of Europe's marginalised communities. The balance of power was constantly shifting, often violently. This book references characters of various marginalised backgrounds, and modern readers will probably note the importance of religion to this story. Religion was, in medieval and early modern Europe, what empires were built on.

I wanted to show that people from different backgrounds *did* exist in Europe's past, but also that not everyone lived a safe or comfortable life. Yes, many European cities were more cosmopolitan and diverse than you might have thought; however, horrible abuses were also carried out against communities and individuals.

This book isn't intended to make light of this, nor does it ignore it (I hope). The characters in this story are overwhelmingly deeply privileged, even when they are otherwise marginalised; I hope this shines through in their stories, and I hope you'll join me to explore that further in Book 2.

To everyone who helped along the way.

ACT 1

SCENE ONE
prologue

The day they sent Crown Prince Hamlet away, there was no sunlight. The air shivered, and thunder roared through the sky like a drum, and the rain came pouring down as if even the clouds wept to see him leave.

A crowd gathered in the courtyard to see the young prince off. Those assembled appreciated the gravity of this moment: the only living offspring of their king, still half a boy, sent away in disgrace. It was terrible. They leaned in to hear his voice better.

Prince Hamlet raised his sodden head. His dark curls stuck fast to the elegant slope of his forehead, like so many curving thorns laid flat against his skin.

"Father," Hamlet said, barely audible over the downpour. The crowd craned their necks so that they could better see the dejected expression upon their prince's face. "Father, I don't want to go."

The king did not respond. He looked down at the boy he called his son with something like disgust and remembered a time when this fool had sat on his knee and played with his crown. There was a time when the boy, named for him, was not spoiled and weak.

The rain pattered against the cobblestones between them. The prince's words hung in the air, unanswered, until the king's hands twitched by his sides.

The crowd paused on a breath: did he mean to hit the boy? No one wanted to miss the moment of flesh connecting with flesh, when perhaps the king's rings might cut the boy's sharp cheekbone and scar it a deep red. That would be a terrible thing to see.

They made sure not to blink.

Disappointingly, the old king only pulled his son into a sudden embrace.

They collided and the father's hot breath stained his son's ear. The prince tensed, rearing back, but his king's hand at the back of his neck held him firmly in place. It was like watching the master of hounds drown the runt of the litter. The boy squirmed, resistance in every muscle; his father held him fast.

In a voice meant only for one, the king murmured, "Bring any more shame on this family and I will ensure that you never return to this castle. Consider yourself no closer to ruling this kingdom than any dog on the street. Do you understand?"

The prince was bundled into a carriage that, despite its rich velvet interior (or possibly thanks to it) smelled faintly of wet animal. When the door of the carriage slammed shut behind him, Hamlet leaned to gaze out the window. He did not dare to shed a tear.

The four foreboding spires of Kronborg Castle pierced the sky in front of him. Its huge square form dominated the skyline and the sea behind. In all his life, he had never gone more than a few weeks without seeing the flags whipping in the breeze above the gates. He had no idea how long it might be before he would be allowed to return.

He forced away the lump in his throat. He had decided, the day he was caught, that he would never again feel anything at all. It was proving more difficult than he had anticipated.

The carriage began to move. It was like a sudden hunger overtook him: he devoured the castle with his eyes, trying to paint its shadows and highlights in his memory. It was only when they had turned away down a narrow street, the carriage bumping over the cobbles, that he realised he should have done the same with his parents, who were by now entirely out of sight.

But there was still one other person he wanted to see before he left Helsingør forever. He didn't need to memorise the angles of her face, the full sweep of her gown. He knew her face better than his own, and still he needed to see her, just once more.

She stood exactly where he'd expected her to: on the steps of the church, in her finest green gown. Hamlet's eyes found her as soon as she came into view, as if drawn there by some supernatural force.

Ophelia's bright blue eyes were cool. Her only acknowledgement was a dip of the chin before she raised her hood against the rain and turned away.

Hamlet withdrew the piece of parchment Ophelia had tucked beneath his collar early one morning, the birds singing furiously in the garden above them, the grass pleasantly scratchy beneath their bare feet. He remembered the furious line of her mouth, her silent anger as she scribbled the words and thrust them at him, where she knew the parchment would scrape against his skin.

It felt like years ago, but in truth it was only a few weeks ago that they'd stood in that garden. The parchment was creased and marked from hasty storage and tears.

It read:

Doubt thou the stars are fire,
Doubt that the sun doth move,
Doubt truth to be a liar,
But never doubt our love.

SCENE TWO
hamlet

The journey to Wittenberg was long and lonely. The rain eased off within a few days, but it did not encourage the young prince to turn his gaze to the outside world. He sat and stared at the interior of the carriage instead, cataloguing the scratches in the wooden seat, the places where the velvet was worn through.

Sometimes a cool breeze introduced the smells of the outside world: the cloying, bittersweet richness of late autumn grass, the rot of the forest floor, more often than not accompanied by the hot, sweating smell of horse dung. He caught sight of the sky sometimes, and heard the occasional exchange of words. None of it interested him.

He was haunted by his father's words: *consider yourself no closer to ruling this kingdom than any dog on the street.*

His crown had been taken from him before he left the palace, its golden laurel leaves smothered in a lead box.

He was not a prince anymore—not in the eyes of his father.

This interested him in an academic sense: being a prince was meant to be something innate. He had been chosen by God, after all: some distant being had placed the elements of him within his mother's belly and decided he would rule Denmark one day. And yet: the crown was gone.

Good fucking riddance.

Hamlet stared at the inside of the carriage. To any onlooker, he must have seemed strange: stock-still, brow furrowed as if deep in thought, yet with eyes glazed and hair untamed, still with a bright bruise blooming beneath one eye. Something inside him had loosened in the long summer days since the incident. Here in the back of a carriage, far from home, he found himself coming undone in a curiously studious way.

Like the scholar he was, he made a list. There were books on the subject of what made a good prince, endless quantities of them: *mirrors for princes*. It was a useful way of teaching the hot-blooded youth of European royalty how to behave themselves, of giving them a way of looking into their own souls and rebuilding themselves.

Hamlet made his list. Then he crossed them out, one by one.

He leaned out the window and flirted with the guardsmen escorting him, who were unreceptive to his many advances. Every time they stopped at an inn to rest, he spent the night getting howling drunk and gambling away what money he'd brought with him, and when any of his escort accidentally addressed him by his title, he reminded them that he had been informally stripped of same, sometimes punctuated by a tearing of his clothes and hair for dramatic effect.

He sat atop a horse on one particularly wet day, divested himself of his tunic, and recited Ovid, although the wind ripped the words away before they could reach his small and horrified audience. He gave flowers to an innkeeper's wife and ate a raw onion like an apple and insisted on stopping to fish in a muddy pond for six hours.

The further from Helsingør they got, the wilder the performances. Some part of him hoped that pinning a young lord's pet bird to the stable door with an arrow might be enough to have him sent back to Denmark; the other, louder part just enjoyed the aftermath: being hauled bodily down a corridor, often cursed at, and locked in his chambers at night.

The guardsmen, who were familiar with the prince but who had never seen him quite so unrestrained as this, found their seventeen-year-old charge eager to make their lives as painful as possible. As a result they fulfilled their obligation to the Danish monarchy to the letter: at the gates of Wittenberg they handed Hamlet his things, gave him his letters of recommendation for the university and the address of his lodgings, and left.

He stood in the street with his trunk full of books at his feet, surrounded by a variety of boxes and bags of nonsense.

"Damn," said Hamlet.

He looked around. It was pitch black outside, with only the light of a few lamps to illuminate the enormous city walls. They glimmered with fresh rain and loomed over him, giving the appearance that the city was being encircled by a large black void. It was an unwelcoming sight: the warm lamplight seemed to freeze as it hit the blue-grey of the cobbles, and the barbican was a gaping maw, through which there was only the unknown.

In the distance a spire pierced the night sky, a black thorn on a navy-grey canvas. He knew little of Wittenberg except that it had a university and some churches, that it was full of red-roofed buildings and swaddled in green fields, with the River Elbe coursing past its walls.

So far, it reminded him a lot of his mother's embroidery. Sharp and pointed and empty of beauty.

There was nothing for it. Onwards, into the black maw of the bar with whatever he could carry. He decided that his books were non-negotiable; the rest could be replaced, and so he left the odd miscellany behind and took only his trunk and one sack of tunics.

The shadows lent a strangeness to everything. He could see no more than a few feet in front of him at any time, and soon his mouth tasted faintly of metal from exertion and he was hot despite the chilly temperature.

He hated to admit it, but he was afraid. The nearest church still seemed miles away. He hoped they might offer him a place to sleep for the night, at least until he found his footing. In the morning he would ask about the location of his lodgings, he decided. The church might offer him something to eat, a drink of wine perhaps. That was preferable to a cold, empty house, alone, perhaps without supplies or servants.

He stopped to push his soaking wet hair back from his forehead. Almost at the same moment, there was a shout. He heard this with cool detachment. People—*commoners*—did not shout at Prince Hamlet, heir to the Danish throne.

Neither did they pick up a clump of street muck and hurl it at him. It splattered into the middle of his chest. There was an audible whoosh of air escaping his lungs, and Hamlet stumbled back a couple of steps, trying to get his bearings.

A hoot of laughter. A word that he had only heard his father use once. *Throne room. Knees burning on the stone, head bowed towards the ground. Tears drying on his cheeks.*

He tried to calm himself. The attackers called again, repeating their insult. There were two of them, but it was too dim to make out their features.

They don't know, Hamlet told himself. *They cannot see what lies within.* The word came again. Hamlet tightened his grip on his case of books and continued walking.

"Where are you going?" one of the men jeered. His German was good enough, sadly, to understand even slurred words. "Going to find a nice man to take care of you, pretty boy?"

Hamlet dropped his bags.

"Going to find a knife," he said, showing his teeth. "I'm going to cut your heart out with it and shove it down your friend's throat."

Mistakenly, he had thought this show of aggression might scare them away. It came as something of a surprise to see their eyebrows draw down into twin scowls. They came forward with their fists firmly clenched.

A newcomer stepped from the shadows of an alleyway.

"Not tonight, boys."

Relief washed over Hamlet. The men, seeing that the match was now even, reluctantly trailed into the nearest tavern.

Their final swear words hovered in the air between Hamlet and the newcomer.

"My thanks," the prince said. He breathed a shaky sigh of relief, his skin tingling. "It was good of you to step in, friend."

"No need to thank me." The other stepped into the light, revealing a young man about his age, perhaps a little older, with dark brown eyes and skin, close-cropped curls, and a square jaw. "These streets can be dangerous. I would recommend keeping to the better-lit ones in future."

Hamlet bowed his head. "I'm new to the city," he admitted. "I don't quite know my way around."

His saviour offered to take a look at the letter noting Hamlet's accommodation address, which he willingly handed over. In the dim light from windows, they discussed the weather while they unfolded the parchment.

The stranger offered to walk Hamlet to his accommodation, and he helped him to carry a bag. It was only then that they remembered to exchange names, and laughed only a little awkwardly at their omission.

"Thomas Guildenstern," the other boy said. "At your service, my friend."

"Hamlet," he replied. "Is that an English accent I detect?"

"Indeed," Guildenstern said, amiably bumping Hamlet's elbow with his own. "My father's family are as English as they come. My mother's side less so: Igbo, Danish, some Norwegian, which is awkward at the moment, you can imagine."

"I certainly can." Talk of Norway made Hamlet nervous. In recent months, old tensions reared their heads. He was not privy to the contents of his father's council meetings, but he was aware enough to know that there were problems, and that they were not easily solved.

"The Kalmar Union caused problems, obviously," Guildenstern was saying. At some point they'd started speaking in French, the cleanest of their common tongues. "As it stands, I can't see Denmark and Norway forming another alliance. Can you? Maybe I shouldn't speak of it—Denmark is your homeland. You will know better than I what the climate is."

The rain, still pattering down, made the cobblestones glint silver in the moonlight. Now that he was not alone, Hamlet could almost see the city as beautiful.

There was a moment in which he wondered whether or not he should disclose his identity. It was tempting to give in to the opportunity to flex his status, to feel Guildenstern's gaze change.

But something held Hamlet back. For the first time in his life, he realised, there was not a guard within shouting distance. And although Guildenstern seemed kind, and was certainly something of a hero, it was probably unwise to trust him too far.

Instead, he shrugged. "I pay little attention," he said, which was not a lie. "I leave those conversations to my father."

Guildenstern laughed. It was a pleasant sound, warm and rich. "Fair enough, my friend," he said, and bumped Hamlet with his shoulder once again. "When I introduce you to Rosencrantz — the fellow I live with — remind me to mention that. He'll argue with you over that for *hours*."

SCENE THREE
ophelia

Ophelia stood in the alcove behind the arras in the library. Her breath warmed the fabric, dampening the loose threads. It smelled dusty and sour with age, like so much in this castle, and she had to fight the urge to sneeze.

At the sound of approaching voices, she forced her chest to go still.

"I begged you to send him to England," Queen Gertrude hissed, her shoes clicking against the stone floor. This did not sound like the beginning of an argument; that was lost in a distant hallway somewhere. No, this was an argument so threadbare there was hardly any of it left. "I told you he would be better off there. What friends do we have in Wittenberg?"

"Wittenberg has good masters, and it is safer than the English court. The boy will do well there," King Hamlet said. He sounded weary. He had looked weary in all the days since they sent Hamlet away.

Ophelia wondered how many times this argument had played out, heard or unheard, over the last few weeks: its own tapestry of violent words.

"The Duke owes me a favour," the king continued. "He will introduce Hamlet to good men who will steer him back on the right course. I'm sure of it."

"But *Wittenberg* of all places—now? All of this preaching, and rioting, and— and—"

"And in England, King Henry has chopped off his second wife's head." King Hamlet let out a bitter little noise of derision. "Is that preferable to you?"

There was a silence, punctuated only by Queen Gertrude's heavy, furious breathing.

"I'll hear no more of this," the king muttered. His footsteps separated from the queen's, going back the way they came. "Maybe Henry has a point. Women and their *talk*."

After a moment, Gertrude followed. Both sets of footsteps faded away.

Ophelia released a pent-up breath and stepped out from behind the tapestry. The watery light of an autumn afternoon streamed into the corridor. It was a welcome relief after the dust and damp of the alcove, but hiding behind artwork was the only way she could get information now.

Without Hal—*Hamlet*, she tried to correct herself, she could not call him by a nickname anymore—she was lost. She had no place in this court anymore.

Father did not tell her anything. Laertes, her only sibling, was away in Paris. And Hamlet was gone.

In the years before, when it was Hal and Fee always, Prince Hamlet and Lady Ophelia, she'd always known her place. She and Hamlet were one person, one unit. The usual rules of the court didn't apply to them. They sat together at mealtimes, went to each other's rooms in the mornings, rode into town on horseback.

Now, it was like a switch had been flipped. Suddenly, she couldn't speak Hamlet's name in public. She couldn't go out alone, not unless she snuck out and hid behind tapestries or went to the chapel. She was not to go riding or hunting or play too much music; she could do nothing that might 'overexcite' her.

All because they had been caught. The memory was painful to her now: the heat of summer, flecks of sweat on a horse's mane, shy glances from a stableboy their age.

She shook it away. She did not want to think of what happened next, because it always led to the remembrance of the pain, the terror, the strike. The memory was knitted together with the image of Hal's carriage drawing further away.

She huffed out a breath of frustration as she re-attached her veil. The king and queen never seemed to have anything interesting to say: it was all pointless words, barbs and thorns. There was little to be gleaned from King Hamlet and Queen Gertrude's conversation. It was a wasted morning.

But there was at least one more thing she could do before the end of the day, despite the lateness of the hour.

Ophelia shook out her hair, wiped the sweat from her top lip with the back of her hand, and went to pray.

Every time she stepped inside, it was the same reaction. The temperature drop made all the hairs stand up on her arms. It was still a shock to the system to see bare wood and marble, where once there had been gold dripping from every surface, beautiful paintings of Christ adorning the walls, ceilings decorated with images from the Fall.

What was left was like a hollowed-out shell. This was Queen Gertrude's command. Good Christians, she said, did not care about earthly things. She had the gold ripped out and melted down. Hal (*damn it*) said some of it was turned into a new set of dinner plates for the royal apartments, and he wasn't sure about the rest. It was probably in the treasury.

Fitting, to send Hamlet to Wittenberg University, the birthplace of this new movement. Ophelia didn't feel particularly convinced by it, but her opinion didn't matter. The new Church of Denmark was only a few months old, but it was already the religion of the court and of the royal family. They were carried on the crest of a wave which was sweeping Northern Europe; now Hamlet was at the heart of it, and she dreaded to think what unwise things he might say to the wrong people.

As she knelt, she had to stifle a laugh: the image of Hamlet debating Martin Luther himself was priceless.

There were only a handful of other people there, and they were all focused on looking pious. Ophelia knelt a few pews behind them and tried to school her expression into the right combination of 'thoughtful' and 'penitent'.

Dropping her hands from their prayer position, she connected her middle finger to her thumb. With her eyes closed and her focus gathered, she could feel it: the strands of magic that wove their tangled web through the chapel, dark and unforgiving.

She could feel how the stone beneath her shrank from it, threatened to crack to flee the darkness; she could feel, too, how the earth resisted it, how the very air quivered in horror at its presence. Magic, raw and unadulterated, threatened everything natural in the world.

But that was alright. She knew how to fix it.

Ophelia opened her eyes and whispered, "*Relinquatis: et non revertatur.*"

She felt the magic—or the shadow that remained of it—clump together in the darkness beneath the pew. Her fingers flexed; the ruined remnants of the magic bent, formed into a thick, deep purple thread, and quivered at the force of her power.

"Relinquatis," she whispered again, more stern now, and finally the purple coil seeped away, seeming to vanish into thin air.

Ophelia wiped her palm on her skirt and repressed a shudder. She hated handling Corruption like that, but when she had to work in secret, there was precious little else she could do. She shoved away the clammy feeling that coated her skin, and also the sensation of pride that rippled through her.

When she'd spend all day cleaning Corruption, she sometimes wondered if the world would be better off without magic. It was woven into the fabric of the earth, yes; but when the offspring of magic was something as evil and twisted as Corruption, it sometimes felt like the world would be a better place without them both.

She had to remind herself: it was not magic that was the problem, but what was left behind when it was used. Magic itself could do wonderful things: her mother had used it to heal people when she was alive. Magic ran in her veins. They just had to be careful, because spells always left a stain.

The more powerful the spell, the more vicious the scars. The traces of the magic that were left behind were initially harmless; they clung to their host, the caster of the spell, like specks of dust.

But in time, they grew strong. Over time, those 'specks' clumped together. The stronger the magic, the faster they could multiply. In time, the Corruption could grow into systems, and before long the magic could become powerful enough to worm its way inside the organs. There, it rotted its host from within, turning the healthy purple flesh to an ashen grey, choked of all life.

To those who could see—truly See—the Corrupted magic was visible as a dark purple shimmer, a potent aura that spelled disaster. The relics of that magic could not be controlled by their host; often, the caster had no idea they were Corrupted until they started to choke up blood.

Left untreated, Corruption would destroy cities, rotting buildings to their very foundations; it would ravage a population with sickness and disease; it would kill every living thing through pestilence and famine.

There were ways of managing the Corruption. It could be cleared by those who knew how, although their numbers grew fewer and fewer by the year. Accused of witchcraft, madness, and insanity, many were killed, and the rest had fled to a secret place long ago, and there they raised their children in the old ways.

The door of the chapel swung open. For a few moments, the outside world intruded: the chatter of the corridor, the draughty breeze. Ophelia's father closed the door gently behind him, and the world retreated once again.

Polonius's gaze landed on his daughter. Open relief: she was at prayer, kneeling on the hard floor, doing what good women were supposed to do.

If only you knew. She wiped her hand on her thighs again, despite the fact that her father could not see the magic. The last woman in this castle with that gift had died, a long time ago.

But not before she'd taught her children to carry on her task. Laertes had faltered; now he was away at university, deciding whether or not magic was a sin. Ophelia alone carried out the task their mother had asked of them. She remembered her mother's rules, spoken every day of their lives on both sides of the mirror.

Stay together.

Keep the secret.

When in doubt, go to Rúnräd.

The first was moot. The second was as easy as breathing.

The third was a temptation she had to resist.

Rúnräd was her safe place, her haven. It was the last thing she thought about at night and, when she woke, it was always a source of eternal disappointment to find herself in bed at Kronborg Castle with a servant laying out her breakfast and not in the little house belonging to her Aunt Hilga, lying near a roaring fire with the smell of Hilga's wife's delicious fresh bread and soup wafting around her.

Her father didn't speak to her, but in his eyes was written his pleasure at seeing her. All his love shone out of his face, as obvious as a child. Ophelia tried not to feel guilty. She let her gaze drift from Polonius's round, happy, proud face back towards the altar, and quietly she started to pray.

SCENE FOUR
hamlet

Guildenstern was right about the other young man he lived with: Rosencrantz spent the first twenty minutes of his acquaintance with Hamlet discussing the importance of making one's own political decisions, and the next five sipping on a glass of amber liquid listening to Guildenstern's light-hearted rebuttal.

Guildenstern had seated himself on the edge of a low table, and Hamlet hovered next to him, his book trunk at his feet. The entire room was shadowed, lit only by the fire behind Rosencrantz, but despite the gloom Hamlet could make out a bookshelf, a couple of other chairs shoved haphazardly into corners, and what looked like a workbench.

It was not the most attractive room, but the company was inviting and soon the drinks were flowing. Rosencrantz had the same slightly standoffish air as a stray cat, but a few more cups of mead and he managed to crack a smile. Guildenstern moved from the table to an armchair, which he draped himself across in a fashion that seemed somewhat risky; next to him, Rosencrantz reclined in his own seat, blinking languidly in the heat of the fire, his pale skin reddening slowly as the night meandered on.

Hamlet tried not to stare at either of them, but they made a striking pair. Guildenstern moved with the elegance of a dancer, demonstrating a kind of trained control from the tips of his fingers to the toes of his boots, and his looks and gestures were carefully exaggerated for comedic effect.

Rosencrantz was almost his opposite: long-limbed and pointed, with a grace that came more from carelessness than study. He was not tall, this didn't seem to matter; it felt, somehow, like he towered over Hamlet and Guildenstern both. Rosencrantz was a little mysterious, closed-off, hard to read; despite the openness of his speech, there was something of a wild-animal-wariness in his eyes, a warning not to move too sharply, to approach with caution. He also had the oddest eyes Hamlet had ever seen: paler than pale, just barely grey-blue, and utterly piercing.

Hamlet moved from table to floor, sprawling in front of the fire. His hair dried and curled over his forehead in fluffy waves, and as he relaxed, he curated a small collection of removable items beside him: his belt, his boots, his small, silver earring. Before long, an invitation was extended to Hamlet to stay the night, and soon he'd accepted.

Nobody asked how a highly-educated Danish man had ended up in Wittenberg in the middle of the night without an escort of any kind. Pressed to answer, Hamlet didn't know what he'd say. They discussed everything under the sun, and somehow he managed to avoid revealing his identity beyond that he was noble and Danish and, as the night began to turn to morning, a Protestant.

"The thing about politics," Rosencrantz said, "is that it's only interesting as long as you aren't caught up in it."

"It must be so hard," said Guildenstern, with palpable sarcasm, "being as victimised as you are."

Rosencrantz shrugged his pointed shoulders. "I'm not saying I'm a victim," he said. "Just that certain discussions have become a lot less entertaining in recent years." Here, he looked at Hamlet. His eyes really were alarmingly pale.

"I am compelled to tell you," said Guildenstern, leaning in conspiratorially, "that our Rosencrantz is a

Catholic. An immovable one, at that." He sighed and fell back in his chair, staring at a mysterious point on the wall above Rosencrantz's head. "Ah, we all were once."

"Yes," agreed Rosencrantz. "Not more than two years ago, if I remember rightly."

"It feels so distant now, those days of our youth." Guildenstern winked, and Hamlet was unexpectedly overcome by a blush that turned him scarlet from the tips of his ears to his collarbones.

"How is it, being a Catholic in Wittenberg at the moment?" Hamlet asked.

The subject fascinated him more than most, and he caught himself leaning forward in his seat.

A shadow passed over Rosencrantz's face. "Fine," he said. "I get along alright, as it stands, although I can't say it's always comfortable. Not while that bat Luther is living comfortably in the university quarter, stirring up various prejudices. I don't have it as bad as some. Horrid, shrivelled old man."

"He's not my biggest fan either," said Guildenstern, and gestured vaguely towards himself. "Can't think why."

A laugh escaped, partially against Hamlet's will. Guildenstern, buoyed by this, continued.

"A white Catholic and a Black Protestant—poor old Luther can't decide which of us he prefers less, although I suspect it might be me."

"And are you really a Protestant?" Hamlet asked Guildenstern. "Or going along with the fashion?"

Guildenstern seemed to find this hilarious. "The fashion! Of course it's because it's the fashion," he said. "Everything I do is for fashion. That's why I'm wearing this strikingly high neckline."

Rosencrantz was smiling. He looked so unlike Guildenstern it was almost comedic. Guildenstern was broad across the shoulders, solid and substantial; Rosencrantz was wispy and almost incorporeal next to him, all elbows and angles in a way that wasn't entirely flattering, and yet suited him.

"Fashion matters in Wittenberg," Rosencrantz advised. "The key is to look as unfashionable as possible. A decade or so behind is really what excites. Poor Guildie can't bring himself to do it."

"We run in different circles, you see," said 'Guildie', leaning in conspiratorially. "It's a strange friendship."

Rosencrantz and Guildenstern went back and forth. They clearly enjoyed one another's company; they were well-matched. Neither could gain the upper hand: they had the same sense of humour, the same sharp intellect, and a matching stubbornness that would not yield for anything.

It reminded him a little of Ophelia, and Hamlet's heart sank. He wasn't very good at missing people: his mind preferred to drop a fog down over the feelings, store them away somewhere he couldn't reach. But he did miss her: her lovely face, her hair and cloak sodden with rain.

"Shall we go to bed?" Guildenstern said eventually, when the wine cups had been empty and neglected for a long time and the fire was burning low. "I have a tutorial in the morning I entirely plan on neglecting."

Guildenstern chivalrously offered his bed to Hamlet. Hamlet knew, dimly, that he should reject the offer, but he couldn't bring himself to say no to the promise of a mattress after so much travel.

"It's no problem, my friend," Guildenstern said cheerfully, although Hamlet hadn't asked whether it was or it wasn't. "A man needs a bed after a long day's journey. Besides, the bonds of friendship are never greater than after sharing a night's sleep."

Something seized and died in Hamlet's brain. *Sharing a night's sleep.* Did Guildenstern mean for them to sleep side by side? He'd done so before, with cousins and friends, bedding down together in a sumptuous tent in the woods in the height of summer, where they stayed awake most of the night, batting away flies. It had never been a problem before. It was, in fact, entirely normal.

But something had changed fundamentally since the last time he'd climbed into a bed with another man, and Hamlet wasn't sure there was any going back.

The sting of a slap. The hot trickle of blood from his cheekbone. His neck, the ache of it, after being shaken and shaken, then tossed to the ground—

But he couldn't refuse. These were the only souls he knew in Wittenberg. Hamlet hadn't decided yet how much he liked these young men, nor how much to trust them, but it was sleep here or find somewhere else—and after the encounter earlier, he shied away from the idea of walking the streets.

"Not untrue," he managed to say, and if either Rosencrantz or Guildenstern noticed his anxiety, they didn't comment.

Hamlet rose. His legs felt unsteady, a combination of the wine and his nerves.

"I'll stay here a while longer," Rosencrantz said, leaning back in his chair. "I'll see you both in the morning. Hamlet, don't leave without a goodbye. There'll be breakfast."

Something unsaid passed between him and Guildenstern. Hamlet couldn't tell what it was: only that

Guildenstern's gaze was sharp, perhaps a little reproaching, and Rosencrantz seemed entirely unbothered.

As he undressed for bed that night, Guildenstern let out a low whistle. Hamlet glanced over, then saw where Guildenstern's gaze had fallen: the mottled bruises covering his arms from the hands of several very angry guardsmen.

"You're a dark horse, Hamlet," Guildenstern said with a wink, and climbed into the bed.

In Guildenstern's bed, space was tight. Hamlet was pleasantly relieved to discover that, despite the fears of his parents and his priest, he was not in fact prone to losing control of his senses and attacking every handsome man he saw.

He lay curled into a tight ball just in case, and he did not fall asleep for a long time. Rosencrantz didn't stir from downstairs. In the morning, Hamlet thought he'd ask what time Rosencrantz slept, and discovered he did not need to: the bags under his eyes spoke louder than words.

SCENE FIVE
ophelia

Bright and early, Ophelia faced her first battle of the day.

"I have to go into the city," she said. Her father glanced up from the letter he was reading, stamped and sealed by some lord. "Can I go?"

Father breathed hard through his nose. "Not today," he said. After a moment, he asked, "What do you need?" which rendered his previous statement invalid. Ophelia repressed her smile.

"I have to collect my new dancing shoes, remember?" she said, which was true. "I'm going back to lessons this week."

She didn't need to mention what had happened to the old shoes. Father had flung them out the window the day she was dragged out of those lessons and brought to kneel before the king and queen. She hardly remembered the interrogation; instead, most of her focus had been on the exchange happening behind her: Hamlet apologising to her father, his words strange and stilted.

"I'm sorry," he'd said. "We'll pay the cost of your daughter's honour."

"Such a thing is priceless," Polonius had muttered, but eventually there was a jingle of coins as a purse changed hands, and the matter was considered settled where Ophelia was concerned.

Father was clearly remembering the same thing. A shadow passed over his face, as he looked down at the letter with unseeing eyes, then around at the servants, then back at Ophelia.

"Bring someone with you," he said, and quickly reached out to pat her on the hand. "I'll ask one of the ladies—or the guardsmen—"

"Alessandra is coming." The lie rolled easily off her tongue. "And Lorenz might join us."

One of the most popular couples of the court: kind, clever, and Italian, Alessandra and Lorenz were the easiest bet.

Father nodded, thoughtful. "And you have spoken to them lately?" he asked.

"In the chapel, only. Alessandra said she would offer a prayer for my return, and said she wanted to walk with me again soon."

This was another lie, but it was the sort of lie her father enjoyed. It was fanciful, the kind of thing women in poetry did; but her father liked fictions, liked to pretend that the world could be examined and explained in black-and-white terms.

"Go early," he said, and turned his attention back to his letter. When he spoke again, his voice was low, the words an afterthought: "I worry less now that that boy is away."

Ophelia rose from the table. Her appetite was gone.

When Father was gone to a meeting, she put on the roughspun servant's cloak she kept under her bed. The dancing shoes could wait. Through the darkest, narrowest halls of Kronborg Castle she went, as quickly as she could.

Her favourite guardsman Marcellus was at the walls. He winked and waved her through the gate. He was always kind when he encountered her here and he never commented on her journeys out of the castle: he already knew where it was she was really going.

The area that stretched between Kronborg Castle and the main body of the town used to be empty, but in recent years it had become the home of wealthy artists and craftsmen from across the world, a place where great minds met. Ophelia avoided it. There were too many people there who might know her, though she longed to go to her favourite shop and purchase delicate French sweets wrapped in paper.

She walked down to the shore, past the spire of St Olaf's Church. The shipyard smelled of metal and brine, and she walked with her face turned to the ocean so that she could feel the cool breeze on her face. Men either paid her no notice or tipped their caps to her, pausing for only a moment in their hauling of cargo, their voices softening in the bellowing of orders.

She liked to take the longer route that ran parallel to the docks, where she could see which of the boats were in and note which flags they flew. Then, she would go back to the castle and search for them in a book, bought for Laertes but now belonging to her, to find out which country they'd come from.

There was a harsh beauty to the docks. Here, all the worlds of Denmark collided: the men with their muscles straining worked in full view of the castle, where royalty shrouded itself in the luxuries brought from the water's edge. Here, the many immigrant communities of the city gathered, rich and poor, hoping to find a ship bearing news of home.

The crews coming aboard didn't often stop: frequently, they were just coming to pay the Sound Tax. It was that money that fuelled the country, that bought Queen Gertrude her glorious gems, that meant Hamlet was bought an entire stable full of racehorses when he turned thirteen.

If she kept walking, past the ships and the fan-shaped city with its bustling streets, she could find the quiet of the forest. There, in the green gloom of it, if one knew their way, they could find the cottage. Ophelia could sniff it out in moments; her brother Laertes had never quite learned the trick of it and was often late to Rúnräd engagements because of it, but Ophelia knew her way, and she crossed the mossy forest floor without trouble.

The cottage's roof was caved in and the wooden beams were scorched, and the stones that formed the wall looked like they might crumble at any moment. If one was brave enough to step inside, they would be met with a strange sight: an empty room, a burnt-out, hollow shell… and a mirror.

She did not have to think, nor pause, nor whisper an enchantment. Ophelia walked through the mirror and out the other side, and she was in Rúnräd.

She was home.

SCENE SIX
hamlet

In the morning, it was Rosencrantz who came with Hamlet to find his accommodation. Graciously, he'd allowed Hamlet to leave his bags on the floor of their living room, so the walk through the streets was easier than it had been the previous night. He had made the mistake of inquiring about servants; Rosencrantz had to wipe a tear from his eye, and spent most of their walk stifling laughter.

"Servants," he said. "That gives us some insight as to your background, I think."

In the daylight, Hamlet had to admit that Wittenberg was pretty. The streets were narrow, but they didn't seem to wind as much as he remembered. He could find the church spire easily. The smell of sausages grilling over charcoal wafted from the market square, and neighbours leaned out of their windows to speak to each other from on high. The sky was blue above them, all of last night's rain forgotten. It was a beautiful autumn day, just warm enough to step out without a cloak.

Rosencrantz talked about Wittenberg as though he'd lived there his entire life. He waved a casual hand at a flock of dark-robed, serious-looking young academics, and privately informed Hamlet they were 'astrologers of the very worst calibre'. He wandered down a narrow, smelly alleyway, hips swaying, and pointed cheerfully in the direction of the city's finest brothel.

He led them through the Elster Quarter, from which Hamlet had entered the city, and it looked significantly more friendly in the daylight. The broad avenue of Collegienstrasse was lined with the homes of salespeople and craftsmen, the front rooms of whom's homes were transformed into little shops. Some had mobile wooden display tables they could fold up and store against their front walls, and those tables were lined with wares, from the simplest shoes to the most intricate stained glass artworks of angels and saints.

"Lovely," Rosencrantz said, when they were standing outside what was to be Hamlet's house. It was tall and whitewashed, with wooden beams and yellow window-shutters and a friendly English housekeeper who introduced herself as Agatha.

Rosencrantz helped him to unpack his small collection of things. There was a firing roaring in the grate, and Agatha busied herself in the kitchen at the back of the house, something delicious-smelling wafting through the halls. But the house still looked very sparse, even with his belongings scattered across the living room.

"It's a good house," said Rosencrantz, when they'd decided in which order to place the books on his shelves. "You'll be very comfortable here."

There was a silence.

"Bored, though," Rosencrantz continued. His eyes slid to Hamlet's, like they were the co-conspirators in some great plot. "I'd go mad, living alone in a big house like this."

Hamlet suppressed a smile. "I think I might," he agreed. "Just Agatha and I... It doesn't bear thinking about."

"I suppose you'd rather that than live with a mad Englishman and a Norwegian, though?"

"Funnily enough," said Hamlet, "I think I would survive it. Might even enjoy it, you know."

Agatha was sent away with instructions to find food and other necessities to stock the pantry, and express instructions to come once a day to cook meals, no more, and she wasn't to worry about cleaning or anything of the sort, other than laundering clothes. Within a few hours, Rosencrantz and Hamlet had moved all of the furnishings from the old house to their new one: 12 Collegienstrasse.

Hamlet's hands hurt from carrying multiple chairs and an entire bookcase across town, but it was a good pain. He rubbed his palms together, feeling the sting of hot, inflamed skin. His forehead was sticky with sweat, his hair plastered to his skin. Rosencrantz was much the same. His fair hair had turned frizzy from exertion, and two spots of pink had appeared high on his cheeks. Currently, Hamlet could hear him clattering around upstairs in Guildenstern's room, boxing up his friend's collection of paperweights.

"Good lord."

Hamlet looked up from where he was standing, in the wreckage of what had once been a perfectly serviceable room. Now it was bare and empty, bits of wood and various belongings lying littered across the floor.

Guildenstern looked around incredulously.

"Are you robbing us or just redecorating?"

Rosencrantz popped his head over the banister. "Sort of," he said. "In that I can't remember what was in this house when we moved in, and what we brought with us. So I'm just going to take the bits I like and leave the rest."

"My paperweights?"

"Oh, I wouldn't leave *them*. I want to laugh gleefully as I throw them in the river."

Guildenstern hummed in acknowledgement. His thumb pressed against the middle of his full bottom lip, as he gazed over the room in deep thought.

"I have a house on Collegienstrasse," Hamlet offered. "Ros and I decided we should live there together."

"Collegienstrasse? Which one's that?"

"Next to St Marien's."

"God," Guildenstern said wonderingly. "That awful place. Nice street, though."

"It seemed alright," said Hamlet.

"Have you seen the Judensau? Now that's *not* nice."

"The what?"

Guildenstern waved his hand. "Pig," was all he said for a moment. He seemed very distracted by the room, which was laid bare before him. "Awful thing. Antisemitic."

"I didn't show you the Jewish Quarter earlier," Rosencrantz said, tramping down the stairs with a wooden crate in his arms. "We can go tomorrow. Guild, here are your bloody paperweights."

He passed the crate to Guildenstern, who took it easily. He stood there a moment longer, framed in the doorway. His shoulders were almost too broad to fit through the entryway.

"I hate that damned pig."

With that, he stepped back out into the road.

"You said Collegienstrasse, didn't you?" he called. "I'll meet you there!"

Hamlet looked at the empty entryway. He could hear Guildenstern whistling as he walked down the road. The task at his feet—the dismantling of yet another bookcase—begged for his attention, and so he crouched down and got back to work.

Agatha exceeded all expectations, and when the move was finished and they had all chosen rooms for themselves—Hamlet got first pick as it was his house—the trio sat around the cosy little table and ate soft bread with pork chops and onions, dipping the crusts into the rich, sweet sauce.

Hamlet propped his feet up on the table when they were finished and leaned back, drinking in the warmth of the fire. Guildenstern and Rosencrantz argued over his head. One single, all-consuming wave of homesickness crashed over his head, then broke; and then it was gone, washed back out to sea, leaving only a trace of itself behind.

Rosencrantz rapped hard against Hamlet's boots.

"Off the table," he demanded, in a pinched voice that reminded Hamlet of his old nursemaid. "That's the most disgusting thing I've seen all year."

"Rosencrantz, they're boots," Hamlet argued. "It's a table. They were made for one another."

"Yes, and *my* boot was made for your arsehole."

Hamlet laughed before he could stop himself. *I need to tell Ophelia about this*, he thought. *She'd love them, and this place.*

He knew she would: she would fill the bookcases with volumes on every subject imaginable, and she'd nail all of her favourite maps to the walls alongside the diagrams she liked to rip out of science books. She'd leave her astrology notes scattered across the table in the mornings, and she'd scold him for spilling candle wax on her parchment.

Hal, she'd say, sighing hard through her nose. *I was reading that book about automatons, and then you went and dribbled wine all over it…*

She was so bright, so beautiful. God, she'd love the university, and the professors would love her too, if it wasn't for the fact of her being a woman. He resolved to write to her as soon as he could, and to include a faithful sketch of Wittenberg life.

She was probably in her room, he imagined. The evening was closing in. Maybe she was praying, or writing something, or doing some embroidery, although that was doubtful—she had no love of it. Come to think of it, he wasn't sure what, exactly, she did in her rooms on boring autumn evenings.

He just knew that he loved her and that this moment, perfect as it was, would be much improved with her by his side, pressed together from shoulder to knee, with her brave, calloused hand holding his.

Resisting another pang of sadness, Hamlet turned his attention back to his newfound friends.

SCENE SEVEN
ophelia

"Tea for three," Hilga sang, pressing a beautiful porcelain cup into Ophelia's waiting hands. Ophelia thanked her, but her words were lost beneath the chatter. She sat in a small room with only two other people, but they were so exuberant that they drowned her out easily. She pulled her colourful blanket over her lap so she could fiddle with it, pulling at the tassles.

She glanced at the clock on the mantelpiece. Only a few minutes ago it had clanged out a new hour, and it now read six o'clock. Father would be worried. Ophelia tried not to stay in Rúnräd for long, but today was an exception.

First, Hilga—her aunt, and one of her only remaining blood relations on her mother's side—had asked her to take a turn down to the well with her. Then it transpired that Laertes was in trouble in some distant part of the magical world for drunkenness and illegal gambling, and he had had to pay a fine. Hilga had discovered this when some tradespeople informed her that her nephew was becoming quite well-known, and not for the right reasons.

"He's your brother," she'd said to Ophelia. "I know it isn't your transgression, but you have to speak to him. It reflects badly."

Hilga supervised her while she wrote a letter, and listened to Ophelia complain that when a man made a mistake, it was always the job of the nearest woman in his life to fix it.

"That's the way of the world," Hilga said. "When a man cocks up, a woman fixes it. Wife, sister, mother, it doesn't matter. When a woman makes a mistake, she deals with it alone." Here she paused for dramatic effect. "Or her kindly aunt calls on the community for support."

It had taken Ophelia a moment to realise what was happening.

"Hilga, you didn't," Ophelia protested. "You didn't tell them about…"

"About your little prince? I did."

"Hilga! I told you not to tell anyone!"

"I ignored you. A woman deals with everything alone in that other world," Hilga said. Her eyes, normally a cool blue, glinted like cold steel. "But that has never been the way in Rúnräd, my dear. We're family."

This was how Ophelia discovered that Laertes was about to receive nine letters, one from every relative and friend in their village. It was also how she'd ended up sitting in Hilga's house clutching a porcelain cup and waiting for the last member of their party to arrive.

Rúnräd was small, as magical settlements went. It was not a place people tended to stay. When Ophelia was a child, her mother taught her about the magical world and the 'other' one, the one where Father was from.

"They are like two spheres," she'd said. In Ophelia's mind, her mother had two long, blonde braids like Hilga, but Hilga said that wasn't true. "One rests inside the other—that's the magical one. But they do not match. That's why we have to be careful when we pass from one world to another."

"But how do we know the mirror will bring us to Rúnräd?" Ophelia had asked. In the memory, she remembered shoving the end of her plait into her mouth, mother's fingers gently taking it away.

"Mirror calls to mirror, my love. They are twinned, our Rúnräd mirror and our cottage one. You must always be careful using a mirror you don't know, because you might travel further than you think. Do you understand?"

"I understand," Ophelia had said, dutifully. And then: "Why is it snowy here and rainy in the castle?"

Mother had laughed and said something about how the magical world was not just a copy of the one above, but a different place with its own weather and landscape, flora and fauna. That was why there was no ocean in Rúnräd, even though Helsingør always smelled like the sea; that was why she didn't need to fear the crocotta in the Aboveworld like she did in the Otherland, because it did not exist.

Now, she sat waiting for the members of her community to come together and 'support' her. She didn't doubt that they would want to help her when they heard what had happened, but she couldn't hide the burning embarrassment, the sense that they might not understand why she and Hamlet had done what they did. That they might look at her with pity and think her a fool.

Hilga, her aunt, played hostess, a role she filled unnaturally in the absence of her wife Solveig. Aaron was already there, sipping his own herbal tea without realising that one of his long, brown curls was drowning in it. He kept glancing at Ophelia, trying to include her in the conversation, but she stayed in her corner.

The door opened, bringing in a gust of icy air—it was snowing in Rúnräd, as always, and Ophelia made an involuntary noise at the chill wind—and Fatma stepped inside. Solveig came in behind her and started to unwrap her wool layers.

"Ophelia! You're back!" said Fatma, beaming as she stripped off her leather hood, revealing a gauzy yellow scarf. "I haven't seen you in months!"

"I haven't been away that long," Ophelia said, standing so she could hug the older woman. Fatma's clothes were cold and wet from the snow, but Ophelia didn't care. "How was Astari?"

"Hot. Full of insects. I got bitten in my sleep almost every night." She shook her coin purse, which made no sound. "I sold everything, and I bought more."

"Did you bring me my dye?" asked Solveig, who was trying to hop out of one boot.

"Do I ever forget? It's at my house. I'll bring it tomorrow when the snow eases off."

Fatma put her arm around Ophelia's shoulders and guided her to sit at the table with everyone else. Aaron passed them both cushions to sit on, and Ophelia sank down reluctantly. It was hard not to accept their kindness, because it was so genuine. She just wasn't sure she could cope when they withdrew it.

"Let's talk," said Hilga, putting a huge vat full of hot water down in the middle of the table. Ophelia reached behind her for her cup and refilled it. The heat against her palms cleared her head, and the steam felt pleasant on her skin. "How are your wards, my dear? Maintaining your sigils as normal?"

Ophelia shook her head. "It's been difficult to get out and renew them. Father's been keeping a close eye." Hilga made a face. "The ones in the queen's chambers have faded completely, and the ones in the chapel are too difficult to renew now that they've taken down all the statues."

A worried murmur went up amongst her gathered family. Fatma clicked her tongue.

"Are these issues renewing the wards anything we can help with?" Aaron asked, looking at her with fatherly concern. "You know you can always come to me for supplies, if that would be useful."

Aaron spent most of his time in Rúnräd, but once upon a time he'd been a successful doctor in the Aboveworld. Now, he mostly plied his trade in the Otherland, travelling to the cities and towns near Rúnräd to assist with birthing babies and treating minor illnesses, but he still knew a lot of useful people in Helsingør.

Sometimes when she was little, she'd wondered if you could have two families: one in the Aboveworld and one in the Otherland. She'd wanted Aaron to be her Otherland father with the seriousness only a child can manage; it was embarrassing to remember now, but she still appreciated his paternal affection.

"Thanks, Aaron," she said, smiling at him. "I'll need to top up my supplies soon, I think."

"Is your father's treatment of you anything to do with this incident with the prince?" Hilga asked, ever blunt. "I assume that's why we haven't seen you at all this summer. It's been weeks since you were last here."

"Not since the last week of July," Hilga's wife said, pouring another cup of tea.

Ophelia swallowed a mouthful of hot tea and braced herself. "I got into some trouble at the castle," she said. She tried to think how to put it in a way that was less embarrassing in front of everyone who had raised her from infancy, and concluded there was no way to ease the awkwardness. "Prince Hamlet and I got into a… situation."

Everyone tittered. "It was bound to happen," Solveig said, settling down between Ophelia and Aaron. She put her arm around her and pulled her into a hug. Solveig smelled like incense and flowers, which should have been overwhelming but it was just comforting. "Surely his mother and father knew you two were close. You've been talking about marrying him for years."

Ophelia turned scarlet. "They—yes, that wasn't… quite the problem."

"Oh gods," said Hilga, who had suddenly stopped clattering about the kitchen area. "You're having a baby."

"Oh, congratulations!" said Fatma. "Or commiserations?"

"You'll have to take a break from extracting the Corruption," Aaron said. Ophelia could practically see the cogs whirring in his brain through his glazed eyes. "You'll need to be eating well, especially as you're so young—"

"Not pregnant!" Ophelia had not meant to shout, but shout she did. Fatma let out a sigh of relief; Solveig began to laugh again, and Aaron looked faintly disappointed.

Hilga whipped round the table to stand above them all. Her hands were on her hips. Despite the colourful apron wrapped around her waist, she cut a terrifying figure. Both of her pale white braids swung with her momentum, and her face looked alarmingly, furiously pale. Two icy blue eyes stared into Ophelia's.

"Stop dancing around the subject," Hilga said. "When you last came to me in summer, in the sweltering heat, you could barely speak and you had a bruise on your face the likes of which I've never seen. Then was not the time for questions. But now is."

Ophelia hesitated. The scarlet burn was beginning again, crawling up her chest. What they'd done was wrong, strange—it was practically criminal, it got Hamlet sent away, and if her Rúnräd family looked at her with half the disgust of Hal's parents, she wouldn't survive it.

"Was anyone hurt?" asked Aaron, impatiently.

She shook her head mutely. Then paused. "Sort of. Afterwards." Ophelia took a deep breath. "There was a boy from the stables… He spoke to me a lot, and we became friends. But I realised not long after that he was… interested… in Prince Hamlet. And Hal was interested in him, too."

There was a lump in her throat now. The sensation of that day settled over her again like a moth-eaten cloak: the heat, the smell of hay, the sting in her cheek and the sticky, stretched sensation of the tears drying on her cheeks.

"I don't mind Hal being with other people," she whispered. "I never have. So I told him that he could see about the stablehand, if he wanted to. And one day he did, in the stables… and I was there too… and we were caught."

A long silence.

"They whipped him," she finished. "Calvin—the stablehand. Father made me watch out the window. I don't know what exactly happened to Hamlet because I was locked in my chambers—before Laertes went away he went between us, but he wasn't happy about it. And then we passed letters inside books, but we were caught again."

"And did anyone hurt you?" Hilga asked. Solveig placed her warm hand over Ophelia's and squeezed.

"The queen." Ophelia pointed to her face, the now-faded bruise over her eye. "And Father."

Tension bloomed like blood at the site of a wound.

Ophelia couldn't look at them, at any of them. She rested her head on Solveig's shoulder because that was the easiest way to stay upright, but her eyes looked wildly around at everything.

The little house's wooden panelling seemed to dance in the light from the open fire; she looked at the shelves full of jars of powdered herbs, dried flowers, crushed shells and other oddities, an array of blue and pink and white. There were blankets everywhere. Tapestries and paintings adorned every wall.

This was the house Ophelia spent so much of her youth in. When Mother died, she came here to cry, to read, to eat, to sleep. In those dark days, when Father couldn't take care of her, no one noticed that little Ophelia and poor Laertes were sometimes missing for days on end. Even Hamlet hardly noticed, swaddled in his mother's skirts, too busy being forced into Latin classes and fencing and mathematics to play every day.

"My dear girl," Hilga said, and sank to her knees. "Come here, my heart."

Ophelia obediently shuffled forward. She still couldn't meet her aunt's eyes.

"If they ever lay their hands on you again," Hilga said, putting her hands on Ophelia's shoulders, "I will carve them up and throw them in the sea. Feel no shame, Ophelia. People like that will never understand how complex love can be. Hmm?"

Ophelia hugged her aunt until the tears she'd been holding in finally fell, and she listened to the others talk, feeling for the first time in a long time like she was not a lamb in a den of wolves.

SCENE EIGHT

Hamlet was gloriously drunk.

It was only eight o'clock and already his skin was filled with a pleasant buzzing. He felt strangely out of control and yet he was aware of every part of his body: the tips of his ears, his hands, the angles of his elbows and knees.

The pub was loud and raucous, a dive of a place with sticky tables and terrible beer, but Rosencrantz and Guildenstern were welcomed there like old friends. They sat in the corner and watched people pass by. Every so often, someone would edge past their table into a shadowy little room, muttering apologies as their drinks shuddered, and they did not come back out.

Hamlet tipped his head back and looked at the ceiling. "Another?" he asked, but Rosencrantz and Guildenstern weren't listening; they had been caught up in conversation with an attractive man with a forked beard, and neither was paying any attention.

"Another," Hamlet decided, and went to the bar alone.

He ordered his pint of disastrously shit beer and stood, swaying, as he waited for it to be poured. Everything felt light and airy and good. It smelled terrible, but it didn't bother him as it had earlier in the evening, and he'd given up on avoiding the table's stickier spots.

He was just clutching his newly-filled pint when someone said: "Prince Hamlet."

That voice. It was enough to almost shock him into sobriety—almost.

"Arion," he said, startling. And then: "Prince Fortinbras, I mean. Forgive me."

The other man laughed. Hamlet turned his slightly confused gaze to him, and was surprised at how far he had to raise his eyes to meet Fortinbras'. He seemed taller now than he had been the last time they'd met. Broader too. Where he'd once been narrow-shouldered like Hamlet, he'd filled out.

Sinewy arms emerging from a worn and dusty blue tunic, faded by use. Hair that walked the line between blond and burnished copper. Hamlet knew that in the sunlight, it would gleam gold.

It felt like they were linked by lightning. Hamlet's veins sung with the singe of it, an imagined smoky tang filling his nostrils. The young man's russet hair curled down his neck in a mop; his face was freckled, his nose high and a little hooked—like his father's, Hamlet thought—and his white skin was marred with a frost-white scar down one cheek, the result of a long-ago fencing accident.

"You're here," Hamlet said. His tongue felt strangely thick, and he wasn't sure that was entirely because of the alcohol.

"I'm here," Fortinbras said. He smiled, stretching the freckles at the corners of his mouth. "I take it you've been having a pleasant evening."

If Hamlet was not mistaken, there was a glint of humour in that tone. Fortinbras looked from Hamlet—his messy hair in need of a trim, his pallor, the smudges under his eyes—to his cup. He wanted to shrivel up and die.

Gently, Fortinbras reached out and took Hamlet's pint. Simply unwrapped his fingers and took it.

"I think that's enough of that for one night, Hal," he said, and Hamlet was almost too shellshocked—Hal, he'd called him Hal, like he always used to—to resist.

Until Guildenstern appeared at his shoulder. He made an outlandish gesture between Fortinbras and Hamlet, mouth gaping. To Hamlet he said: "My friend, you've been robbed! By a prince of Norway, no less!"

A wave of pride and childish embarrassment washed over Hamlet. He felt, suddenly, like a child again; like he was once again in the fencing ground with Arion, Prince of Norway, and the master was telling him again that he needed to move like Arion, strike like Arion, think like Arion.

And here Arion stood, just like he had then, with his gentle hands and his bright eyes and his conqueror's smile, and he looked at Hamlet with a fondness that bordered on cruelty.

"I think he's finished," Fortinbras said. That smile didn't flicker, didn't change. "Why don't you have it instead?"

He passed the cup to Guildenstern, who pressed it back into Hal's hand. He felt, as he often did, like things were happening to him and he was powerless to stop them. *Go here. Say this. Take this, drink it, all in one.* He did as he was instructed and Guild laughed.

When Hamlet looked to Fortinbras again, the smile was gone. His gaze drifted from Guildenstern, who he looked at with mild disapproval, to someone else over Hamlet's right shoulder.

Rosencrantz.

Hamlet had never seen such plain dislike written over Fortinbras' features. He looked at Rosencrantz the same way Hamlet looked at simpering dignitaries.

"Prince Fortinbras," said Rosencrantz, and extended one delicate, long-fingered hand for Arion to shake. "To what do we owe the pleasure?"

"I came for a drink with a friend," Fortinbras said. "And found another friend here waiting. How do you know Prince Hamlet?"

"We met him two days ago," said Rosencrantz, "and as of yesterday, we live together."

Again, Hamlet felt that strange sense of being buffeted by opposing winds.

"*Prince* Hamlet," Guild echoed.

He looked at Hamlet, then at Rosencrantz, who simply pulled a face that meant: not surprising. Hamlet felt sick. Whether it was because of the alcohol or the anxiety or the fact that the room seemed to be rapidly turning into a sauna, he wasn't sure.

Fortinbras looked as if he was about to say something, but then he seemed to catch sight of Hamlet, his pallor, and the way a bead of sweat was now trailing down his forehead, and his gaze softened.

"Apologies if that was a secret you had planned to keep, Hal. That was thoughtless of me."

"It was," Hamlet said. Sickness and frustration made his words feel like bile washing up his throat. "You should think before you speak, Prince Fortinbras."

"I didn't mean any harm."

"It hardly matters now."

A beat. Someone cleared their throat. It took Hamlet a moment to understand: this was the friend Fortinbras had come to meet.

What was that feeling that made the room spin? He refused to call it jealousy.

"Arion," the newcomer said. "Everything alright here?"

Italian, based on the drawl, with pale brown skin and an obstinate expression framed by shaggy dark hair. Poor clothing that was patched in places, shoes that had clearly seen better days…

"Ah—allow me to introduce you," Fortinbras said. That smile emerged again: he was doing his best to break this strange tension, to dissolve whatever made Rosencrantz stand as still as marble, made Guildenstern look between the bar and the door like he couldn't decide which would be a better escape.

"This is my dear friend, Horatio," Fortinbras said, and clapped the newcomer on the shoulder.

He was not sure why he did it. Later, lying in bed, he reflected on his words with a sense of shame that made him toss and turn, unable to rest. He tried to pretend that he hadn't said it: maybe he'd shook the newcomer's hand instead, or he'd just given him a peaceable nod, and the man would have nodded back, and Hamlet would have avoided what came next.

"A pet commoner," he said, plastering on his most genial smile. "How very continental of you."

Fortinbras did not take kindly to the insult. Hamlet saw the storm clouds beginning to descend. When they were boys, a remark like that would have brought them to blows, and he was already curling his fists in preparation when Fortinbras instead shook his head, cleared his throat, and turned away.

"My apologies, Horatio. It seems that my cousin has not quite grown up."

He did not look at Hamlet again. They turned and left.

SCENE NINE
ophelia

Ophelia hurried back through the ice and snow, back to the mirror and the autumn air, which felt hot against her skin after Rúnräd's chill. It was dark. She was running late, so late; she would be lucky if her father hadn't stirred up hell and convinced the guards to look for her.

Before leaving Rúnräd, she'd spoken to Fatma about the level of Corruption in the palace. Fatma said what Ophelia had expected: if the quantity kept rising as it was, Kronborg would soon be uninhabitable. Fatma travelled the world, speaking with other communities about the ever-present issue of Corruption. If she was worried, Ophelia was worried.

The potion fit into the palm of her hand. It was the sort of thing most people wouldn't have kept out in the open. Admittedly, most people wouldn't even have made this particular potion, just to avoid the risk of the wrong person taking it.

It had been easy to swipe but harder to hide. When her aunt's wife Solveig saw her slide the potion bottle into her pocket, Ophelia had expected her to say something. But Solveig, with her pale Seer's eyes, had only smiled and nodded once, encouragingly, as if to say: *I expected this.*

It was reassuring in a way, to think this was planned somehow. Better to believe that than to see this as her own choice, to see the consequences as relating to her own actions.

She hurried down the main street. Better to be safe, where it was well-lit and uncomplicated, than to go by the sea and risk the dark. She kept thinking of the threads of Corruption she extracted from the chapel, the dancing room, her father's chambers: invisible, until she beckoned it. She rushed past the open door of an alehouse and kept her head down as she dipped through the light spilling from the open door.

Fatma said her efforts to remove the Corruption were, more than likely, all for nothing. It didn't make a dent in what was a catastrophe waiting to happen, a plague in the making, a tidal wave about to come crashing in.

Kronborg was not long for this world, if Fatma was right, which she almost always was. And if Kronborg fell, so would Helsingør, and then Denmark: a fatal game of dominos, a dangling thread waiting to be severed.

Ophelia's skin did not hurt yet after drinking the potion. That would be the first effect, the burning, as if she'd been out in the sun too long. Then the burning would move inside, tracking along her veins, searing her from the inside out. Then her organs: the plump, purple muscle of her heart, her liver, her lungs. Soon, her muscles would quake as a fever took over. Her eyes would roll back in her head, showing only their whites; if an ordinary physician came to see her, he would think she was dying.

But then it would pass. The strength would enter her limbs again and her body would recover—except for her eyes, which would start to turn pale, until eventually, maybe not for years, they would lose their blue and turn entirely white.

And the world she saw when she woke would look entirely different.

The process of becoming a Sight Guide—someone who could see Corruption—was not meant to be painless or easy. It was the sort of thing that could not be undone, not by anything. It would change her utterly into someone who could see the threads of magic and alter them in ways few could.

It was meant to be frightening, sickening. But if it meant better protecting Kronborg... If it meant keeping her home safe, she would do it.

There was the spire of the church, pointing at the dimming blue of the sky. The castle was still far away, and she couldn't stop herself from imagining Father's panic. Their evening meal was long past; maybe her plate was cold on the table, the fat from the meat congealed into a cloudy puddle. She couldn't erase the image of his worried face from her mind: his teeth gnawing at his lip from behind his little white beard, his darting gaze flickering between her empty chair and the door.

Beyond the city limits there was no one around to see, so she ran. Ophelia found to her concern that already her muscles felt like they'd been wrung out. Her mother's face swam before her, her eyes paler and paler by the day; she remembered her father clutching her hand as she slipped away into fever.

Influenza, not the Sight Guide ritual. The disease had swept through the palace, taking the queen's sister and the head physician and half the kitchen down with it, but Ophelia recalled the murmurs of her Rúnräd family, their fear, and finally, their absence as the way to the Otherland was shut.

Through the gate. The sky was getting darker and darker, the stars beginning to show themselves through the cloudy gloom. Marcellus was still there, but he was distracted speaking to another guard and didn't notice her. The great doors creaked open for her, pulled by some unseen servant. The golden glow of the entrance hall washed over her: the fire flickered in the grate, warm and inviting, and the lanterns swung gently in the cool breeze she'd admitted.

She took the stairs two at a time. Left by the tapestry representing a fleet of sailing boats, right past the library doors, up a narrow spiral staircase…

Ophelia paused outside the door. It was quiet inside; perhaps Father had gone looking for her, and now he was gone. But she didn't even have to search for the key in her purse to let herself in. The door swung easily open, revealing their little sitting room.

Father sat in his favourite chair, warming his feet by the fire. He didn't look up when Ophelia entered. He didn't acknowledge her at all. His only action was to flip over the letter he was reading to see the other side.

She didn't pause to acknowledge her disappointment. Ophelia just dropped her basket and went to bed.

Before dawn had a chance to illuminate her bedroom—the overstuffed bookcase, the cushions, the dried flowers hung on the walls—she was writhing in pain. But Ophelia did not cry out. She was too stubborn for that.

She squeezed her eyes shut as hard as she could through the pain and pressed her face into the pillow, until the blood that oozed from her cracking lips stained the fabric crimson red.

SCENE TEN
hamlet

It was dawn, and Hamlet was alone. The room was mostly dark, only the barest sliver of light filtering in through a tiny window. His one candle only illuminated one patch of desk, its effusive glow no match for the steeped-tea shadows that drenched every surface. He felt alarmingly sober.

Outside, Wittenberg was quiet. Rain was falling—he could hear the quiet, soothing sound of it splashing against the cobblestones, the gentle rattle of it against the window panes. His limbs itched. He always felt restless after an intense rain, but going out into the streets and running endlessly wasn't the most appealing of ideas.

Hamlet had just moved to pick up his quill when Rosencrantz spoke from the doorway.

"I heard you were caught in the armoury with your trousers down," he said. Tall and lean, he looked a little like a predator standing in the doorway, with his strawberry curls falling over his face and his strange eyes: pale like opal, which lent him an odd, starved look that was not as off putting as it should have been. "With a boy, is what I heard."

Fear seized Hamlet's heart in a vice-like grip. He tried to calm it, to repress it, and leaned as nonchalantly as he could against the edge of his desk. The rapid rise and fall of his chest betrayed him.

"I don't know what you're talking about."

Rosencrantz stepped further inside. Here, the candlelight deepened the shadows beneath his eyes, the hollows of his collarbones. He looked, Hamlet thought, like something from another world. Like he had been carved from marble, not made of flesh and blood like the rest of them. He, too, did not seem to feel the effects of the night's inebriation.

"Don't worry," he said. "I don't care whose trousers you're untying. But tell me: is the story true? If it is, I may have something of interest to show you."

Hamlet couldn't think what to say. To admit it was to offer Rosencrantz a part of his soul—to tear out his own heart and present it, beating and bleeding, on a silver platter. To deny it felt the same, except at least Hamlet was the only one tearing himself to shreds.

"It's safe," said Ros. "Guild knows too, if that convinces you. Lord knows he has more sense than I do."

Guild knows too.

"It was a stable," Hamlet managed. His mouth felt dry. "Not an armoury."

He would offer his heart, and risk it being hurt. He could not, in this little room, with the candle burning and his ink bottle opened and the rain pattering outside, seem to pursue any other option.

Ros's mouth twitched. "I had a feeling."

"Tell no one."

Amusement. "Not even your future wife."

"She already knows that part," he replied, and relished the moment of confusion that flashed across Ros's features.

He partially expected Ros to question him, to dig deeper. It came as a shock to see him turn away instead, wandering over to the corner and staring into the little mirror which hung there, peering into his own features.

"You surprise me," Ros said, after a moment. "But I understand. Regardless of whether you're looking for an attachment or not… Nordsee is safe. There are more people like us in one place than I've ever seen in my life."

They met eyes. A thrill of understanding darted between them.

"Where is this Nordsee?" Hamlet asked, rubbing the back of his neck. His skin felt hot and clammy, and he was still uncomfortably sweaty from travel. "Is it far from here?"

Ros's hand reached out to brush the gold-gilded frame. It was an unwieldy, clumsily-made thing, but expensive. To Hamlet's surprise, Rosencrantz lifted the whole thing easily and placed it flat on the ground.

"A mirror," he said, rolling up his sleeves and glancing at Hamlet, "is a wonderful thing."

He stepped forward, and when his feet hit the glass, he disappeared.

Hamlet jolted backwards and slid, landing in a heap on the floor. The desk rocked, the quill rolling onto the ground, parchment fluttering. bed and he fell sideways, landing in a heap on the floor. The room was quiet and empty. The mirror's surface was undeniably still.

Rosencrantz was gone.

Hamlet's hand went to the rosary around his neck. He squeezed its wooden beads between his fingers. All the prayers were gone from his head, whisked away; it was just him, and the rain tapping at the window, and the mirror.

Until Rosencrantz's arm came scrabbling back through the glass.

"Jesus," Hamlet said, squeezing his rosary tighter.

Rosencrantz grabbed the edge of the mirror and hauled himself out like he was dragging himself from a deep pool. He lay on the floor on his back, his hands propped behind his head, and gazed peacefully at the ceiling.

"The angle of entry is unfortunate," he said, pushing his hair back. There was a smudge of dirt on his cheekbone and a smear of something dark, like ashes, across his tunic. "The nearest full-length mirror is a mile away, but this does the trick in a pinch."

Rosencrantz rolled his head to the side and examined Hamlet.

"You can drop the rosary," he said. "I thought the same at first. Devilry and dark magic. But it's nothing like that, I promise you."

Hamlet slowly released the beads.

"What is it," he asked, "if not that?"

Guildenstern spoke from the doorway, and Hamlet jumped. He hadn't seen the other man appear.

"It's magic," said Guildenstern. "The good kind."

ACT II

SCENE ONE
ophelia

She was made of fire, of heat. Her limbs were wood to feed the fever. Her skin turned black and cracked, splitting like overripe fruit. The place where her back met the bed was hotter than the fires of hell, and as much as Ophelia tried to resist screaming, she could not.

It was five more days before the fever tossed Ophelia from its grasp. She woke up rasping for breath from a mouth that tasted like death itself, wrapped in a blanket that was soaked through with sweat. There was no one in the room.

She sat up slowly, testing herself. "Father?"

No reply. Ophelia carefully manoeuvred her legs out of bed. Despite the longest three days of her life (apart from those where her mother sickened and died), she felt… alright.

She'd expected everything to look different, but so far it was all the same. Same rickety chair in the corner, same red and blue bedding, same woven rug on the floor. Same pile of books in the corner, delicately balanced with their plain leather bindings facing out.

There was a little bottle of something resting on her dressing table. Ophelia reached for it and misjudged the distance. It toppled, spilling everywhere. Oil.

She salvaged an unfamiliar brown book before it could be stained by the mysterious liquid. Everything felt strange and dreamlike, like she was surrounded by a cushion of air. Nothing seemed to really touch her.

She flipped open the Bible. It landed on the Book of Judith.

The oil. The Catholic Bible. The sweet, heavy smell of incense in the air, and the strange, gluey sensation on her forehead. She touched the skin there and the pads of her fingers came away shiny.

Extreme Unction, her brain supplied.

The last rites for the dying.

"Father!" she called again, and tried to stand. "Father, I'm awake!"

A pause like a held breath. She was certain for a moment that she was alone—that Father had thought she was dying, that she was dead, and he had left her in her bed with the last rites and gone to do business—but then the door clattered open, and it was not only her father but her brother came running in.

Father took her face in his hands, telling her to get back to bed, ridiculous girl, your fever has broken, you look so much better, do you think you can eat?

Ophelia reached out with her weak hands and stretched towards her brother.

"You came home," she said. "Oh, Laertes—that beard looks awful."

And then she passed out.

When Ophelia woke up again, Laertes was sitting in the little chair in the corner. He was leaning with his chin in his hand, reading something. He had shaved, and now he looked a little more like the brother who'd left not so very long ago.

His blond hair hung in ringlets that trailed over the neck of his tunic. There was a furrow in his brow, and his cheeks were a little red and wind-brushed from time outdoors. His eyes were the only ones in the world the same colour as Ophelia's now that their mother was gone; when hers changed to the misty grey of a Sight Guide, he would carry their mother's eyes alone.

He must have noticed her staring, because his eyes flicked up from his book to meet hers. Laertes smiled.

"If you wanted me home," he said, "you could have just asked. No need for the dramatics."

"That wasn't dramatics."

"Father thought you were dying. The physicians didn't know what to do. He snuck in a Catholic priest to smear that oil on your head, by the way, so you'd better be grateful and sinless for at least a few weeks."

Ophelia's mouth twisted. "No one saw, did they?"

"Not that I'm aware," Laertes said.

Carefully, Ophelia sat up. "You were coming here anyway," she accused, when she had got her breath back. "How else would you get here so fast?"

"On an enchanted sailing vessel through the Otherland," was Laertes' speedy answer. "It cost a pretty penny, but I did think you were dying. Now I know you're not, you can pay me back."

She bit back a smile. "I can offer you three marks and a bit of old ribbon."

He pretended to consider her offer. "Done."

Carefully, Ophelia tested her feet again. She felt a little more steady in the muscles but was still fiercely light-headed. More than anything, she was craving cheese. Hopefully, she asked Laertes if there was any, to which the answer was no, and that the physician's orders included no dairy for a week.

"I've already told Hilga and Solveig that you're doing well," he said, offering her a miserable-looking disc of dry, tasteless bread. "They send their love, except Hilga also sends her rage, and I'm not convinced she and Solveig are speaking. You wouldn't happen to know why?"

She managed to get to the windowsill. The castle courtyard was almost entirely empty. In the distance, Ophelia could see the rooftops that made up the city, their beautiful orange-red roofs, the same colour she imagined desert sand to be when she read about it in her books.

The castle looked no different. Ophelia's stomach sank. Solveig had warned her to be prepared for the world to look different after she woke from the fever, and yet nothing had changed. The same blue sky, the same gulls crowing overhead, the same cobblestones worn soft and silver by a thousand tramping feet.

She rubbed her eyes. The eyelids were swollen, and she could already tell that they would remain red and raw for days. Her looking-glass showed her the truth of it, as well as how pasty and strange her skin looked, how lank her hair had gotten.

She needed a bath. She needed to brush her hair and wash her face and make herself smell less like a corpse.

Then and only then she might be able to work out the mystery of why her Sight Guide ability hadn't kicked in.

It was strange. When she pinched her fingers together and whispered the words, her nightly routine for so many years since Mother died, the Corruption didn't feel right. It was like trying to grasp an eel with her bare hands, like it was slithering and writhing from her grip and into the current.

Ophelia looked into the darkness. Maybe she was imagining things, but something did seem… off. Like the magic that was always there for her to grasp was sliding out of reach, and like the stain it left behind was growing stronger, more solid, taking form…

She shook her head and went back to bed but all night she couldn't stop looking into the shadows, waiting for something to stir.

SCENE TWO
hamlet

P hilip Melanchthon was a man who refused to admit that he was going bald.

His reddish-brown hair had thinned to a fine dusting, most of it confined to a few curly wisps at the front, the rest scraped over the glistening top in greasy strings. He had a very pointy chin and thin lips, through which he talked almost incessantly for three hours about theological issues. This would have been fine had it not been for the fact that his lecture was entirely in Latin (Hamlet despised Latin), sprinkled with Classical Greek (Hamlet also despised Greek), and made no sense whatsoever (this Hamlet could support).

Hamlet's classmates were a lost cause. In a stuffy room in Melanchthon's own house, deprived of light and fresh air, Hamlet sat at a rickety little table while they all gazed, wide-eyed, at their professor like he was a god descending from the clouds.

Magic is real, he wanted to scream. *None of this matters because magic is real.*

Their adoration only served to heighten Hal's irritation, so that when his lecture was finished he packed all of his things as loudly as he could and clattered out before anyone could try to engage him in painful Latin conversation.

It was a dismal introduction to the scholarship of Wittenberg University, and it made him wonder why he had bothered to attend in the first place. It wasn't as if he needed to go; Father would be furious when he found out Hamlet wasn't attending, but with any luck he'd just drag him back to Denmark and they could be done with this charade.

His day only worsened when he got outside the classroom and found Prince Arion Fortinbras waiting for him.

"That bad?" Fortinbras asked, falling into step beside him.

Hamlet wanted to ignore him and brush him off as he would an annoying fly, but he found that he couldn't. His old fondness for Fortinbras stopped him.

Reluctantly, he pressed down his disappointment: he'd been planning to go home and catch Rosencrantz, who'd promised to give him another magic demonstration, maybe even to show Hamlet how to put a hand through the mirror like he did.

"It's just new to me," Hamlet said. He wasn't sure which he was really speaking of: the lessons or the magic. "I'll get the hang of it."

The awkwardness of the evening at the tavern hung between them like a thick mist, but Fortinbras seemed to move effortlessly through it. At no point did he question where they were going. He seemed content to walk beside Hamlet without any aim or meaning.

Fortinbras talked about the weather and his lessons. Hamlet was aware that his responses were stale, maybe even rude, but he couldn't seem to produce anything else. He wished he could have something interesting to say, but here he was again, as always seemed to happen: he was out of control of his own mind, his own tongue, and his surprise at seeing Fortinbras was not enough to stir him into proper speech.

His brain rebelled most of the time. When he wanted to be calm, his mind would race; when he wanted to speak, it withheld all words and forced him into silence. He took in what Fortinbras was saying, acknowledged it and understood its meaning, and there was some kind of response in his own mind, but not one that anyone else could understand. Sensations, shapes and colours, not language.

Fortinbras noticed, as he was always going to.

"You must be tired," he said. Hamlet gnawed hard on his bottom lip until he drew blood. "Shall I leave you?"

"No, no," Hamlet managed. "I mean, yes. If you want to."

Fortinbras shrugged. "If it makes no difference to you, then I'll stay. Can I show you something?"

Whatever Fortinbras wanted to show him was beyond the walls on the southern side of the city. Fortinbras seemed happy not to speak, and Hamlet felt more comfortable observing his surroundings. They left the city and passed the rickety little houses that had accumulated outside the main centre, the temporary markets and the cobblestone streets.

Now they walked across a flat plain with the breeze at their backs. The sun was low in the sky, the autumn light shimmering across the grass. Out here, the smells of the city vanished. No more food and sweat and urine, no more smoke, no more iron tang from the blacksmith's.

Hamlet breathed it in and felt his shoulders relax minutely. He hadn't realised how much he'd missed this:

the simple pleasure of walking without feeling the hard stone under your feet or following the path set out for you. He let the long grass brush his shins over the tops of his boots.

"It's nothing special," said Fortinbras, who had taken off his cloak and was now carrying it draped over his arm, a bundle worth more than five of the ramshackle houses behind them. "Just a nice view and a good place to sit, but it's helped me when Wittenberg becomes too much."

"You find it overwhelming too?"

Fortinbras cracked a smile. "Very, Hal. It's a busy place. No one has time to stop and enjoy anything, except us students, who have all the time in the world and we still don't. Although, speaking of which, most people don't come down here very often—I should really swear you to secrecy or it'll be overrun. Promise you won't tell anyone?"

Hamlet looked around. It was a simple place: the ground must have sloped gently downwards, because when he looked back they were sheltered somewhat from the view of the city. A broad river spread out in front of him. Even from here, he could hear it burbling and the splash of a carp jumping somewhere downstream.

"Why is it so quiet?" Hamlet asked. He couldn't resist wandering towards the bank. The sound of water reminded him of home, only missing its briny smell and the shriek of gulls.

"It won't be this evening," Fortinbras said, "but this time of the afternoon is usually pleasant. Hardly any vessels stop here, and most of them sail through early in the day."

Hamlet shrugged, then sat cross-legged on the grass. "It's a nice place. Peaceful"

Fortinbras sat down beside him, stretching out his long legs with a sigh of relief. Hamlet's eyes were drawn to him, as they always had been in the sliver of childhood they'd shared.

Prince Arion Fortinbras, so concerned about keeping a patch of grass and a stretch of river private.

Fortinbras rolled his neck, like his back was hurting him. "Truth be told, I brought you here as a bit of a… peace offering."

Hamlet's insides shrivelled into dust. "About the other night," he started. "I was drunk. I shouldn't have said what I said about your… your friend. It was unkind."

"It didn't befit your status."

He was right. It wasn't the kind of thing Hamlet could imagine his father saying—his mother maybe, who'd always had a temper that couldn't be tamed, but not Father. And whatever Hamlet thought of his father's parenting abilities, he had to give it to him: he was, at the end of the day, a very good king.

Father was calm when it mattered, energetic when it was needed. He could embrace a grieving widow and clatter his spear against three hundred shields in the same day. Old King Hamlet treated his emotions like something to be tamed, to be controlled and brought into submission, and he expected the same of everyone around him.

Father was so in control of himself that he couldn't understand why Hamlet struggled. It made no sense to him: one day, his son could sit still as a stone all day long, staring out of the window at nothing; the next Hamlet's limbs would twitch with energy and his eyes would dart ceaselessly and the longer he stayed in his chair the more he felt like his skin was on fire.

Hamlet admired that control, craved it, would never have it.

"I'm sorry," he said, and poured as much genuine emotion into the words as he could. "It was a stupid thing to say, and I would like to apologise to your friend properly."

"I can arrange it," Fortinbras said. He seemed pleased, and abruptly he lay down to look at the clouds. They remained there in silence for a long time, long enough that Hamlet became acutely aware of the feeling of his own heart drumming violently in his chest.

When they parted ways, he thought—hoped—it might be as friends.

SCENE THREE
ophelia

"Ophelia, do I look like a fool?" Polonius asked. A wry little smile darted from beneath his moustache, then swiftly faded as he smoothed his jerkin and looked once again into the mirror.

Yes, Ophelia agreed privately, but in reality she just brushed the lint from the crushed velvet of his gown and hummed. Gown and jerkin both were a faded and unbecoming shade of green that reminded her of sickly leaves. The jerkin was too big and even when it was fastened as close as possible he swam in it, and the shirt beneath was gaudy and decorated with clashing red thread.

"I have nothing else, you see," he said, twisting this way and that to find a better angle. "The moths got into my good clothes."

"You look perfectly fine, Father." She kissed him on the cheek. "Please don't worry."

It tore at her to see him like this, embarrassed of his appearance. She reached out to pick another piece of fluff from one of the creases in his puff-sleeved gown, as if that small improvement might shift things for the better. It didn't.

"Apparel often proclaims the man. That's what I always say," he muttered, mostly to himself. "And here I am, dining with the king in clothes the colour of bile. What that says about me, I don't want to know."

That got a laugh from Ophelia, and she was relieved to see Father smile again, wider and for longer. He took one last look in the mirror, then reluctantly turned away. Father's kiss to her forehead was momentary, but even then she felt slightly sick from the smell of his perfume.

He went, the door closing behind him with a snap. She used her moment of privacy to cast her eyes around the room, but nothing was out of place. There was no Corruption, not that she could see. There was no other magic either. It was just the same as it had been before she drank the potion, and that disappointed her more than she cared to admit.

Moments later, a serving girl appeared with a message for Ophelia: Lady Alessandra would be with her shortly, and she hoped Ophelia would be willing to come and join the other ladies in a dancing lesson.

Ophelia dismissed the girl and changed victoriously into her dancing clothes.

The first thing Ophelia had done when her hand was steady enough to write was pen a letter to Alessandra. Alessandra was an Italian lady at court, a gentlewoman, and had been a handmaiden to the queen for four years. Only a month ago, Alessandra had been married. Ophelia had hoped to attend the wedding, but everything happened with Hamlet and no one would speak to her and the idea languished, too silly to even speak aloud.

For a long time, Ophelia had treated Alessandra like an older sister. She'd even harboured secret imaginings of Laertes marrying her so that they could be real sisters. It was a lovely dream, but never to be true: Laertes and Alessandra butted heads more than any other pair at the palace, and there was no hope of any attachment there.

Anyway, Alessandra married Lorenz, who was one of the loveliest men at court and a fellow Italian to boot. They made a gorgeous pair. Two of the tallest people at court, they swept around like a pair of swans: both long-haired, hers dark and his light, both tanned, both with that secretive, permanent smile that seems to say: I have this figured out.

They were beautiful and lovely and kind. People adored them, and not in the the uncomplicated way she'd thought they loved her. No, people loved Ophelia when they thought she was clean and angelic, and now they saw that she was an imperfect human made of flesh and blood and the illusion shattered like glass, along with their 'love'.

But Alessandra and Lorenz… Beautiful. Kind. Powerful.

That was where the admiration flowed from: not from some sentimentality, but from the cold, hard truth of money and connections. Alessandra and Lorenz were two of the most entangled people within the palace web, the best connected, the most vital.

So Ophelia wrote a letter and begged forgiveness. More than that: she begged tutelage.

I can't fix my mistakes alone. You know that I can be stubborn and silly, and that sometimes my mind is difficult to change. I have no one to guide me away from my errors.

Would you help me? I have always trusted and loved you like my own blood. You would never steer me wrong.

Help me to be better and to be loved again. It's all I want.

Alessandra liked to help. Liked to take in waifs and strays, the newcomers to the castle, the thirteen-year-old girls with no Danish and no friends.

Begging made Ophelia's teeth grind, but clearly it worked.

She stripped quickly down to her shift and re-dressed in a simpler gown, one that made her look younger than her age. Innocent, the way these women liked. It was a delicate rose colour that accentuated the flush in her cheeks and, more importantly, the colour was muted; she wasn't flaunting wealth, or beauty. She was just there to dance.

If she got to Alessandra, she thought, quickly braiding her hair back, she could perhaps get back into the queen's good graces. And then she could resume the work she'd been doing tirelessly, which now felt so very pointless: removing those tiny strands of Corruption from all the darkest corners of the palace. A job she could do better with the Sight, which was stubbornly resisting her.

The royal wing was the most important part to ward and cleanse. Royalty had a way of attracting Corruption. Her wards could only do so much. Painting ingredients onto the walls in rigid symbols prevented the Corruption from 'sticking' to surfaces, which made it easier for her to remove. The caveat was that walls where the Corruption was already deep-rooted wouldn't hold wards for long, the sap that stained them flaking into sad, magic-less snowfalls.

Wards were good when done well. So was cleansing the Corruption, teasing out its strands and dissolving them with magic. In a normal household, those things would be perfectly effective.

But, although the Sight clearly had not taken, she could feel that her work was doing almost nothing in Kronborg. Every time she tried to ward a wall, the spell fragmented instantly; every time she cleansed her room or herself, she felt like she was only grasping a tendril of a larger thing, the tail of a beast that slipped easily out of her grasp.

Without seeing the exact strands and knots of the Corruption's tendrils, she would never untangle them.

Her hand slipped. Ophelia clutched her head, swearing. The last pin to fasten her headdress had gouged her in the scalp, and the sting was unbelievable.

"Not language befitting a penitent young lady," came an amused voice from the doorway. "I hope it's not bleeding; with fair hair like yours, it'll show."

Ophelia blushed scarlet to the roots of her hair, which was, in one thin section, turning the same colour. Before she could explain herself, Alessandra was beside her. The other woman's hands were cold as she began to expertly remove the pins from Ophelia's hair.

Her gown was made of luxurious black and grey fabric, thick to keep out the cold. A low, square neckline showed her collarbones beneath a thin white chemise and her hair was nested within a silver capigliara. She looked thoroughly Italian. Amidst the other court women, who were mostly Danish, Alessandra always stood out. That seemed to be the intention.

"I'm still quite weak," Ophelia offered into the silence. "I've been ill."

Alessandra hummed. "Your recent confinement made me believe you were with child. I assume I am incorrect?"

Ophelia let out a very undignified squeak and tried to shake her head, but the vice-like grip Alessandra had on her hair prevented any movement.

"Not pregnant," Alessandra said, in a slightly wondering tone. "Miscarriage?"

"Never pregnant," Ophelia insisted. "I have never been with child."

The very thought made her want to be sick. As much as she loved children, she was never able to stomach the thought of having her own. Sex didn't appeal to her. Pregnancy and the confinement that would come with it seemed like a prison sentence. All of that to birth a child, and in the process risk her life, risk leaving the baby motherless, or to go through it and leave with no baby at all…

"That is a mistake," Alessandra said, which was not what Ophelia was expecting. None of this was what she'd anticipated, actually: Alessandra's firm hand holding her in place, re-pinning the headdress, talking so abruptly. "You should have made sure of it. They would not have been able to stop him from marrying you, then. You would be a princess by now, wouldn't you?"

Her surprise must have shown on her face, because Alessandra chuckled. The final pin slid into place. Ophelia's head still hurt, and she was sure the blood was still flowing, but at least the black headdress would cover it.

"There is no reason to treat you like a child anymore," Alessandra said, and tapped Ophelia gently on the cheek. "Before, you were in that strange time, where the world cannot decide if you are a woman or a girl. Now, we have decided."

"I wouldn't have done that," Ophelia said. She rose from her seat and slipped on her shoes. *She must think I am innocent*, she reminded herself. *She must trust me enough to vouch for me to the queen.* "Truth be told, I wasn't thinking. I couldn't have… planned, like you suggest."

Alessandra just shrugged. "Perhaps not," she said.

Her warm, brown eyes swept over Ophelia from top to bottom. Whatever she saw, she didn't feel the need to share. Ophelia tried to pretend she wasn't thrown. This was not the Alessandra she remembered.

Alessandra was not simpering or saccharine, but she was not so… blunt. Ophelia wondered if this was just a change that came now that she was married, then shook the thought off; simple and childish to think saying a vow could change a person that way.

Perhaps it wasn't that Alessandra was fundamentally altered. Maybe it was Ophelia who had changed. As she'd said, the court had decided: she was grown now, an adult woman, not the half-child she'd been for so long.

At just seventeen, her childhood was done.

Alessandra's dark skirts rustled as she turned towards the door with finality. She swept across the little sitting room, pausing only for a moment to pick up Father's book and turn it over in her hands, and then glanced behind her.

"Do hurry up, dear," Alessandra said. "If you're late for your first dancing lesson back, even I won't be able to save you."

SCENE FOUR
hamlet

At the same moment as Ophelia was struggling through the steps of a complicated dance, Hamlet was watching Ros levitate a ball of water between his palms.

"Some would say this is bad magic," Ros said. The orb of water swirled, bright blue like it was lit from within. His elbows were propped on the table, his sleeves rolled up to protect the cuffs from dragging in the liquid. "Some say you shouldn't use magic to manipulate anything outside the self."

"Then what's the point?" Hamlet asked. He reached out to touch the water and Ros tutted, whisking it away.

"They say it's because magic can leave a mark." As Hamlet watched, the water turned from blue to a deep, inky purple. "You have to think of magic like a physical thing. When something is brushed by magic, a residue is left behind."

"So that water will be left with traces," Hamlet murmured. "Would anything happen to me if I drank it, for example?"

Ros pondered the question for a moment before he answered. "It's possible, but the effects would be so minor they'd practically be non-existent. The residue might stay, but it's impossible to see or feel, and it has no magical capabilities of its own."

Hamlet watched the water swirl between Ros's palms. It was beautiful, but something about that shade of purple unsettled him. He preferred the blue, and he told Ros so, but the orb remained the same strange shade.

For the past few days, he'd hardly thought about anything but the mirror. He'd asked first if it was possible for him to pass through it as easily as Ros did, to which Ros had answered in the affirmative. Then he'd begged to go, to which Ros said no. Or, rather, not yet.

"Why not?"

"Because," Ros said, "I need to think about the implications."

Hamlet felt this was an unnecessarily mysterious answer. He was also annoyed, because he had received an invitation from Fortinbras to come for dinner which he'd declined because Ros had promised to show him some potions. The potions didn't materialise, and an evening with Fortinbras would have been nice, odd as it was to admit it.

"Do you think I could do that?" he asked. He still found it hard to believe that anyone—*anyone*—could do magic, even when Ros told him so over and over.

Ros didn't even bother answering, just rolled his eyes.

Magic is everywhere, all around you. It's in the air you breathe, the water you drink. It lives in you. All you have to do is learn how to use it, to bend it to your will…

He wanted to cradle an orb of water. He wanted to manipulate a breeze through their little sitting room, stirring up paper and parchment into a whirlpool; he wanted to imagine objects into being and turn himself invisible and make himself immortal.

He didn't know if those things were possible, but he was determined to find out.

"Watch carefully," Ros said. He wrenched his hands back from the orb, as if it took an enormous amount of force. The purple water hesitated a second, then seemed to distort itself. It fell in a perfect disc and splattered on the table, soaking everything nearby.

Hamlet picked at the laces of his shirt, examining them. As the water rolled over the fabric and dried against the warmth of his skin, it lost its purple sheen and became perfectly clear, all its magic lost.

"Thanks for the warning," he muttered. He stripped off the soaked shirt and got up. He was drenched, most of the water having rolled off the surface of the table and into his lap. "That's the end of this evening's lesson, I take it."

Ros smiled. "I think so."

His eyes skimmed over Hamlet's bare chest. Hamlet let them. For a moment, he wondered if Ros was going to stand, to say something, to do something.

Something low in his belly uncurled itself, woke from a deep sleep that had lasted through the late summer months, and wriggled into his skin.

But Ros's gaze slid off Hamlet's bare skin and back to his face. His eyes were unreadable through that pale, silvery sheen.

"Magic is delicate," he murmured unexpectedly. "It takes a strong will to tame it, to force it into shape. To fear magic is to admit that it is your master. To see it as something to be avoided, to be cleansed, is to deny that magic is natural, and so is what it leaves behind. I don't like to think of it that way: like something that stains."

Rosencrantz raised his right hand, fingers splayed.

In the centre of his palm, a kernel of black forged itself out of the air. That kernel sparked, grew, devoured fuel from nowhere, and burned into a flame of pure, solid purple.

"Using magic is easy," he said. "But using what it leaves behind? That's power."

And power is what I need, Hamlet thought. Here, alone in Wittenberg, he felt it suddenly: that feeling he'd always noticed in Denmark but never been able to put a name to.

Wear the crown. Come to the meeting. Don't speak. School your expressions. Listen to your mother prattle on about etiquette while you watch the girl you love leave the room, dragged by a father's hand.

What had he done of his own volition in his entire seventeen years of life that had not ended in punishment?

Kings and princes were meant to be powerful. It should have run in his veins, impressed into his being by a god he wasn't sure existed, a god who had never answered his prayers to be stronger, to be better, *please let me be good, let me be the son my father wants me to be.*

Every prayer unanswered. Every encouraging word from Father cradled close to his chest, every piece of advice, all of it crumbled to ashes in the heart of a son who could not seem to make himself better.

But power thrummed from Rosencrantz, and Hamlet recognised it now: the unearthliness of him, the way he seemed almost like a shade walking this earth. The faraway look in his eyes, like he was always gazing into another world, scrying for ghosts. The same lost energy emanating from Guildenstern.

They moved through this world with the knowledge that none of it mattered against the power that flowed unseen around them. There was a force that could not be contained in books or maps. There was more to the world than heaven and earth, more than existed in all these pointless philosophies.

"Teach me," Hamlet said, his mouth dry. "Teach me how to use the magic, how to bind it to my will. And I swear to you, Rosencrantz, I'll remember it when I am king."

"I'll hold you to that," answered Rosencrantz, and the flame went out.

SCENE FIVE
ophelia

A strand of Ophelia's hair escaped her braid and pasted itself to the back of her neck. She could feel it every time she twisted her head to echo the other women, every time she moved with one shoulder forward, her opposite hand trailing behind her, fingers carefully manoeuvred to look light and airy. It hurt like hell.

Portraits of Hal's ancestors gazed judgmentally down at her. Her foot landed wrong and her ankle rolled a little, but there was no time in this dance to stop and correct. She pushed through, hopping on one foot, turning with her partner, and trying to ignore the cramping in her chest from holding her breath.

"*Relinquatis*," she muttered under her breath as she clasped Lady Agard's wrist for the next step.

Agard looked at her, her forehead pinched in confusion. "Did you say something?"

"No, no!" Ophelia said brightly. She pasted the smile back onto her face. "Just trying to remember the steps."

Lady Agard didn't seem convinced, but then she whirled away. Momentarily, a purple thread dangled between them. Ophelia yelped, "*Et non revertatur!*" and the thread dissipated. She glanced around as she danced, but no one seemed to have noticed.

She may not have been able to see the Corruption, but when she pinched her fingers and muttered the words, it was certainly there. In fact, it felt like there was more of it: the threads were thicker and stronger than they had been before. Internally, she kicked herself. If she hadn't been caught with Hal, she could've kept peeling the residue from these women.

In the physical world, she stepped on her own foot and made a pained noise. Alessandra caught her eye and tutted, smirking playfully. "Darling, where is your lightness gone? You've always danced beautifully."

"I haven't had a chance to practice," Ophelia muttered. The music came to an end, the musicians lowering their instruments and reaching for cups of water.

Ophelia's entry had startled everyone. Alessandra ignored the looks, the slightly widened eyes, the parted lips;

Ophelia did not. The women didn't say a thing, not to her face, but Ophelia knew they would talk when the dancing was done.

Dancing lessons were always something she'd enjoyed. She hadn't been since she and Hal were caught, those dark days when she was only let out for a brisk walk in the afternoon and Hamlet was kept inside until she was finished. She'd tried to catch sight of his window so many times and failed.

She saw the lad from the stables once but he was working, walking with a limp and with red welts peeking out from the collar of his tunic, and the sight made her so sick she had begged to be allowed to go back inside.

The pause in the music provided the perfect opportunity for them to chat, but no one approached Ophelia. The women hung back, as if to invite conversation was the same as courting scandal. For a moment, it bothered her. These people were meant to be her friends. Heat came to her cheeks and she felt herself draw inwards, away from them, to somewhere their odd looks and whispers couldn't hurt her…

But then she shook that off, pushing her shoulders back. She, unlike them, had a purpose, and that purpose was to save them.

They were not her friends, but she would rather kill them herself than see them swept up in a wave of Corruption, see their skin rot and blemish, watch them be buried in a mass grave like had happened in so many places.

They weren't her friends, but she wasn't the arbiter of life and death. She couldn't decide who deserved to have the Corruption removed from their skin, their hair, the soft tissues of their organs. She could only offer them mercy and let God and the world do the rest.

Ophelia adjusted her skirts and padded across the room to join them.

Clara had a fresh rose in her uncovered hair, and Ophelia reached out to brush the petals with a fingertip. She was a pretty girl, a few years older than Ophelia but with a small stature and fidgety, bird-like demeanour that made her seem younger.

"This is so beautiful," Ophelia said. "Where did you find it this time of year?"

"I grew it indoors," Clara said, colouring pink. "I've tended it for months and months, but it was time for it to bloom."

"It suits you." Ophelia pinched her fingers together behind her back. She could feel the Corruption there, gathered thick and ropy like gory purple tendons.

The music struck up again.

"*Relinquatis, et non revertatur,*" Ophelia said, turning away.

"What was that, Ophelia?" Clara asked. Her bird-like head was tipped to the side, making her look even more like a little robin perched on a branch.

"I just said it's beautiful, Clara," she replied. "Would you mind partnering with me for this dance?"

The room warmed to her slowly. Alessandra's acceptance was enough for them to tolerate her; before long, she was giggling with Clara, both of them laughing too much to dance the steps, and Lady Agard smiled at the two of them, and before long the tension had melted away. By the time they were finished, sweat marking their foreheads and the underarms of their dresses, Ophelia felt that once again she might be one of them.

The other girls fussed over her before she left, legs aching and a victorious warmth in her heart. They admired the new buttons stitched onto her old dress, pink and in the shape of little flowers, which were a gift from Laertes. He had them made for her the week after she and Hamlet were caught, and handed them to her with promises that the next man to lay a hand on his sister would find himself short a few fingers.

These dancing lessons were the first step towards being accepted back into society. And she needed them to accept her again, not just for her own selfish reasons, but because she needed their knowledge. She needed to know when they would be away, so that she could slip into their rooms and daub protective sigils on their walls; she needed to know if they were ill or weak, so she could report it back to Aaron and Fatma.

In her chambers that night, she rubbed her eyes until they watered, hoping to see something, anything. The Sight stayed stubbornly beyond her reach, the true extent of the Corruption unimaginable.

Her skin prickled. Something was wrong, but she couldn't put her finger on what. Removing such small threads of Corruption shouldn't have bothered her, but as she stood in the middle of her bedroom she felt drained, like all the energy had come soaring out of her.

Maybe the potion hadn't just failed.

Maybe she was losing the only thing that gave her purpose: her magic.

SCENE SIX
hamlet

The next day, Hamlet received an invitation. A portly, balding messenger, who looked constantly shell-shocked, stood at the door with his hands clasped behind his back, awaiting a response. Hamlet groaned. Judging by the seal, it was from the Electors of Saxony.

He scanned it wearily. He was right; it was an invitation to some 'friendly displays of swordsmanship' to be held in his honour, as a welcome present from Johann Friedrich and Johann Ernst, the Electors themselves.

"Good job we found out you were a prince all along, eh?" said Guild, reading the invitation over Hamlet's shoulder. The messenger looked like he wanted to protest, but instead he just turned steadily redder. "Can you bring a guest? And can that guest be me?"

"It says no," he said, pointing to the line that specifically requested only invited attendees to come along. "Maybe next time?"

"You have a geometry lesson that day," said Ros, also peering down at the invite.

"That settles it." He scribbled his acquiescence on the back of the scroll and returned it to its messenger. "It could be incredibly boring, but it will absolutely be more interesting than geometry."

The morning of the fencing competition dawned bright and cool. Hamlet left a message for his master with Guildenstern, who very reluctantly went to ferry it to its intended destination even before their breakfast was delivered. Hal's stomach rumbled as he clambered into the waiting carriage. It was bare and empty on the inside, with a cross hanging up on the wall. Definitely Johann Friedrich's then.

They trundled along the city streets, past Luther's house and through the gates into the countryside. The carriage was anything but comfortable, and by the time they reached the long driveway leading to the Elector's house, Hamlet could hardly feel his buttocks.

He hopped out as soon as the house was within sight. The remains of a morning dew made the track slippery with mud. It smelled fresh and bright, and he had to reluctantly admit that yes, it was nice to be among trees again.

The house was enormous, quite like the manors he visited once on a trip with his mother to visit cousins in France. It was large and square, with ornamental gardens in the front that looked strangely dead against the backdrop of the wild trees.

"Oh no, not my main residence, no," someone was saying as he approached the steps of the house. "Goodness, no. In Torgau, my usual place. This is a *nice* little spot for events and such…"

The man trailed off.

Johann Friedrich was tall, broad in the shoulders and gut, with a big red beard and small, watery eyes. He was dressed all in orange, with a funny cap that sat low on his round head and a fur-trimmed cape over his shoulders. The most interesting part about him was the shadow who trailed along behind him: his brother, Johann Ernst.

Ernst, who ruled alongside his brother, was rather smaller, with sad and drooping eyes that reminded Hamlet of the donkeys that bayed out in the fields. His clothes were all black, and he wore a funny little ruff around his neck that made it look like his head was popping out of a misplaced shirtsleeve.

Hamlet nodded to them both. "Prince Hamlet of Denmark," he said. "Pleased to make your acquaintance."

Ernst bowed at the neck.

"Fyrste Hamlet!" Friedrich said delightedly, using his Danish title. "Good man, what a pleasure. What a delight! I'm so happy to see you in good health…"

The other guest—and the other brother—was ignored in favour of Hamlet, who found himself taken rather roughly by the arm and brought around to the back of the house.

"By god," Friedrich said as they walked, "You look so much like your father did at your age! I remember him well. A good man! An excellent man!"

Hamlet forced a nervous laugh. "He is, sir."

He pushed a hand through his hair, trying (and failing) to tamp down his curls. His doublet felt uncomfortably tight across his chest. He realised with a sick feeling that he'd actually never been to an event like this alone.

He was always tagging along with his father, or trailing behind his mother, or, when he was very small, hiding with his sister before the influenza took her away. Never had he gone to one of these stupid things without a soul he knew.

The event was already in full swing around the back of the house. Men gathered in good clothes, weighing up weapons. Racks of swords glimmered in the light. Hamlet's eyes were drawn to the rapiers, which were in the corner being ignored.

"The English still disdain fencing for the most part, but I think it can be *very interesting*," Friedrich said, catching where Hamlet's attention had gone. "Are you a fan of it, Prince Hamlet?"

"I've studied," he said.

"The schools?"

A crowd of older women huddled nearby, talking indistinctly. At the sight of him, their heads drew together. He was glad he had a knife tucked into his sleeve, even if the absence of a sword at his waist made him feel naked; amongst this crowd of lions, who knew when he might need to defend himself with more than a barbed tongue.

"The Danish style, but mostly Italian," he said. "I was blessed to have Achille Marozzo as my tutor for a time."

"Ah, so did one of our other guests!" Friedrich said exuberantly. "Let me see, where has he got to... Ah! Prince Fortinbras trained under Marozzo too." Then Johann Friedrich's gaze sharpened. "I hope having the Norwegian prince here is not awkward for you. It is not my intention to revive the strain between your nations."

Hamlet forced himself to school his expression. But his traitorous heart leapt, and his equally traitorous eyes searched the crowd, and that strange creature in his lower belly unfurled itself when it caught sight of copper hair and freckled arms wielding a longsword.

Friedrich was about to call Fortinbras over when the other prince caught sight of them. He smiled, and in a moment he'd deposited his sword with a servant and was loping up the lawn towards them, rubbing the back of his neck with one large hand.

"Hamlet," he said. "Good to see you."

"And you," he said, mouth dry, but couldn't seem to find the words to say anything else.

"I'm glad to see you're already acquainted," Ernst said mildly. Hamlet hadn't even realised he was there. Yes, he was certainly the sharper of the two brothers: Hamlet caught his watchful gaze and knew that, no matter how fast he'd smoothed his own mixed emotions at the mention of Fortinbras, Ernst had caught it. "We'll leave you."

Ernst bowed and walked back towards the house. Friedrich hovered a moment, mouth working as if he had something to say, and then he made a hasty bow and followed in his brother's footsteps.

Hamlet stood, unmoored. The wind ruffled his curls, blowing them across his face in mockery.

"They're good hosts," Fortinbras said finally. "They did the same for me when I first arrived."

"I appreciate it."

"You should mingle. These men are all here to meet you." Fortinbras smiled. "They all want to say they knew the King of Denmark when he studied in Wittenberg."

The King of Denmark. "And the King of Norway," he said. "Is that why they're all watching you now?"

"I think they're watching us," Fortinbras said, "to see what peace between our nations could look like."

The tension between Norway and Denmark would never dissipate in a day. It was impossible. For generations, it had simmered; now Norway claimed some of Denmark's land, and Denmark claimed some of Norway's in return, and they made truces that came to nothing.

They were in the middle of one such truce now. Five years, it had lasted: that made it six since Arion Fortinbras came to stay at Kronborg Castle with his father, first to forge an agreement, then to celebrate it. Six months he'd stayed, lanky Arion three years older than Hamlet.

A year later, Hamlet went to stay with King Fortinbras and his family, again to celebrate. He stayed by Arion's side and trained with him, attended his lessons, sat with him during long dinners, as Arion had in Helsingør.

Three months in, Hamlet's mother—Gertrude was there in place of Father, who was dealing with a Protestant uprising in the north—took him to one side.

"Darling," she'd said, brushing his curls back from his face. "Don't you think you should give Prince Fortinbras a little bit of room to breathe?"

Hamlet squirmed away. "What do you mean?" he'd protested, trying to escape her hands, her motherly touch.

"He's at an age," Mother had said. "He doesn't need you nipping at his heels every day, my dove."

"Arion doesn't mind," he'd said confidently.

"He does mind, Hamlet," Mother had said. "He told me so."

He'd been so embarrassed that he'd mostly avoided Arion for the next three months of the stay. It made him miserable. Their lessons together were particularly unbearable: Arion was always kind, always patient, always smiling. Hamlet, at barely thirteen, felt like he was dissolving under that soft gaze, burning up every time Arion offered a helping hand with his sums or adjusted his grip on a rapier.

He was miserable and depressed and utterly infatuated, thirteen years old and still capable of feeling everything.

He looked at Arion Fortinbras, but he never looked him in the eye.

Now he was seventeen, and he still looked at Arion Fortinbras like he'd created the warmth of the sun just for Hamlet to bathe in. He looked at Fortinbras like he'd whispered every star into existence, like every flower bloomed at his command, and the gaze was out of his control.

He felt it all again, the pain and the pleasure, and he could not understand how love could feel like this, how it could take the heat of two palms and turn it into a forest fire. It was so different to Ophelia's steadiness, her softness. He loved them both, but Ophelia was *forever* and this was *for as long as it takes to destroy us both*.

Fortinbras smiled at him, the corners of his blue eyes crinkling.

Hamlet felt himself fall.

"Peace between our nations," he echoed. "You think we can achieve that at a swordsmanship contest?"

"I think we can make a start here in Wittenberg. After all, I have no hatred towards you. I want our people to be happy and our kingdoms to work together. Why should we fight each other?"

It seemed so simple, yet something in Hamlet resisted. All the years of conflict, of turmoil, all the grey in his father's hair resolved by… deciding not to fight?

"I've always been fond of you, Hal," said Fortinbras. "And now that my brothers are dead, you're the only one I have left."

"I'm not your brother."

"You've always been one to me," he said, like it was the simplest thing in the world.

What are you to me? Hamlet thought. *Something else. Something you can never be.*

"Come," Fortinbras said, and clapped him hard on the shoulder. "Let's have a friendly match."

Hamlet let himself be steered away.

It was too simple. War couldn't be avoided with a handshake and a clean slate. It had to be harder than that, it had to be more.

But Fortinbras seemed so sure as he guided Hamlet to the ring and they took up their dulled blades. He seemed sure even when Hamlet got under his guard and, with a well-aimed jab, knocked him off his feet.

Fortinbras stayed on his hands and knees, panting. And then the other prince lifted his visor, and Hamlet saw that he was grinning.

"An excellent match," Fortinbras said. "You always were more talented than I."

Hamlet stretched out his hand and helped him up.

He had always thought peace was unreachable. It was a moment, a temporary state of being. Peace was just the break between wars, a held breath, the silence before a storm.

But in this moment, peace was a handshake, a smile. Peace was Fortinbras standing in front of him and the future stretching out before, and it was a choice, and it was his to make.

But it was not his to keep.

※

Four hundred miles away in Denmark, a messenger was welcomed into Kronborg Castle.

He bent the knee to greying King Hamlet and produced a large roll of paper from within his Norwegian coat.

He read out a declaration of war, and all hope of peace shattered.

In Wittenberg, Prince Hamlet of Denmark kicked off his boots. He took off his sweat-stained shirt and stretched. His back popped in three places as he stretched, cat-like, and then padded back downstairs to pick at some food.

He smiled to himself. It was nice to see Prince Arion Fortinbras again, and nice to relive their youth together. He felt satisfyingly heavy-limbed, a pleasant buzzing in his ears from fresh air and exercise.

He and Fortinbras had spoken all afternoon. He thought about writing a letter to his Father expressing such a thing, but then decided it was childish. Father didn't need to know; he had his own diplomacy to attend to.

It was nice, Hamlet decided, to have Prince Arion Fortinbras as a friend.

SCENE SEVEN
ophelia

A shudder ran through the spine of the city of Helsingør.

In a moment, all the air disappeared. The place became soundless like a specimen beneath a cloche. At the moment of war—did war have an exact moment of beginning, a time of birth? It felt like it did—the city was frozen, a marble mimic of itself, devoid of its usual colour and sound. It shrank into its own shell, and Ophelia shrank with it.

Funny, how there was no real fanfare about it. The usual skirmishes had been no worse than usual in the weeks prior to the declaration, and it seemed that this war was entirely brewing behind closed doors. Odd, that the private letters of kings could cause the entire city to shut its gates in a day.

In Helsingør, people wrote letters to distant families and friends. They packed bags and stepped onto the rocking decks of ships without a sound. Officially, no one responded to the absences; from behind a tapestry dampened by her own breath, Ophelia heard Queen Gertrude call it cowardice.

But it was not so simple for most to leave.

War raged between the Grand Duchy of Moscow and the allied Lithuania and Poland. Word of a revolt came from the north of England, and French armies joined with Ottoman ships against the Italians. Though they did not know it, Spanish and Portuguese ships sailed into the New World dripping with Corruption of a concentration never before seen.

"It feels like a wave is about to crash over us," Laertes said, as they sat in the dark waiting for Father to return from another late-night meeting. "Like this is only the first flecks of what is to come."

Quietly yet desperately Ophelia re-entangled herself in court life. She walked in the gardens with Laertes and asked questions of the ladies they met: no-one asked who was staying or going, but she found they were often content to proffer the information themselves when they realised they would not be judged.

The number of women at Kronborg Castle shrunk by half within a week, so the garden walks were rendered mostly obsolete. Then Alessandra's friends left, so she attached herself to Ophelia instead, and soon she didn't need Laertes to escort her between rows of dying greenery.

Alessandra was staying because her husband Lorenz had been asked not to leave. She could have gone to the countryside like so many of the others—and who could blame them?—but instead she stayed.

"Anyway, the queen needs me," Alessandra said, squeezing Ophelia's hand tighter as they walked, shoes squelching in the mud. The more autumn slipped into winter, the more the garden transformed from an idyll into a sea of brown and faded sickly green. "If it carries on like this, she'll have no one left to dress her. And how would she survive?"

Ophelia tried her best to disguise her laugh as a polite cough, but failed.

Alessandra clicked her tongue. "Now is the time," she said, and squeezed Ophelia's hand again. "I think the queen still feels offended about your situation with the prince, doesn't she?"

Your situation. "I think so," she said, biting back a far sharper reply. "I want nothing more than for her to forgive me."

"Write to her," Alessandra urged. "She will forgive you more easily now because with the other handmaids leaving she will see that she needs you."

The thought of writing to Gertrude, who hadn't addressed her directly since she was hauled into the throne room that day, didn't sit right with her. But she had very little choice, and if war was really here then she needed to know what was happening. She needed to be able to help.

"What do you think I should say?"

Alessandra shrugged. "I don't know. But whatever you decide, say it quickly. If you wait until the prince comes back, she will think you're only doing it to please him."

Ophelia's ears filled with a pounding noise, like the hum of a thousand birds taking flight. Her heart beat like a battle cry.

"He'll come home now that we're at war," she repeated. "I hadn't thought about it."

"Not for long, I imagine." Was it her mind playing tricks, or was Alessandra watching her with particular sharpness? "When the battles begin in earnest, I'm sure he'll go to fight. Lorenz, too."

Hamlet is coming home, Ophelia thought.

Hamlet is going to war.

At the chapel that night, her father left her alone to pray. When she emerged and pulled the veil from her hair, her hand tingling from drawing free the Corruption, he laid his hand on her shoulder. It was as big and warm as she remembered it being in her childhood, only the hairs were tinged with silver.

"You've changed since Prince Hamlet left," he said, the first time he said Hal's name since the incident.

The throne room; that same loving hand pulling her hair, dragging her down the aisle; the maids combing through the tangles later as Ophelia cried, the tell-tale silence when they found blood.

It was the first time her father had ever done anything akin to hitting her.

"I mean it, Ophelia. You're much more yourself," he said, and sighed. "It's time your old father apologised, I think. I should have seen that he was changing you. I should have seen that you needed to be protected from that boy and his... *proclivities*."

"I don't need protecting," she said, but the words came out half-hearted.

She couldn't defend Hal, not if she wanted Father to keep his hand on her shoulder.

"You only think that," he said, "because no one has been there to protect you. Not since your mother passed. She would have saved you from him, helped you to understand the lies men speak…"

He talked on and on, but Ophelia could not listen. Every fibre of her wanted to tear his hand away, which no longer felt like the loving press of a paternal palm and now was like a brand, the heat of his skin burning through the sleeve of her dress, the dampness of it raising in her a bone-deep revulsion.

"You see," Father said, "men say these things, but what they mean is…"

Liars say these things, she thought. *Men or women or anything else they might be. Lies are the work of liars, and they come in all genders.*

But explaining this to Father was a fruitless exercise.

Often as a child, she'd been punished for asking the wrong questions. Mother always told her that Aunt Hilga had a wife, and that in Rúnräd that was okay, and they lived together as a couple.

She'd asked Father if she could marry a lady when she grew up, and he'd laughed at first, then looked confused, then threatened to lock her in her room until she learned to keep quiet about 'deranged things'.

It was why they fought, often and loudly: Ophelia's life was shaped by the people she knew from Rúnräd. They were her beautiful, loving family, by blood or by choice. They had loved her mother better than anyone in Kronborg Castle ever could, and when she died they poured all that love into Laertes and Ophelia, filled the cracks in their broken hearts with it and stitched them back together.

Father kept talking about men and their tricks until they were back in their chambers, sitting in front of a fire. Ophelia drifted away from the room, back into the recesses of her mind. When she noticed Father go quiet, she stirred herself.

Laertes crouched in front of her, the fingers of his right hand drumming out a gentle rhythm on her knee.

"I'm sorry," he said quietly. "Forgive Father. He wants you to be happy."

Laertes was always best at the magic of undoing things: knots, enchantments, corsets. Ophelia felt her tension seep away a little, drawn out like poison from a wound by her brother's knowing gaze.

"I want to be happy. That's what he can't seem to understand," she whispered back. "I'm not trying to make my life miserable. In fact, I'm doing all I can to make it bearable."

The drumming stopped.

"Tell me why you want to be a Sight Guide." He said it carefully. There was something hiding behind those words, a secret waiting to be unmasked. "Explain it to me."

"Because someone has to," she said desperately. "Because someone must learn to do what Solveig used to, and what Mother did after her, and cleanse the Corruption, and the little I can do without being able to see it is useless. Because this war is the least of our problems. Because when the Corruption infects us all with a plague, there will be no soldiers left to fight."

"When you can see it," Laertes said, "it will start to drive you mad. Like Solveig."

Ophelia sucked in a sharp breath. "Solveig isn't mad," she admonished. "Don't say that."

"But she would be. If she lived here and walked through the Corruption every day, it would kill her," he said, which was irritatingly true. "That's why Sight Guides end up living in Rúnräd forever. You would never be able to live in Kronborg again. You would never see Father, or your beloved Prince Hamlet…"

In his eyes, identical in shade to hers, there was a challenge.

"What did you do?" she breathed into the silence between them.

They were always so similar. Their hair was the same golden colour, so alike that Mother would sometimes braid it together as a joke. My little twins, she would whisper. They had the same chin, the same pointy elbows, differing only by the scrapes on their knees.

The same stubbornness, too.

"I wanted to give you time," said Laertes, out of a mouth that matched hers almost perfectly.

"What did you *do*," she repeated, but this time it was hardly a question. She shot up from the chair, nearly knocking him over.

Her room felt like a void. She stepped inside the threshold and it sucked the energy out of her. It didn't feel like a weight or a punch to the stomach: it just felt like nothing, like emptiness, like total and complete stillness. It felt like sitting alone in a room with a corpse and suddenly becoming aware of the morbid beating of your own heart.

"Tell me what you did," she hissed, turning on a heel. She jabbed him hard in the chest. "Undo it, Laertes!"

He shushed her furiously, waving in the vague direction of their father's chambers.

"I don't care," Ophelia hissed. "*I don't care!* Undo it!"

"You're not old enough to throw your life away to contribute nothing," he hissed back, and here it was: the fire and the flame, the secret hidden in his eyes. "No Sight Guide can help Kronborg. I've spoken to a hundred people and they all say the same—there is nothing to be done now. The scales are tipped. The Corruption will win, and eventually it will burn itself out, but the only thing we can do before it does is leave while we still can and cleanse ourselves of it!"

When she spoke, she poured the ice of seventeen Danish winters into every word.

"How far do you think we should run?" she asked. "How far do we need to go to outrun a plague? France? Brazil? China? It won't work. Denmark—specifically this castle—seethes with Corruption and no one knows why. Something has happened, or is happening, to make it this way. I am the only person who can find out what is going on and make it stop."

"And you'd give up your life to do that?"

"You're going to go to war, aren't you? If you're asked to go, you'll do it!" she said, louder than she meant to. She took a breath, lowered her voice again. "You cannot tell me not to put myself in danger when you're about to join an army on the march to go and wave swords at Norwegian soldiers. Whatever you've done, undo it. I've made my choice: I'm doing what I can to help Denmark, as are you."

Laertes said nothing. His features hardened, and he went to her bedside and got down on his knees.

From beneath Ophelia's bed he withdrew a small cloth bag, heavy with what looked like stones.

He whispered a word, and the Corruption came flooding in.

I can see you, she kept thinking, as Laertes wordlessly caught her as she fell. *I can see you now.*

He laid her down in her bed and pulled the covers over her, and once again he took up watch by her bedside.

The Corruption burned where it touched her skin.

I can see you, and I will destroy you, she thought, before she fell into unconsciousness.

It did not take long. There was ice, and there were flames; she was born and remade again, but it was only a shadow of the previous days of agony that felt like years ago; and in the morning, her nerves so burned out she could hardly feel a thing, the world was made new.

Her fingers trailed across the wall, following the grid-like lines of magic that held up the world. The threads of magic were gold and as fine as gossamer thread. She lay still for a long time, just examining how it shimmered and moved, a network of threads running through all things.

Her eyes followed it around the room. They were beautiful, the unbroken strands of magic, but in the corners they turned strange and grey, like ashes. In the corners of the room, purple Corruption curled like snakes lying in wait. Where the Corruption twined itself around the golden threads, it turned colourless and crumbled.

Corruption was not the still mass she had always imagined. No, this was restless. Magic was stillness, steadiness; the Corruption twisted and shivered and twitched, a thousand glistening worms tossing in the corner of her room. She was overcome with an urge to cleanse it, to take those purple strands and destroy them in a burst of flame.

Her limbs shook. She reached out, pointing with a quaking finger, and whispered a spell she'd only ever heard Solveig use: *ut in lucem.*

A trail of purple fire erupted. Every purple thread flared, a burning pyre invisible to almost anyone else, from any world.

Ophelia watched the Corruption burn, and she smiled.

It didn't matter if no one else could see.

This was power. This was how to change the world.

SCENE VIII
hamlet

"Why won't you let me come to Nordsee?"

It was not the first time he'd asked the question. If the answer was not what Hamlet wanted to hear, it wouldn't be the last.

It felt like years since Rosencrantz dropped through that mirror, when in fact it was only a week or so ago. Every day, Guildenstern told him to be patient, that it was up to Rosencrantz for reasons he could not explain. Every day, Rosencrantz said no.

Guildenstern was there now. Hamlet had watched him step through the mirror with a wave and a sympathetic smile. He'd worn a nice tunic, and said he might not be back until morning. Then he winked and was gone.

"Ros," he said, impatient. "Why?"

Rosencrantz paused in his examination of the bookshelf, his back to Hal. Hamlet swallowed the lump in his throat. The question shivered in the air between them.

Ros breathed hard through his nose and dropped his arm. When he looked at Hamlet, it was with more than mild frustration.

"I've told you before," he said. "Be patient. It's not really my decision to make."

"Guild says it is."

"Guild's only saying that so you'll bother me instead of him," said Ros.

Hamlet flinched. Ros didn't appear to notice.

"It would be easier," Ros continued, "if you didn't insist on being Fortinbras's best friend. I wonder if that other fellow is jealous yet. What was his name? Hortensio?"

"Horatio."

Hamlet hadn't seen Horatio, not since the night in the tavern. Fortinbras mentioned him at the river, and again at the swordsmanship competition: little nods to his existence, nothing of note. They lived together, Hamlet gathered. Horatio was, indeed, Italian. He hated mathematics lessons about as much as Hamlet did, but Fortinbras had always enjoyed them.

When Fortinbras offered up an anecdote about Horatio spending hours identifying flowers with the aid of a century-old book, Hamlet told him about Ophelia, the dried flower collection that hung in carefully-organised rows on her bedroom walls.

If Ophelia wanted to go to the Otherland, Hamlet wouldn't keep her waiting. He would lead her in by the hand the very day she found out about magic, show her around, teach her a trick or two. He wouldn't tease her with a hundred tiny spells and throwaway remarks, then deny her access.

"I don't see what Fortinbras has to do with anything," Hamlet said, pushing his shoulders back. "He's a friend, but it's not as if I'm going to tell him."

Ros looked at him, eyebrow raised. "Oh, I'm not worried about that," he said archly. "You wouldn't be telling him anything he doesn't already know."

Ros turned back to his books. Hamlet's world seemed to collapse in on itself for a moment, then glued itself back together the wrong way around.

"Fortinbras knows?"

"He knows," said Ros, in a tone that said that answering Hamlet's question was the verbal equivalent of swatting away a flea. "It was difficult enough for *him* to get to the Otherland. People there don't love princes coming and meddling with magic. I'm afraid Fortinbras has taken the princely spot, and it's making it hard to convince anyone to let you in."

A book floated from the shelf into Ros's waiting hands.

"You see why it's dangerous, don't you? Two princes from rival houses with access to the world's magical arsenal… I know you're friends now, but if that changed, it could be disastrous."

Hamlet's mouth worked soundlessly for a moment before he managed to say, furiously, "What do you think I'd do? Levitate him off a roof?"

"I hope not, because that would be *very* messy," Rosencrantz replied. He turned back to face Hamlet again, and this time his pale eyes flickered with amusement.

"And you can't just take me through the mirror… why?"

"Because there's only one mirror in the Otherland," Ros explained. He still sounded bored. "It's watched over day and night. And only those with their names on the list are allowed entry."

"And they won't let me in because of Fortinbras?"

"They won't let you in because they don't want open magical war on either side of the mirror when the peace between your countries eventually implodes again," Rosencrantz said, in the sort of tone one might use to explain a complex topic to a toddler. "It's only a matter of time, I suspect."

Ros ignored the outrage on Hal's face. He crossed the room to stand in front of Hamlet, far too close to him. Ros was taller than him and he had to crane his neck to meet his cool gaze. This near, he could see each individual eyelash, smell the soap he used to wash his clothes, practically feel the displacement of air as Ros's chest moved up and down in time with his breathing.

Hamlet's arms prickled with goosebumps. The moment was too long for comfort yet too comfortable to back away from. He wanted to move, but his desk dug into his back; if he stood up straight, his face would collide with Ros's shoulder.

Cool fingers curled around his wrist.

"You have to understand," Rosencrantz said quietly, and now his tone was as soft as satin, gentle as a caress. "You have to understand that I'd like to take you there. I'm doing the best I can. Give me more time."

"Is there anything I can do?" he asked. "Anything that might convince them?"

"Staying away from Fortinbras would help," Ros said immediately. "I don't trust him. He has too much sway. If he thinks you shouldn't be allowed into the Otherland, he will make it so."

Hal's eyes tracked across Rosencrantz's face. What he saw there was something he was used to noticing only in himself: a hunger with teeth.

"Consider it done," he breathed.

Rosencrantz stepped away, and the air around Hamlet cooled with the absence of him, and the creature within him shivered and fell back into an uneasy sleep.

⋙ ⋘

In the night, he slipped out of the house alone.

The streets were mostly quiet, punctuated with sudden bursts of sound from open doors and drunken groups of students. Hamlet blended in amongst them with his dark clothes and darker thoughts.

His feet took him to his destination as his brain remained in a daze. He rapped hard on the door. He waited.

The light that slipped around the edges widened until Horatio's face peeked through. He looked Hamlet up and down, squinting, and then ushered him inside.

"Arion," he called. "Arion, Prince Hamlet's here."

Hamlet said, "You know too, don't you? About the mirrors?"

Horatio replied, "Who do you think told him?" and quirked his chin towards an exhausted-looking Fortinbras trailing down the stairs.

He was wearing a robe open to his bare chest, and his feet were uncovered, and he looked so baffled and confused to see Hamlet that his chest welled with something disgusting, and suddenly he wanted nothing more than to cry, not because he was sad but because Fortinbras was beautiful, flesh and blood, standing in front of him rubbing his eyes and saying, "Hamlet, what are you doing here? It's late."

"Nordsee," said Hamlet. The firelight flickered over Fortinbras's skin, warming Hamlet's face. "Please, Fortinbras."

He didn't know why he said 'please'. What was he asking for? He wasn't sure.

"Hal," Fortinbras said gently, "Who told you?"

"Rosencrantz," he said. "And Guildenstern."

Fortinbras sighed. "I worried about this. Listen, Hal… I don't know what they told you, but it's not all it's cracked up to be. You're better off here."

"Please, Arion. I just want to see—I just want to *know*…"

Horatio's sleep-roughened voice said, "Know what?"

Hamlet could not explain it, the void inside him, the thing that had always been there.

"Everything," he said instead, desperate, pleading. "I want to know everything."

And for some reason carved so deep into his flesh that he couldn't put a name to it, Hamlet sank to his knees.

"I need to know what else there is," he said. The words were still not enough, not quite right. "I need to know if there's something there that can make it go away."

Horatio looked horrified: Hamlet on his knees, supplicant, every word a strain coming from a throat drawn tight against tears.

But Fortinbras did not look horrified. Instead, he came to his knees in front of Hamlet, so close their skin touched. Like this, bathed in firelight, he looked as strange and otherworldly as Ros. Was that something that happened when you went to that other place? Did every fibre of you change, become something else, whisper to the world: *I have seen everything, and you have only seen half of what there is.*

"Make what go away?" Fortinbras asked. "Because the Otherland is just a place. It can't make you into something you're not."

Fortinbras's hand on his cheek. Hamlet hadn't realised he was crying.

"What is it," asked Arion Fortinbras, "you need to know? What are you trying to escape, Hamlet?"

He didn't even have to speak.

The look was enough, how he gazed then at Fortinbras with something that was half-frenzied, half in love. It was all there, written on his face, the truth he did not want to admit: that this was who he was, that this creature lurked in his ribs, that it was always hungry. That it came alive when he looked at Guild, when he felt the brush of Ros's hand against his, but that that was no match for what happened when he looked at Fortinbras.

"Ah," said Fortinbras, quietly. "Nordsee cannot cure you of that, I'm afraid."

"And neither can he." Horatio pinched the bridge of his nose. He really did look exhausted. "Tell him, Arion."

"Hal, I'm honoured." Arion's hand disappeared. The second time today the absence of another's touch turned him to ice. "Really, I am. But…"

Fortinbras looked at Horatio.

Horatio put his hand on the back of Fortinbras' neck. A simple touch, made possessive.

Whatever his moment of madness was, whatever the creature that lived in his ribs wanted, it vanished. Hamlet sank back on his heels. He lowered his eyes and took a breath, then another.

"I want to go to Nordsee," he said calmly. "I want to understand. I want to go somewhere I can *be understood*."

He took hold of his mind.

Ophelia's words resounded around his head. In the moments when his body ran away with him, when he couldn't think beyond the itch in his skin and the need to move, to go, to flee, she would take him and lie him down in a dark room and into his ear she would whisper:

Doubt thou the stars are fire,
Doubt thou the sun doth move,
Doubt truth to be a liar,
But never doubt I love.

Whatever Fortinbras thought of this episode, he didn't say. He just gathered himself and stood up, then offered Hamlet a hand. He took it. He was unsteady on his feet and the warmth of the fire was suddenly too much, but he swallowed hard and rocked on the balls of his feet until he felt better.

"You can't deny him that," said Horatio quietly. He was speaking to Fortinbras. "Where would we be if we hadn't had the mirror?"

Their whispered conversation continued for long moments. Hamlet, dazed, concentrated on a dark spot on the far wall. He felt like he'd just run a marathon. His entire body was heavy, drained of all energy, and his mouth was as dry as a desert. He paid no attention to what Fortinbras and Horatio were discussing. His mind buzzed with competing emotions: embarrassment, disgust, shame. Relief.

Finally, Fortinbras agreed.

"Let me get dressed," he said. "We'll make our appeal in person. Horatio, bring the mirror down, would you?"

As the clocks struck three, Hamlet stepped through the mirror.

SCENE NINE
ophelia

Her mind was crackling. Funny snapping sounds filled her ears, like a smouldering fire, and everywhere she looked, she saw purple.

She could not see any threads of gossamer. It was all ropes as thick as she was, enormously heavy, running across every surface like an invisible web. Walking through the palace halls felt like running through an endless litany of obstacles that no one else could see.

Wherever she went, the thick walls of Helsingør were draped with ribbons of thick purple fibres. Muscular growths emerged from the cracks between paving stones in the courtyard. Every beam on every part of the ceiling was decorated with them, a thousand tiny filaments and ropes as wide around as her waist, all of them wriggling and squirming and reaching for something, hungry and seeking.

Never before had she seen the need to ward herself, but here she was: a charm bag around her neck, a ward scratched into the meat of her thigh, runes written in red ink on the seams of her undergarments. It was the magic of her family, the magic of a dozen generations putting their heads together to whisper spells to their ancestors.

No books, no guides: just words around the fire, lessons in the forest, the fragile survival of a delicate magic that would so easily be forgotten.

Laertes, walking alongside her, gave her a filthy look: his leg also bore the mark of her concern, and the air around him shimmered with golden threads, the mark of someone freshly cleansed. It would not last long, not in this cacophony of Corrupted air.

She ducked her head to avoid another twisting arm of it emerging from a doorway, despite the fact that it could not physically touch her; Laertes snorted quietly, unaware of the creeping tendrils already trying to affix themselves to the soles of his shoes.

I walked through this darkness every day, Ophelia thought, staring wonderingly around her. *No wonder my mother could not cleanse it all.*

Every mirror, once an impossible entryway to Rúnräd, barely considered, now felt like temptation. She wanted to run from this, to go where she knew she would be safe. There were no Corrupt strands there. It was why Solveig stayed there, refusing to leave. Ophelia understood, in a new way, why Solveig had chosen that life over this one.

As she approached the corridor of her chambers, she heard the march of a dozen feet. A flock of people could only mean one thing: royalty. Laertes grasped her arm, tugging her to one side. They pressed their backs to the wall to allow the group to pass unencumbered.

Ophelia bowed her head, wishing her hair was uncovered so that it could shield her. The ground was a constantly-moving thing now that she could see the Corruption and the magic: gold and purple battled, a million tiny fronds waving in every breeze. It made her feel slightly dizzy.

The fronds suddenly changed direction: they reached, as one, towards the group rounding the corner. The king's ancient and hulking secretary stomped along, writing as he walked on a large roll of old-fashioned parchment. The king walked alongside. A wave of cold sickness washed over her when she finally dared to lift her eyes.

The king was swarmed with Corruption. It followed at his feet, clawing up his legs to grasp at his knees. It was a wonder he couldn't feel the weight of those thousands of wriggling, writhing tendrils dragging him down.

The king was not speaking, she realised, as she curseyed as deeply as she could. He was instead nodding, deep in thought. The man whose words were being noted down was not someone she recognised.

He was tall and fair-haired, of an age with the king but a little less care-worn. He was dressed plainly in brown travelling clothes dripping with rain. He spoke with an articulated albeit clipped tone, the tone of a man who was used to saying few words and repeated fewer.

But what was most interesting about this man was that he, like Laertes, bore the golden aura of someone who had just been cleansed.

Her heart leapt. If there was someone else like her in the castle, someone else who could understand magic and who could help her with her cause…

"Who was that?" she whispered to Laertes, when the king and his entourage had disappeared. "The man who was speaking."

He gave her an odd look. "Prince Claudius," he said. "I suppose you were small when he was last here. He's here to help organise the army, if rumour is to be believed."

"He knows magic," she said, trying to contain her excitement.

Laertes frowned. "Are you sure?"

"I saw it," she insisted, and described it to him. "Maybe he's a Sight Guide too. Maybe he can help!"

Laertes made a wounded noise. "I could help you," he said. "If you taught me how."

"I've asked you to do the wards before and you've always said no!"

"That was before I knew the entire palace is basically one big Corruption-creature with nine thousand arms," he hissed back, just as a servant rounded the corner. He smiled placidly at her, waited for her to be gone again, then turned back to Ophelia. "Your description is going to give me nightmares for the rest of my life."

"Help me, then," she said. "You know the wards."

"I'm going to Rúnräd tonight," he added. "I'll see if anyone knows anything about the prince."

Ophelia's satin slippers made quiet hissing noises against the stone. She was being dragged along the hallway by the arm at breakneck pace, but the warmth of victory made the discomfort worthwhile.

"You are such a leech," Laertes muttered. "For God's sake, if you're going to act like you're glued to my side, you could at least keep up. One evening to myself in Rúnräd, that's all I ask…"

"I'm trying," said Ophelia, wriggling out of his grasp and hiking up her skirts. "I'm actually trying to help you, you know. I'm saving you from yourself."

"And how are you doing that?"

"Stopping you from going all gooey over Fatma again," she said, knowing she'd hit a weak spot. Laertes huffed furiously and walked faster. Inwardly, Ophelia cheered.

They walked through the town and out into the forest. Laertes pushed her through the mirror; she grabbed his sleeve as soon as he emerged and yanked as hard as she could, knocking him off-balance.

"Be nice to your sister," said Hilga, who was waiting. Laertes sputtered. Hilga winked at Ophelia as soon as he wasn't looking.

It was a lovely evening, the snow falling in thick flakes the size of a fist, candlelight twinkling in windows, the smell of pine trees wafting through the air. It was even quiet enough for a leucrota to emerge from a distant clump of trees, sniffing at the ground with its horse-like head. When it saw them, it transformed instantly into a quivering white stone.

They drank tea while the members of their strange little family trooped in and out: Aaron popped his head in the door, but he was on the way to treat a patient and couldn't stay. Fatma was at the house when they arrived but left soon after: she was sailing to a place called Nordsee to meet with their authorities about Denmark's rising Corruption.

Hilga already knew about the war.

"Oh, I come and go," she said, as she tried to stack another tray of food onto the already-cluttered table. "It's a bad business. Does that mean that prince of yours will be coming back?"

Laertes began to talk very loudly about how Prince Hamlet couldn't lead an army of lambs, let alone swordsmen, and Ophelia ignored him as hard as she could, purely because she knew that would annoy him more than anything.

"This other prince, though," said Laertes finally, when he was finished lambasting Hamlet. "He's interesting. Claudius, the king's brother. Do you know of him?"

Hilga looked over her shoulder at Solveig, who was perched in the corner knitting something. Her fingers, however, had stilled on the needles.

"Stay away from him," Solveig said, very sharply. "He is a danger to us all with his wickedness."

Wickedness? Ophelia explained what she'd seen that day, the lack of Corruption around him, but with each word her heart sank a little bit further. Whatever hope she'd had of help from Prince Claudius, it was clear she'd been mistaken.

"When it was me and your mother in that castle," Solveig told her, "that man was the bane of my life."

Solveig did not talk about her time as a Sight Guide on the other side of the mirror. The hairs pricked up on the back of Ophelia's neck.

"He was smothered in Corruption, soaked in it. Everywhere he went, it trailed after him. I used to hate to meet him in the halls because it would make me sick for hours and hours, and your mother felt it too."

Solveig drew in a shuddering breath.

"He left for England with enough Corruption around him to bring the castle down on all our heads. I don't trust it: someone so immersed in Corruption cannot be cleansed like that, cannot be cleared of it. It should rot the flesh from the inside out. It would take years to remove, and even then, he should still bear the scars…"

She shivered.

Ophelia looked at Laertes. He reached over and linked their pinky fingers together, the way they always used to when they were little and Mother was telling them a scary story. She used to sing a song they both hated, but she found it funny: *They bore him barefaced on the bier; Hey non nonny, nonny, hey nonny; And in his grave rain'd many a tear: Fare you well, my dove!*

They would link fingers like this, Laertes scowling, and Mother would laugh and apologise, then come and pinch their cheeks.

It was Laertes throwing himself forward that jerked Ophelia from her reverie. He caught Solveig mid-collapse, guiding her limp body carefully to the floor. Ophelia dropped her teacup and threw herself down beside him. Hilga shoved a blanket under Solveig's head, the better for her to thrash around on.

Her mouth had gone odd and slack, her jaw hanging loose. It was Ophelia who cradled her head while she trembled and shook. Solveig's spit slicked her hand. She brushed Solveig's hair away from her pale, trembling lips, and waited for the vision to end.

Years, since Solveig had had a full-blown vision come on so suddenly. Ophelia felt terrified: first for Solveig, whose whole body seemed drawn so tight it might snap, and then for herself. She hoped, desperately, that the Sight Guide magic stirred nothing like this within her.

"No!" Solveig shrieked suddenly. "No, no!"

Hilga took her wife's hand, but Solveig began to thrash and she was forced to let go or wrench her arm off.

"No," Solveig gasped. Now the air sounded like it was caught in her throat, as if her airways were closing and this was her last gasp for air. "She cannot! Ophelia of the lilies!"

Ophelia's heart pounded against her ribs.

"In the cold ground," Solveig whispered. Somehow, the hissing of her voice was worse than the shrieks. "In the cold ground, and the skull in his hand, and the flowers on the water."

Solveig's eyes opened. For a moment, they were blindingly purple.

"My dear," Hilga breathed, taking her wife's hand again between hers and rubbing warmth into her fingers. "What did you see, love?"

Solveig shook like a leaf. She sat up, and Ophelia had the distinct feeling that her aunt's wife was trying to get as far away from her as she could.

"I saw a world as dark as a raging river," Solveig said softly. "I saw a girl crowned in flowers, floating in the water—a boy with a grinning skull for a face, and he was drenched in blood—I saw... I saw a graveyard with rows upon rows of fresh graves, and yet more to be dug. And the air smelled like death and roses, and Kronborg Castle flew a different flag."

Laertes wordlessly draped a blanket around Solveig's shoulders.

"But what can it mean?" Hilga asked quietly.

A girl crowned in flowers. A boy with a grinning skull for a face. It couldn't be her, surely. Solveig would have said. Except Solveig's eyes still weighed heavy on her, gazing at Ophelia as if her life was thinning before her pale eyes.

"Was the girl me?" she whispered. She didn't bother to hide the fear in her voice from the Council. "The girl in the water, I mean."

"It was."

"And the boy?"

Solveig's breath hitched.

"The prince," she breathed. "The boy with the skull… I feel sure it was Prince Hamlet."

SCENE TEN
hamlet

Hamlet sucked in a deep breath, and then he stepped through the mirror.

Instantly, he felt his feet go out from under him. He tumbled what must have been at least six feet, before landing curled in a heap with an audible thump. He groaned.

"—bringing every lad in Wittenberg through that damned portal," someone was saying. Hamlet clawed his way onto his hands and knees, panting, and looked up. The girl in front of him was tall and broad-shouldered, with an enormous book propped on her lap.

She reached out with her boot-clad foot and prodded Hamlet in the forehead.

"Is this the other princeling?" she asked. "I thought we already declined two appeals from that Rosencrantz person."

"You did," said Horatio. "Arion thinks he can change Jinlian's mind, for some reason."

Hamlet clawed himself off the ground. "Pleasure to meet you," he said, and extended a hand. "I'm Hal."

She snorted. She was quite pretty, he realised, under the brim of the enormous hat she wore, which cast her face half in shadow. Her accent was as smooth as butter, Spanish but not the courtly inflection he was used to.

"Hiba," she said, tilting her head so he could see even more of her face. She had the complexion of a sailor, with ruddy cheeks from wind and salt and an uneven tan across her skin.

The room was bare and empty—just four walls, a large free-standing mirror, a desk, a chair, and a grumpy woman. The floor was just compacted dirt. The chair was really the only thing worth looking at, because it was extremely fine: the arms were carved so that sea monsters seemed to be peeking out from under Hiba's white knuckles.

There was a quiet sound from behind them, and Hamlet turned. It was only Fortinbras striding with purpose through the mirror. He looked Hamlet up and down with red-ringed eyes, but there was still a look of fondness on his face.

"Don't worry Hal. It takes practice," he said, and brushed some sandy dirt from the front of Hamlet's tunic.

He turned red, but before he could respond, Fortinbras hit Hiba with his brightest smile.

"I need to speak with Jinlian," he said.

"Hamlet stays here," said Hiba, eyes narrowed.

"Hamlet comes with me," Fortinbras responded. That same easy smile stayed in place. "Jinlian won't mind."

Hiba muttered something under her breath and pulled an enormous ledger out of her desk drawer. She scrawled something on it in large letters from a quill dry of ink; somehow, letters still appeared, the ink fresh and wet as if she had just dipped it into a pot. It looked a lot like it said *I hate monarchies*, but Hamlet couldn't be sure.

"You get fifteen minutes," said Hiba finally, putting down her quill with a click. "You cause any trouble, you're out of Nordsee forever." She looked at Hamlet, and her eyes went very cold. "He causes any trouble, he's going to be very familiar with the catacombs. You understand?"

Fortinbras slipped a ring from his finger and pressed it into Hiba's hand. "My seal," he said. "In fifteen minutes,

I'll collect this ring and bring Hamlet back through the mirror. You have my word."

"The word of princes is good for almost nothing," Hiba muttered, and then she unbarred the massive wooden door next to her. "One minute late and I smelt your ring into a nice pair of ear studs."

"Sounds lovely," said Fortinbras, and he ushered Hamlet out into the night. He wasn't sure what he'd expected, but it wasn't this: stepping out into a wall of warm air, the stars glinting high above, the sound of trickling water somewhere nearby.

The street they stepped into was cobbled, sand gathered in the cracks and every stone worn to a smooth polish by thousands of feet. As far as the eye could see was an inky blue sky studded with stars, and it was only when Fortinbras and Horatio turned, paying the view no mind, that Hamlet realised the little shack stood on the outskirts of an enormous walled city.

The city was built out of shimmering yellow stone. Torches flickered in the parapets, and shadows across the top of the wall walked in twos and threes: they were not guards, from the sound of laughter and revelling. The enormous wooden gate stood open. Unlike any other city Hamlet had visited, there was no shabbily-constructed market around this gate, no cluster of tents and stalls. The wide street was empty, the bustling city contained within its stone shell.

"Fifteen minutes?" said Horatio. He walked close enough to Fortinbras that their shoulders brushed, and Hamlet wondered how he had never seen it before. It was there, in every glance, in every word. It should have taken a second, a fragment of a moment, to figure it out.

"It can be done."

Horatio glanced at Hamlet. "I hope you're not afraid of the dark."

"Or skulls," said Fortinbras cheerfully. "Catacombs are full of them."

Fortinbras walked like a weight had lifted. The shadows under his eyes seemed to evaporate. His skin glowed under the light of the moon and a dozen lamps. Even his clothes seemed to hang differently on his frame. He looked more beautiful than ever.

Hamlet gazed wonderingly around. The road they walked ran along a hilltop, and to either side there was water, the waves of the ocean lapping at their land bridge. The city of Nordsee was on a peninsula. He breathed in the salty sea air and looked up at the stars, tipping his head all the way back to take in their full scope, and without even realising it, he laughed.

When Hamlet was a child, he used to stand at the docks with Ophelia and watch the merchant ships come in. His older sister was their babysitter before a bout of influenza stole her away. Ida would point to a ship's sails on the horizon and weave such a story about where it came from based on the design of its prow, the style of its sails; when it arrived at port, she would accost the sailors and demand to know every detail of their journey, every port they had traded at, every story they had to tell.

The stories were not always good, or bright, or kind. Sometimes, humans were among the cargo. The slaves brought to Denmark came most frequently from Eastern Europe, but in truth they came from all over the world; most often, they were bought at the slave markets in Naples or Florence, where they arrived from all over the globe, and they came north from there.

It was a miserable day when those ships came in, and Hamlet knew even as a little child to go with his sister when she hid behind the port wall rather than speak to the sailors.

But then there were the ships that came in with silk and spices, and the ones that left bearing everything Denmark had to offer. One day, a ship landed in the port—Danish crew, but sailing from Portugal. At the markets there, they'd been overwhelmed with goods from China. There were rolls of silk, he remembered, that were embroidered with delicate swirls of colour, telling stories he did not know.

He'd liked how the buildings looked in them: their roofs with their angular eaves, the rows of clean panels that made up the walls, the reds and yellows and blues, and he'd convinced someone to buy it for him. Come to think of it, it was probably still somewhere in his room, never used or looked at.

When they passed through the open gates and into the town, Hamlet saw that these buildings were like the embroidery—some of them, at least. They crowded together on one side of the street, one of them standing above the rest, with a golden twisting spire pointing towards the sun. Then on the other side there were some buildings that looked vaguely like the drawings that speckled one of his travel books: a minaret stood proudly, with small, square buildings gathered nearby.

He saw nothing in the Danish style, but there were many buildings here and there that looked similar to the ones in Wittenberg, only less crowded together. Clay and wood warred with stone, and the plainer buildings stood out against the highly decorated ones that dotted the landscape. It was a cacophonous collection of styles and shapes and colours, and he loved it as soon as he set eyes on it.

"Not bad, is it?" Horatio said, coming to stand at his shoulder. "You can thank the Golden Spiders for the market, and half the goods sold there." He pointed down into the valley, where a Roman-style forum stood. Even from here, Hamlet could see it was thick with people.

"Golden Spiders?"

"A women's fleet of... opportunistic sailors. They run most of Nordsee."

"Pirates," said Hal, raising an eyebrow.

Horatio's lips quirked into something resembling a smile. "Yes," he said. "Pirates."

"Lucky for you, their captain is also the woman who decides who comes in and out of this city." Fortinbras paused in the loosening of his tunic strings to point at a high tower just inside the walls. "Jinlian Feng. Very formidable, and fiercely protective of the city she's built."

"Best to keep your mouth firmly shut, I think," said Horatio, and again that half-smile made an appearance. Hamlet returned it.

The salt air on his skin, a warm breeze ruffling his curls... It was not what he had imagined, but it was beautiful nonetheless. Something about the strange raw-ness of the night buffed away the sharp edges of Hamlet's speech and smoothed Horatio's stern features.

Perhaps it was what they had in common: the man walking ahead of them with his shoulders back, his head held high. A head made to balance a crown. Hamlet glanced at Horatio as they approached the tower, and for a moment, he glanced sideways. His eyes met Hamlet's.

They exchanged a look of understanding: *he is to me what he is to you.*

The moment passed. Hamlet stepped into the cool darkness of a tower, and there he met the Pirate Queen herself.

Moments later, he emerged back into the night.

"And?" said Horatio, who had hung back.

Hamlet smiled.

The night's strangeness slipped away once and for all. Now all he could think of was that need that followed him everywhere, the hunger, the want. He ached for something he had never been able to name, and then he named it magic.

But even after it gained its name, the feeling grew and grew.

But standing in a tower in the middle of a warm night, a pirate had looked him up and down from beneath the brim of her large brown hat, and she'd sucked her teeth for a moment, and then she'd said:

Arion, I warned you.

And Fortinbras had said: *I know. But trust me.*

It's not you I'm worried about.

I trust him.

That was all it took. Three words.

Hamlet turned his face towards the gates. What he had once assumed was a silent evening had blossomed into something else in the moments since Jinlian wrote his name into the book. Where there was quiet and the sound of birds before, now there was music and singing and the sound of laughter, of clinking cups, of money jingling, the smell of food wafting through the gates.

"Stay close," said Fortinbras. "And don't touch anything. The most vicious magic is the hardest to spot."

With that warning, Hamlet entered the city of Nordsee.

⇢⇢⇢ ⇠⇠⇠

In Wittenberg, a Seer pressed his hand to his forehead. Rarely did the visions come. Rarely did he pay attention to their ramblings.

Tonight as he tripped through his arithmetic, he kept seeing the same two faces. The vision was unclear, faded, probably because he kept drinking potions to push it away. He did not care for these images: a boy holding a skull, a girl wreathed in flowers.

They meant nothing.

Rosencrantz sighed, closed his book, and went to see if Hamlet was awake.

ACT III

SCENE ONE
ophelia

Ophelia fussed with her curls, squinting through tired eyes. The November sun was not yet in the sky, but the queen preferred to take her visitors early. Ophelia suspected it was to catch them half-asleep, when their guard might be at its lowest, but maybe that was Hal's suspicion of his mother creeping into her thoughts. She suppressed a shiver of tiredness, her stomach clenching. The corridor was chilly, and the dress she'd put on was one of her finest, but it did nothing against the cold.

Despite her exhaustion and the nightmares that had plagued her since Solveig's vision, she couldn't avoid this audience. She needed it. Having her old position back meant more than just the opportunity to smear protective sigils on the walls. It meant status, which meant knowledge, which meant having the opportunity to act.

With the aid of the Sight, Ophelia could see the tangled web of Corruption that knitted the castle together. But without getting close to the royal family, she'd never be able to follow that trail, to creep through darkened hallways without suspicion.

The door began to creak open, painfully slowly. Ophelia stood to attention, the hairs standing on the back of her neck.

"Frøken Ophelia, you can come in now."

A little girl stood at the door to the queen's private chambers, her arms held tight behind her back.

"Thank you, little one," said Ophelia. She racked her brains for the girl's name, but came up empty. Judging by the tiny bird etched on her sleeve—and her chin, which resembled her father's almost entirely—she was the daughter of one of the minor lords at court.

There was a telltale stillness on the other side of the open door. The queen was listening.

"Have you been in the castle long?" Ophelia asked, as kindly as she could. Queen Gertrude loved children. She would appreciate the kind words more than the child herself did. "I don't think we've met, have we?"

"No, Frøken Ophelia. Only a fortnight."

"Well, I hope to see far more of you. You'll make a very fine lady's maid one day, if you work hard."

The girl blushed, and Ophelia pressed one hand gently to her little shoulder as she passed, and pulled a strand of Corruption away when she lifted it again.

The queen was sitting up in bed, her head tipped back against the wall. Her eyes were closed, but Ophelia had no doubt that she was listening.

This early in the morning, her skin was free of makeup but it still glowed. She had always been beautiful: when Princess Gertrude of Pomerania arrived in Denmark, poets wrote that her skin glowed in the moonlight, that her eyes were made of green glass, and that her hair was crafted strand by strand with gold.

The older she got, the more beautiful she became. Hamlet's mother had a strong, elegant neck, a soft curve to her jaw, plump cheeks, arched brows, and a long Roman nose, down which she usually looked at her handmaidens. She was where Hamlet got his fine-boned features from, the smoothness of his skin, his musician's fingers. There was little of his father in him.

Alessandra was bent over a little table in the corner, preparing the queen's dressing area for the day. She smiled at Ophelia as she tucked fresh flowers into a vase, perfuming the air with their sweet, fresh scent. Around the flowers was arranged a wealth of jewellery, enough to feed a peasant family for their entire lifetimes.

The room was full of Corruption, but it was nowhere near as bad as Ophelia had anticipated. She steeled herself against the wave of dizziness that came over her, a combination of Corruption sensitivity and nerves, and curtseyed.

"Ophelia, dear," Gertrude said, opening her startling green eyes. "It's so lovely to see you. I heard you were ill."

Her voice was soft, and for a moment, Ophelia remembered so many mornings like this over the last few years: mornings when she would perch on the edge of Gertrude's bed and read to her, or they would smell new perfumes together and line them up in order of best to worst, or they might sample some treats from the kitchen together and then take a stroll with Hamlet, who was always hardly out of his first lesson.

He would saunter through the rose garden with a book in hand and ink-stained fingers and a smile, and Gertrude would let him stay until halfway through the next lesson, when she would send him off with an apology to his tutor.

There was nothing left of the ease they used to share. It made Ophelia embarrassed thinking about it now: how she'd thought Gertrude looked at her like a daughter, how she'd imagined her joy when her beloved son announced his intention to marry her.

"I was sick, Your Majesty, but I have recovered."

"What are you here for?" Gertrude asked. The pillow rustled beneath her head as she looked Ophelia up and down. "I think I know your mind, but I should like to hear it from your lips."

"I wanted to know if you would admit me to return to your household, Your Majesty," Ophelia said. "I would be honoured—"

Gertrude sighed and closed her eyes again, pinching the bridge of her nose as if Ophelia had said something painful. "My dear," she began. "I would *love* to, but you must see where my hesitation comes from. Alessandra, my milk."

She accepted a cup and took a long sip. Her face smoothed out, and she sighed like a difficult weight had been lifted.

"Goodness," she said. "Darling Ophelia. How you distress me. You need to understand—a girl I love, a girl who was as much a daughter to me as my own poor departed girl, betrays my confidence in the most terrible way. A dalliance with the crown prince, my own son. The poor boy thinks he's in love with you!"

Ophelia's cheeks flared as the queen's laughter echoed throughout the chamber. She wished furiously that Alessandra was not there, trying to busy herself in the corner with her back turned.

"You seduced my son. A strange relationship... I always thought you saw him as a brother, and that makes it worse, I fear."

Heat encompassed her. Her dress felt too tight across the chest all of a sudden, restricting her breaths. This was worse than she'd imagined. Father had said the same, in the worst of his outbursts: accused her of incestuous thoughts and unnatural inclinations, of sodomy and wantonness and witchcraft. That night, when Laertes had come to comfort her, she hadn't even felt able to look him in the eye.

"You betray my trust," Gertrude continued, smoothing the blanket over her lap. "You betray the innocent love I allowed you to share with my son. You draw him into scandal, and then you come to beg me for a position in my household." She broke off, putting her fluttering fingers to her throat as if the words choked her. "The questions I had to endure! Oh, everyone wanted to know what had happened—they were all dying to hear what my poor son had done to be sent to Wittenberg, after I spent the last five years refusing to let his father send him away to some draughty school or university."

Tears sprang to Ophelia's eyes. Here it was again: the shame she hated feeling, washing over her like an oil slick.

"Forgive me, ma'am," she managed. "I never meant anything by it, ma'am."

That was the wrong thing to say. Gertrude's gaze became razor-sharp, her lips thinning into a harsh line.

"So you played my son like a fiddle for no reason then? You didn't care for him at all?"

Ophelia's head jerked up. "No—no, ma'm, I mean I never meant any offence! I—I cared for Fyrste Hamlet, of course. But I see now…" She swallowed hard. The words tasted bitter in her mouth. "I see that perhaps my attentions were misguided, and that Fyrste Hamlet deserves more than I could possibly offer."

"Little to offer as a wife, but you think you're a valuable maid?" Gertrude hummed. "My mother always told me a lady's maid is in training to become a wife. If you're a poor maid, you'll have an unhappy husband; I suppose a poor wife would make a poor maid too, if that is to be believed."

Ophelia gritted her teeth.

"Ma'am, I promise I will do my best to serve you." Finally, she swallowed her pride. "I will take any position, as long as you accept me back into your household with love. That is all I desire."

The formal words sounded uglier and less truthful than she'd anticipated, but Gertrude let out a hum of contemplation.

Finally, she gave in. "You always were good with the flowers," she said. "Ensure your duties are done well, or you will be suitably punished."

Ophelia furiously nodded her thanks.

Queen Gertrude swung her legs out of bed and threw her blanket to the side. Her nightclothes were rumpled, and Ophelia could see where she had been sweating in the night.

"When Fyrste Hamlet returns from Wittenberg, stay far away from him. Is that clear?"

She nodded again.

"He will not be back for long." Now Gertrude's eyes seemed to bore into her, waiting for a response. "He will come for Christmas on his father's command, to boost morale. Then he will go back to the safety of Wittenberg, and he will not return until this damned war is over. You will have few opportunities to get your claws into him again, girl."

Ophelia ignored the way those words felt, the acknowledgment that this woman would stand between her and Hamlet forever, that they would never have a love that was uncontested.

"Yes, ma'am," she said, and she left the room as quickly as she politely could.

It was an uneasy victory. She was a fool, she realised, to think Gertrude would forgive and forget so easily. But as she walked down the hall, she realised the stares had lessened already, even without Gertrude's blessing. She could move freely again, and soon she would be back to repainting the sigils in the royal corridors, and perhaps she could bring Kronborg Castle back from the brink of destruction.

So long as the war didn't destroy them before the Corruption could.

SCENE TWO
hamlet

The market was packed. A dozen languages surrounded him between the narrow rows of tables loaded with the ordinary and the bizarre. He lost track of how long they'd been in the market: hours or days, or maybe just minutes.

In Denmark, he had access to every fine thing on earth. Here, Hamlet found his eyes landing on things that could not be earthly. A glass display showed tiny serpents slithering in the water, with short stumpy wings at their sides. They looked like the sea monsters from his map collection at home.

Then there were the glass bottles filled with mysterious liquids, things that shimmered, pearlescent, in the strange and never-dimming sun. Powders were weighed on scales etched with bizarre symbols; elsewhere, a tired young woman with three children at her feet stabbed those same symbols into people's arms with a needle and ink.

Although the market was small, it was crammed so full of stalls that once he was inside, Hamlet couldn't find his way out. He stayed close to Fortinbras, who was thankfully about a foot taller than almost anyone else at the market, and tried not to lose Horatio, who was hardly taller than he was.

He found himself listening in to hear what snippets of conversation he could: nearby, two old men in long tunics argued about the price of some sort of dried, salted meat, while elsewhere children happily threw stones at one another, each one shouting excitedly in a different tongue.

"What can magic do?" he asked Fortinbras as they lingered by a stall, where Horatio was examining a tiny silver knife. The Italian's dark eyebrows were drawn down as he turned the delicate weapon over between his fingers. He pressed something and, without warning, the blade extended until it was the length of his forearm.

"It's less powerful than you're probably thinking," Fortinbras said, without flinching, "and there's less of it here than you'd expect. Nordsee is mostly used as a trading spot. It's quicker and safer to sail here than to travel in the world above. As long as you don't run across any sea serpents, of course."

He winked. Hamlet tried to tamp down a renewed childhood fear of sea serpents.

"So magic is only used to come to this place?" he asked, looking around. "I thought magic would be more… tangible."

The corner of Fortinbras' mouth quirked up. "It can be. But there are old stories about magic, superstitions… Some people believe in a thing called Corruption, which as far as I can tell is a story to dissuade people from using spells left and right."

"So people don't really *use* magic here?" he asked, trying to hide his disappointment.

"People don't tend to use it for anything more than a bit of fun in Nordsee, no. Party tricks. Bursting into flames, making figures out of shadows. Horatio once drank one that made him cough up flower petals for a day, but that's another story entirely."

Horatio returned to Fortinbras's side, tucking his new knife into a pouch at his waist.

"Hamlet wants to know about magic," Fortinbras said. "You know much more about it than I do."

Hamlet had thought as much. Horatio moved much more naturally through this space than Fortinbras—as if it was part of him, more home than Wittenberg. He wondered if Fortinbras was one of the many people Horatio had taken to this place, and he wondered why anyone would ever share something so wonderful. If he had this secret to himself, he'd tear a man's throat out before he led him inside.

He supposed he was lucky Horatio did not have that same instinct.

"It's complicated," Horatio said. His eyelashes were so long they brushed his cheekbones as he scrunched up his forehead in thought. "People have been studying magic for generations and we still don't truly understand it or its limits. Here, try."

Horatio had plucked a cup of food from a passing peddler, swapping it for what looked like three miniscule coins on a string. He picked up a piece of brown meat smothered in some kind of rich sauce and held it out. Hamlet hardly had time to think before he was parting his lips for Horatio to feed him, but even as his cheeks flushed, he was closing his eyes to savour the flavour. Buttery, garlicky, with a hint of lemon and something earthy he didn't recognise... It was delicious.

They ate the rest between the three of them, the conversation dying in the face of the nicest food Hamlet had ever eaten. When they were finished, Fortinbras led them to a small tap on the side of the building, where they washed their greasy hands. He linked his fingers with Horatio's when they were finished, easily, as if there was nothing unusual about this.

And there wasn't. It was one of the first things Hamlet had noticed on their arrival to the market. He was used to the cosmopolitan mélange of Helsingør, but never before had he seen so many religious symbols worn openly. About half of the women wore their hair uncovered, and of those another half wore trousers instead of skirts. There were long tunics and high-necked embroidered shirts and buttoned gowns in all the colours of the rainbow, and many of the people in the market held hands, and for some of them, he couldn't even decide on which gendered word to use.

"It's a good place," Fortinbras said. "Strict, but I don't suppose Jinlian has much choice."

"She has to be," Horatio agreed. "I don't know much about this Corruption rumour, but if Jinlian is worried, then so am I."

"So this Corruption," Hamlet said. "It's some kind of dark magic?"

"Not quite," Horatio said. "It's a very traditional idea. Something about magic being unnatural, or leaving something unnatural behind—"

"Magic," said a familiar voice, "is as natural as breathing."

Rosencrantz stood there like an apparition. Fortinbras and Horatio both shifted, their body language changing: the relaxed stances turned into something more tense, wound like a spring, waiting for a reason to strike.

"People will tell you that it's complicated," Rosencrantz continued. "They'll tell you there are all kinds of magic, and that some types are dark and corrupt and others are perfect and pure. But that's mostly a lie. If you want to make beautiful things with it, you can. You can poison someone, or make them bleed through their eyes. Kingdoms have fallen over magic, and they probably will again."

Hamlet's skin tingled. The way Rosencrantz looked at him, with open curiosity that bordered on predation, made him shiver.

"Magic's just another force," Rosencrantz said. And then, like it was nothing, like they were the only people left in the marketplace: "I can teach you magic like that, if you want. Was going to anyway, eventually."

Fortinbras said, "Be careful, Rosencrantz."

Hamlet's mouth felt oddly dry. "How did you find us?"

"Had a feeling you'd be here," Rosencrantz said, stuffing his hands into his pockets. He changed the subject as easily as breathing, like his appearance hadn't just changed the very air. "Magic's not about waving your hands in the air and whispering words, nor is it about pretty enchanted knives." He gave Horatio a disdainful look. "It's gambling. It's combining the right ingredients, over and over again, and seeing what happens. It's—"

"Dangerous to treat like a game," said Horatio. "Alchemy? Really, Rosencrantz?"

Rosencrantz shrugged. "You use magic however you like," he said. "But my magic is about power. Not playing games and making things disappear in a puff of smoke."

"If Jinlian knew you were practising alchemy again, she'd never let you back through that mirror," Horatio growled. "Not when you're on thin ice already, after that little episode in Felltree."

Rosencrantz smiled. "We've discussed it. She accepts it."

Fortinbras and Horatio both glared, but they clearly had no rebuttal.

"Ros, stop it," Hamlet said. He wasn't even sure what he meant: for Ros to stop speaking like that, to stop putting that expression on Fortinbras's face? Or for Ros to go away, to undo the tension, unwrap it like a heavy blanket and bring back the easy conversation of earlier?

He did not like being on the receiving end of one of Ros's glares, he decided. It felt like being frozen, like being pinned to a board by a spear in the gut and examined.

"It's funny," said Ros. "I'm surprised to see you together. Aren't your countries officially at war?"

"No," said Hamlet. "No, we're not."

But Fortinbras's stony silence remained, and Horatio grimaced and looked away, and Ros leaned back against a stall, arms folded, looking victorious.

So it was true.

"We are not at war," Hamlet repeated. "We can't be. I would have been informed."

"But you are," said Rosencrantz. "It's been a few weeks, actually. Long enough for an urgent message to reach Wittenberg. But your family didn't send you a message, did they?"

Hamlet felt like the breath had been knocked out of him. His mind was full of visions of armour and smoke, of blood and white flags.

"Fortinbras received a missive," said Ros. His voice had dropped to something barely above a whisper. "Well over a week ago, if I remember rightly."

"That was a private communication, Fortinbras said. His tone was a warning in itself. "I could have you jailed for eavesdropping. In fact, I could drag you back to Norway and have you executed for treason."

"You could," said Rosencrantz.

"But you won't," said Hamlet. His right fist curled and uncurled by his side.

He didn't want to look at Fortinbras, but at the same time he couldn't look away. Those blue eyes, that smile, working together to hide a war.

Hamlet couldn't believe he had been so blind. Sitting in Wittenberg attending lectures, following Fortinbras around like a lost puppy, staring at Rosencrantz's jaw or Guildenstern's arms, letting the world outside shrink until it contained only him and them and somewhere, a pinprick on the horizon, Ophelia.

Now here he was: the prince of a nation at war, ignorant and impotent.

It was not possible that Father simply sent a messenger late, or the message failed to arrive. No, this was the natural continuation of years of being the imperfect son: too scrawny for swordsmanship, too twitchy for archery, too dreamy for politics. Hamlet and Arion Fortinbras should have been evenly matched: princes on either side of two warring nations, almost of an age, formed by one another.

Instead, it was like this: Fortinbras was told, and Hamlet was not.

"You will not threaten him," Hamlet said. He disliked the smugness on Rosencrantz's face, but he liked it better than what he saw in Fortinbras's expression: pity. "Is this true, Fortinbras?"

"It is," he said, quietly. "I thought that you might know. I wondered, at first, if that was why you came to see me tonight."

"It was not." Embarrassment. Throwing himself at Fortinbras' feet like an animal, weeping. Begging for a look, a touch. The thing inside him that had warmed to Fortinbras shivered and died. "You should've told me when you realised I didn't know. That would have been the honourable thing to do."

"If you feel that you cannot remain civil with Fortinbras, I understand," said Horatio. "But if this is about taking sides, choose your own. Not Rosencrantz's. Trust me, Hamlet."

Hamlet bared his teeth. "You misunderstand me," he said. "The side I choose is Denmark's."

And then he turned to Rosencrantz.

"Teach me," he said. "Or I'll find someone else who will."

Hamlet turned on his heel and left. After a moment, Rosencrantz followed.

He wrote a few lines and had them sent to his father as urgently as possible.

Coming home soon, he wrote. *I heard the news. You should have told me.*

Three days later, he received a letter from his uncle.

Have spoken to your father. You are to lead. Be home at Christmas.

SCENE THREE
ophelia

Father roused Ophelia early in the morning.

"The king has called an assembly," he said. "Come. Your brother is already there."

Father hurried off, a stack of books and papers under his arm and his jerkin buttoned up the wrong way. Ophelia dressed quickly in the half-light, her hands clumsy with sleep. When she was ready, she stepped out into the hall.

The throne room was thronged with people. The tapestried walls seemed to shimmer in the watery light from the narrow windows. It made it look like all the cloth horsemen were moving, riding into a never-ending battle, and at the other end of the room the throne stood empty. So did the smaller, less adorned chair beside it.

Hal's chair stood abandoned to one side, propped up against the wall and gathering dust.

Ophelia could see her father standing at the head of the crowd. His grey-streaked head was tipped close to another courtier's, and he was gesticulating wildly enough that the other man kept having to dodge out of the way. Laertes was somewhere nearby, looking torn between embarrassment and ambivalence. He waved half-heartedly when he saw Ophelia, but it was so closely packed that she couldn't raise her own arm to return the gesture.

She stretched her neck to try to see over the heads of the crowd. She saw Father as he was approached by a servant and ushered into the antechamber behind the throne. Ophelia watched the metal-studded door swing shut behind him, and felt dread sink into her belly.

Had they surrendered in the night, she wondered? Or had there been some attack from Norway before Denmark could properly fortify its defences? Danish boats could be approaching Helsingør, or maybe some other nation had decided to weigh in on the conflict, or perhaps they were going to be under siege…

"Before you ask, I know nothing," Alessandra said, appearing beside her. She was a vision of beauty as always, dressed in lush purple, but her eyes were red. "From how poorly Lorenz slept last night, I assume the news is bad. Has your father told you anything?"

"Nothing," said Ophelia. "Truth be told, I've hardly seen him since Norway visited."

That was what they had taken to calling it. Not 'since war was declared' Instead, they said, 'when Norway visited', because that sounded less like their entire world was falling apart. Funny, the things humans would do to avoid the truth.

"Lorenz is the same," Alessandra said. "Last night was the first time he has been home and in bed before dawn. That is what worries me." She looked around, wrinkling her nose with disdain. "What news is bad enough that the king orders his men to get a good night's sleep?"

Ophelia took Alessandra's hand and squeezed. The warmth of her skin was a decent substitute for the hand she really wanted to hold at this moment.

If anything has happened to Hamlet, she thought, *I will never forgive a single soul in this court for sending him away.*

Everything pointed to tragedy. Even in wartime, there were usually torches burning on the walls, a fire in the grate. In Kronborg now, there were no ribbons hanging from the walls, no bouquets lingering in the corners. And she was right that the room was more dimly lit than usual: when she glanced around, she realised that sconces had been left empty. The only light came through the stained glass windows, tinting the room a forested green.

A rumble grew among the gathered courtiers. She turned with them, looking not at the king's door but at the one they had all entered through. Someone important had arrived, but she could not see them. Ignoring all appearance of propriety, she stood on her tiptoes and peered over the crowd. She could only see a head of blond hair streaked with grey, a man's forehead; that was all.

Alessandra gasped and bent low to whisper in Ophelia's ear. "I know him from his portrait," she hissed. "The king's brother, Prince Claudius. He hasn't attended court in years."

Ophelia pretended surprise, as if she hadn't already seen him. Again he was the only person in this entire room who was free of the Corruption, but this time she looked at him with a more suspicious eye. She remembered what Hilga had said: that man was smothered in Corruption, soaked in it. She noticed now what she had missed before, when she was so distracted by the aura of emptiness that surrounded him.

He had strange yellow-gold eyes and a stern demeanour, a neatly-trimmed beard, and this was interesting, because it gave a full view of the strange scar that twisted across his face. Ophelia was no stranger to scars:

she had plenty herself, and almost every man at court had nicks and marks all over him from battle or training or any manner of things, but this one was strange: it was almost like he had been hit by lightning. The white scar tissue rippled across the right side of his face in a branching path.

Whatever the injury, she felt sure it could not be anything natural. In fact, she had a sneaking suspicion that a scar like that could only be as a result of magic.

Claudius disappeared into the antechamber, followed by the murmurs of the crowd. It was a long time before anyone emerged, and when they did it was in a quiet, solemn stream. Lord Emberlin dabbed at his eyes with the corner of a handkerchief. Ophelia spied her father and noted the way he rubbed his nose repeatedly, the way he always did in high emotion.

"It will be alright," Alessandra said quietly. "It will be better when we know. It is more painful to imagine the possibilities than to know the truth."

Ophelia didn't reply. She couldn't bring herself to agree. She wished she could stay in the comforting unknown for a while longer, but then the crowd began to shift and change, and before she knew it, she was curtseying for the king and queen's arrival.

For a long time, Old King Hamlet just sat upon the throne in silence.

King Hamlet was a broad, weathered-looking man. Usually his eyes were very bright, blue as the wildflowers that dotted the meadows in spring. Today, it was like a raincloud had passed over them. His beard was uncombed, although he still wore his rich robes, his fine cloak; it made him look half-dressed, like someone had clambered through the windows of the royal wardrobe and decided to play dress-up.

"Speak, husband," the queen whispered, her hand squeezing at his wrist.

King Hamlet heaved a deep sigh. "You know," he started, "that our enemies, Norway, have made unscrupulous efforts to conquer our lands and take what rightfully belongs to the Kingdom of Denmark."

He sounded, Ophelia thought, the way he did when he spoke to Hamlet from the dais the day he left. Calm, but with the possibility of fury running through it like a current. It lay just beneath the surface, waiting for an opportunity to erupt, a thin river of magma under a calm rock. She shuddered at the recollection, feeling the ghost of the rain on her skin once again.

"King Fortinbras has advanced once more. His words of war were not folly. Our attempts to broker peace have failed.

"I heard four days ago that Norwegian ships had departed from Kristiansand. It was my belief that they sailed for Hirtshals. I had no reason for concern, although there was fear in my heart, and I admit today that my lack of action has failed my people grievously."

He raised his head, staring down at the assembled court.

"Fladstrand has fallen to the Norwegians. They laid siege to the city and within a day—after the supply wagons were stopped and a skirmish occurred beyond the walls—the town was forced to cede control to the invaders."

Silence. Ophelia felt numb, her body someone else's. She imagined fleets of ships, swords held to throats in the salt chill of the coast, boots scrambling over rocks. She imagined houses ransacked, food raided, screaming and sobbing.

"We have always known that Norway laid covetous eyes upon the Skagerrak cities. It is my fear that Norway intends to continue to Aalborg and attempt to take the city, as part of their larger plan to consume our kingdom and subdue our people beneath a foreign power." Here,

King Hamlet paused for breath and squeezed the queen's hand. "If I had spoken a few days earlier, I would have asked this of you: to prepare yourselves for the war and to pray for peace. Now, I must say: war is here, and we will defend our kingdom. I do not doubt that any man here will offer his best service in the name of Denmark, but still it pains me to ask you to make so great a sacrifice."

Laertes. She felt sick.

"A final word: I know many in this court have friends and countrymen in Norway. I do not ask you to put aside your love for them. I merely ask you to be wary. Anyone who offers information or aid to Norway in this time commits an act of grievous treason, and you know the consequences of such an act. You will be punished with the utmost severity."

Claudius stepped forward. Up close, he and the king were obviously brothers, similar in stature with the same nose, the same square jaw, but here the differences between them seemed more pronounced. King Hamlet was large and strong and physically very powerful; but Claudius had the look of a man who had gained strength not through a routine of training but through a lifetime of scars.

"It is my honour to lead the army northwest," he said. His voice rang clear and true; he had the voice of an orator, the kind of voice that could not help but be listened to. "I intend to march as soon as supplies have been arranged."

Murmurs rose throughout the hall. Ophelia grounded herself through her feet, feeling the sturdy floor beneath her. She breathed deep.

Winter was approaching fast. Soldiers were going to die of the cold before they ever reached Aalborg. When the war was over, no matter who won, there would be a trail of frost-bitten bodies left along the march. Would Laertes be one of them?

Ophelia was suddenly fiercely glad that Hal was away. She recalled his mother's words: he would return for Christmas, and then he would go back to the shelter of Wittenberg, and all would be well.

If anyone in Kronborg Castle had a brain, they would keep the war a secret from him for as long as they could. If Hamlet caught wind of it, he would go, and he would hate it or love it, and she didn't know which one was worse. Hamlet would pierce himself on a spike if he thought his father might acknowledge his bravery in doing so. He'd nail himself to a cross for his father's love. She could see it already: Hal, blood-spattered with bared teeth, knee-deep in corpses. They said war changed people, but she didn't want Hamlet to change. She wanted him to remain as he was, with no blood on his hands.

Claudius continued to speak, but she wasn't listening. Alessandra slid her gaze sideways, then smiled wanly.

"It is as bad as we thought, then," Alessandra whispered. There was a hint of relief in her voice. "I'm glad it was only what I imagined, and not anything I could not."

Ophelia smiled and squeezed the other woman's hand. "You make a good point."

She scanned the room, and her brief smile flickered and died on her face. The men stood together, talking despite Claudius's flowing speech. The younger men were grouped together like a herd: she spotted Alessandra's husband, the ever-smiling Lorenz, looking lost among them. His eyes were somewhere very far away.

They were going to the slaughter. She knew this with a sudden, sharp certainty. Norway was powerful. If the cold didn't take them, the battles probably would. And if Aalborg was only weeks from being besieged, then there was no guarantee the Norwegians wouldn't have increased their strength and holdings by then.

A horrible feeling overtook her. Helsingør suddenly felt tiny: a pinprick in the map, a tiny spot in an ocean. What hope did they have if an invading force sailed around the strait and attacked from the east instead? They would be swallowed in an instant.

Alessandra nudged her gently. Ophelia came to her senses and realised everyone was leaving, filtering out into the hall, and Claudius had retreated to stand at his brother's shoulder, and Old King Hamlet was sitting with his chin in his hands, lost in thought. She glanced back at her father, but he seemed to be staying behind with the rest of the privy council.

"Come along, dear," Alessandra murmured. Her hand rubbed little soothing circles on Ophelia's back. "Why don't we take a walk together?"

"That sounds lovely," she managed. "Yes, let's take a walk."

That night, thoughts of a fleet sailing around the coast wouldn't leave her mind. It tormented her to the point that she rose and wrote a few lines to Hal—nothing of the war or the battles to come, but just to say that she loved and missed him.

The kind of thing he'd made her promise not to write.

It's for the best, Fee, he'd said. *I'll be back before long, and then things will be back to what they were. But for now, let's leave it.*

Father caught her writing it and burned it immediately.

"I thought we were beyond this," he said, holding the paper over the candle until it caught. "I thought you'd come to your senses. Heaven forbid…"

Ophelia watched the paper burn with little other than resignation. She had had a feeling it wouldn't make it out of the castle, but she had to try. Try as she might, she couldn't summon up anything more than exhaustion. It was not yet dawn.

"I never want to be harsh with you," said Father, sweeping the ashes into the grate. "I never wanted to speak plainly, but it seems now that I must."

Ophelia wished he would reach his point a little sooner. It was going to be the same as always: *he wants only one thing from you, and when he has it, he will abandon you, he will neglect you, you will watch him marry a queen and you will linger always in her shadow, all your beauty faded, all your life wasted, the fruit of your youth rotting in your hands.*

"He wants only one thing from you," Father began, and Ophelia turned back to her mirror to finish fixing her hair.

SCENE FOUR
hamlet

"Teach me," Hamlet said again. They stood at the edge of the market, away from the crowd, but he still felt like they were all watching.

Rosencrantz rolled his head first one way, then the other. "I hope you don't think I owe you thanks for that," he said. "In fact, I think you owe me an apology."

"For what? Speaking to Fortinbras?" Hamlet scoffed. "It's my country that's at war with his. With *yours*."

"For fraternising with the enemy."

"Fraternising…" It was comical, but Rosencrantz's face was deadly serious.

"Behind my back, might I add," he said. "Maybe I should have been more direct with you: Fortinbras and I detest each other. Any friend of his cannot and will not be a friend of mine."

"Why is that?" he asked.

"None of your concern."

"I think it is my concern," said Hamlet. "And you may have noticed: Fortinbras and I are apparently at war, which you have known for weeks. You failed to mention it. Don't you think you owe me an explanation?"

Now it was Rosencrantz's turn to scoff. He started walking, strolling into the warren-like mass of streets. Hamlet thought about going in the opposite direction, but he had no idea where he was. So he followed.

"Fortinbras and I disagree on a number of the finer points of magic," Rosencrantz said finally. "He believes there are things magic shouldn't be used for, such as altering the body or the mind."

"And you think it's fine."

"I think it's fine, and I think Fortinbras is an enormous hypocrite for any number of reasons, namely that he regularly blasts fire out of every pore." Rosencrantz said this as if it was an absolutely reasonable thing to say, and not completely bizarre and slightly terrifying. "He can blast fire out of his arse and I can't grow myself a set of balls? Idiot."

Hamlet decided not to even ask.

"He can set himself alight," he said. "At will?"

Rosencrantz nodded.

Hamlet's mind filled with images of the battlefield.

Fortinbras will leave Wittenberg soon, he thought. *He must. And he will go to war with my father, and if he can do this… then Denmark will burn.*

He thought of the soldiers he knew being crushed under waves of flame; he thought of fiery spears piercing his father, bursting through his belly, his chest, dissolving him into so much ash.

Fortinbras would not use magic as a weapon, surely.

But Hamlet had no guarantee that he would not.

"If you're thinking," said Rosencrantz, "that he will use that power against you, you're right. And there is so much more that he can do."

"But if it's as you say," Hamlet said, thinking it over desperately, "and he thinks some magic is evil… why use it at all?"

"Because he's already sinned half a hundred times," said Rosencrantz. "What's a couple more?"

"What can I do against that?" Hamlet asked, dry-mouthed. "No one would believe me. Not unless they saw it themselves, and then it's too late."

"I'll teach you everything I know," Rosencrantz replied. "I'll make sure you're stronger than him. I'll teach you everything you could possibly need to help Denmark in this war."

For a moment, he was elated.

Then he realised he was missing a crucial piece of information.

"Why?" he asked. "You're Norwegian, after all. Why would you want to help Denmark?"

Rosencrantz just shrugged. "I'm a gambling man," he said. "And I'm betting on Denmark to win."

"You have no qualms about fixing the match," Hamlet said, which made Ros laugh.

It was only later that he realised he'd never asked what prize it was Ros expected to be awarded for such a great victory, or what specifically made him so sure he could lead Hamlet to winning a war. It was an oversight he would deeply regret.

They had only days before an entourage was set to arrive to bring Hamlet safely back to Denmark. He abandoned his lessons. No one questioned it: by now, word of the war had become common knowledge in Wittenberg. He couldn't understand how he's missed it: it was like he'd been living in a dream. He spent sleepless nights reading through books on magic and spellcraft with Rosencrantz, not speaking except to point out anything that might be of use.

It made no sense to Hamlet. Magic was a natural force, apparently, and everyone could use it, except some people struggled more than others, and spells were inefficient and seemed to involve lengthy Latin chanting, so no one bothered with them. Magic was all around, but you could only use what was stored in your internal 'well', according to Rosencrantz. If the well dried up, your spells would collapse until you refilled it.

"Some wishy-washy people say you shouldn't be using your well at all and your magic should all come from outside, from nature," he said with a sneer. "And that's why they're still daubing sigils on cave walls and chanting about Corruption."

This was a word Rosencrantz used a lot, usually derisively: *Corruption*. Hamlet wasn't sure what it meant: sometimes it sounded like a disease, at other times like a physical thing. Rosencrantz said it wasn't something to be particularly worried about.

"Oh, we're all riddled with it. There's no avoiding it," he said cheerfully. "Might as well accept it."

Within a day, he had Hamlet excavating his well, digging deep into it to feel the magic coursing within. It was strange: for what felt like years but was really just weeks, he'd ached to do magic. Now that he was doing it, it was almost… pedestrian. Making a pebble quake against the tabletop was nothing in the face of the fiery explosion he kept imagining coming from Fortinbras, a poison arrow, a weapon of utter destruction.

Rosencrantz made him learn how to empty the well and refill it. He made Hamlet experiment with forcing the magic into different limbs: how did it feel if it was all concentrated in his lower body, in his arms, in his fingertips? How did it impact the use of it?

Hamlet found that it worked best if he encouraged the magic to flow from his belly up into his chest, then down into his arms and out through his fingertips. It felt more directed, sharper.

But Ros was disdainful. "You're making it into a spear," he said. "What you need for strong spells is for the magic to act as a shield. It needs to come from every pore, not just leak out your fingernails."

He tried to copy that, to send the magic radiating out of the entire front of his body, but all that happened was that he lost control and made all of Rosencrantz's books go flying across the room and then set them alight.

Guildenstern was almost non-existent. When he did appear, he walked straight past the mess on the table and up the stairs. Hamlet got the sense that he knew everything that had gone on, and had chosen not to be involved. He also got the sense Guildenstern wasn't sleeping, because neither was he and neither was Rosencrantz, and many times in the middle of the night he heard Guildenstern's bedroom door creak open or heard his quiet swear as his candle burned too low to be revived.

Sometimes, particularly when something went wrong—such as the books flying across the room—Hamlet became distressed.

"Ros, he knows about magic. If he uses it—"

"He'll hang if anyone sees," Ros said sharply, collecting rocks from where they'd struck the far wall. "And so will you, so I hope you're going to be careful. All eyes will be on you now, Hal."

"What if I can't do it?" Hamlet whispered. His miserable, pathetic voice cracked and shook, as fickle as his desperate feelings towards Fortinbras. "Fortinbras is clever. His father is one of the best strategists I've ever met. They'll crush us."

Ros pulled his hands away from his face. He was on the ground too, kneeling in front of Hal.

"You'll be fine because I'm helping you," Ros said. His gaze was intense, swaying; Hamlet couldn't take his eyes off him, his strange, grey-white eyes, the thousand freckles that studded his cheeks. "I'm here, Hal."

Ros's knuckles brushed Hal's cheek. The touch was so gentle Hamlet could've cried.

He pressed his forehead to Ros's warm, bony shoulder, felt the fabric of his tunic, the heat of his skin. He forgot sometimes, touch-starved as he was, that humans were not made of stone: that, when you touched them, the flesh was soft and gave way. Even Ros was not sculpted entirely from unfeeling marble.

"I told you I'd help you to win this war," he said. "Have a little faith, Hamlet."

"It's not you I have no faith in," he muttered, and sat up. "This isn't working. I'm not learning fast enough."

He expected Rosencrantz to disagree, maybe assure him that they had plenty of time, but instead Ros just made a thoughtful noise.

"You're right," he said. "We may need to try another tactic."

"Such as?" Hamlet said. "Whatever it is, Ros, I'm willing to try it. If it gives me a chance against Norway…"

Ros looked up through his lashes. "It wouldn't be very noble," he said.

"I don't care, as long as it means winning the war."

"Oh, you don't need to pretend you really care about the war," Ros said casually. "You care that Fortinbras and your father didn't tell you about the war. But that's besides the point."

"That's not true."

"Funny, that," said Guildenstern, who was just passing through. "Fortinbras and your father in the same sentence. It's almost like your bizarre obsession with the crown prince of Norway is actually just a reflection of your paternal issues."

"Christ, Guildenstern," said Rosencrantz.

"What are 'paternal issues' meant to be?" asked Hamlet.

There was a pause.

"Anyway," said Guildenstern, "I'll leave you two to it. 'It' being planning war crimes, or something."

He ascended the stairs. When the sound of his footsteps faded, Ros turned back to Hamlet.

"I worry that you're more concerned about proving yourself than actually winning this war," he said. "There are things people will do to prove themselves, and those things are usually horribly noble and lovely and romantic. And then there are the things people do to win, the things no one talks about when the war is over. I need to know you're willing to do *those* things."

Hamlet said, again, "I'll do anything."

"Well then," Ros said, "I think you should murder Prince Fortinbras."

SCENE FIVE
ophelia

Ophelia trailed after the queen wherever she went, sitting at the edges of the room at dinners and wandering the rose gardens with the rest of the flock in the afternoon. They went to chapel twice a day and accepted the body of Christ onto their tongues, bland and mealy-tasting.

When she was around the queen, Ophelia's head throbbed as if someone had hit her over the head with a plate. Queen Gertrude was predictably wrapped in Corruption magic, but so were some of the other lady's maids, and the sheer volume of it stuck to the walls in her chambers almost drove Ophelia to despair.

But when she went outside, and she travelled down to the water or walked alone in the gardens, there was enough beauty to keep her going.

In those places, she could hardly see magic. When she looked closely at a rose, sometimes she could spot the finest of threads, golden tendrils that grew up through the ground and made its way into that blossoming bud. In the water, it floated sometimes, like escaped fabric amidst the sea foam. More often than not, she saw no magic, and she liked that. It reminded her that there was more to life than seeking out Corruption. More to life than trying desperately to save the city.

Every night, she brought a basin of water to her bed and did the necessary movements to cleanse herself. She washed her hands, and she whispered the magic words. She washed her face, and murmured her mother's song, a song of cleansing. She washed her body, and she willed herself clean.

But always, the Corruption hovered. Sometimes more, sometimes less: but when one was living in the den of sin, it was impossible to stay away from it.

You were always complicit.

The Corruption was getting worse and worse, and it was blocking out the light, and most of the time she felt like she was trapped underwater without any air.

But that didn't matter for the moment. Now, she was doing one of the only things she knew how to do in the face of Corruption. Today was a sigil-marking day, and Ophelia's bloodstained fingers smeared the wall red.

She reached once more into the leather pouch and felt the thick liquid contents make way for her. A shudder worked its way down her spine. In the corner of the alcove, hidden behind the tapestry on the king's hallway, she left her bloody mark.

It was just as Hilga instructed and just as Mother had taught her—drying brown on the stone, hardly visible in the dark. But the fish blood wouldn't flake easily thanks to all the other unguents mixed with it to make this paste. Fats thickened it so that it was more blood suspended in oil than liquid, and the herbs Ophelia had helped to grind lent the mixture its speckled tone.

She wiped as much of the blood off on the strips as she could and grimaced, tucking the fish-blood-stained cloth back where it came from. Then she withdrew the water skin she kept tied to her thigh and dripped as little of it as she could over her hands. If anyone wondered how it got so wet behind the tapestry, they would assume someone from the court was too desperate to wait for a chamber pot. It did little to clear the grime, but it made it easier to wipe the blood off on the strips of cloth tucked into her underpants.

She hated wearing them—so constraining—but they helped to hold her menstrual rags in place, and that was exactly the effect she needed to create: that she was having her monthly bleeding.

Ophelia tucked away all her little bags where they belonged. These sigils could be ineffective at worst, but at best they might keep the walls from crumbling when Norway came.

She listened for a moment, then slipped out into the hall behind a group of other girls. Within a moment, she was among them, as if that was exactly where she belonged. They were going to the chapel, and she agreed enthusiastically that she was going there too, and that they should all pray together.

The chapel was busy. A crowd had gathered outside, mostly men waiting for their wives to finish their prayers by the looks of it. Ophelia and Alessandra bowed their heads as they approached and the men did the same, muttering greetings under their breath.

Ophelia caught the eye of Antonius, the Kammerjunker, and of Sir Stellan, the Master of Horse. They stood shoulder to shoulder outside the chapel, talking of something that was evidently not meant for a house of God by their bawdy laughter.

Ophelia pulled her veil forward so it covered all her hair and allowed Sir Stellan to open the door for them, casting him a small smile. Inside, it was dimly lit with candles. The small altar at the top of the chapel was uncovered, ready for a priest to adorn it for evening mass. She knelt at the back, Alessandra sinking to her knees beside her.

In the dark, it was easy to think. She could hear the quiet rustle of a prayer book somewhere, the hushed whisper of a psalm from someone to her right. With her hands clasped in front of her face, Ophelia bent in prayer. She breathed in the dusty, cloying smell of incense. It reminded her of the smell of her mother's clothes, freshly scented with flower water and herbs.

She tried to ignore the clinging Corruption on the walls. A rope of it wiggled past her knee, and she tried hard not to flinch. Quietly, she whispered a spell; it gave one final wriggle and burst into sparks before it finally disappeared.

The other women prayed, their heads bowed over their clasped hands. Alessandra was already whispering under her breath, hushed Italian Ophelia couldn't make out.

She turned her attention to her own prayers. What would she pray for? She could be here all night, if she didn't focus. There was everyone in Rúnräd to think about—they all looked stressed and harried, Aaron most of all. He worried over every cough and cold. He remembered the plagues, and he knew the dangers that came with them. Perhaps she would pray for him to get a good night's rest.

And then there was Hal, who was undoubtedly carousing in Wittenberg. She wondered if he'd seen the inside of a church in the last few months. Probably not.

She could pray for Lorenz, who looked more worn than ever, even with a smile on his face, and for Alessandra, who was so clearly worried for him. They deserved a better start to their marriage than all of this uncertainty. Laertes needed a thought, because if he wasn't careful he was going to find himself in trouble.

Was there room in her heart to pray for herself?

She breathed in hard through her nose, and began.

Pater noster…

And then something struck her in the back of the head.

She was falling, falling, too far to be possible. She did not have control of her body. In front of her was only darkness and behind her was something too terrible to conceive of. She could see nothing, but she knew that she was being hunted. She didn't need eyes to hear its slavering mouth, to feel its hot breath on the back of her neck.

"Whatever you are," she screamed, "I will burn you to ashes! *Fiat lux!*"

The thing did not speak in words. It only growled, making the same wet sounds a hunting dog might when greeted with a running deer. Her eyes adjusted, and she saw that the walls of the cavern were a deep red, the colour of blood. Shadows clambered from the stone, reaching for her with claws and fingers, talons and beaks. She screamed, and her voice bounced off the walls and returned to haunt her.

It felt like falling through space.

Hell was empty, and all the devils were here.

And then, with a feeling like she was being dragged over hot coals, she heard Hal's voice echoing in the chasm around her.

"Mother, you have my father much offended," he said, seeming to speak from very far away. Then—and his voice was altered now, still his but raspier, driven through with a fury so cold she could not bear it—Hamlet said, "You wretched, rash, intruding fool. Farewell—I took you for your better."

A wet noise, like a carving knife through meat, and a stoppage of breath…

And again, Ophelia's body burnt to a crisp, her skin shrivelling, the flesh pulling back from her nails, her teeth, leaving her ash and bone and nothing more…

"Ophelia, darling!" Alessandra was saying, shaking her. Something smelled terrible: incense, she realised, wafting directly into her nose. She sat up in a hurry, coughing and pressing her cold hands over her mouth to keep herself from gagging all over the chapel floor. Nothing had struck her, she realised. The pain was gone.

"Poor girl," someone murmured—one of the ladies, but in her state Ophelia knew not which. "Someone must carry her out, surely."

"I am quite well," croaked Ophelia. "In a moment or two, I will be walking."

"Are you sure?" Alessandra pressed a hand to Ophelia's chest. "Your heart races. You must be ill, dear…"

"No illness," Ophelia told her firmly. She forced herself to soften her tone then, to speak kindly and patiently, even though she wanted nothing more than to scream with frustration. Her swoon had left her feeling terrible, like an awful dread was seeping into every corner of her mind.

"Please call a maid to help me to my quarters," Ophelia said, and one of the other ladies—Daphne? Daffodil?—practically skipped out the door to do as she was bid. The disgraced Ophelia passing out at prayer? Another day, another scandal.

They were going to think she was possessed, Ophelia thought wildly, or being tempted by the devil. She had to do something else, say something to get herself out of this situation.

"I dreamt of the most beautiful thing," she said, affecting a smile. Alessandra's forehead puckered. "I saw Helsingør's victory, and the flags waving in the summer sun, and I saw the Lord himself bless our city with his noble hand."

Alessandra gasped, her hand flying to her mouth. Her eyes were unchanged: she knew, as well as Ophelia did, that this was nonsensical. To be frank about it, it was bullshit.

"Really?"

"Really." She hid her face by pulling herself to her feet, making a show of straightening her skirts. She really did feel dizzy. "Would you take me to my rooms? I need to rest a while. I feel very weary."

But then, before Alessandra could respond, Prince Claudius stepped over the threshold. Ophelia's stomach lurched and for a moment she felt feverish, like she was back in her vision, but no. It was just the dread that seemed to strike her so often whenever he was around.

Claudius offered her his arm. "I can walk you, Lady Ophelia," he said. "Lady Alessandra might accompany us, as she knows your part of the castle better than I would."

She looked at his arm—his unblemished, aura-less arm, not even a shimmer of any kind of magic clinging to him. When she took it—reluctantly—it was warm and firm, and she found herself leaning on him more than she wanted to as she found her feet. The hallway was too bright in contrast with the chapel and for a moment Ophelia swayed, pressing the back of her free hand to her forehead.

"You gave us all a fright," said Prince Claudius. He slowed his pace when he saw that she was struggling to keep up, and for that Ophelia was grateful. "I'm very glad to see that you're well, albeit pale."

Purple and gold wove around the corridor. It looked like a cavern dripping in stalactites, coated in lime.

But Claudius was untouched, as usual.

Ophelia smiled to hide her fear. "My thanks for your help," she said. "I think I will feel quite well after a rest and some private prayer.

Claudius smiled at her, the lines around his eyes crinkling. It surprised her. He didn't seem like the kind of man to have smile lines, and yet he did, lines as deep as her father's that were etched there from some joy he must have found outside Helsingør

"I know times are hard," he said, lowering his voice a little, "but you must keep your strength up. Women are the backbone of Helsingør, Lady Ophelia. We will need your fortitude in the days to come."

"Is the privy council meeting over, sir?" Alessandra asked. She walked a respectful pace behind the prince, her head bowed. "Only, I am waiting for my husband."

Claudius pulled a face. It was unexpectedly light-hearted. Ophelia wasn't sure if it was encouraging or uncomfortable to see him display such emotion.

"I think it will finish soon," he said. "I hope it will finish soon. I only stepped out for some air."

They walked on in silence, but not the kind of silence that is waiting to be filled with words; the sort that is comfortable, well-known, a quiet agreement between two souls not to speak another word.

When they reached her door, Claudius allowed her to withdraw her hand.

"Good evening," he said. "Get some rest."

When he was out of sight, Alessandra leaned close.

"He seems nice," she said. "Perhaps you shall have a prince after all, Ophelia."

Ophelia's stomach roiled at the thought, but she forced out the laugh Alessandra was expecting and brought herself into her rooms, where she could at least sit in the quiet and try, desperately, not to go over the vision over and over again until she started to forget what was real and what was not.

"Interesting," Alessandra said, very quietly, following her despite the distinct lack of an invitation. "I was going to tell you—perhaps you already know—but... there is something you should hear, if you would permit me."

It was a relief to sit down, where the spinning of the world could not quite get to her.

"It is about Prince Claudius, and about you," Alessandra said. Her stormy eyes were filled with concern. "The queen was on one of her rampages this morning. She was furious—Prince Claudius came to visit her in her chambers, which I thought was odd, and he made a joke... He said something about picking his future brides well, and the queen said..."

"Said what?" Ophelia asked faintly.

"Said you are a ridiculous choice," Alessandra said. "And he laughed. But he had not mentioned your name until that point, Ophelia, so they must have discussed it already."

Ophelia sank back into her chair. "Good Lord," she said. "Oh no. But he's only just arrived!"

But Father, full of hot air as he could be, knew a good opportunity when it fell into his lap.

She wished she could tell Alessandra the whole truth, about magic, about the Corruption. It would at least explain away the horror that showed so clearly on her face. But she knew better than to risk it.

"Let me see what I can discover of him," Alessandra assured her. "I'll find anything that can be found, my dear. You can count on it."

SCENE SIX
hamlet

"Well, I don't want to dispose of Fortinbras in any way that might be messy," said Hal, peering at his fingernails as though they belonged to someone else. He was imagining them with blood beneath them. It wasn't a pleasant thought. "But if this magic of yours can't just dissolve him into a dew, what next?"

"Don't worry about that side of matters," said Rosencrantz.

Probably for the best, Hamlet had to admit. His stomach did an anxious flip.

It wasn't that Fortinbras deserved to die, he told himself. It was just that he had to.

Ros had explained it in a way that made so much sense. This was one of those things that happened during a war that would never be celebrated, but it would matter. It would make a difference. And yes, it made him want to be sick every time he thought about it, and yes, he had spent most of the night outside in the dark scrubbing his hands with water from the jug, trying to wash Fortinbras' phantom blood away, but that was a small price to pay for victory.

"In many ways," Rosencrantz had said, "it's the ultimate sacrifice. No one can ever know you did it. No one can know how much you contributed to Denmark's success."

But the thought of it still scratched at him. Could he really do it? Was he really capable of looking Fortinbras in the eye and killing him?

"No," Ros said flatly, when Hamlet expressed this concern. "Which is why you're going to poison him instead."

Rosencrantz secured hemlock, which he carefully ground down into a powder and placed in a tiny glass vial marked C. maculatum. The same day, Hamlet received a message informing him that the soldiers who were to accompany him home would arrive in three days, perhaps four if the weather continued to worsen.

It started to snow.

Hamlet came downstairs one day to an innocuous bottle of wine on the table, Ros and Guild sitting in front of it. They were both looking at it with vastly different expressions: Ros looked vaguely proud, while Guildenstern looked like he wanted to push the bottle off the table and onto the floor.

"Are we celebrating?" Hamlet asked, picking up the bottle to examine it.

Both of his friends made noises of horror.

"Hemlock!" said Guildenstern.

"Fortinbras can celebrate with it. Or at least, that's the plan."

Hamlet put the wine down and closed his eyes.

It all felt too quick: the war, the poison, the murder. It was happening faster than he could make sense of it. He could not think about Fortinbras without thinking of the slide of a blade between his ribs, the light resistance of the flesh, the duller scrape of bone chafing against metal. He saw Fortinbras thrashing on the ground by that favoured river spot, choking from an invisible poison.

"How are you going to get it to him?" Guildenstern asked, sounding resigned.

"You could bribe someone," Rosencrantz suggested.

"No." Hamlet touched the bottle again with a fingertip, drawing shapes on the glass. "I don't want anyone else involved." Hamlet said. "I'll give it to him myself."

He couldn't imagine sitting in this small, hot room, waiting to hear if the Prince of Norway had died in the night. It was unthinkable. He could consider no other option than to look Prince Fortinbras in the face as he handed over that innocuous bottle, a parting gift between maybe-would-have-been-friends.

Snow covered the city in a pale blanket. Hamlet peered out of the window, watching men stumble past with crates of goods loaded into their arms, women trudging up the slope with buckets and babies balanced at their sides. It was a drab day; even the sky was a pale haze, the only colour coming from the lights burning in the windows.

I am making the right choice for my kingdom, Hamlet reminded himself, picking up the bottle. *I'm removing a threat from the world, not a man.*

A fraction of a second could change everything. A breath was the only divide between life and death.

Fortinbras would die, and the shock of it would ripple through Wittenberg for a few days until it was forgotten. Hamlet's hands would be red for a lifetime, but worse things were done every day for the love of a crown.

It was not difficult to find Fortinbras's house again. It was much more of a challenge to convince his hand to raise and his knuckles to rap against the wood.

This is ridiculous, he thought. *It's the most obvious play in the world.*

The door swung open. Arion Fortinbras looked as though he'd only just woken up from a long sleep. His hair was a mess, flattened curls on one side and frizz on the other. There were pink-red lines on his cheeks from where the pillow crushed his face.

Hal's heart pounded like it was trying to leap out of his chest.

"I brought you something," he said without preamble. "A gift. I wanted to… to apologise."

Better to cut straight to the point, he thought, and make it look like an apology for his rudeness the other day, for Rosencrantz's insults. In his heart, he knew it was an apology for what was to come.

His mouth felt like it was stuffed full of cloth.

Forgive me.

"You don't have to apologise to me, Hal," said Fortinbras. "But if you came inside… I'd like to explain a few things to you. About Rosencrantz, I mean. There's something you should know…"

He was so earnest. In a few hours, those eyes would betray no emotion. They would be glassy, probably bloodshot, staring at the ceiling.

Fortinbras reached out with his free hand. Hamlet took it, absently. He was horrified. Fortinbras felt warm. He was made of muscle and sinew. Under his skin, although he couldn't feel it now, there was a pulse.

"It's cold," said Fortinbras. "Come on. Share a glass with me."

"No," Hamlet said. "No, I should go home. I have… things to do. I have a lecture in the morning and I haven't done my reading." They exchanged the shared smile of coasting students. And then, before he could think better of it, he said, "Goodnight, Arion."

"Goodnight, Hamlet."

Hal's heart ached.

You lovestruck fool, he hissed to himself, where no one could hear. *You idiot, you've killed him.*

But deeper down, in the part of him that only knew how to speak the truth, he ached.

"Hamlet," Fortinbras called, when he was halfway down the road. Hamlet looked over his shoulder at his enemy, framed in the warm candlelight spilling from his doorway, clutching his poisoned wine in one hand.

He raised the bottle like a trophy and winked.

"Nice try," Fortinbras said, and the glass shattered on the ground.

Hamlet turned back and kept walking, the snow settling on his shoulders. He wasn't even angry. He just felt relieved. He walked through the dark and winding streets of Wittenberg, watching as the snow began to glimmer against the cobblestones.

It was a beautiful city really, when it came down to it. In his short time there, he had come to love it: its strange narrow buildings with their slanting, high-eaved roofs, the markets that remained open day and night, the warmth emanating from a tavern as he walked past its open door.

He resolved not to tell Rosencrantz or Guildenstern the details of the evening: they could see Fortinbras walking around town for themselves, and draw their own conclusions.

SCENE SEVEN
ophelia

Ophelia was eating supper alone when her father arrived. He looked around for somewhere to put down his armfuls of notes, muttering under his breath, the wisps of hair on his top lip fluttering against silent words.

"Daughter!" he said finally, sitting down opposite her. "I heard you had quite the experience in the chapel this afternoon." His eyes shone with mirth. Ophelia wished she could laugh, truly. It was difficult, when she kept imagining him selling her off like livestock to the highest bidder.

"Yes, Father. It was… unpleasant."

"Fainted, did you? Hmm. Where did your little vision of victory come from?"

A servant came, bearing a large bowl of something steaming on a platter. Another followed, with bread and wine. One of the perks of working for the king night and day: eating in your chambers.

"I didn't want the ladies to think ill of me," she said, leaning back to allow the servingwoman access to her bowl. The soup was thick with autumn vegetables, and the smell was warming to her heart. "I assumed they'd spread some rumour about... oh, I don't know. Possession, or something terrible like that."

"You're looking after your image," Polonius said, nodding approvingly. "I'm glad of it, but I know that my daughter can make a more impressive blag than 'visions from God'."

"I'm sorry, Father."

He hummed and dunked a fluffy chunk of bread into his soup. Ophelia tried to eat more—when the war truly began and the army were on the march, would there be extra portions to spare?—but she felt nauseous and tired, and the headache that was threatening to burst through her skull wasn't helping matters. She forced herself to eat half the soup her father had served, but it tasted of nothing.

Her thoughts swirled, and the bread turned to dough in her mouth and sat heavy on her tongue. She almost let it block the words from emerging, but she knew she couldn't. She had to ask.

"There are other rumours about me, Father," she said delicately. "That's why I worried, when I was taken ill…"

Ophelia's heart pounded in her ears.

Father raised his eyebrows. "What rumour was that, dear?"

"Someone mentioned that someone was… well, that I have a suitor, but if I had, you would have to approve. And you would have told me, wouldn't you? You would not have kept a secret like—"

"You are my only daughter." Polonius's voice was firm. There was no touch of fatherly affection, no warmth. Only the cold, clear voice he used when he was speaking of figures and numbers. Profit and loss. "You have been involved in a scandal with the crown prince. It was made clear to me long ago that my daughter was not a suitable candidate for marriage to Fyrste Hamlet, and so I have searched for others who might ignore the stain upon your honour."

His voice grew fuzzy, like it was coming through a long tunnel.

"You're a woman grown now, Ophelia. It's time to prepare yourself to become a wife. I am trying to do the best I can by you."

She put down her spoon and sat back in her chair, straightening her back. "And if I will not accept a husband?" she asked, but even she could hear her voice shaking.

Polonius held up his hands. "I cannot and will not force you, but I can't promise you my protection either. You will have no money if anything should happen to me—you know that. I can't guarantee that your brother will take care of you—"

"Laertes loves me!" Ophelia interrupted. Unbidden, the tears that lay just beneath the surface were springing to her eyes. "He won't mistreat me. He'd never do that to me."

"And if I'm dead, and Laertes has a wife and children to take care of?" Her father sighed, exasperated. "He will have to put them first, Ophelia, and you never know when a man might find himself short of coin. If Laertes ran out of money, who would he feed first? His starving children or his spinster sister?"

"Then allow me to have some income!" she demanded. "There are ways, Father! Land!"

"That's for princesses, Ophelia! You know I cannot afford to buy you some estate so that you might—might rest on your laurels and become a… a tawdry, disgraced mistress to a king someday!"

She seethed. "And if that is the life I choose? Who are you to stop me?"

Her father flinched as if he had been hit.

Polonius's chair scraped against the floor. He stepped away, shaking his head.

"Clear this away!" he shouted suddenly, banging on the wall behind him with his fist, and Ophelia jumped. She got up so fast that the chair tumbled back behind her, crashing onto the floor. Two attendants entered and started to clear away the mess of their abandoned dinner. One of them stepped behind her and righted the chair, placing it against the back wall of the room.

Her skin was covered in a cold sweat. She felt, as if it was happening again, the twist of her father's hand in her hair.

For the first time in her life, Ophelia was afraid of what her father might do.

"So it's true then," she said through her fear. "Claudius—"

"—Is interested in marrying you? Yes. And I have informed him that he's welcome to pursue you."

Ophelia's voice shook with disbelief. "He is Hamlet's uncle."

"He is a member of the royal family, and a damn sight better than any suitor I thought you'd have after the scandal you've caused."

Ophelia took a long look at her father. She was lost for words. He looked so calm, even though anger drew his thick, grey eyebrows down over his eyes. Yet his moustache trembled.

"I would not marry you to a man who I thought unsavoury," he said, quieter now. The attendants were almost finished, and the quiet clatter of silverware was a flickering annoyance in the back of Ophelia's head. "Marriage is the best way a father can protect his daughter in this world, my dear. You know this."

She knew. She knew, and it felt like a blow to even admit it. The king's words echoed around her skull, the way they had ever since the day she and Hamlet were discovered: *my son will never marry some quivering little hussy, daughter of yours or not.* Her father's fingers had tightened in her hair and she must have screamed, because the king's eyes flickered to her. In them, she saw remorse.

That only made her hate him more: did he see the little girl he allowed to play with his son? The girl who ate apples on the floor of their private apartments and who came into court with leaves in her hair, her hand in

Hal's, and who the king sometimes lifted high in the air, laughing with her until she cried with joy? Did he see that girl, or did he see someone else?

Just because her body changed, just because she grew curves and valleys and bled once a month, did not mean she was tainted. The king would never see that, not now... but maybe her father would.

"Please, stop this," she said firmly, stepping forward, stretching a hand out towards him. "I'm not ready to get married, not yet. It hasn't been so long since Hal went away—"

"And soon he will return for the winter," Polonius said grimly, "by which point I hope you will be firmly engaged to another man." He pointed at her. "If I see one glance between you and Prince Hamlet when he returns, I will make this marriage go ahead. Regardless of your will, Ophelia."

"Father, wait!" she called, but he had already turned and slammed the door to his private quarters. She heard the snick of the bolt sliding across. Furiously, she slammed her fists against the wood, then stormed to her own room. The attendants moved out of her way. The bed was turned down already and the candles were freshly lit; a maid stepped out of the shadows and Ophelia turned around, allowing her to start undoing her dress.

"Get me ink," she said. The maid's fingers stilled.

"I can't," she murmured.

"Then you're of no use to me," Ophelia said waspishly. She pulled away. "You may leave me. I can undress myself just fine."

Alone, she stood in the puddle of her overdress, staring at the flickering candlelight. She strained hard, but there was no sound from her father's room. At least if he was furious and throwing things, there would be a reason to hate him.

Could she hate him for this? She didn't think so. He was only trying to protect her. For any other girl, an arranged marriage of this sort was exactly what they aspired to. And they worked, often! She sat down heavily on the edge of her bed, still staring at the trailing smoke. All you had to do was look at Alessandra and Lorenz. They didn't meet until four weeks before their wedding day, and they'd spent perhaps an hour in each other's company before the marriage.

And now they were inseparable.

But Ophelia… couldn't seem to stomach it. At least with some lesser nobleman, she might be able to make excuses. He could get a child on some other woman and Ophelia would happily raise it as her own, and no one would have to be any the wiser.

But the wife of a prince… needed to be seen pregnant. Needed to be visible.

They would dissect her marriage bed with Claudius, and there would be no avoiding her duties. The thought made her physically sick.

No, she couldn't bear it.

She needed to be in Rúnräd.

Outside, Ophelia nudged past a servant carrying a bucket of pig slops and paced quickly towards the castle's back gate. In the narrow alleyways of the city, it was easy for her to lose herself. She passed through the mirror, ran down the muddy path, and rapped at Hilga's door. It smelled of ashes and burnt fennel.

Solveig crouched before the firepit, striking a flint, and above her, drinking cups jostled for space on a crowded shelf amongst glass jars and medical implements. Clothes hung from metal spikes driven into the wooden beams, hanging on the walls like shadows. Aaron was in the corner, smiling beside Fatma.

She wrapped her arms around herself and leaned into the heat of the fire, feeling embarrassed.

"I told you, Tove," Hilga was saying, yanking unceremoniously at her daughter's knotty braids, "when you leave these too long, and you roll around in the dirt all day long—"

"I hunt! There will be dirt!" Tove insisted.

"Then clean your hair more often," Hilga grumbled. "Ophelia, something dire must be happening if you're here. You never come to visit otherwise."

She nodded, looking at the floor.

"Well, what are you waiting for?" Hilga clucked. "Are we going to stand in silence until the rivers run dry?"

Tove snorted quietly from behind her mane of blonde hair. She was thirteen and precocious, with a fascination with wolves and a love of all things hunting. She was, all in all, terrifying, and she was rarely in the house, preferring to stalk the woods and creep in early in the morning to sleep on the floor. She was somewhat feral, a magical child of the magical world.

Ophelia took a deep breath, steadying herself. Hilga was a witch and married to a woman; they had a child who was surely born of some kind of magic. They would not think her odd, she told herself. They could not.

"Father wants me to marry Prince Claudius," she said, deciding to start with the worst offence. "Also, I passed out in the chapel and had a vision."

The little room was quiet apart from the crackle of a fire, and even Tove didn't sigh or roll her eyes.

"I might be sick," said Hilga.

"The vision—did it make sense? Who was involved? People you knew?" asked Solveig.

"Are you sure you didn't hit your head?" asked Aaron, already reaching for his bag of supplies.

"Me too, yes it made sense, I heard Prince Hamlet, and no, I haven't hit my head," she said patiently. "It was strange. Hamlet was so angry. Furious. I've never heard him sound like that in life, but it wasn't as if I was imagining it. It was too... too perfect."

The whistle of the pot made her jump. Solveig took the kettle from its peg and began to pour water into four small cups. The herby scent of nettle tea was inviting, and she felt her shoulders drop a little bit.

"And is that all you saw?" Hilga asked. Her voice was gentle, so much gentler than that day in the shop or any time since. "Nothing else?"

Solveig came over and cupped Ophelia's cheeks in her hands, the way she used to do when she was a little girl.

"It must be difficult to face such a transformation in the palace, where things are already so dark," she said. "But to be a Seer and Sighted is a blessing. You're truly very lucky."

"I don't understand," Ophelia said wildly. "Surely having one vision does not a Seer make!"

"Oh, it does," said Hilga. "Now, it might be the only one you ever have. But it does mean something."

"So what I heard in the chapel..." Ophelia pulled at her braid. "That's in my future?"

"It's in the future," said Solveig, not unkindly. "Often, what we see does not concern us in the slightest."

If it concerns Hamlet, it concerns me, she thought, but she knew Hilga would laugh if she said it aloud.

"It's nothing to worry about," Solveig murmured, smoothing her loose hairs back from her forehead. Ophelia leaned into the touch. She needed gentleness, on a day like today. "It is not uncommon for the Sight Guide process to uncover little things like that. Take heed of what you see, but try not to obsess. In time, if you have more visions, you'll learn which threads are most important."

"And there's no way of seeing something in particular?" Ophelia asked glumly, although she knew the answer. Solveig shook her head, and Ophelia sank down next to the fire and pulled the comb out of Tove's hands.

With the war on the horizon, with Claudius as her suitor, with Hamlet so far away... If she could see, if she could watch Hamlet and wrap herself around him from the past and keep him safe—keep them both swaddled from whatever the world wanted to throw at them, from whatever obstacle threatened to keep them apart now—then maybe she could reach the dream they shared since they were little children.

Two crowns. Linking hands between their twin thrones; an older Hal looking at her and smiling. He is content in this future she imagines, with happy lines by his eyes and as many lovers as he desires and ten times so many friends. And she is happy too, basking in the glow of the country they will rebuild together, poring over maps and papers with the finest of musicians strumming in the background.

"I fear Helsingør is not strong enough to hold if Norway does advance," Ophelia murmured, dropping into a cross-legged seat on the rug. Her hands clutched the warm cup to her chest like a lifeline. "I don't know which is worse: a life married to Hamlet's uncle, or a future in which Norway wins."

"There is little enough I can do for you, girl," Hilga said. But then she smiled, and Ophelia felt her anger dissipate a little. "Before you go, let me put a few things in a bag. It will protect you against unwanted affections."

"And I'll give you something to bring on cephalalgia," said Aaron, rooting around in his pockets. "Good for avoiding visitors."

Ophelia laughed. She let Aaron check her over, as he always did, listening to her heart and testing the pulse at her wrist. His careful, calloused fingers found a burn from a candle and smoothed salve into the skin. As he did so, without raising his eyes, he said, "We're always here, Ophelia. Whenever you need us, you can call."

She fought back the tears that threatened to overwhelm her. "Thank you," she managed.

Being cared for in this little room felt exhausting. She was a raw nerve, an open wound. The slightest affectionate touch was a sharp beam of pain that threatened to tear sobs from her throat. She felt, for perhaps the first time in her life, that she would have rather been in the stone halls of Kronborg Castle than in this house with people who loved her.

At least in Kronborg, no one would give her tea or treat her childish injuries. No one would coax tears from her eyes, and she could hide in her chamber and carve sigils on the walls and go nights without sleep and, now that Hamlet was gone, not a soul would notice her flame dwindling slowly to nothing.

SCENE EIGHT
hamlet

"I saw Fortinbras in the marketplace today," said Rosencrantz, his arms folded across his chest. "Alive, I should say."

Hamlet shrugged and continued spooning hot beef stew into his mouth. The gravy was delicious, bursting with savoury flavour, and he forced his thoughts to stay on how the cook had achieved it instead of acknowledging Rosencrantz's words. Odd, beef stew for breakfast. An unusual start to the day.

Ros snorted. "Lord, never go into acting."

"Wasn't planning on it," said Hamlet. "He mustn't have had the wine."

"I have an answer to that," said Guildenstern unexpectedly, without looking up from his own bowl of stew.

Hamlet's stomach dropped. He remembered the stain of the wine on the freshly-fallen snow: had Guildenstern seen, somehow? Had he followed him?

"It turns out our friend Fortinbras recently gave up drinking," Guildenstern continued, and Hamlet repressed a sigh of relief. "Probably some sort of bizarre pre-war cleansing of the soul, or something like that."

"Oh, well I am pleased he's found God," said Rosencrantz bitterly. "Good for him. You couldn't have mentioned this sooner?"

"Nah," said Guildenstern. "Didn't want to be involved in all that murder business. I do still count myself as a Christian, you know."

Maybe Guildenstern is the only person here with any brains, thought Hamlet. *Or a moral compass.*

He was quietly grateful to his friend, who had melted into the background these last few days. Rosencrantz, with all his heady confidence, suddenly seemed like such a precarious character. He stood over them, observing, the cold light of morning turning his skin as pale as the frost outside. Guildenstern ate industriously, and he only slid his eyes across to Hamlet once, a secret glance not shared with Rosencrantz.

Until Rosencrantz suddenly burst out, "Christian! You consider yourself a Christian? Then you should stop playing with magic, and men. And stop having sex altogether, until you're happily married to a nice woman. Even then, should you wish to lie back and let your lady love take her pleasure, you might want to think twice."

There was a moment's confused silence. "Are you scolding me or making a point?" Guildenstern asked.

"Just a gentle reminder that that the church won't even let a man fuck between his wife's thighs without calling him a sinner and a sodomite," Ros said. "I'm no heretic, but perhaps—given you *are* still living in the house of two 'murderers'—we should take the church's words with a grain of salt."

Guildenstern rolled his eyes, shaking Rosencrantz's bad humour off like a horse twitching its flank to ward off an annoying fly. "I'm starting to think my mother was right when she said you were a bad influence."

"Is this it, then?" Ros asked impatiently, turning his attention back to Hamlet. "One failed attempt to win the war and you're giving up? Just like that?"

Rosencrantz's foot tapped furiously against the wooden floor. Energy seemed to radiate from his very pores. He was wound tight like a spring, and there was something accusatory in his gaze, a challenge. Not for the first time, Hamlet wondered if Fortinbras was the first person Rosencrantz had ever attempted to kill.

He took up his spoon and carried on eating his stew, one bite at a time.

"Wasting my fucking *time*," Rosencrantz spat, and stormed outside into the rain.

Inside the little house, there was only the noise of Hamlet's cutlery scraping the inside of the bowl, the crackle of the fire, and Guildenstern shuffling in his seat.

"Thank you," Hamlet said. "For… For that."

"Good choice," said Guildenstern quietly. He said nothing more; just rose and went upstairs to bed.

Hamlet waited a while, in case Rosencrantz might return and want to pick up the argument, but he didn't come back. Hamlet went to his room and began to pack his things. Hardly two months had passed since his arrival into Wittenberg; now his departure felt achingly premature.

But at the same time, he ached to be at home. For a part of those few weeks, Wittenberg sang with the promise of a fresh start. This was a place he could grow and make himself anew. Now he felt that he was leaving worse off than he'd arrived. Whatever this place was, it was not a haven. It was not a home. It was a rest stop on his journey, a port in a storm, but it was not the end.

Whatever Fates had guided his father's hand to send him here, they'd done their job well. Now his bridges with Norway were well and truly burned; now, he felt that he understood, with fresh eyes, the cost of the war that was closing in on his future.

He could probably count on one hand the number of nights he'd slept more than a handful of hours since coming to Wittenberg—since leaving Helsingør, really. It felt like such a long time ago that he'd stood in that courtyard and begged his father not to make him leave.

The door downstairs opened and closed, the telltale tread of Rosencrantz's footsteps echoing up the staircase. Hamlet looked at the disaster strewn across his floor and decided it was a problem for the morning. He climbed into bed, but he couldn't sleep. Voices from downstairs rose to meet him: Guildenstern, low and solemn; Rosencrantz, angry and hissing. An argument, then.

He lay awake, trying to make out their words, but he couldn't. Even when they faded away, he stayed staring at the ceiling, watching as the candlelight made the shadows dance.

His escort arrived a day early.

Hal's room looked bare without his belongings strewn about. He stood by the little window and gazed out at the street, fingering the rough fabric of the curtains. The snow was thick. The journey to Helsingør would be long, and he hoped they didn't get stuck in a snowdrift on the way. The last thing he wanted was to be trapped in a carriage in a blizzard with two guardsmen and a war on the horizon.

But at least he would be home soon. Rich food, warm fires… Ophelia. He hoped she was getting on alright. She probably had plenty to do, with the war and everything. Sewing uniforms, more than likely. Or embroidering Mother some commemorative handkerchiefs. That was exactly the kind of task she'd give Ophelia, expecting her to hate it, but Ophelia liked making things.

When they got married, she could make things all day. She'd have all the money in Denmark to do whatever she wanted, and no one could give her orders.

He just hoped that fool of a father, Polonius, hadn't gotten it into his head to marry her off.

"What on earth are you smiling about?" Rosencrantz asked. Hamlet jumped. He hadn't seen Rosencrantz since the previous night's tantrum, and he half-expected to see the remains of his anger lingering on his face, but there was nothing.

Instead, there was just his usual placid politeness, the cool façade he displayed to the rest of the world.

Not to me. The thought was enough to make him recoil. *He doesn't look at me like that.*

"I was thinking about Ophelia," he admitted, trying to shake off the remnants of that realisation. It went nowhere: it stuck stubbornly to him, and the more he thought of it the less he could bear to look at Rosencrantz's face, the chill of it, the medical coolness as a physician.

He crossed to his overstuffed trunk and opened it for something to do, rifling through his old shirts and books. "It'll be nice to be home, although I daresay my father's welcome will be colder than I'm imagining."

He straightened just in time to catch a strange look passing over Rosencrantz's face. It was there for barely a second until it was replaced with that emptiness again.

Hamlet decided to risk it.

"Is everything alright, Ros?" he asked.

"I'm fine, Hal." Ros's fingers were very cool when they unexpectedly clasped his hand, drawing it gently to his chest. Hal's breath caught in his throat. Ros's chest was as warm and flat as his own.

There was a strangeness to that, but not because of his gender. It was odd to think of Ros, who was usually as casually cold as a mortuary cadaver, having a warm, beating heart beneath his ribs.

Hal's own heart pounded a discordant rhythm in return.

"I have these episodes," Ros said quietly, calmly, still holding Hal's hand firmly to his shirt. "My heart races like a wild thing. I think it's tiredness that causes it, or maybe stress."

"Have you seen a doctor?" Hamlet asked. His voice came out strange and husky. "You should, you know. If it's worrying you."

"Worries Guild more than it does me." Ros laughed and dropped Hal's hand.

"Regardless, you should look after yourself."

Ros smiled. It showed his crooked front teeth, the black one to the side where he hit his jaw on a stone as a child and the tooth died.

"I'm sorry I couldn't teach you more," Ros said. "But I put some books into your bag. Don't be caught with them, or you'll end up dead before you ever get to the battlefield."

There was a polite cough from the hall: one of the guardsmen, and Hamlet stepped back. The guard helped Hamlet to pack. His uniform was crisp and clean: they'd clearly polished everything before they arrived. It was not quite the same as when he'd arrived in Wittenberg, deposited with scorn. There was a deference in how this man—far older than Hamlet—took his belongings and carried them down the stairs, placing them carefully into the carriage.

"We should leave before we lose the light, sir," said the head of the escort when Hamlet's room stood bare, bowing his grizzled head.

Hamlet turned to Ros and Guild. He rapped once, gently, on one of the beams criss-crossing their little sitting room.

"I suppose this is goodbye," he said.

"We'll meet again," said Guildenstern, but the words were of no comfort to Hamlet. He knew an empty phrase when he heard it.

So this is how it ends.

Hamlet nodded at the guard at the door, dressed in Helsingør colours; the other man grabbed his case and took it for him, sparing him the burden. The carriage was ostentatious in the middle of this small Wittenberg street. It hadn't felt so out of place when he arrived, but then again, how was he to know what was out of place?

He had arrived a prince; he felt like he was leaving as something else, but he didn't know quite what. The second guardsman opened the door and Hamlet stepped up, settling into the lush, comfortable seats. They wouldn't be so comfortable in a few hours, but they would do for now.

At the gates, where the streets opened up so that they sprawled wide on either side, there was a hold-up. At first, he thought it was other students leaving. But that couldn't be right: there were long queues of carriages and horses and carts, people carrying baskets, merchants with their wagons loaded for a long journey.

"What's all this?" asked Hal, leaning out of the window. "Is something wrong?"

The guardsman to his right shook his head from atop his horse. "Nothing, sir. Just bad luck."

An hour later, they had hardly crept any closer to the gates. Hamlet was thoroughly uncomfortable by this point. He yanked at the neck of his travelling tunic, which itched uncomfortably at the collar, and leaned out the window once again.

Only to see Horatio standing outside, next to the open door of another elegant carriage. Hamlet looked away, hoping the other boy hadn't seen. Out of the corner of his eye, he saw his guardsman leaning down to speak with someone.

Someone rapped on the carriage door. He looked out and saw Fortinbras standing there. He was dressed in travelling clothes too, Horatio glowering at his shoulder, and when Hamlet looked further he saw that more than the usual number of bags were piled onto his carriage.

"Prince Hamlet," Fortinbras said. "You're going home."

It wasn't a question. Fortinbras didn't smile, but he didn't look murderous either.

He looked far kinder, and far more grown up, than Hamlet would ever have expected.

"So are you." Hamlet raised an eyebrow. "I imagine we'll meet again on a battlefield somewhere."

Fortinbras' usual energy seemed to have faded. Hamlet looked more closely at his old enemy, taking in the bags under his eyes, the messiness of his hair, the way his skin was reddened and sore in patches like he was picking at it.

"I know that times are hard, Hal, but I do care for you, and I respect you. When you're ready to talk, write to me. We can arrange something, I'm sure."

Horatio's stony expression did not change, but something drew Hal's attention anyway. He was fidgeting. It was unlike him.

Hamlet tipped his head. "And you?" he asked, ignoring Fortinbras. "I admit, I'd be surprised if you chose to fight for Norway."

"I don't fight for a country," Horatio muttered, his jaw clenched tightly. "I fight for Fortinbras. That's all."

Hamlet swallowed again. He tried to gentle his tone. He meant well, although his own embarrassment and shame made it easier to lash out than to speak with soft words. It was easy for an animal to bite, when it was used to being beaten.

"What I mean to say," Hamlet corrected, quietly, "is that there is a place for you at Kronborg, if you need it. Write to me, and I'll send you a letter for the border."

Horatio tilted his head slyly. "Because I'm Jewish," he said. "Tell me, Prince Hamlet: when you're king, will you change the laws for everyone like me? Or do you just feel ashamed of yourself, and you want me to drown you in gratitude so that you feel better?"

"The former," he said. And then, because he felt the need to defend himself further: "It's always been my plan. I am not... I am not my father, or my grandfather."

"Well," said Horatio. "I'll believe it when I see it."

Hamlet shrugged. "The offer stands."

They were all quiet for a long moment. The sun beat down on them—surprising on a cool December day. It was going to melt the snow and make the roads worse. The crowd swelled, then pushed forward: the main gate was finally open, and now the traffic moved along quite quickly. They stood alone amongst the swirling crowd, ankle-deep in churned mud and snow, the fresh smells of cool air and horse shit rising like a tide.

"We will meet again," Fortinbras said quietly. "In better days."

He stretched out a hand towards the carriage window. There were ink stains around his fingernails, blue smudged almost the wrist; a freckle perched over the knuckle of his middle finger.

Hamlet could not bring himself to care about the magic, about the danger, about the threat to his kingdom. Not now that Fortinbras stood before him, more boy than man, with his ink-stained hand held out in hope of a brighter future.

Hamlet shook it. He took in everything he could about Fortinbras in that moment: the calluses on his palms, the firmness of his grip, the way the veins stood out in his slender wrists. His hair was a froth of coppery curls, and his eyes were like twin sapphires in his face.

Hamlet committed it all to memory.

One day, someone was going to plunge a blade through that chest, and he wanted to remember Fortinbras as he was: handsome and perfect and *alive*.

The guardsman called out. Hamlet climbed back into the carriage. He felt like he wasn't really in control of his body. Everything was dreamlike. There couldn't be a war, surely: not on a beautiful, bright day like this. The horses began to move, their hooves clattering on the cobblestones. Hamlet watched Fortinbras grow smaller and smaller behind him.

The nights that followed were long and hard. First they travelled north through the Holy Roman Empire, past Berlin, past Neubrandenburg, through a sliver of Pomerania, and finally to Świnoujście, where their ship set sail for Denmark.

Hamlet stood at the prow and watched the dark waves roll beneath the boat. For a moment, he thought he saw an enormous, dark shape threading its way through the water beneath. Its scales seemed to shimmer in the moonlight, the only bright thing in the entire damned sea.

And then it was gone; nothing but an illusion.

He shook his head. He spent too much time thinking about magic, and that was no good when the war was just on the other side of the water.

He reached deep inside himself, looking for that spark of magic he now knew lay there, fizzling beside his heart.

Concentrating hard, he imagined it turning into a shower of sparks, into flames, into nothing at all.

The magic hissed. It curled around his heart, warm and alive, and unbeknownst to him, the edges of his heart singed and turned a deep, dark shade of purple.

SCENE NINE
ophelia

Ophelia was helping one of the younger girls collect the queen's clothes off the floor when the news came.

The Overhofmesterinde urged them to hurry, and then she gathered all the ladies maids of all ranks together in a small, unused chamber above the queen's bedroom. She stood by the window and gazed out at the snow as the other girls shuffled their feet. More and more women filed inside until everyone who made up the queen's household was there, fussing with their skirts and waiting for the news to come.

There was an air of change in Kronborg Castle. Ophelia could feel it prickling her skin, raising the hairs on the back of her neck.

By the time the snow cleared and spring came sweeping in, Helsingør was going to be a very different city.

"The queen has decided that you should all be informed, as this affects you as much as anyone else," said Ulrike. Her lips were pinched in a thin line, making them all but disappear. "The army is marching west from Kronborg as soon as the Christmas celebrations are done."

There was a quiet gasp, not of disbelief but of acceptance. This was the news they were all waiting for, the news no one wanted to hear.

Flags burning. Stones crashing to the ground. A city starving, demanding blood.

Ulrike held her hands up to silence them all. The room fell into a hushed quiet. They were puppets on the end of a string, waiting for Ulrike to tell them what to do, how to act.

"This is not the most important thing for you, ladies," she said. "The men will leave us, they will all know when by now... What you must know is that during Christmas, we will host a farewell ball."

"Must we speak of balls now?" Alessandra said, in an uncharacteristic display of irritation. She was standing by the fireplace, her dress dangerously close to the flames. She didn't seem to care. A look of utter derision, cold enough to freeze an ocean, was painted on her face. "We have just been reminded our husbands, brothers, fathers, and sons will be sent to war in a week. I can't bring myself to care for dresses and ribbons."

"Dresses and ribbons are not the point of a ball," Ulrike said, nostrils flaring. "It will be a long, hard winter for those men who march to defend us. Good food and pleasant company will make those first few days lighter for them. And, must I remind you, Alessandra, that not every man will return. Memories. Morale. Lifting spirits. That," Ulrike finished, "is our role in this. That is what the hands of women are made for."

Slowly the crowd dissipated. So few words, and yet so much said. Alessandra came to the window and rested her cheek against the cold stone wall.

"I knew already," she said eventually, when they had already been standing there for long enough for the other girls to have left. "Lorenz has been asked to be an officer. He's been told to start packing."

"Fighting in winter is a terrible idea, surely," Ophelia murmured. "Hopefully it'll cause Norway enough problems that they'll turn around and go home."

"May every Norwegian soldier catch frostbite," Alessandra muttered, "and lose the ability to grip their sword. And yes, I mean that in both senses of the word."

They watched the flakes swirl past outside. The trees were bare now. They'd shed their leaves all at once. It was like all of Helsingør went to sleep one day in autumn and awoke in the depths of winter. The garden looked like a graveyard.

"At least your father is on the privy council," said Alessandra. She rested her cheek against Ophelia's shoulder. "He won't have to go."

"And Laertes will be close to Lorenz, I imagine," Ophelia said.

"Certainly, if they go alphabetically by first name."

It was a poor attempt at a joke, but Ophelia still laughed.

There was that, at least.

If nothing else.

Later, she had tea in Alessandra and Lorenz's apartments. It felt distressingly normal.

"Claudia's intended is a fine thing," Alessandra said, scooping up a cake and popping it into her mouth. She was almost back to normal, although a little pale. "I've seen the portrait he sent—a tiny thing inside a locket. Very romantic, I think."

"Very," Ophelia agreed. "He's English?"

"I think his mother is from Granada—she's very pretty, and by all accounts incredibly clever, which is always a dangerous combination. And you know how the English treat Spaniards."

"In this day and age," Ophelia said, shaking her head. "It's the fifteen hundreds, for God's sake."

"It was quite the affair in the English court when they got married, but the son is something of a favourite to the king."

"He's the one who grew up in Constantinople," Lorenz added. He was sprawled across the couch with his long legs crossed at the ankle, swilling a glass of red. "He visited Kronborg—two summers ago, I suppose? Short, stocky boy, red-haired."

"The one with the sunburn!" Ophelia remembered. He was a nice boy, if a bit arrogant. He swore up and down he couldn't get burned in the Danish sun, because he was so used to living in a far warmer country. He spent the rest of his trip scorched and rubbing wet rags on his neck.

She had never been so far south as Constantinople. She imagined it as a city of pillars and spires; mosques and cathedrals crowded together under the heat of the sun. In the drawings she had seen in books and, once, on a decorative clock, the skyline of the city had seemed beautiful.

If she could choose a life for herself, it would be this: to travel across land and sea with Hamlet by her side, without a worry in the world. No titles, no fears.

"Speaking of marriages," said Lorenz, "I wanted to warn you, Ophelia," he said, in a low tone of voice, "about conversations I've overheard lately."

"I've already told her!" Alessandra said, swatting her husband on the shoulder. "Honestly, Lorenz. Listen to the words that come out of my mouth, please!"

Lorenz took a long draught of his wine. "I'm glad you already know—I didn't want to be the one to tell you. You told her about the other wife, my love?"

"No," said Alessandra. "Not yet."

"Other wife?" asked Ophelia, leaning forward. "What other wife?"

"Nothing to stop you marrying him, I'm afraid," said Alessandra apologetically. "Claudius was married once before but she died shortly afterwards—the sweating sickness."

She couldn't hide her disappointment. "Have you heard anything else… unpleasant?" she asked. "Do you know why he didn't visit Denmark for so long?"

Alessandra shook her head. "I know only pieces here and there, and nothing is enough to put together the picture yet. But fear not—I think he plans to wait until this war is won before he courts you properly."

"He thinks he'll be back by the end of spring," Lorenz said. Ophelia tipped her head to look at him. He was smirking. "I think not. This war will go on for at least a year, probably longer, unless something dramatic happens."

Her heart sank just as fast as it had flown. "Why do you think that?" she asked. A year of war—how many lives would be lost in that time? Surely thousands.

Lorenz shrugged. "Our armies are evenly matched," he said. "It's going to be a war of attrition: who can erode the other's forces the fastest? Wars like this are always slow."

Surreptitiously, she wound a sprig of Corruption around her finger and pulled. It unravelled, like a thread from Alessandra's dress, and she hid a cough while she muttered the words. It dissipated into mist.

The battlefields were going to be rife with it. She wondered what the Council was going to do. Probably allow the Corruption to mount while Ophelia tried to cleanse the castle in the absence of the men.

With a war happening, causing more and more Corruption to gather in the world, how much more could they bear? How long before another plague, a tidal wave, or something worse came to deal them a reckoning they wouldn't survive?

What was she meant to do? Sew marks into everyone's clothing in the hope that might protect them a little longer? It made no sense.

"Don't worry, Ophelia," Alessandra said, misinterpreting the worry on her face. "There is still time to discover more about him. Maybe we'll discover that he isn't so terrible after all."

On the way back from Alessandra and Lorenz's apartments, Ophelia crossed paths with the queen.

She felt Gertrude's presence before she saw her: that strange, sulfuric Corruption smell; the way her hairs rose up on her skin. But today, there was something different. The queen rounded the corner, and Ophelia shuddered from head to toe.

She shrunk back against the wall, the same way she had when the king crossed paths with her, the first time she saw Claudius—but it wasn't enough. It felt like someone had just dunked her in cold water, or placed a row of leeches on her spine.

The queen's body was entirely arraigned in a mass of purple magic. This was normal: Gertrude collected Corruption the same way the king did, and Ophelia hardly noticed it anymore. But today, the Corruption nipped at her heels like eager sea creatures, draping from the hem of her dress, and something on her arm pulsed and moved, a writhing purple mass like a beating heart attached to the delicate skin beneath her wrist.

Queen Gertrude was wearing a bracelet Ophelia had never seen before. Its stone was brilliantly purple, even without its Corrupted haze. Anyone without the Sight would think it an unusually large amethyst, worn to protect against nightmares or some other melancholy.

But that was no amethyst. It was a rotnastān.

It was made of pure Corruption.

It took everything in her body not to run after Getrude and rip the bracelet from her arm. She stayed pressed against the wall until the queen's attendants had fluttered away, and then she crept back the way she'd come.

There was a servant's passage she could take—if the queen was going back to her quarters, as she suspected, she could probably get there before her. She needed another glance at that bracelet to confirm her fears.

There were no rotnastāns in Denmark, or at least there weren't meant to be. They were only found in the other world, deep beneath the mountains. No one was supposed to touch them—no one was supposed to mine them, much less make jewellery from them. They were cursed, rotten to the core, capable of burning flesh from skin if someone unaccustomed to Corruption came across one. In a way, it was lucky Queen Gertrude was so Corrupted: that was the only thing stopping the stone from rotting its way right through her arm.

She ducked through the narrow passage with her head bowed. It was dim and damp and smelled faintly of mould. She dodged out of the way of a couple of servants having a chat, whose faces paled at the sight of a lady in their part of the castle.

She emerged in an empty hallway, her legs burning. The door to the queen's chambers was opposite her, and just down the corridor was a tapestry hiding a narrow alcove, one of the many places she'd discovered to place her sigils. She waited for the queen to pass by so she could catch another waft of that dark magic, just to confirm her fears.

Footsteps became audible. Ophelia scurried across the hall as quickly as she could, tucking herself into the alcove. For a moment, she could breathe easy: this was only two sets of footsteps, not the posse that followed the queen. But then their voices became audible, and she realised who it was.

"…a fool's errand," said Queen Gertrude, rounding the corner. Ophelia bit her lip almost hard enough to draw blood. "And after all of that, you tell me you plan on marrying that little court wench? My son's whore?"

Cheeks burning, Ophelia pressed her back against the cold wall.

She had little doubt Gertrude was talking about her.

"It's an excuse for me to stay at court when the war is won. You know this already." Claudius's voice was wheedling, like a father trying to convince a toddler of its bedtime. "No one will cast any doubt on the match—I have seen to that. Her father practically threw her at my feet. And the girl is the best choice. She has eyes only for the prince. Once I've gotten an heir on her, there will be no reason to concern ourselves with her any further."

"And she'll be free to carry on entrapping my son, distracting him from a marriage of any merit." Any love Ophelia had left for the woman faded in an instant. "She was always a sweet girl, but too sly for her own good. Sneaking around, hiding in stables and up trees, stealing books far beyond her understanding, dragging poor Hamlet along behind her…"

I never dragged him anywhere, Ophelia screamed inside her head. *We have always been of one mind. You never understood that.*

Claudius's steps stopped first, then Gertrude's.

Not here, for Christ's sake. Ophelia tried not to breathe, but the more she thought about it, the harder it became.

Claudius spoke first. "As I have said: when the girl has given me an heir—and perhaps a spare, given Helsingør's remarkable propensity for breeding diseases—we will no longer have to concern ourselves with her. I'm sure I can find some quiet country estate to send her away to. She'll nurse the children while I handle the real business here."

When Gertrude spoke again, her voice was rough.

"You won't leave me again," she said. Not a question. An order. "You won't fall in love with that ridiculous girl."

Claudius laughed. "Never. I can promise you that much freely." Quiet, and then: "I cannot give you a ring, my love, but did I not find you something better? A peerless bracelet for a peerless woman."

The sound of a kiss, one both long-awaited and well-practised, echoed through the hall. Ophelia's blood turned to ice.

The queen and her brother-in-law were having an affair.

Claudius wanted to get married and 'get children on someone', on Ophelia, and then spirit her away where she couldn't inconvenience him with her existence.

Or he could just kill her, and have the children raised by a nanny. Hairs raised themselves on Ophelia's arms. There was no reason not to. It wasn't as if the idea was unheard of. Done well, a murder was impossible to trace. He wouldn't even have to hide her body. Just dose her with poison, perhaps for a few weeks to give the effect of an acute illness, and then she would die and he'd play the tragic, mourning husband.

Husband. The word made her want to get sick in her mouth.

"Mind yourself, sir," Gertrude said lustily. Ophelia's horror was enough to keep her on her feet a moment longer. "It does not do to tempt a woman so. You know our natures run hot."

"Then you have set me alight," Claudius murmured. His voice was husky with want. "For I have not stopped burning since I met you, dear Gertrude."

The door to the queen's chambers opened. Here was the reason for the lack of guards, the silence: they must have been dismissed. Two sets of footsteps disappeared into the bedroom.

Ophelia crossed herself.

The rotnastān belonged to Claudius. He was the one who had gifted it to the queen. He who was always so clean of Corruption… She felt sure that he knew what the stone truly was. How could he not? He clearly knew something of magic.

The rotnastān needed to be dealt with before it could burn through the skin of an innocent handmaid.

But Ophelia could not think of anything but the way Claudius had said he would get an heir on her, and before she made it back to her chambers she had to stumble into yet another alcove and be heartily sick.

SCENE TEN
hamlet

Kronborg Castle loomed on the horizon.

The guardsmen bowed at his approach. It was dark, but the windows of the castle were illuminated with light. Snow drifted down, flashing momentarily as it caught the light, some of it evaporating in the escaping heat.

"A ball, Prince Hamlet," one of them explained. "It's Christmas."

Of course.

"Thank you, Barnardo," Hamlet murmured.

Somewhere in this behemoth of a castle, Mother and Father waited in their best clothes. Somewhere, Ophelia danced in her best dress in front of a warm fire, her hair glowing like a flame.

Hamlet swallowed. He reached, once more, for the flicker of magic in his heart. For bravery, maybe, or strength, or just to feel for a moment like he had a grasp on who he was, in this home that no longer felt like home.

As he approached the enormous wooden doors, they were thrown open.

It was not Father who greeted him, nor Mother, nor was it Ophelia.

"Ah, Hamlet!" his uncle pronounced, beaming. "Finally, you have arrived. Come, come!"

Claudius walked him through the halls, pointing things out, as if Hamlet had never seen the inside of this castle before. He tried to squirm out from his uncle's grip, but the arm he had around his shoulders was too heavy and his fingers too sharp against the tender skin of his neck.

"The ball is in full swing," said Claudius, smiling. "You can change before you join us. In fact, I think you should—it's become quite the formal affair."

Hamlet picked at his travelling clothes.

"You're right," he said. "I should change."

"Well, come and join us when you're ready," said Claudius. "I'll tell your mother and father you've arrived safely." He released Hamlet finally and stepped towards the door of the ballroom. "When you come down, why don't you come and sit with me and my betrothed? I'm sure you know her already—perhaps you can teach me something about her, eh?"

Hamlet frowned. Travel tiredness was setting in, and he wanted nothing more than to lie down and go to sleep.

"I was not aware that you were betrothed, Uncle," he said. "Who is she?"

Claudius smiled. "Oh, I hear you've met," he said, teasingly. "It's your lovely Ophelia. Do come and join us when you're ready. I'm sure she'd *love* that."

Before Hamlet could process what he'd said, Claudius was gone, swallowed up by a sliver of open door and a crowd.

ACT IV

SCENE ONE
ophelia

Her new veil glimmered in the light. Alessandra's cast-offs were always better quality than anything Ophelia bought for herself, and this scarf was made of pale gold silk that rippled gently as she moved this way and that. It matched her underskirt, and the beaded red brooch pinned into it shone beautifully in the light.

She wore a red overdress on top, embroidered in delicate white thread at the sleeves. She'd had to do it herself this morning: there were stains on the cuffs that wouldn't come out, and it was easier to hide them with a floral pattern than to repair them.

No one was quite in the mood for a ball, but then again maybe that was why everyone threw themselves into it so relentlessly. Everywhere she looked was gauzy silk and colourful ribbons and makeup smeared on various surfaces. That morning the servants had decorated the halls with brightly-coloured holly and green stems, but all she could see was their thorns.

Hamlet was not back yet. His ship was due in three days ago, and there was no sign of it yet. The seas grew rougher by the day, and there was ice gathering along the shoreline. Harsh, freezing winds threatened to tear boats apart every day. Even the queen spent most of her days praying in the chapel, and Ophelia had dark rings under her eyes from standing watch by the queen's bedside last night as she begged God that her son would come home.

But even as Gertrude knelt in prayer, Ophelia couldn't scrub her sultry tone from her mind. She kept replaying the queen's interaction with Claudius in her head. Once, she even substituted herself into the scene in place of Gertrude, and that made her feel so queasy that she had to miss dinner.

To make matters worse, she'd gone to daub her usual sigils on the walls and found half of them were gone. Not crumbling, like they usually did when they needed repainting; gone, wiped clean.

She didn't like it one bit.

"Anyone catching your eye?" Alessandra asked, brushing against her. "Now would be the perfect time to find yourself a true firecracker of a suitor. Someone who would fight a duel for you."

"I'm worried Claudius would win," Ophelia muttered, and took a long sip of her wine.

He was somewhere in this room, lurking. Since that single conversation when he guided her back to her chambers, they hadn't exchanged words. He clearly didn't feel the need to convince her; Claudius seemed like the kind of man who would court her father more than he'd court her.

And he clearly didn't think very highly of her, if that conversation with Gertrude was anything to go by. He didn't appear to think she had any thoughts that weren't about Hamlet.

This was all the more annoying because, for days, all of her thoughts had been on Hamlet.

She spotted Claudius finally—he was slipping in from the hallway. Her heart started to beat harder, but not from attraction. She didn't like the look on his face, the way he made a direct line for his brother and put his arm around his shoulders. He was probably up to something nefarious, but she hardly had the energy to care.

The level of Corruption in the palace was making her head spin. She tried her best to ignore it and avoided the temptation to remove strands here and there; it was a pointless exercise, and too dangerous in such crowded surroundings.

"I do wish we didn't need to wear red," said Alessandra despondently, smoothing her own dress. "It isn't my colour at all. Even Lorenz admitted it, and he always says I look stunning."

"You do look stunning. I look like a funeral bouquet," said Ophelia.

Alessandra snorted. "And isn't that a cheery image for Christmas? I'm sure that's exactly what the queen wanted when she picked this ridiculous theme."

It really didn't feel like Christmas at all. The energy at the ball was frenetic. Most people were already steaming drunk a mere hour into the celebrations, no one was eating, and at some point, one of the other lady's maids had broken down in floods of tears and had to be guided out by Ulrike. The only humour in the situation was the way Ulrike had pinched the girl's wrist between thumb and forefinger, like she was afraid the disease of 'crying' might be catching.

Ophelia's heart twinged. When she was a child, her mother used to sneak her and Laertes out of the palace for a few hours. They'd go through the mirror and celebrate Christmas with the rest of Rúnräd. They were a small community: they joined in each other's celebrations, no matter what they might be, and most of Ophelia's fondest memories took place among a muddle of festivals and feast days.

On a day like this, she should be curled up on the floor of Hilga's house with a blanket, playing some kind of dice game with Laertes and Aaron and Solveig. Not hovering on the edges of a ballroom, waiting for a prince who was never going to appear.

The queen appeared to a round of applause, alongside her friends and the lords attending, and took her seat next to the king. Claudius sat down on his other side. It was, Ophelia thought, rather ironic: the two lovers separated by the physical and metaphorical thorn in their sides.

"Lady Ophelia," a page whispered. She vaguely recognised him as the son of some Scottish lord, but she couldn't for the life of her remember whose page he was. "Prince Claudius requests your presence at the high table."

Oh.

Yes, that would explain the two empty seats on Claudius's right.

Ophelia became vividly aware of Alessandra turning away, leaving her there.

"I couldn't," Ophelia said instantly. "It wouldn't be proper, would it?" She looked where Alessandra had stood, but in her place was her brother. The only sign he'd been whisked over at high speed was the way Alessandra hovered just behind him, pinning him to the conversation. "Tell him we're honoured, but—"

"I don't think you're allowed to say no," the boy whispered back. "He said to get you, and if you said no, to ask your father instead."

He shot a quick, frightened look at Father, who was indeed fluttering amongst a crowd of aristocrats. They were all wearing terrible ruffs, twice as large as they needed to be. Laertes said it was going to be the fashion in a few years; for Ophelia, it only heightened the nightmare this evening was rapidly becoming. Alessandra made her apologies and went in search of Lorenz.

"Don't worry, Father told me," Laertes grumbled, shouldering his way through the crowd. "If Claudius tries to speak of weddings, I'll start coughing."

Sitting at the high banquet table was nothing new to Ophelia. As children, she and Hamlet used to sit together during formal dinners. She was always smiled on by the king. Queen Gertrude would tuck the stray strands of her hair behind her ear and feed her morsels from her own plate.

This was when Ophelia's mother was still alive, and Hal's sister and grandmother too, and they would all sit together long after everyone else had left, the fire blazing and the wine still flowing. Ophelia never forgot the feeling of safety of those nights: half-asleep on her father's shoulder, beaming at Hamlet who was sitting in his mother's lap, their parents' drunken laughter, Laertes tossing bits of string and broken toys to the cats who hung about in the shadows of the hall.

It was very different now. Laertes, thank God, insisted on sitting between her and Claudius. Ophelia was glad she wasn't directly beside the prince, but she still felt... discomfited to be there. The queen ignored her, as Ophelia had expected; the king kept shooting her strange, darting little glances she didn't understand but hated anyway.

She picked at the food on her plate, but hardly noticed how it tasted. The conversation flowed around her, leaving her like an island. She was never good in a crowd, not without Hal, whose quiet, clever comments made her bold.

"Paris must be interesting, these days," Claudius was saying, gesturing with his fork. He tilted his head; his tongue darted out to touch his upper lip. Something hungry shone in his eyes, and it was not directed towards the meal. Whatever he was about to say, Ophelia felt sure she didn't want to hear it. "You must have some trouble there as a Lutheran, I'm sure."

Laertes shrugged one shoulder. "Not much," he said, but his ears were turning a tell-tale shade of pink.

Oh, you bastard.

Claudius's eyes darted to Ophelia, just for a second. When he spoke again, his tone was private—but not soft enough that the king would not be able to hear.

"I shouldn't pry into the relationship between you and God, my good man," he said. "But Paris—a fascinating choice of university. What a brave time to choose France for your studies."

"It's a wonderful city," said Laertes, a muscle jumping in his jaw. "I've always wanted to study there."

"Wasn't it just last year that all those reformers were arrested?" he asked. "I thought France was moving in the same direction as us, but it seems it's becoming a Catholic stronghold once again."

Laertes said, very quietly, "That was two years ago, sir. And I'm afraid I don't take your meaning."

"I'm told you were quite the devoted Roman Catholic in your youth," said Claudius. His eyes dragged across Laertes, settling on Ophelia. "As was your sister. And your father."

A muscle jumped in Laertes's jaw. "We all were," he said tensely. "The Church of Denmark isn't a year old."

"Yes," mused Claudius. "There were rumours, you know. About your father. He was apparently reluctant to convert... Some say he may not have, in the end. That he leaves the castle and goes outside the walls for hours, and when he returns, he reeks of church incense."

The blood drained from Ophelia's face. Under the table, Laertes grabbed for her hand. He squeezed her fingers hard enough to hurt, but this was better than stabbing Claudius in the thigh with a fork, which was what would happen if her hand was free.

The king's eyes slid sideways, lingering on Laertes a while.

He was listening.

"I don't know what you mean, sir," Laertes managed. He swallowed his anger—Ophelia saw his throat bob, reluctantly, like he was drinking poison. "I assure you, my father is an honest man."

"Honest, yes," Claudius murmured. "I'm quite sure of that."

Relief flooded Ophelia's body when the door to the banquet hall slammed open and the room turned towards it, wondering who this intruder might be.

The room seemed to grow colder, but maybe that was just the draught.

Hamlet stood in the doorway. His hair was a ragged, long mess that stuck to his face with melting snow; his clothes were dry, but they hung off his body as if he'd shrunk in the time he'd been away. His face was sallow and pale. He looked like he had walked to Helsingør on foot across an entire ocean.

But that was not the thing that made her gasp.

Hal's heart throbbed outside his chest. No one else could see its pain, but she could. It was a tortured, dying thing, wrapped in a lead coffin of Corruption that stilled its every beat.

It squeezed him like a vice, and she watched it swell in his lungs, emerge from his throat like a swarm of demented butterflies. As it did, she watched the Corruption in the room respond. It rose up from the floor, crowding around his feet; it gathered into pools on the walls and around the door, reaching for him, craving whatever rotting magic sat deep within the prince's heart.

He was a plague all on his own.

She stood, but she found her balance wasn't right. It wasn't just the wine. The sheer force of Hal's Corrupted heart knocked her off-centre, making it hard to stand up.

He was still staring at her, wide-eyed, and even from a distance she could see how travel and Corruption had worn him. His face was thinner than it had been before he left. The healthy glow of his skin had been sapped away, leaving only dark shadows around his eyes and hardly a trace of a freckle.

He was not the young man who had left Helsingør—or perhaps he was, but he was not the Hamlet she had grown up with, who she had sat in that stable with what seemed like years ago, whose touch she knew like a secret halved. That man was dead, and his months at Wittenberg had not brought him back to life.

In trying to protect him, they had only succeeded in damning him more completely.

Slowly, painfully, Hamlet dragged his eyes away from her.

"Welcome back, my son," Gertrude was saying, clapping her hands together. The king must have spoken already; Ophelia had not noticed. "Come and sit with us; you must be weary."

Hamlet cleared his throat. "Very weary, Mother," he said. If Ophelia was not mistaken, his eyes lingered on Claudius. "For that reason, you must excuse me."

He turned on his heel and left.

Gertrude looked as if she hardly knew what to do with her hands. She dithered, looking at the door through which Hamlet had already left. Then she sat heavily and gestured furiously to a serving man for more wine.

"I must go," Ophelia breathed, looking towards the door. Laertes pulled her back into her seat. "I have to go, Laertes."

"You can't," he hissed back. He nodded at her father, who sat at a lower table facing them. His face showed that same mix of anger and fear as the king's: emotions for something that had not happened yet, but might. His eyes slid to her, and she could practically hear his voice in her head as he mouthed: sit.

"Forgive me," she said.

Ophelia picked up her skirts and ran.

SCENE TWO
hamlet

Hamlet knew Ophelia's footsteps as well as his own—better, probably. He stopped walking, the moonlight streaming in through the hallway's narrow windows and colouring him in a strange halo. His shadow scarred it, cutting across the floor like a blade.

"Fee," he said, taking in her wide blue eyes, the familiar set of her shoulders. Before he knew it, she was in his arms. He buried his nose in her soft hair. She shook in his arms. She was crying, he realised, the kind of deep, wracking sobs that usually mean grief.

He held her back by her arms, then swiped tears from her cheeks with the soft pads of his thumbs.

"Don't cry," he said, grinning like a madman. "Don't cry, you're being ridiculous. I'm home."

"You look awful, Hal," she sniffled, wiping her nose with her sleeve. "Were you attacked on the way?"

Hamlet smiled. "No incidents," he told her. "Of course, if there were any bandits en route, I would have fended them off single-handedly."

"Oh, of course. I can see you fighting off three grown men at once. Like a beetle turned on its back." She sniffled again. "You need to tell me everything about Wittenberg, Hal."

"First, tell me: is it true?" he asked, seeing it already—the ceremony, the gown, the candles flickering in applause. "Claudius has made some agreement with your father?"

"They won't let me say no."

Her eyes were desperate, and Hamlet knew Ophelia's father. When Polonius got an idea into his head, it stayed. And especially now, with Ophelia's name dragged through the mud on his account, how could he blame them?

Any shred of love he had for his uncle shrivelled and died in an instant.

"Let's hope he dies on the march," Hamlet said. "I don't like the idea of you becoming my aunt."

Ophelia grimaced. "Nor do I, believe me."

Before he could say anything, a skirmish drew his attention. Ophelia's father and brother seemed to be fighting to get out of the door at the same time, and that scary Italian woman—Eleni? Alice?—and her husband were looming behind them. Whatever her name was, she looked ready to commit a crime.

"Oh dear," Hamlet said, stepping backwards. "Ophelia, as much as I'd love to catch up, I think your brother wants me dead."

"Laertes!" Ophelia growled, turning sharply, but then withered when she saw her father approaching too. "Prince Hamlet, you do look very tired after all—why don't you go to bed?"

"An excellent idea."

"My hero," she said drily, over her shoulder. And then, to Laertes, "You expect me not to check on him, when he looks as if he's on death's door? We've been friends since we were children!"

Hamlet didn't linger long enough to hear what else was said. Judging from the fact that he could hear Polonius shouting from the far end of the palace, he supposed it wasn't good. He felt faintly guilty, but deep down he knew it'd be worse if he stayed.

Hell, he was surprised his mother hadn't yet emerged to join the fray. Although, she did usually like to wait until a drama had died down before blowing on the sparks again.

He went through a servant's entrance beneath the stairs, frightening a maid when he appeared out of the dark and snatched a fruitcake from her tray. It was busier and stuffier down here near the kitchens, with trays of food and drink constantly flowing between these rooms and the banquet hall.

He emerged through another indistinguishable door on almost the other side of the castle. His rooms were up a private staircase on the first floor, as was befitting a prince: Ophelia's chamber three floors up always felt like they were brushing the servant's quarters.

Inside, Hamlet stepped on to a carpet of thick furs. He smiled, kicking off his boots and slamming the door behind him. The fire was blazing merrily, a tub of hot water already steaming in the corner. News of his arrival must have travelled fast. Even the things on his writing desk were carefully arranged: fresh ink pots, fresh quills, a pile of expensive paper. It had an Italian seal on it when he held it up to the light, a faint impression of a sickle moon stamped into the page.

It was building. All through the ride up to the castle, and again the hallway, he'd felt it coming: the ache that had haunted him since leaving Wittenberg. It had only grown worse with distance, a rot at the centre of him. He felt a terrible pain in his head, like someone was jabbing a long needle right into his brain. It was so painful that he fell to his knees on the furs, clutching his head. His blood rushed in his ears. The headache got worse and worse, pulsing, like the needle had been set alight.

He lay, face-down and drooling, and waited for the pain to ebb away like it always did.

The headaches had started almost as soon as he left Wittenberg. At first, he'd assumed it was from the travel. It wasn't comfortable, being jolted around in the back of a carriage as they traversed the rocky country roads day and night in their hurry to get to the port. Since then, they'd gotten considerably worse.

There wasn't a single evening in the last five days when he hadn't ended up banging his head against the floor, biting his tongue so he wouldn't scream. Fear trickled down his back, mingling with his cold sweat.

"I'm not dying," he muttered to himself, gathering his limbs into his abdomen, so he could curl on his side in the foetal position. "It's nothing but stress."

The pain redoubled. He squeezed his eyes closed and moaned like a wounded animal.

"Hal?"

It was Ophelia. One of her cheeks was redder than the other. Hal, curled on the floor, felt like a monster.

"Did he hurt you?" he said as fiercely as he could manage, forgetting his own pain for a moment. "If he raised a hand to you, Ophelia—"

She shushed him and slipped inside, closing the door quietly behind her. "You're bleeding." She crouched by him, touching the corner of his mouth. Indeed: he was leaking scarlet-tinged drool. How romantic. "What happened?"

"You shouldn't be here," he said. "We need to be careful."

"Tell me."

Hal's breath stilled.

He couldn't tell her about the magic. Could he? He looked at her in the flickering firelight: her loyal, serious eyes, her slowly reddening cheek. Another wave of pain threatened to undo him, and he pressed his face into the furs so she wouldn't have to see him gag.

"I missed you," he whispered, his voice cracking. *Fuck*. He was going to die at sixteen from a brain haemorrhage and Mother was going to go entirely wild, and Father would more than likely get killed on a battlefield, and—

"For God's sake, Hal," Ophelia said sharply. "This is magic, isn't it? I can see it dripping out of your mouth. What on earth did you do?"

She might as well have punched him in the face. He was so shocked he jerked upwards to stare at her, and then the pain rocketed through his forehead like a lance. He collapsed with an embarrassing noise, while she tutted and laid her hands on the burning back of his neck.

His vision went funny and white as Ophelia started to talk, strange words in Latin that meant little to him. He understood their basic meaning—Latin might as well have been his second language, he used it so frequently—but the words made no sense together.

She kept talking about drawing things out, about lifting, about corruption and cleansing. What she said was vaguely reminiscent of the sort of thing Rosencrantz tended to sniff at. He brushed away the thought: he didn't want to think of Rosencrantz here. It felt somehow wrong, like mixing oil and water.

Ophelia spoke of fire, and when she whispered the words, Hal's heart nearly burned itself right out of his chest.

"It's not working," she muttered to herself, smoothing her hands over his back. His tunic was drenched in cold sweat, and he still stank from travel. It was not, he thought blearily, a great start to their reunion. "The Corruption isn't coming out, and I don't know why—it's like it's stuck to you… How did this happen?"

"I don't know," he whispered. He recognised the word *Corruption*, but only from Rosencrantz's dismissive commentary. "I only went through the mirror once. You know about the mirror?"

"I know about the mirror," she confirmed, and went back to chanting in Latin.

"Really, Fee," he felt the need to say again. "I did only go there once."

He couldn't look at her, but he could hear her: the rustle of her skirt as she stood, the quiet slither of its hem across the ground, the frustrated way she breathed out through her nose, what Mother always called her dragon's breath. Ophelia was always so bad at hiding her frustration.

"Someone must have done this to you," she muttered. "You were fine when you left, you must have been…"

Hamlet gazed at her. "You're not surprised. You know about magic," he said. "You never told me."

"I don't understand," she muttered. "Why isn't it clearing?"

The headache finally faded enough for him to sit up.

"When did you find out?" he asked. "Was it while I was away? Who showed you?"

Ophelia stopped in her tracks.

"I've always known," she said quietly.

Betrayal lodged itself inside his chest, like a knife.

"Always?" he asked.

"Always." Her tone was guarded. "My mother is from… from the other side of the mirror. A place we call Rúnräd."

"You never told me."

"I'm so sorry, Hal." She reached for him, but he crawled backwards away from her. "I wasn't allowed to."

"When did that ever stop us?" he asked, and Ophelia flinched as if she had been hit.

Something between them changed. He felt it shifting, like a cavernous gap was emerging. To think he'd feared the months of not speaking, the distance of Wittenberg, when in fact this was a gap that had existed unseen by him for their entire lives.

"But I told you everything," was all he could think to say around the sudden appearance of a lump in his throat.

It was all coming together now, the horrible reality of it. The mysterious trips into town, the disappearances, all the times he went looking for her and she was gone. Hours spent wandering the halls, searching for her behind tapestries, inside the trunk in her father's room. She was never anywhere to be found, because she wasn't anywhere at all.

Not anywhere on this earth, at least.

"I couldn't tell you, Hal. I just couldn't," she said. She reached for him, and he let her fingers touch his cheek. They came away wet with tears. "And I don't regret it," she whispered. "I protected you for so long, I took the Corruption away when you weren't looking, and now *this*..."

"I've heard all about your *Corruption*," he said. Words, like cannonballs, lined up to find their mark. Daubing sigils on cave walls and chanting about Corruption. Rosencrantz's words came back to him. "It's ridiculous, Ophelia, the idea that magic can stain..."

"It's not ridiculous, it's true!" she said, puffing up with anger. "I can see it! All around you, in your heart, I can see it!"

Hamlet looked down at himself. Sure enough, there was nothing there: no magical bloodstain, no mark, no fuzzy aura. "It's made up," he said again, calmly, because he knew that would annoy her more. "It's just a story invented to stop people from exploring the true power of magic."

"Who have you been talking to?" she asked, with a tone of such naked disgust that Hamlet felt sick. "Did your uncle tell you this?"

Claudius? Knowing about magic? The thought was ludicrous.

"Did you tell him?" Hamlet asked, which felt like the only logical conclusion to draw. The agreement between Ophelia and Claudius… Did it somehow involve magic?

"No," Ophelia replied, nostrils flaring, and Hamlet saw his life flash before his eyes. 'No, I did *not* tell your uncle about magic. He already knew about it when he arrived. Now answer me: who told you Corruption isn't real?"

"A friend in Wittenberg," he said. "The same friend who showed me the other side of the mirror. A more honest friend than you, clearly."

A white lie, but nothing in comparison to the lies Ophelia had told him. She didn't need to know about Rosencrantz, and he didn't want to tell her. In fact, there was something in him that shied from telling her a single thing about his life in Wittenberg.

"I'm not your friend," Ophelia said fiercely. She stood, her skirts rustling around her. "I'm the love of your life, and I'm trying to protect you."

"I didn't ask for protection—"

"I've known about magic for as long as I can remember," she said, fire burning in her eyes. "I grew up with it. My mother helped to cleanse this castle, and my aunt, and their mother before them, and their father. My whole family's lives have revolved around keeping this place clear of Corruption to keep Denmark safe, so don't you *dare* tell me that it isn't real! Don't you dare speak on it!"

Hamlet mimed sewing his lips together. Ophelia rolled her eyes and made for the door.

"I'm finished talking to you," she said. "I'm sure you must be tired from your travels, Prince Hamlet. Goodness, it must have been *so hard* being at university with your friends doing God knows what... I've just been sat here, twiddling my thumbs, looking at the wall while I waited for you to return and *explain magic to me*."

Ophelia saw herself out.

That night, Hamlet tossed and turned in a bed more luxurious than any he'd seen in months, and yet less comfortable. The very air of Helsingør felt wrong. Everything was off-kilter. It was as though, as soon as he'd turned his back on the city, it had scrambled to change itself into a form he couldn't recognise.

Ophelia being from the magical world. His uncle apparently knowing about magic... Ophelia being promised to his uncle. He shuddered, and sat up so he could wrap his furs more tightly around his narrow shoulders. No, this wasn't right. This was some kind of parallel world. He must have launched them into it when he kissed that stableboy, and now everything was broken and twisted and damned.

He screwed up his face. Deep in his gut, he could feel the burning sensation he had become used to these past few weeks, in that place Rosencrantz called 'the well'. His well, unlike Rosencrantz's, was not easily drawn-up; his was filled with fire and flame.

The very thought of Rosencrantz was enough to make him nauseous. He wished more than anything that he'd been brave and spoken to Guildenstern, those heady weeks where he and Ros sat and planned a prince's murder. What was Guildenstern thinking, all those days he'd lingered like a wraith, tight-lipped, incorporeal, refusing to meet their eyes with anything but stark invulnerability?

Hamlet wondered, not for the first time, if Guildenstern was the only one out of the three of them with a whit of sense.

His stomach lurched, and with it the flames rose into his chest, curling around his ribs. Hamlet curled into a ball and let out a moan like a dying man. He could feel the heat radiating off him. Rosencrantz, if he was here, would probably tut and say Hamlet lacked control. He would say Hamlet didn't deserve magic, if this was how he let it behave.

The anger rose to a crescendo and he twisted, intending to throw the furs off himself—except, before he could, he smelled smoke. He looked down at his lap, staring in horror at the ashes that covered him. There were no flames: only the black, shrivelled remains of his furs, singed and twisted into something terrible.

He leapt out of bed, pushing the furs off himself. He yelped, leaping back and pressing his palms against the cold stone wall.

Furs didn't burn easily. They were designed not to. The acrid smoke smell of them brought tears to his eyes—as the animal skin burned, it had the terrible scent of charred leather mixed with fat. He stood there for what felt like a very long time, long enough that a servant came in, stopped when they saw the wreckage, and came back with a bucket and a shovel to scrape away the remains of his bedding.

Whatever magic Rosencrantz had, it was more easily controlled than this... thing that lived within Hamlet, this creature of smoke and talons. He shuddered in horror.

The servant looked strangely at him from beneath a shock of orange hair.

"Pardon me for asking, sir, and if this is rude, sir, forgive me," the servant said, and made to go on in this vein, probably for quite some time. Hamlet waved a hand, as if to say, *skip to the good part*.

"Well, sir," the servant continued, cheek twitching. They were around the same age, Hamlet noted, with disconnected interest. "I was just wondering, sir... if you were quite well? I can send for the physician...?"

The servant licked his lips as if his mouth was drying up. He stood there, and Hamlet looked at him—*really* looked at him—for the first time. A shock of red hair cut bluntly across the forehead, clean uniform, a pockmark over his fair eyebrows, a few spots on his jaw.

"I'm perfectly well," said Hamlet. "You're dismissed."

When he was once again alone, he went to the small mirror he kept propped on his desk. Same blue eyes, same dark hair, same frightened face staring back.

Except now, as if through fresh eyes, he saw it: the hollows in his cheeks, the darkness that swallowed those eyes so that they appeared dull and lifeless. He looked like a corpse walking.

Hamlet went to find Laertes.

SCENE THREE
ophelia

"I cannot believe," Ophelia said, sitting in her nightgown in the empty library, "that you would conspire against me like this, Laertes."

"Don't be so dramatic." Laertes reclined, legs up on the long reading desk that ran the length of the room. "I can't believe you're already arguing. This must be a new record. He's been back... what, five hours?"

"Something like that," said Hal. "Can you stop talking about me as if I'm not here?"

"No," Laertes replied, and turned back to Ophelia.

Out of sheer habit, she shot Hamlet a look that meant, *my brother is the most annoying man in Denmark and perhaps the world.*

Candlelight softened the edges of the room, lending it a dream-like quality. Soon, the sun would begin to rise and the castle would wake, but for now it was so deep in the wee hours that even the servants slept, and only a few guardsmen wandered the halls. They knew by now, even after Hamlet's long absence, to expect Ophelia and her brother to emerge for a walk and to see the prince returning to his chambers hours afterwards.

Ophelia sighed. Her hard work was being undone before her eyes. She knew with certainty that the guards would talk. By morning, the servants would all know, and by mid-afternoon her father would be drawing her into their apartments and shouting the walls down, red-cheeked and furious, and she would have to repress her laughter at the way his little moustache twitched with sheer rage.

She'd also have to repress the shame of it, of loving and being loved.

Not that this evening felt like love.

"I'm bored of enabling this," Laertes was saying, massaging his forehead with his thumbs. "In all honesty, are you two *sure* you're in love? Because to me it looks like you want to kill each other every five minutes."

Laertes is my brother, Ophelia thought. They used to braid each other's hair as children. When he was in Paris, he saved up wildflowers and dried them and sent them to her in paper sealed with wax. *I do not want to kick him until his shins turn black and blue.*

"Laertes, please explain to Prince Hamlet that, first of all, Corruption is real, and that, secondly, his uncle knows about magic."

Laertes swung his exhausted gaze around to meet Hamlet's.

"I'm not even going to indulge the former with a response."

"But the latter?" Hamlet asked, leaning forward. "My uncle?"

"Knows all about it," Laertes said, dragging a hand down his face, so that his eyes popped wide open and his mouth distorted. "Committing evil deeds left, right, and center. We think, anyway."

Ophelia, who had been sitting with her eyes closed, waiting for the moment Hamlet inevitably apologised and begged for her forgiveness, felt a bolt of ice slide down her spine. Her eyes shot open. Hal looked like he'd been smacked over the head with something heavy.

"There's something strange about him," she explained in a rush, paving over her brother's blunt words. "It's... I can see the Corruption. It's a gift that was given to me, and in theory it should make it easier for me to remove it and to see when it rises to dangerous levels. But Claudius has no Corruption around him, none at all. And my aunt said she knew him, when she used to live in the castle, and the Corruption used to… follow him around. It was at its worst around him."

"So… what? My uncle was covered in this Corruption, so he must be evil. What does that say about me? Am I evil too?"

Laertes hummed noncommittally. Ophelia *did* kick him this time, sliding down in her chair to catch him right in the meat of his thigh, and savoured the way he doubled over in pain.

"It's not," Ophelia said primly, when she had enjoyed her victory for long enough, "as simple as that."

She explained it as best she could: that Corruption was a natural by-product, but when it built up, it caused problems. That certain spells could cause more of it, and those spells tended to be powerful, and the most powerful spells held the power of life and death. Spells that were more permanent created more Corruption: in this way, a harmless temporary trick to turn a friend's freckles blue might create a tiny puff of Corruption, infinitely small, but the same spell made permanent could cause the Corruption to bloom beneath a watchful eye.

When she had finished explaining, Laertes leaned forward.

"Is there really a spell," he asked, "to turn freckles blue?"

"Shut up."

"You couldn't think of a better example than that?"

"Shut your mouth, Laertes."

"Benighted *freckles*."

"*Benighted*. What does that even mean? Oh, I'm *Laertes* and I live in *Paris* where we use brand new words we *just made up*––"

"What exactly are you accusing my uncle of?" Hamlet interrupted, jiggling his knee impatiently. "Removing the Corruption sounds like a good thing. He's saved you a job, surely. And maybe it could help me."

How to explain that her worries came from nothing concrete, just a feeling, without sounding mad? The feelings of a woman, and her aunt, and apparently her mother––that was all she had to go on, all she had to prove herself. And her suspicions, all of which were unfounded: the damaged sigils, the way he looked at her, like he knew, somehow, that she understood magic.

She fumbled her way through an explanation that made no sense and yet would convince any of the women.

"In conclusion, I don't know," she said. "I don't know what exactly he's done or is planning to do, but I just have a feeling he's going to do something, and I don't know why."

They sat in silence for a while, all of them in nightclothes with cloaks thrown hastily over the top, in the flickering light from the candle. Hamlet was playing with the melting wax without even seeming to notice what he was doing, dipping his fingertip into it, peeling off the dried shell, flaking it over the tabletop.

Ophelia cast her gaze to the books. She wished she had one to show them, a volume with written evidence and a handy illustration of Claudius she could point to and say, 'Aha! Here's the villain now!'

But no such volume existed. They had nothing to go on except her word. Agitated, she got up and went to the shelves, drawing her fingers across the leather spines, feeling the chill of their metal clasps against her skin. She whispered the words and drew tiny strands of Corruption away, watching them dissipate.

Even if all she had to protect was this library, she couldn't do it. Was it always such a pointless slog, she wondered, or was this the impact of having no Sight Guide since Solveig left years ago, when Ophelia was only a child? Was her job always meant to be so utterly impossible, or did she just lose the draw, facing the worst possible odds?

"Are you taking it away?" Hamlet asked, quietly. "The Corruption, I mean?"

She nodded.

"Is it bad?"

She nodded again, lips pursed. If she didn't hold her words in, she might cry.

"Is there anything I can do to help? I can't help you to remove it?"

She shook her head again. Hamlet rolled his neck, thinking.

He was so dear to her. She wished she could see him again without the ring of Corruption surrounding him, without those writhing tentacles of it at his feet turning him into more monster than man. She hated that her eyes were drawn to them instead of to his proud, lovely face.

"Then what can I do to help? Do you need me to speak with my uncle?"

She shook her head. "I need you to keep an eye on him," she said. "And I need you to tell me if he says anything, anything at all, that so much as hints he's using magic."

"Alright," he said. "That sounds… easy."

Laertes coughed and flapped a hand in the air. "The other thing," he said, his voice muffled by the fact that he once again had his face in his hands. And then: "I am so tired."

"Yes. The other thing." Ophelia took a breath and faced Hal. "I need you to help me get into his chambers."

This time, it was Hamlet's turn to pinch the bridge of his nose and sigh.

"Fine," he said. "But only because I owe you an apology for earlier."

"You'd help me anyway," she said, and she felt the beginnings of a smile appear on her lips.

Laertes slammed his hands against the desk. Ophelia yelped.

"Now can we *please*," her brother said, "all go to bed?"

Ophelia did go to bed eventually, guided by Laertes through the dim halls. They only encountered Barnardo on the way, who pinched his bottom lip between his teeth but let them pass without a word.

She tucked herself into her blankets the way she always did: bound like a corpse, the sheet tight around the outline of her limbs, so that she could hardly move. She sighed in relief, wriggling further into the mattress.

In the dim light, against all odds, it was her cross that caught her eye. Hung above the door, the crucifix was usually easy to ignore. She hardly noticed it was there most days, the dull copper fading into the wooden beam that held it up, equally exhausted shades of brown.

But tonight, it caught her eye. Not for the first time, she wondered what would happen to her when she died.

Exodus 22:18. Maleficos non patieris vivere.
Thou shalt not suffer a witch to live.

Sometimes, she wondered how it was possible: to live the life she did and still believe in God. It was, to her, one of the central confusions about her person that she would never be able to explain to another living soul.

How to love a God that can't love what it created?

But love Them she did (because God was a Them, to her). She loved Them because she believed, in her heart, in forgiveness. And maybe it was the ultimate act of forgiveness, to look God in the eye and say, *I will love you in spite of it all, and I believe that, in the end, you will love me too.*

In the other room, she heard Father clearing his throat, the shuffling of his papers as familiar and comforting a sound as a bright morning's birdsong.

Ophelia swallowed the tears of an emotion too big to be named, and she took her eyes off the small bronze cross, and she went to sleep.

SCENE FOUR
hamlet

Lack of sleep was Hamlet's eternal nemesis. It made him clumsy and forgetful, fidgety and overheated, and it was always accompanied by the feeling of a thousand frantic ants running around beneath his skin. Just now, he felt like the ants were holding no fewer than five separate conferences in different parts of his body, and they were all very angry.

He had tried, during the voyage home, to cover up the sickness welling inside him. It was difficult, though, when he was exhausted all the time and his arms and legs became marked with yellow-green bruises and he spent his mornings throwing up, his afternoons eating everything within reach. The ants found their favourite place in the hollow at the base of his throat, where they scrabbled and bit and did their best to silence him.

He tossed and turned, and eventually had to open the door at the other end of his chambers that led to a small staircase down into the private orchard. The breeze that came in rustled everything on his desk and sent scraps of paper fluttering on top of his wax tablet and styli rolling onto the floor.

Hamlet groaned and sat up. It was mid-morning. His father's voice called out from the orchard, demanding wine and bread from some overwrought servant. It was his custom to spend the middle of the day there when the weather was fine, eating and drinking first, then sleeping, surrounded by the trees and the sound of birds.

The weather was not fine, not today, but Father clearly desired the fresh air and silence that came with having a private garden. For a moment, Hamlet wondered if he should go and join him. When he was a child, he was never invited to join Father in the garden. Now grown, he still didn't. The idea simply hadn't crossed his mind.

Midway through swinging his legs out of bed, a wave of fire somewhere in his gut swept over him. He tumbled to the floor, gritting his teeth in pain.

But he was used to this, after the long and arduous journey from Wittenberg. He knew to store something nearby he could bite down on, and he took the leather cord in his hand and shoved it between his teeth. His stomach gave a lurch, then another; he pressed his forehead into the rug as hard as he could, indenting his skin with the woven pattern. He knew exactly where this pain came from, although he couldn't understand why.

Deep in that well of magic Rosencrantz had helped him to create, something was growing.

He bit down harder into the leather, hard enough to hurt his teeth, as another wave of pain crashed over him. It felt like the magic Rosencrantz had helped him to nurture was angry with him. It flared up at the strangest moments, like when he was angry, or dehydrated, or in that wonderful warm stage before he fell asleep, and it was always fire that leapt to his fingertips when the pain came, fire that burned through his belly and shot from his pores.

The magic leapt up in him, tingling through his skin, and the fire jumped six inches with it. Then, like the steady roll of thunder, other things began to respond: the ashes came flying out of the grate, whipping around him and covering his chamber in a layer of soot; the carpet rolled itself up and shot beneath the bed; his pillows flung themselves apart and tore into pieces, sending feathers all over his blankets.

Hamlet wished this strange magic that lived inside him would leave him alone, but it would not. It had turned feral and strange, and now it ignored his attempts to restrain it and rein it in.

He thought about writing to Rosencrantz to ask for his opinion on the matter, but he was too proud. And Ophelia… She would worry, and she was worried enough. He recalled her face in the library, the trembling of her bottom lip as her finger dragged across the spine of a dusty tome. The seriousness of her voice as she spoke about her task, her duty, the cleanse Denmark of Corruption.

To save them all from an evil he had unknowingly made worse.

No, he wouldn't tell her. He would fix it alone, without Rosencrantz or Guildenstern, without Ophelia. He could, at the very least, do that.

The final wave of pain coursed through him and back out again. He tested his weight, found that he could hold himself up on his palms and move so he was kneeling. He panted there for a few minutes in a position that made a mockery of prayer. In a moment of desperation, he looked up.

God, if you're listening, make it easier to bear.

There was no reply, no wave of understanding.

Just a knock at the door, and one of his servants appeared.

"Nathan," Hamlet said, trying to look like he wasn't sweating profusely and tasting bile in his throat. "Good to see you again."

"And you, sir." Nathan bowed his head. "We missed your company while you were at Wittenberg. Pardon the interruption—were you praying?"

Hamlet got to his feet and stretched. "I was," he said. "I had just finished. Is something the matter?"

Nathan had been serving Hamlet for three years. He was quite a bit older than Hamlet himself, perhaps in his late twenties. He was the son of some country nobility—a place in the king's court was an impressive achievement, and a position serving the crown prince even moreso.

"It's a summons for you, sir," Nathan said. "Your mother would like to see you in her sitting room."

Ignoring the dull ache that still resided in his belly, Hamlet flung open the door of his garderobe. Three sets of fine armour stood to attention at one end of the room; he briefly considered putting on the gold set just to see his mother's face, but instead he selected a doublet and jerkin that had seen better days and began to dress.

Nathan came to help him with the fastenings, but Hamlet waved him away.

"I dressed alone in Wittenberg," he said. "I'll manage now."

Tactfully, Nathan did not mention the weeks after the incident with the stableboy—or was he a kennelboy? He couldn't remember—when Hamlet wouldn't allow anyone to touch him. He remembered feeling horribly like he was diseased; like Nathan laying his hands on him to tie his laces might awaken that sleeping beast within.

He dressed himself and splashed his face with cold water. It only served to stick his hair to the sides of his face, which made him look even more drawn and tired than he already was.

"How did she seem?" he asked Nathan, as he finished lacing his shoes. "Was she alone?"

Nathan hesitated, but that was all it took.

Hamlet groaned and cast one final look at his bed—it was so tempting just to climb back in—and he went to meet his fate.

※※※

Mother was decidedly not alone. She had invited all of her favourite ladies to sit with her, and the married ones were noticeably missing.

The usual disappointment cascaded over him. Before Wittenberg, scenes like this made no impact. He was used to being bought and sold, used to the fact that

Mother would more often call on him to wheedle a proposal out of him than to just… talk.

Now, a few months out of practice, it did sting. He never disliked Mother when she was on her own. It was when she was with other people that she became overbearing, obsessive, moody, and difficult to please.

He often wondered if it was a side-effect of how she lived her life: the constant need to soothe everyone around her, to maintain serenity, to be polite and entertaining and kind and funny but not too funny, to tell the right anecdotes. Her life depended on being liked, on being enjoyed, and she was most certainly not a natural at it.

Maybe that was why she treated him so strangely. He was the extension of her, her child, the son she so desperately needed to secure the line. But in being a son, he had everything she never had: freedom. The freedom to make mistakes, to be undutiful, to do what he wanted instead of what was necessary.

He found her exhausting. He found her pitiable. He loved her, and yet the reek of her simpering, her desperation to be liked, to be needed, all of it made him feel sick.

"Oh, Hamlet!" Mother said, standing to welcome him. She pulled him into an embrace. He was happy to see her, but he hated so many decorated eyes on them, so much makeup and perfume. His headache lingered in the background, waiting to pounce once again.

He wished she had summoned him in private, for their first real conversation in six months. He wished the way she stroked his hair back from his forehead didn't feel like it came with conditions attached.

She guided him to his usual seat, a rigid, velvet-covered chair, where he sat uncomfortably stroking the fabric between finger and thumb.

"I wanted to speak with you in private," Mother said, beaming, like these ladies were dolls instead of people with ears. "You must be so tired, my dove."

"Very, Mother," he said dutifully. "It was a long journey."

"And was it safe? You had no trouble along the way?"

"Perfectly so."

With so many people watching, it was hard to speak naturally. He sat there, mind utterly blank: whatever thoughts were there, they were something between a feeling and an image. There were no words to string together into any meaningful sentence.

"It is a good time to be home," Mother said. "It will raise morale, for the people to know their prince is safe and well in Denmark."

Hamlet shifted uncomfortably in his chair. "I suppose," he said. "Would it not raise it more if their prince joined them on the march?"

Mother sucked in a breath through her teeth. "No," she said. "No, no. That won't do at all. They would worry, Hamlet."

Privately, Hamlet was sure most of Denmark cared not a whit about where he was or what he was doing, but saying so was out of the question.

There was a knock at the door. He breathed a sigh of relief for the respite it afforded from the tense conversation. Sometimes, he felt like he'd lost the trick of talking to his parents—like somewhere in this palace there was a guidebook gathering dust, waiting for him to stumble across it, abandoned during a childhood game and lost ever since.

Uncle Claudius stepped inside, ducking his head at the assembled women. He did not bow to Hamlet, but strode over and put his heavy hand on his shoulder instead. Hamlet leaned very slightly away, partially out of loyalty to Ophelia, and partially because there was some sort of brown-red dirt on his uncle's fingers that looked very unappealing.

"Forgive me for interrupting," Claudius said. His eyes darted between Hamlet and his mother. "Good to see you, Hamlet. I stopped by your chambers earlier this morning, but you were dead to the world. Unsurprisingly, I suppose."

He wrinkled his nose. "It was a long journey."

Claudius laughed loudly. Even Mother let out a titter, although Hamlet couldn't see where the joke was.

"You were up late, I'm told." Claudius winked. "You know, a lesser man would knock you out for that. But I accept that you had her first."

Mother gasped. "Hamlet, you didn't! How many times have I told you to keep away from her? At night, unaccompanied—"

"Not unaccompanied," Claudius said, shrugging. "With Laertes, I hear. An odd thing for a brother to condone."

"Well, they always were uncomfortably close," said Mother, turning her face away, like she found the whole conversation so unpleasant that she wanted to escape from it. "Going around whispering in hallways, turning up with twigs in their hair, singing those nonsense songs their mother taught them…"

Hamlet stood up.

"I don't think," he said, trying his hardest to repress his anger, "it's helpful to bring their mother into this. And nothing untoward happened last night. In fact, Laertes asked to speak with me, and Ophelia demanded to come along."

"And you've never denied that girl anything," Mother scoffed. "That's why she thinks the whole world bows to her!"

"She thinks no such thing!"

"Hamlet, Hamlet." His uncle rested both hands on his shoulders and pressed him back down into his seat. "As long as you don't get a child on her, I don't care what you do."

Hamlet turned his head to look at his uncle, with what he hoped was a dangerous glint in his eye.

"You're not marrying her," he said. "I won't allow it."

Hamlet didn't stay to hear whatever insults his mother had for Ophelia. As he stormed towards the door, he heard the women whispering; he heard Claudius say something in an undertone, and the sounds of many skirts rustling as the ladies got to their feet.

It was lucky, he thought, tamping down the rage that threatened to burst out of him in the form of ten-foot flames. It was a blessing, really.

Because Father was in the gardens, and Mother was in her chambers, and Claudius was with her.

Which meant his uncle's chambers were empty, and there was no one to stop him from finding Ophelia and walking right inside.

SCENE FIVE
ophelia

"God's bones!" Hal swore, rubbing the top of his head with an injured expression. He crawled out from under Claudius's desk, muttering under his breath. "Nothing. I even checked for secret drawers, but all I found was a drawing of his dead wife and a very big spider."

"It's no use," Ophelia said, looking around. For once, what she was seeing was… normal. It was like her Sight Guide powers were gone, vanished into thin air. Claudius's chambers were just a series of rooms. There were no purple tentacles, no slithering, writhing purple worms.

The most Corrupt thing in the room was Hamlet, who was at this moment tentatively lifting the corner of his uncle's bedding between his index finger and thumb, grimacing, and placing it back down.

"I'm trying to remember where all the hidden bits are," he grumbled, getting back onto his hands and knees.

"All the hidden bits?"

"Every room in the castle has little secrets." He flashed her a grin. "Laertes has a secret cupboard in his bedchamber, and he used to put a flower in there for every time Alessandra looked at him."

"No, he did not!"

Hamlet nodded somberly. "Indeed, he did."

"Bless him," Ophelia said, and started knocking on sections of the wall at random.

"Don't forget to check behind the tapestry," Hamlet advised. "There's always something behind a tapestry."

It was a very ugly piece of embroidery, actually, and not a tapestry at all. It had some writing on it in what looked like English, but she couldn't make it out. The centrepiece was what looked like a very drab English battle of some kind, with lots of horses and men and dogs all trying to leap over one another and tear one another apart.

Ophelia opened her mouth to say that she did, in fact, know all about things being hidden behind tapestries, since she was usually the one who put things there, and to correct him on his textile knowledge, but her mouth opened and closed without a word escaping.

Behind the embroidery, there was a large, square alcove. It was about as wide and as deep as her forearm, and there was a monster in it.

She leapt back as something purple and slimy emerged, trying to wrap its tentacles around her wrist. She must have screamed, but then Hamlet's hand was over her mouth and his arm clutched her to his chest protectively, tugging her backwards.

"Don't scream again," he said quietly, his breath warming the shell of her ear. "It's just a hole in the wall and a… basket?"

There was, indeed, a basket. From the basket emerged a tentacle that seemed, horribly, like it was watching their movements. It swayed slowly. It was as thick around as her thigh and shiny with moisture.

She wanted to cry.

"You can see that, can't you?" she whispered, forcing him further back, until there was nowhere to go and his back hit the wall.

"Just a basket." His voice lowered. She didn't dare to take her eyes off the tentacle to look at him, but she could see his face in her mind's eye: his brow furrowed, his jaw clenched. "What are you seeing, Ophelia?"

It's protecting the basket, she realised. This… Corruption-creature, it was drifting back and forth, waving its enormous body around in front of that basket. It was almost comical: the enormous muscular growth emerging from the wall, sticking up at a right-angle, twitching…

No, it wasn't funny at all. It was terrifying.

"It's some kind of Corruption-creature," she said, trying her best to keep the tremble out of her voice. "I think we need to get to that basket."

She felt Hamlet relax at her back. "Well, that's fine," he said, and gently tugged her around so that she was standing behind him. "You stay here. I'll go and get it."

"Hal, no—I don't know if it can hurt you! I've never even heard of something like this before."

"I can't even see it," he reasoned. "Stay here. I'll get you the basket."

He took a step forward and she tried to clutch his hand. He drew his fingers away, smiling over his shoulder.

Hamlet got within arm's reach of the tentacle before it struck.

Within an instant, it grew a round mouth full of teeth. It reeled back, poised to strike. Ophelia darted forward and grabbed Hamlet by the back of his jerkin, but not quickly enough: the creature struck true.

Hamlet clutched at his chest. The Corruption-creature's jaws left no physical mark, but his face went horribly pale.

It aimed for his heart, she realised, dragging him back to the far corner of the room. *It aimed for his Corruption.*

Hamlet stayed doubled over for a long moment. When he finally raised his head, he did his best to smile.

"I saw it for a second," he said. "Just a flash. It's extremely ugly."

She swatted him. "I don't know what to do," she admitted.

"Try your Latin?"

She looked doubtfully at the monster, which waved back. It was moving faster now. It seemed... confident? Ophelia tried mumbling a few words of Latin, but her tongue felt heavy in her mouth, and the words did nothing at all.

"Okay," said Hamlet. "Alright. I have an idea."

He unbuttoned his jerkin and threw it on the ground. His doublet followed, dark green fabric pooling on the ground. Carefully, he rolled up both sleeves.

"You are not," Ophelia said, "going to try the exact same thing again."

He nodded.

"Hamlet, that's ridiculous."

"No, it's not. I'm prepared this time."

He marched forward, blind to the way the tentacle coiled back, ready to strike.

"On your left!" Ophelia yelped, as the tentacle lunged.

Hamlet leapt to his right, a true fencer; the tentacle just missed its mark and wound back for another shot.

"Back!" she called. Hamlet jumped backwards, landing with a little *oof*. "Okay, move forward—it's tired—*left!*"

Hamlet ducked to the left and, seemingly deciding to go with his gut, made a grab for the basket. He got his fingers around the handle and threw Ophelia a lopsided grin over his shoulder, turning on his heel—

Again, the tentacle lunged, except this time the wound was not invisible. Hamlet swayed on the spot. The basket tumbled from his slack hand, his eyes focused on a point somewhere over Ophelia's right shoulder as blood blossomed across his white shirt.

She dove for him, but at the same time, the basket hit the floor and what felt like a hazy purple explosion ricocheted through the room. She put her hands over her head, the pins from her hair poking her palms as she curled into the smallest ball she possibly could.

Her skin was on fire. She reached out, looking for Hamlet, and found the back of his head, the soft curls at the nape of his neck. She buried her fingers in them and tried to speak, to say something along the lines of, *everything will be okay*.

Except, for what felt like the hundredth time that day, she was interrupted.

Hamlet's body sent a wave of flame coursing through the room, great gusts of it burning up seemingly everything except him and Ophelia and the basket, which she realised was toppled next to them on the ground.

Amidst the fire and the scorching heat, she reached for the little cloth bundle that had tumbled out onto the floor.

This time, when she unwrapped the contents and saw a human heart lying there, still beating, she did scream.

Three nights later, Ophelia waved her hands over another dying woman in the dark. There was no spell to stop the influenza from spreading. There was nothing she nor her magic could do against the invisible plague, the miasma that spread across the castle like wildfire in the wake of the enormous explosion of Corruption that occurred in Claudius's chambers.

She remembered very little of what had happened once the heart had emerged from its bundle. She recalled, with a jolt, Claudius appearing in the doorway. He'd snatched the heart from the ground and wrapped it hastily in the sheet once again, shouting something to dismiss the guards outside. The room was no longer clean of Corruption. It had been soaked in it, flecks of it spattered across every surface like the aftermath of a grisly murder. In the corner of her eye, the Corruption-monster thrashed and flailed.

She touched her hand to the dying woman's parched lips and whispered the only words of healing she knew, the only part of healing magic her mother had ever taught her.

"*Requiem*," she whispered. The tense muscles in the woman's throat relaxed; her jaw slackened, and her hands loosened from their tightly-closed fists.

She would sleep now, and in a few hours, she would die. But first, she would rest.

Ophelia tiptoed around the room, offering respite to those she could. There was little she could do, and less to protect herself. She knew Aaron in Rúnräd would wear a hole in the floor with pacing if he knew that she was in this sickroom, breathing in the stale air.

But he would go into the rooms, she knew. He had, when it was her mother who was dying. The only time Aaron ever broke his rule of isolation during the outbreak was to give her mother this very blessing, to stroke her too-warm forehead, and to ask Ophelia if she wanted to say the word.

Requiem.

Aaron said isolation was the best way to treat a disease like this, and she knew he was right. Once the Corruption helped the sickness to grow, there was no cleansing charm that could take it away. It was not Corruption anymore. It was something else, and all they could do was let it burn through those who were infected and try to spare the rest.

But tonight, she walked the halls. Tonight, she gave rest to those who needed it, and then she would go to Rúnräd and lock herself in the small empty house that had once belonged to her mother, which Aunts Hilga and Solveig kept clean and tidy even though neither Ophelia nor Laertes ever set foot in it.

Ophelia rolled her neck one way and then the other, trying to shake off the soreness of a night bent over the dying. The first death had occurred only hours ago, but she knew there would be more. Still, the men would march next week or the week after, depending on how many in their number fell ill. They were needed to take back what Norway had gained.

She hoped Hamlet was sleeping peacefully somewhere. The wound in his chest was not as bad as it seemed at first: a perfect ring of puncture-marks, which rapidly turned purple with bruising, not Corruption, and swelled around the edges. His Corruption-laden heart had practically burst out of his chest at the moment the creature bit him though, and that was what made him collapse to the floor.

Despite her best efforts, Ophelia hadn't been able to see him since. Laertes said the court physician was visiting him hourly.

How on earth he'd explained them being in Claudius' chambers, she didn't know. But so far, there were no questions from her father, no strange looks from courtiers. Just Claudius's unnerving yellow-brown eyes on her at mealtimes, distracting her from the coughs that spread around the dining hall.

Ophelia gathered her cloak around her and picked up her basket, which she'd filled with a few things to keep her company during her isolation: a book, a blanket, some embroidery she was half-finished with. She slipped out of the sickroom with one last look at the fifteen poorly people spread out on pallets, unnaturally sick unnaturally fast.

She made her way through silent streets, her only company the call of the early seabirds and the wash of waves against the shore. Water was replaced with the rustle of trees, pebbles with moss underfoot. She knew Laertes would be furious when he found out she'd gone away, and she wondered how he would explain it to father. She could imagine him already, standing in the snow outside the Rúnräd cottage, blustering from outside.

When she found the mirror, she reached in—

And her fingers brushed cold, smooth glass.

The way was shut.

SCENE SIX
hamlet

Hamlet pushed the physician's bony hand from his chest.

"I don't need you," he said, swinging his legs out of bed. "Leave me be."

"Your Highness, I think His Grace is suffering the effects of the sun with the planet Mars," said Master Frederik, turning to Getrude with an expression of utter seriousness. "This conjunction can be positive, but in His Young Highness's chart, I believe it heightens that, shall we say, ill-temperament…"

"His patience has been thin," Gertrude agreed. "You don't think it's this illness, then? Just the planets in motion?"

"Mother," said Hamlet. "This is nonsensical, and you know it."

"I have always said," said the physician—who moonlighted as the Court Astrologer and it showed—"that His Grace's temperament has too much of the hot and dry."

"Hot and dry," Hamlet muttered. "We'll see about that, when I lie down in the snow to die, unless you leave my chambers *now*."

"Hamlet!"

"To speak of self-slaughter is a *sin*," Master Frederik said, face pale. "A terrible sin, the worst of them—"

Hamlet dressed himself, batting away the old man's reaching hands. Mother apologised over and over again to the physician as Hamlet called for Nathan, who came in from the hall with the distinct look of someone who had been listening at the door and had no interest in participating in what they had overheard.

"I'm going for a ride," said Hamlet, without stopping to hear any ideas to the contrary.

Mother and the physician tripped over one another trying to follow, and were so caught up in their apologies that they fell behind, and soon their voices faded out of earshot.

The halls were near silent. Three days since he'd been out of his chambers, and the castle had shifted its mood once again. It was as if normal life was on hold, as if Kronborg Castle was a hunk of amber and they were the flies frozen within it, waiting for the world to begin moving again.

Only the guards were out now, everyone too shaken by the sudden and swift bout of influenza that had struck them. Unnatural, Mother had said. Never had she seen anything like it. The castle was in a state of perpetual night, of cautious glances, of hushed voices and footsteps that echoed into the voids in the arched ceilings.

Guilt felt like a jet blade slinking between his ribs, thin as a shadow.

"Your Grace," said Nathan, jogging to keep up.

"Just Hamlet is fine, which you know," Hamlet replied, giving Nathan a sharp look he didn't deserve.

"Yes, sir," said Nathan, entirely ignoring him. "I'm not entirely happy about this sir, and it would get me in a lot of trouble if anyone found out, but I have a message for you from Lady Ophelia."

He shoved a scrap of parchment into Hamlet's hand. Hamlet paused, unfolding it and scanning the words there. Ophelia's handwriting slanted awkwardly across the page, and her looping scrawl was hurried, as if she'd written her note in a rush on a hard surface that wasn't a desk.

He crushed it in his palm.

"On second thoughts," he said, "I have a headache. I'm going back to sleep."

He left Nathan standing in the hallway and went to find the nearest mirror.

It wouldn't let Ophelia in, sealed from the other side. But her hunch was right: the spell on the Rúnräd mirror was automatic, blocking off entry to those who were shrouded in dangerous levels of Corruption. It had sensed the waves of it coming from her body, the aftereffects of whatever was wrapped in that bundle in Claudius's room, and it locked her out.

Hamlet was doused in equal levels of Corruption.

But when I look at you, she'd said, *it's inside you, not outside, like the others. I wonder if the mirror will recognise it the same.*

His fingers slipped through the glass the way they once had in Wittenberg. He took a deep breath and steadied himself for the fall. And he entered the Otherland.

※

On the other side of the mirror, all was quiet. He was inside a tiny building, and this time there was no guard. It was very cold.

Outside, through the open maw of the doorway, he could see snow falling in thick clumps. Stars glimmered overhead. Time was not the same here, it seemed; wherever he was—Rúnräd, she had called it—it was the middle of the night.

Hurriedly, he pressed his fingers back through the other side. They went, and he breathed a sigh of relief that he was not trapped in this strange place.

Rúnräd was nothing like Nordsee. There was no bustling market. The air wasn't scented with the sweet, heady mixture of spices and wine, nor were lights strung everywhere to illuminate the warren-like streets. No high walls surrounded Rúnräd, no musicians played on every corner, no tavern spilled its customers out onto the street after a raucous evening.

Hamlet pulled his hood over his head and stepped out into the tiniest village he had ever seen. There were six or seven houses, none of them large enough to have more than two rooms. They were all situated in a large clearing in the middle of the forest, into which vanished four paths, one leading off in each cardinal direction.

Behind one of the houses was a large shape covered in an enormous stitched leather sheet: a boat. Apart from that, there was very little to see. Some silent, empty beehives; a coop, presumably for chickens or quail; a few more unremarkable outbuildings which gave nothing away as to their purpose.

So this was where Ophelia grew up. This was where she chose to spend her time, instead of in the winding halls of Kronborg looking for secret rooms and hidden treasure. He could see the charm in it, but he could not say he would have made the same decision.

Just as he looked around, searching for the house with the paintings of birds encircling the windows, a door swung open. The woman framed in the weak candlelight looked to be about his mother's age. She had black hair that hung beyond her waist and a pale, noble-looking face, with high cheekbones and deep-set eyes: eyes that were as pale as an opal, gleaming in the dark.

She pressed one long-fingered hand to her forehead.

"I could feel it from inside," she said. "What are you?"

Not who. *What.* Hamlet absent-mindedly pressed his hand against the bite mark on his chest. This woman, it seemed, was like Ophelia. She could see what lay within, and she did not like it one bit.

"I have a message from Ophelia," he called. He lowered his hood despite the snow, hoping this woman might see that he was not some kind of monster—just a man. "She can't come through the mirror. It won't let her in."

A rustle, then another woman emerged from the house. Tall, broad, with flyaway hair and the same set to her jaw Ophelia got when she was prepared to fight.

"Stay back, boy," said this woman, a little dangerously. "Stay where you are." A moment of recognition, and then a narrowing of the eyes. "I suppose you're the little prince."

He straightened his spine. "If you like," he said. "And you are?"

"Solveig," the dark-haired woman offered. "And Hilga. Ophelia's aunts. Tell me: is she well?"

He bent his head. "She's fine. But there's a lot you should know—things she wanted me to tell you."

Another door cracked open.

"Aaron, stay away," Hilga warned. "Solveig says the boy is drenched in Corruption."

"But the wards—"

"Kept Ophelia out, and let him through. Or so he says."

Solveig stepped barefoot into the snow. Hilga put a hand out and tried to stop her, but the other woman shook her away.

"Something has been done to you," said Solveig. Her eyes were two white pools, into which Hamlet could not stop staring. "Who did it? Who took it from you?"

Hamlet wanted to step away, but something stopped him. He felt rooted to the spot by her.

Her eyes, he realised, reminded her of Rosencrantz.

"Solveig," the man warned—Aaron. "Solveig, stay away from him. We don't know how he got through. He could be dangerous."

"You *should* stay away," Hamlet advised. "There's a disease spreading in Helsingør again. Ophelia says—she says it's 'like last time'." He shrugged. "I don't know what she means, but she said you would."

Aaron's lungs seemed to empty of breath. He pressed a hand to his doorway, brow furrowing above his glasses. But Solveig came closer, and her hand reached out to touch Hamlet's chest, just above the bite of the Corruption-creature.

His teeth chattered from the cold, and icy water soaked into his boots, but he didn't move. Solveig tilted her head, bird-like.

"No," she murmured to herself. "Nothing has been taken. Something has been placed."

He asked what she meant with a heavy tongue, but she didn't answer.

"Ophelia," Hilga called from the safe distance of the house. "Tell us of Ophelia and go, boy."

He reached into his pocket, wary of Solveig's proximity. Her hand dropped into the space between them, but she looked at him still, brow furrowed.

"She said to tell you… that the illness is back, that the men will still march." He scanned the hasty lines, trying to parse her frantic words. "Her wards… are disappearing faster than she can write them. She needs more powdered mandrake root and she wondered if you knew anything to treat the influenza, although she knows the answer is no."

Aaron laughed wetly, and Hamlet realised with a rush of hot embarrassment that the man was crying.

"The last thing," he said hurriedly, reading over the final line. "She asked if you could tell us anything about 'the man who took his lover's heart'." He frowned. "She said it's very important."

"I knew it," Hilga said. "Solveig, get away from him!"

"The boy's done nothing," Solveig said over her shoulder, sharply. "Your uncle is Claudius, is he not?"

He nodded, once, sharply. Solveig once again turned her pale eyes on him. Whatever it was she was searching for, she must have found it: she opened her mouth, and she began to speak.

Once, there was a man. He did many terrible things in his life. He used magic too powerful for him and he came to rely on it, until one day he realised that he was dying. No spell could cure him, only slow his demise, for the Corruption was embedded in him and nothing would remove it now.

He had a wife who had never known another soul. He kept her locked in a room with all that she needed to live and she never saw the sun, and because she knew nothing else, she thought she loved him. When she saw that he was dying, she was distraught. She knew no life apart from him. How would she live?

She asked her husband, when he came to visit her, weak and sickly and rotting from the inside out, if there was anything she could do to help him live.

He did not wait to answer. The man stabbed his wife in the belly, cut out her beating heart, and gripped it in both hands.

"*Quod tuum est, meum est*," the man said. What is yours is mine.

The heart, once lively and healthy, began to shrivel. He poured all the Corruption of his own rotten heart into her innocent flesh, and he felt his own chest grow lighter, his legs stronger, and his mind more evil.

He kept the borrowed heart somewhere safe, for until both hearts were destroyed, the man could not die.

"It's treason," Hamlet hissed, "to accuse my uncle of this."

"Ophelia believes it is truth. Perhaps it's both."

Solveig reached out again, this time to touch his cheek, but Hamlet flinched back. He was cold and wet and yet his skin burned with an internal fire he could not, would, not, stamp out.

There was a sizzling noise: where he stood, the snow melted in a perfect circle.

"May I give you some advice, Prince Hamlet?" Solveig looked at him long and hard with her eerily pale eyes, and again he had the distinct recollection of squirming beneath Rosencrantz's gaze. "Leave Helsingør. Don't come back, not for a long time. Stay far from magic and hope that whatever you have rotting inside you dies, and it does not take you with it."

This was not an option, and so Hamlet turned and walked away. Back through the mirror, back into the castle, back into his chambers where he could change mechanically into dry clothes and, eventually, he could climb down onto the floor and sit, staring, until someone came to retrieve him for dinner.

SCENE SEVEN
ophelia

Rain lashed against the castle walls for three days without stopping. It was a constant downpour, sheets of water falling from a sky that shook with rolling thunder. In some ways, it was nice: it was easier to pretend that staying inside, sequestered from each other, was a choice due to weather rather than due to a rapidly-spreading sickness.

Four people in the castle had died of it now, and there would be more. This was just the first wave of illness, the people who caught it first, the ones more susceptible. Ophelia stayed in her chambers and sewed herself a little green bag, which she decorated with glass beads and yellow thread. She tucked all of her sewing supplies inside, and she did her best not to think about anything other than the task at hand.

Every night she heard Father come in from meetings of the king's council, which were continuing despite the situation in the castle. He and Laertes sat together in rickety chairs by the fire, talking about numbers and figures, routes and roads, the right way to fletch an arrow. They never spoke about the war directly, or whether they thought Denmark would win or lose. They focused on the figures.

The third night of rain, Father returned in an unusually optimistic mood. Ophelia, who was rearranging the dried flowers that hung from her ceiling beam for the fifth time in as many hours, could hear him humming as he kicked off his boots. He sighed as he sank into his favourite chair, and inwardly, she smiled: he was so predictable.

"Still not coming out, Ophelia?" he called.

She answered in the negative.

"Goodness gracious," Father said, the same way he had for three days now. "You're young and healthy! Spare a thought for this old man who only wants to see his daughter's face."

She went to the door and opened it a crack, peeking through. "Are you happy now?"

"Much improved." He offered her a platter, on which was a little pile of her favourite treats. "I thought these might help your condition."

She tiptoed out of the room and accepted the tray. "I think I can come out now. It's been three days, and I'm fine."

"I don't think you've been afflicted with this mysterious illness," Father said, and pointed her to the chair where Laertes usually sat. She perched there, nibbling at an almond cake. The honey glaze melted on her tongue, filling her mouth with sweetness.

They sat together in contented silence for a few moments. Father had someone come and light the fire, and Ophelia tucked her feet out of the way so that the servant could get on their hands and knees to do it. She ate her way through several cakes before it was lit, and had several more while Father read over correspondence and muttered under his breath.

"Money," he complained. "When you're old and grey like me, Ophelia, all anyone ever wants to talk about is money. And there really is nothing else to be bothered with, that's the problem. That's why a man must make a fortune in their youth—in hopes of better conversations in old age. That's what I say."

"And how am I going to make my fortune?" Ophelia asked. "Maybe I'll become an adventurer, or a scholar, or join a pirate crew—"

There was a crash as the door flung open and hit the wall. Father shouted, "O-*ho!*" and practically leapt out of his seat, which made Ophelia jump far more than the slamming of the door.

"I need to speak with you," said Laertes, addressing Ophelia. "Urgently."

"This clattering about isn't the behaviour of a noble person, Laertes!" Father scolded, red in the face from embarrassment. "It is buffoonery. A man should be patient, and cautious in his movements. He should think his actions through and have restraint in everything he does, except in battle, when he should—"

"Father, this is a wonderful lesson for another time." Laertes scowled in a very ignoble way. "Ophelia, now."

Ophelia rose from her chair, put the platter of cakes down, and brushed a few crumbs from her skirt. There was a bead loose on her bodice, which she plucked at, and a hair on her shoulder, which she removed. She took her slippers off and put them back on again. She found another crumb, which she plucked from the fabric with the same caution a surgeon might use to remove shrapnel from a wound.

Ignoring Father's protests and blustering, she followed Laertes out into the corridor and closed the door behind them. She folded her arms across her chest, ready to tell him off for being so overdramatic.

"Prince Hamlet," Laertes hissed, "went through the mirror. He's been to Rúnräd, and Aunt Hilga is not happy."

Ophelia did her best to look surprised. "Goodness," she said. "Is the mirror-way open again, then? We can go through?"

"You sent him through the mirror," Laertes said, leaning so close they were nose-to-nose. "Ophelia, have you gone entirely insane? You sent a prince who is riddled with Corruption to our home?"

For a moment, all she latched onto was *our home*: rarely did Laertes acknowledge Rúnräd as anything other than the place their other family lived. It was not home to him, even though he was older than her. It was the place Mother was from, the place they went sometimes to get away from the castle. That was all.

She was overwhelmed with the urge to throw her arms around him. Then, her nostrils flared as she processed the rest of what he had said.

"I had no other choice. I needed to tell Hilga something important about Claudius, and I needed someone to go straight away—"

"Me!" Laertes nearly shouted, spinning away in fury, arms cast into the air like a ragdoll tossed at the far wall. "God's blood, Ophelia, why didn't you just ask *me?*"

That was a very good question, and one for which she had no answer. The only thing she had to say was that she hadn't thought to ask, and it was better to say nothing at all than to admit that she'd thought of Hamlet before her own brother.

But he read it in her eyes, and she saw that it wounded him. Laertes turned his back on her, his body taut as a bowstring. When he looked back, he was as open-faced and vulnerable as a child.

"You never even thought to ask," he said. "You endangered our entire family, everyone we've ever known, to send a prince who knows nothing through that mirror. He didn't even believe Corruption was real until a few damned days ago! They opened the way for us! Because they are willing to sacrifice their safety so that we have somewhere to go! And you are incapable of asking for help!"

She looked up and down the hall before she risked speaking. "Listen: I sent him because he was there in

Claudius's chambers," she hissed. "He saw what I saw: a monster made of Corruption."

"But you saw something else," Laertes said. "Something you didn't tell me. You saw a heart."

Footsteps approached; Laertes leaned as casually as he could against the wall, and Ophelia folded her arms demurely in front of her. Some nameless courtier drifted past, clearly deep in their cups, and when their footsteps had faded away Ophelia and Laertes resumed their former positions.

There was no way to explain away what had happened: that she had not thought to ask Laertes, that she had sent for Hamlet first when she was in a panic, that she had trusted him to help her above her brother. But the entire argument frustrated her: there was more to worry about than who went through the mirror.

There were monsters made of Corruption in this castle, and a disease spread through the halls, and Hamlet's heart was practically beating out of his chest, and that was not to mention the very real heart undoubtedly hidden in some other secretive, safe spot in the castle, moved from its previous comfortable lodgings.

What was the point in wasting energy on petty arguments? It seemed utterly infantile, all of a sudden, to even be having this conversation. Soon Laertes would leave for war, and Hamlet would not. Hamlet would be here to help her dispose of Claudius and his evil magic; Laertes would be gone, fighting his own battles in western Denmark.

She told her brother all of this, trying hard to keep her voice from shaking with anger and with fear.

She didn't expect his eyes to soften with something that looked a lot like pity.

"You don't know," Laertes said.

Her heart stilled in her chest.

"He's coming on the march," Laertes said. "So Prince Hamlet won't be here to help you, Ophelia. You'll have to do this on your own."

Laertes was a very powerful young man. He was broad in the shoulders with the lean build of a fencer, the kind of tell-tale tendon-strings in his arms that spoke of long hours training with a sword and a bow. He was not, by any means, unfit, and he would likely have considered himself one of the strongest men of his cohort in Kronborg.

Nevertheless, he couldn't hold Ophelia back when she stormed across the castle and down the steps to Hamlet's chambers. All he could do was follow in her wake, half-jogging, occasionally pulling at her shoulder and begging her all the while to stop what she was doing and come back, for God's sake.

Ophelia shook him off and walked faster. The men she knew, she had decided, had a number of flaws they almost all shared. Chief among them was a constant desire to throw themselves headlong into danger for no discernible reason other than that it might look impressive to some distant onlooker. This onlooker would inevitably see their name on a scroll of the dead and wonder how such a strapping young man could have died so tragically.

However, in this situation Ophelia was the onlooker, and she had no intentions of mourning quietly at this particular funeral.

She walked straight past the guards at the prince's door, who were so accustomed to the Kronborg rumour mill that they didn't even flinch. Laertes followed her in, apologising all the way.

Hamlet was sprawled on his bed reading some kind of philosophical tract by candlelight. He sat up, bleariness transforming into wariness before her eyes.

"You are not," she said dangerously, "joining the march. Do you understand me quite clearly?"

Hamlet set his book aside and stood up.

In an equally dangerous tone, Hamlet said, "Your aunt told me an interesting story about hearts. I can't say I found the implications pleasing."

She didn't mean to do it, or she did, but she hadn't thought it through. It was not planned. Her hand simply raised itself from her side and smacked Hamlet clean across the face with a sound that echoed like a crack of thunder. Hamlet stumbled backwards and sat down on the edge of the bed, more from shock than the force of the blow.

There was an eerie stillness. Hamlet touched his cheek, fingers tracing the edges of a bright red mark. He looked, wide-eyed, up at Ophelia. His eyes seemed to ask her what she had done, and she was asking herself the very same thing.

The rain continued to hammer down and the fire crackled, and for a long moment, Ophelia could think of nothing but the way Hamlet prodded his own skin, feeling for the edges of the wound.

"For God's sake," Laertes said, and perhaps for the first time, Ophelia realised the gravity of the situation. She had thought she understood, but faced with Laertes's furious face, Hamlet sprawled on the bed with his Corrupted heart twisting, something dug its nails into her spinal cord and pulled. "For God's sake, this is bigger than us."

He meant it in every sense: the slap, and the silence, and the war raging outside the walls. Ophelia took a step backwards, hand reaching for her own cheek, a startled mirror-image. She felt, as if it was happening again, the sting of her father's hand across her cheek the day she and Hamlet were caught. She felt again the horror, as if it would burst out of her chest, of having trusted and having that trust shattered.

Hamlet cleared his throat. "What do you mean?" His voice came out hoarse, and his eyes did not settle on Laertes, but darted around the room as if looking for somewhere to rest.

"For once in your life, just try to accept that you aren't the centre of the universe," he snapped. "And I mean that for both of you. This isn't about your star-crossed love affair, and it isn't about finding some kind of happy ending. This is about the survival of Denmark. It might even be about more than that. This is about making sure we don't all die of a plague."

"And you do that," Hamlet said, a shadow of his previous fury crossing his face, "by accusing my uncle of treason? That's how you save Denmark?"

Laertes was looking at her, and Ophelia could not stop thinking about the collision of her palm with a cool cheekbone, about the sound of flesh against flesh, of bloodied hearts and mirrors.

She watched the next words brew in Hamlet's mind. She knew his face and all its myriad expressions, but this one was new to her. There was something cold in his eyes that she'd never seen before: the heat of fury was replaced with ice, with a freezing distance, with a wall she could not hope to climb.

His blue eyes were, in a moment, the eyes of a stranger, and his left cheek bloomed red with the mark of her palm, and the way he looked at her nearly killed her. She wanted, desperately, to cry.

"If this ends with you asking me to kill my uncle," Hamlet said, "you might as well leave now. Because I was with you all the way, Ophelia, but I can't follow you if that's where this path leads. Laertes is right: this is bigger than us. This is about Denmark, and my family is Denmark. They come first."

There was nothing else to say to that, really.

She left, and she managed to hold her tears in until they reached the halfway point of the stairs. Laertes held her silently as she cried against his chest. There were no words for this, for what felt like the ending of the only constant she saw for her future.

It was sudden and sharp and blurry enough that it might not be an ending, not really. But she couldn't help but to feel, in her heart, like whatever she and Prince Hamlet had had was over. She wasn't ready to say goodbye.

But, she thought bitterly, this was bigger than her. And even if it felt like her heart was breaking, she had a job to do.

She would just have to do it alone.

SCENE EIGHT
hamlet

Mother screamed at him when Hamlet told her he was going to war, but Father patted him on the back and sent for someone to make a new winter cloak, one suited to the long journey west. He took to riding every morning to build up his strength for the journey, and he became very good at performing an emergency dismount with a blinding headache. He rode out to the forest often, and would stand and stare at himself in the mirror in the little shack until his eyes blurred.

The days melded together, a mélange of riding and eating and sleeping and pacing, of reading without seeing, of setting little curls of paper on fire because he could. The magic in his belly roiled less frequently, but that made things worse: he worried that his tenuous, novice grip on magic was slipping already, and found himself calling on it four or five times a day.

Often, he tried to do things he'd seen Rosencrantz do, but those tricks never worked. He couldn't hold a bubble of water in the air for minutes at a time, nor could he create a cloud of constellations between his palms or make the air smell of roses. All his body knew to do, it seemed, was light fires.

He didn't know why it latched onto that: perhaps it had something to do with that story Rosencrantz once told him. *Fortinbras regularly blasts fire out of every pore*, he'd said, with a poisonous wryness to the words. What was it that he'd said? That Fortinbras would not hesitate to use that power against Denmark, if that was all it came down to.

Maybe that was it: some deep-rooted issue in his psyche connected to that monstrous feeling that constantly rooted around in his ribs. The same feeling that made him get on his knees before Prince Fortinbras of Norway, that made him beg for something he could not name. The same thing that made him flinch from Nathan, that drew him to that stableboy.

His body, for whatever reason, bound itself to flame. He drew on that well and he learned to control it, to some extent: to understand which part of his body would burn.

He brought spare clothes with him any time he left the castle, in case he might burn the ones he had.

He looked for Ophelia, and he did not find her. The court grew bored of the disease and re-emerged, only to hide away again when another bout of influenza took hold and, in one week, the three youngest pages in the castle succumbed to the illness.

In the absence of court dinners or taverns with friends or long evenings spent with Ophelia, Hamlet went to the library. It was reliably quiet apart from a monk called Brother Leo who took care of the books and could usually be found painstakingly copying, by hand, whatever interesting new volume he had secured.

Brother Leo was the only Catholic monk left in the city of Helsingør, and that was only because he hardly spoke Danish, and no one had the heart to explain in broken English or schoolboy Latin that he needed to leave and never return. Brother Leo seemed content to sit in the same corner of the library every day, and Prince Hamlet sat in the other, so that they were as far apart as physically possible. He couldn't see the monk from his habitual seat. He could only hear him: the infrequent turning of a page, an occasional cough, the sound of a quill-tip against an ink bottle.

Hamlet pulled a book on occultism off the shelves, and he began to read. He read throughout all of those days the court emerged from their rooms, and he read throughout all the ones they retreated back to safety. The books, however, were of no use. None of them spoke of magic the way Ophelia did, the way Rosencrantz did. He tried all their spells and they did nothing.

Nothing strengthened his sword-arm as promised. Nothing took his fear away, nor did it make him faster or better with a bow or less likely to come unseated on his horse. And he needed all of these things, because truth be told, he was terrified out of his mind.

He researched late into the night, searching for something that might make him braver, brighter, more brilliant. But there was no spell in these books that could do that for him, it seemed.

On the ninth day of trying and failing, Claudius told him they were going to march soon, before the days could get any darker, while the unseasonal warmth had turned soft snow to thick globules of rain. Hamlet, privately, couldn't stop thinking about the risk of taking horses over hard-packed slush and snow, their hooves sliding on ice, but he said nothing. His uncle, for all his flaws, knew the ways of war.

Hamlet felt nauseous. He felt weak, and impotent, and alone.

And so, he wrote a letter.

The messenger must have reached Wittenberg in record time, because Prince Hamlet was being introduced to his squire for the first time when the reply came. He dismissed the boy—who was distressingly only three years his junior, but it felt like far more—and unfolded the letter with shaking hands.

He sank onto the edge of the bed, trying to steady his breathing. For a moment, he was horribly embarrassed: he remembered the hastily-written scrawl of his initial letter, that whining, begging tone, the requests he had made.

The reply was short and to-the-point, just four words.

Kolding. See you there.

But the plans went awry before they ever got off the ground, and the word went around that the march was being delayed. Hamlet breathed a sigh of relief, but the temporary respite was not to last: every day came with the possibility that they would be told to dress and saddle the horses.

Men arrived in the city to fight, more and more each day, and they became restless. The temporary camp outside Helsingør expanded its borders until getting to the forest required riding through it, and Hamlet had no real reason to do so. He stayed within sight of Kronborg when he went out and he kept to himself.

Fights broke out and were settled; his father was tied up from dawn until dusk, mediating between soldiers or discussing donations of bread to the hospital, whose beds were rapidly filling up. Soon, the poor would have to be accommodated elsewhere, and that was another of his father's problems to solve.

Mother was equally busy: now that it was wartime, officially, she ran the household with a firmer hand. She analysed the account ledgers until the wee hours of the morning, and she wrote correspondence to Denmark's most respected families every morning. She even inspected the kitchens one day and gave all the servants a fright.

Hamlet, however, found himself at a loose end. He was hanging in the balance, waiting for the order to march, unable to act on anything else. In his brief snatches of time with his parents, they tried to offer him tasks: Mother suggested he write to a variety of important sons of important fathers; Father asked him to sit on this committee, to research this subject.

But he could not act, try as he might. His limbs were frozen. He moved through the world like the air was made of treacle. Nothing was fast enough for him. He also felt, bizarrely, like the world flowed around his limbs, like he was sitting in the eye of a storm. He was a part of life and not, an observer inside a glass orb but also keenly, desperately aware of everything going on outside.

This was not the first time he'd felt this way, betrayed by his own body's refusal to act. He got out of bed every day without trouble, fed himself, and kept himself clean and tidy. Apart from that, he did nothing but sit in the library or pace the gardens or, for reasons he couldn't explain, sit in the dim silence of the chapel and wait for some bolt of inspiration to strike.

When word from Odense finally arrived, Hamlet was already having a terrible day. Nathan had not appeared for his duties that morning, and it transpired that he was sick with the flu and couldn't rise from his bed. The rumour in the air was that they would march the following day, and Hamlet hadn't seen Ophelia in two weeks, although he'd seen Laertes the previous day and failed to ignore his look of scorn.

The first clue that something was wrong was when a messenger approached Kronborg on horseback. Hamlet, who was out for his morning ride, this time accompanied by Barnardo, approached with caution: the messenger threw a scroll to him, eyes rolling back, and slid from his horse. When he and Barnardo returned to the castle with the (somewhat revived) messenger in tow, the scroll was taken into a private meeting of the Rigsråd. Hamlet was not invited to join them.

He had just bathed and changed his clothes when the summons did eventually come: the court was to convene in the hall, where important news would be shared. For a few moments, he wondered if this was peace—a surrender, or an offer? But the messenger wore no Norwegian flag, and there was no formal seal on his scroll, so it seemed unlikely. He quashed the selfish thought, put his shoes on, and went downstairs.

He stood at the back wall behind his father, looking out over the heads of everyone else. Father was taking an awfully long time to start talking. He just sat on his throne, looking out at the crowd. Not looking over them, like Hamlet tried to do: looking at them, in the eyes, like he was trying to see into their souls.

His stomach gave a lurch: there was Ophelia entering the room, her brother by her side. His focus turned entirely to her. They were deep in conversation, Ophelia and Laertes, and he could see from here that she was questioning, her hands motioning the words, her forehead crinkling. Wondering why they were all here, more than likely. He was wondering the same thing.

He turned his attention back to a distant point on the opposite wall, and tried to ignore the very bad feeling beginning to grow in his gut.

There was no fanfare. Father cleared his throat and the room fell quiet, an audience hungry for news of the world outside. He saw people cut off their greetings but nudge one another, saw secret, half-hidden smiles. Many of them had not seen their friends in weeks, emerging for the first time from bouts of illness or a quarantine or both. He also heard a lot of coughing and sniffling and blowing of noses, which did not bode particularly well.

"I have kept much from you," said his father, "and I cannot apologise for it. There is something that happens when a man is made king: he is rendered the sword of his people, but also the shield. I have tried to wield both with accuracy. But the time is right for the shield to be lowered. Now, you must understand the force of the blow we have been dealt."

Hamlet eyed the back of the throne and wondered if it would be a good place to get sick.

"You know of Fladstrand and how it fell to the Norwegian invaders. Some of you will know of Aalborg, of the resistance they raised, of how it was quashed. Aalborg, Hjørring, Tårs; all fought bravely, all have surrendered.

"Here is what I have kept from you: the Norwegian force split into two. One army was led by servants of the king; the other by his son, Prince Arion Fortinbras."

Hamlet's stomach clenched, as something icy cold trickled down his spine, like the fire inside him had been doused with freezing water.

"We expected the force to continue southwards towards Fredericia, where they might gather their strength. This, they did—except the force led by Prince Arion, who sailed to Sejerø at an uncommon speed and overcame our people there, then carried on to Saltbæk."

Sejerø—an island off the coast, barely defended. It was in the Kattegat Sea, small and defensively useless. Except now. He wondered over his Father's words, the 'uncommon speed' of the approach: magic, skill, or just pure luck?

Sejerø was small, tactically a strange choice. But, as his father's words echoed in the horrible silence, Hamlet realised the wisdom of the decision. A small, carefully chosen group of soldiers could easily take a place like Sejerø in a matter of a day. The island was hardly inhabited. It had few links to the mainland. A takeover was easy, and more importantly, could go unnoticed for a few days; from there, more Norwegians could join them. They could stealthily collect themselves and make their way to the mainland. They could launch a brutal surprise attack.

"When they had gathered enough men, this small skirmish force sailed for the mainland, advanced south and intercepted the men sent to fight our cause by the barons of Funen. Their losses were severe, and they retreated with their tails between their legs, but we lost many of our best fighters, and a great many more are wounded."

Father rose from his seat. Hamlet watched him, then watched the crowd: how their chins rose a few almost imperceptible millimetres to watch the king's expression, how they stood a little taller as he raised himself up. Hamlet had always thought there was something of stagecraft to his father's role, and this, he believed, was the most important performance of a great actor's career: to counsel his people through their despair and to coach them not to anger but to righteous fury; to bring out their rage, their sorrow, and their sacrifice and transform it into something that Denmark could used on a battlefield against its enemies.

Father spoke of duty and of honour. He spoke of the boy Arion Fortinbras once was, the boy many of them knew from his short time at the Danish court; then he spoke of a killer, a villain, a miscreant who refused to fight with honour and would not follow the commands of his own father, the king of Norway. He painted Fortinbras, luridly, as a barbarian prince, a youthful rogue, a cruel, cold-hearted beast of a man.

In a few lines, Prince Arion Fortinbras was made the chief enemy of Denmark, and that, Hamlet thought, was one of the most spectacular feats of fantasy he had ever seen enacted on the stage.

Because Fortinbras could not be the man his father painted him to be—was not, he reminded himself. Fortinbras was kind. He was clever. He had handed Hamlet the keys to a different world on the weight of a promise, and he had seen Hamlet's greatest shame and raised him up despite it. Had forgiven it, even.

And yet, some things were true. Arion was somewhere in Denmark, in Hamlet's country, with a crown and an army and a sword at his hip. He was somewhere, his bright, bold face smeared with dirt and Danish blood, the hollows of his cheeks brought out by army rations—there was no world, Hamlet believed, in which Arion Fortinbras ate roast pork while his soldiers starved.

Was Horatio with him too? His nameless second-in-command, written in shadow because of an ordinary birth and a suspect faith? What was he doing? Was his sword wet with Danish blood too?

He remembered a garden, the gleam of sunlight, the weight of the eyes of strangers. *I think they're watching us to see what peace between our nations could look like.*

Uncle Claudius was speaking now, addressing a thinning crowd. Everyone was leaving, everyone except the men between the ages of sixteen and sixty, the ones who had agreed, implicitly by their birth and sex, to go and fight on some faraway battlefield. The words felt dream-like.

Hamlet was imagining running Arion Fortinbras through with his sword: the pressure that it would take to sink a blade through tense skin and tight-knit muscle, to find a spot where the metal would not be impeded by bone. The give, when finally the fibres of muscle and flesh tore apart and the weapon would sink into a medley of organs and blood.

If I die because of Fortinbras and his magic, I'll never forgive myself. And if Fortinbras dies because of me, I won't forgive myself either. So what am I to do?

He replayed it over and over in his head: the splash of viscera and how it would mark his armour, how he would take the breastplate off at the end of a battle and find the clothes beneath smeared and stained despite it, because blood, he knows from the stories, can find its way into any crack or crevice.

He felt sick. His eyes burned with tears. He noticed, in the muscles of his arms, a clenching, like they were practising for the real thing.

"What are you waiting for?"

His uncle slapped him hard on the back, jolting him back to reality. Hamlet blinked away visions of mud and salt. The hall was almost empty, only a few stragglers. He had missed his uncle's entire speech.

"Get your armour on, boy," his uncle said. "Wear the finery now; you can change on the other side of the trees. Better not to attract too much attention, hmm?"

It was the most his uncle had spoken to him since the incident with the Corruption-monster. Hamlet looked at him, speechless and wordless: they had almost the same pattern of flecks in their eyes, he realised, despite their differing colour.

Claudius squeezed his arm, not forcefully.

"It is forgotten," he said, like he knew just what event Hamlet was thinking of. "When all this is over, I will explain it to you. But not yet."

It was not until his uncle's footsteps had vanished, leaving the prince alone in the hall, that he thought to ask what all this meant: the war, or the magic, or both?

SCENE NINE
ophelia

Ophelia tried to pull away from Alessandra's grip, but the other woman's firm grasp on her wrist was relentless. They had left the hall even before the king's speech was finished, before Ophelia could even process the words being spoken. Alessandra tugged her out into the hall, the servants closing the door quickly and quietly behind them.

"What are you doing?" Ophelia hissed as Alessandra released her. She rubbed her wrist. "That *hurt*."

"Come with me."

"What... Come with you where?"

Alessandra bit her lip. "Firenze," she said: an admission. She was not just leaving: she was fleeing. "Ophelia, darling, come with me. Imagine how lovely it would be! You could meet my mother, my sisters... I know several young men who would be very intrigued to meet you. Won't you join me?"

Alessandra didn't look like herself. Her face was very pale, and her beautiful eyes were wide with panic. She reminded Ophelia of the horses when they came in from a hard ride, sweat wicking their skin.

Alessandra was not well.

"Why don't we go and sit down somewhere?" Ophelia tried. "I need to think. It's a lovely offer, and so kind, but we should talk about it."

Alessandra was not coughing, not choking, but she was sick, and the Corruption rolled off her in waves. Ophelia had no idea if removing any of it would help, but she'd tried it with the people she'd treated in those first few days. Half of them had died. The other half had recovered.

"We should go soon," Alessandra whispered, mostly to herself. She brought her beautiful, elegant hands up to her face and stared at them like she had never seen them before. "My mother says she always knows by the nails. My nails are dull and brittle now: look."

She thrust her hands out: Ophelia took them and pretended to inspect them. The nails were dull: it looked like Alessandra had been biting them. Gently, she brushed the pad of her own thumb across her friend's knuckles.

"We need to speak to Lorenz, surely. He will arrange it all—"

This was the wrong thing to say. Alessandra began to sob: it came over her in an instant, the tears bubbling up from where they clearly lay just under the surface. Her friend—her wonderful, fashionable friend, who did everything with one eye on the court—sank to her knees and cried like a child.

Ophelia dropped down to join her, hurriedly tucking her skirts under her so she could sit. She touched Alessandra's veil, her shoulders, her cheeks. Her forehead burned.

"Oh, Ophelia," Alessandra sobbed. "I didn't want to tell you… I was afraid, I thought you would hate me…"

"I could never hate you," she murmured.

Alessandra's fever-bright eyes met Ophelia's. Her hands went to her belly.

"I am with child," she whispered. "We tried to avoid it, but now I am, and Lorenz is going away. He cannot stay—he asked the king, and the king said no." She took a deep, gasping breath. "I am alone, Ophelia. My entire family is in Firenze. I must go to them."

"You can't travel like that, surely?" Ophelia whispered. She racked her brains for the little she knew of pregnancy. "Alessandra, what if something happens on the way?

It's too long a journey, it'll take weeks, and how on earth will you come all the way back with a baby?"

"That is why I am asking you." Alessandra touched Ophelia's cheek. "I know, Ophelia. I have seen you—marking the walls with symbols and treating the sick with powders and poultices. I've heard you whisper strange things in Latin. I *know*."

The Otherland hung between them, an enormous unspoken idea. Ophelia tried to find the words: *is it your home too?* Suddenly Alessandra's idea of travelling all the way to Firenze made more sense. There were faster ways to travel in the Otherland, and the world was smaller. You could get from one place to another in half the time, if you found the right ship, the right carriage.

"You're a healer, aren't you?" Alessandra whispered. "A witch."

Cold shot through Ophelia's chest. Witch was not a word her family used, not ever. But maybe it was different, in whatever part of the Otherland Alessandra was used to. Maybe witch was a good thing, and not utterly damning.

"Tell me, Ophelia," Alessandra said, desperate. "You must know ways of making the passage easier: herbs for the sickness, something to stop the baby coming early. I can pay handsomely, and we can stop as many times as you need, to gather what you wish. There are places in Firenze with healers like you—perhaps you can set up a shop, be independent, run a business. You would love it!"

"Stop," Ophelia heard herself say. "No, Alessandra, you've got it wrong—I don't know what you saw, but that isn't—that's not correct."

Alessandra knew nothing of magic, real magic. That much was apparent. But she had still seen Ophelia, seen enough to join the right dots together to come to this conclusion.

Ignorance was more dangerous than knowledge. In this moment, Ophelia would have taken another run-in with Claudius's Corruption-creature, rather than face the eyes of an ordinary woman who thought she knew something about magic.

Alessandra looked at her, long and hard.

"You will not come with me?"

Ophelia shook her head mutely. There were no words: only sheer panic.

The doors to the hall opened and Alessandra sprang up. She brushed off her beautiful skirts. Her tears were entirely dry, not a trace left behind.

"Well," Alessandra said, and there was the proud tilt to her chin again, the steely look. Except now, they were levelled at Ophelia. "I know what I saw. I will tell no one, but I will say this: you think you understand this court, but you are wrong."

"Alessandra, I can't come with you––I don't know what else to say," she said desperately, glancing at the open doorway.

"I have tried to help you, but I see that our friendship ends here. I could take you away from this––but you will stay because you cannot abandon your little prince."

"I can't abandon my family and my home to run away to Firenze with you and be your––your nursemaid!"

"I have tried to warn you about the dangers of this infatuation. I have tried to be a friend to you, and you have never reciprocated, never sacrificed, never given me a moment if your *beloved* Prince Hamlet needed you!"

"Alessandra, I'm sorry, I never meant to make you feel––"

"What has he promised you?" Alessandra asked. There were tears in her eyes, pleading tears. Ophelia hated the very sight of them. "Did he promise that you'll be queen? If he truly loved you, my darling, do you not think he'd promise you something more realistic? To leave his position? To abdicate? But no, he promises something he does not have the power to give you without his family's permission, and that will never happen as long as they draw breath."

Ophelia looked around, shaken. "Please, speak quietly," she hissed. Alessandra's eyes felt like a brand, scorching through her.

"I want you to be happy, dear," Alessandra whispered in the tense silence that followed. "And I do not see happiness if your future is with him. I do not see a friendship between us either, if you will not help me."

Ophelia tore herself away, anger and embarrassment tearing through her. "Focus on your own future," she managed, in a quavering voice, "and I will focus on mine."

She stayed in the chapel for hours. It was empty. It would fill up, when the men had marched out, but for now her peers were spending their last hours with their loved ones. She should be with Laertes. She knew that, and yet she knelt and looked at a rough-hewn, simple crucifix, and she prayed for someone to tell her what to do next.

She felt him before she saw him: the weight of his steps, the sound of his breathing. She knew him like she knew herself, knew his face like looking in a mirror. Hamlet knelt beside her.

The muffled sounds of the castle found their way into the heavy darkness. It all sounded so normal: hurried footsteps, the clatter of a tray, a door slammed in a distant corridor. A child cried, and a woman's voice hushed it, soothed them back into quiet.

Hamlet said, in a rough voice, "Doubt thou the stars are fire."

She stared straight ahead. Her eyes welled with sudden tears. "Doubt that the sun doth move."

"Doubt truth to be a liar," he said, and his hands left their clasped prayer position by his chest, by his Corrupted heart. She shivered when he touched her. The heat of his hand seared the juncture of her neck and her shoulder.

"But never doubt I love," she finished, and she reached up to entangle their fingers.

His head leaned to rest on her shoulder, his curls pressing against her cheek.

"I was meant to put my armour on an hour ago," he said dully.

"Why haven't you?"

He turned his face into her skin, shook his head against her shoulder. "Makes it real."

She tried to cry silently, but she shook and then she was being held, her head against his chest. He hushed her as she buried her fingers in his shirt and sobbed. She wanted to tell him about Alessandra; she wanted to tell him about every morning for the last three weeks, about what she'd eaten, what she'd worn, about the birds she heard singing through the rain that morning.

She could tell he was doing the same thing. They were holding back, both of them, and she didn't know how to bridge this gap anymore. The only way forward was through to their separate destinies: his on the battlefield, hers at home. And her destiny seemed to involve killing his uncle, which she didn't foresee as something that might bring them back together.

I can't follow you if that's where this path leads.

"I don't think I can say goodbye," she whispered.

"Then we won't."

She swallowed hard against the lump in her throat.

"I should go," Ophelia said. "I should find Laertes."

They both stood. It was awkward, neither of them quite sure what to do with their hands. Ophelia genuflected on her way out of the chapel. Hamlet sauntered ahead, but it was put-on, falsely arrogant. They stepped out into the hall. Ophelia blinked furiously against the sudden influx of lamplight.

They looked at one another.

"I should put my armour on," he said.

"I'll be outside. In the courtyard, I mean." She swallowed. "I'll wave."

He ducked his head in acknowledgement, but he did not meet her eyes. She drank him in once more: the dark curls over his forehead, those stormy eyes. She wanted to see once more the shape of his mouth when he smiled. She was afraid that, even if he returned, he might leave those smiles behind on the battlefield.

It was Hamlet who left first. She watched him go with an empty, numb, anticlimactic sort of feeling; and then she went to find her brother.

The evening's gathering was a show, a performance. Gilded armour, decorative swords, glorious horses snorting in the cold air: all of this showed their wealth, their strength, the glory of Denmark. It was still early, and it would be dark for some hours yet. The rising sun hadn't even touched its paintbrush to the sky.

The king mounted his enormous brown destrier. He called something out and the men began to fall into line. Laertes gave Ophelia a hug, pressed her painfully tight to his metal chestplate.

"I love you," he said. "I'll be safe. Good luck."

He looked meaningfully at Claudius.

Ophelia's eyes burned with tears. Saying goodbye to Laertes when he went to Paris was bad enough. She'd cried for days. And now here he was, returned to her and leaving again, all armoured up and gleaming like a hero from a story.

"Be careful," she whispered, but that was all she could get out without bursting into tears. He gave her a fleeting hug and left. She got the sense that he, too, wasn't sure what to say.

Hamlet stood with his father and uncle in a beautiful set of armour decorated with gold flowers and vines. He was eye-catching. His sickly thinness was transformed into lithe power with the help of a full casing of metal, and a silver circlet gleamed in his hair. His uncle, dressed in court clothes, looked small and narrow beside him. Old King Hamlet, dressed in cold, unadorned steel, held a battleaxe like one might hold a child.

There was a boring and painful speech by Hal's father, which seemed to go on unceasingly for hours, announcing that his brother Prince Claudius would be his regent in his absence, which was a thought that filled Ophelia with brittle hope: maybe Claudius would be too weighed down with paperwork to do anything else.

With half-hearted fanfare, the king gave the order to march. The men turned as one—but their loyalty didn't overcome their need for goodbyes, and soon the ranks were all out of order as people reached over one another and clambered to hug their loved ones, to take a token with them to remember them by.

Most of the men here were on horseback, and the grooms came out in streams leading horse after horse, sweating with the exertion of running to and from the stables. The flagstones were smeared with hay and horse shit by the time they left, and the snow melted from the heat of hundreds of bodies.

A glint of gold: that was Laertes swinging up onto his horse, a much more sensible rouncey, uglier than Hamlet's steed but twice as useful. Ophelia felt a sudden rush of resolve. She clambered to get a foothold on a nearby column and pushed herself up, so that she was a head taller than any of the other ladies.

She waved wildly, tears streaking down her cheeks.

When they had left, she stayed in the courtyard. The grooms came with their brushes and cleaned up the dung and straw. More came with buckets and started to scrub the stones clean, dousing the ground in water, melting the thin layer of snow and scrubbing it away, then salting it to keep the ice from forming.

Within a day, there'd be another half foot at least, and it would be like none of this had happened at all.

SCENE TEN

They rode long into the night, and in the darkness he lay in a wagon and was pulled, and in the morning he rose and climbed astride his horse and rode again.

Coughing and heavy breathing. The smell of hay, of grass, of smoky fires. Stories: frostbitten fingers, dying horses, sick and dying men far back in the line, their bodies like markers along the road.

There was no going back.

Hamlet thought of Ophelia and of betrothals, of flowers strewn on top of snow.

⊸⊸⊸⊸ ⊷⊷⊷⊷

Somewhere in the dark, Prince Fortinbras reached out a hand to touch soft skin and hard muscle, the knot of Horatio's shoulder. His partner shifted in his sleep, curling further into the one thin blanket they were allowed. His thoughts were all of Denmark, these days. Somewhere, an army marched towards them: a line on a map, a trailing black snake of ink, curling across peaks and valleys, rivers and fields, until it reached them.

He brushed his lips against the tender skin, the rose-petal softness of it.

With an anger that was already more cold ash than flame, he thought, *There is nothing in Denmark that is worth this.*

And in another place, Rosencrantz looked out over the water. The ship cut through the dark waves like it was nothing, like it was air.

The woman beside him glowered from beneath the floppy edge of her wide-brimmed hat.

"I do not like this," she said. "I do not like this at all, Seer."

Rosencrantz shrugged. "And what," he asked, "did you think all those favours were for? They were for this."

Jinlian hardly made a noise as she walked away. They did not call her the Silent Captain for nothing, and one did not become the leader of the Golden Spiders without learning a thing or two.

Guildenstern said, his voice rough from sleep and the sea air, "Come back to bed."

And, turning his pale eyes towards the distant shore once more, Rosencrantz did.

ACT V

O phelia opened her eyes.

Solveig hummed and removed her cold fingers from Ophelia's temples. She started to rearrange the things in front of her: stones and bits of wood and bone counters, a spindle whorl, a spool of thread.

Ophelia wrapped her blanket around her shoulders even more tightly. The storm outside rattled the windows and doors, and she wished more than anything she could just sit by this fire all evening with nothing else to do.

"Nightmares can simply be nightmares," Solveig said finally. She picked up the spindle whorl and weighed it in her palm. "I think your mind is heavy, child. The Corruption is wearing you down."

"Are you sure?" she asked through chattering teeth. An interesting mixture of exhaustion and cold made everything feel… terrible. Her eyes seemed to throb, and her fingertips kept going numb, and her back hurt all the time. "They were very vivid."

"Not visions," Solveig repeated. "Another cup of tea?"

Ophelia nodded gratefully and stretched out her hand for her mug to be refilled. "It's just odd. I keep seeing these two men," she said. "It's always the same: they're in a big hall, but it's empty. And one of them is a Sight Guide, and he says something I can't hear. But then the other one says, I can't do it. And that's all that happens."

Solveig sighed. "Not every dream," she said, "is a vision. And not every vision is important. One of the curses of being a Seer, Ophelia, is that we do not get to choose the futures we see."

"So you *do* think they're visions!"

An impatient noise. "They are what they are: a sign that your mind is tired, and you need rest. Here. Away from the Corruption."

This was a conversation that had started in the early afternoon, when Ophelia made her first foray into the Otherland since she found the way closed to her. It had repeated itself three or four times since, and each and every time Ophelia responded in the same way: a wordless sound of despair, the thunk of her head hitting the wall behind her, and no real answer.

Because there was no real answer, because it wasn't a real question. There was no world in which she could make an excuse to stay in Rúnräd; there was no world in which she left Father on his own in a draughty, disease-ridden castle wondering where his daughter had gone.

Despite the tumult of their relationship, she loved him. She couldn't leave him, not with Laertes gone too.

"You know the toll it can take. That's all I mean," Solveig said gently. Ophelia didn't reply. She knew: she felt it in the tiredness of her limbs, the lethargy of her mind. She felt it in the way her heart skittered unexpectedly at times, and in how she could close her eyes for a moment and sleep for several hours.

The Corruption was wearing her down. Even with an ordinary quantity of Corruption, a Sight Guide would eventually struggle. But in Kronborg Castle, it was a miracle she was still standing.

She knew this. Solveig knew this. Hilga, seated silently in the corner like an angry spirit, knew this.

Ophelia took another gulp of her too-hot tea. The skin on the roof of her mouth cried out for help.

"I'll be fine," she said, putting the cup down on the tabletop and beginning to gather her things. "I always am."

She pulled her cloak on. Despite the heavy snow and the wind beating at the door, all of a sudden all she wanted was to be on the other side of the mirror, where no one would know how close to the edge she really was.

"A word of warning, Ophelia," said Aunt Hilga without looking up from her crochet project. The mess of lurid yellow wool at her feet twitched. Ophelia prepared herself for the inevitable moral fable that would come, but she was wrong.

"Fatma said there are rumours: that boy, the one who took out most of Felltree with a bit of dodgy spellwork… He was in Wittenberg for a while, not long back. Nasty piece of work, and a Sight Guide to boot."

"You don't think Hamlet might have known him?" Her breath caught in her chest. She remembered, even though she had only been a child, the terrible events at Felltree: how even Hilga, who at the time seemed as strong as an ox, had to sit down when she heard.

It was one of those events grown-ups only whispered about in her presence. She remembered her mother and Aaron sitting at this very table: her mother resting her cheek on her hand, frowning. Aaron removing his glasses, like he needed a moment away from the world.

Felltree wasn't far away: half a day on horseback, probably. It was bigger than Rúnräd, perhaps five times the size. It had a marketplace and a town square, and they had a summer festival Ophelia used to beg to go to but was not allowed to attend.

Some thirteen-year-old boy no one knew set up shop, played with the wrong potion ingredients, and blew up the town centre. He survived, in some miraculous turn of events; the only thing that changed was that his eyes were a pure, blinding white, where before they had been piercing green.

It was the first known case of someone making themselves into a Sight Guide.

"You'll have to ask him yourself. I can't remember his name—he found himself a patron, Fatma said, some English family… Guildenstane, I think? Something like that."

Ophelia picked up her basket.

"I can't ask Hamlet," she said. "They rode out last night."

"Oh, good," replied Hilga, perking up. "Then you can dispose of his uncle in peace, hmm?"

Solveig tutted quietly, and Hilga protested her wife's annoyance, but Ophelia wasn't listening.

Ophelia was wondering what it would feel like to sink a blade into a man's heart.

Twice.

SCENE TWO
hamlet

Hamlet gagged, pressing his forehead against the trunk of a tree. He curled his body in on itself, praying that his seizing muscles might relax, but the spasms didn't end. Around him, he could hear the sounds of the march: men pissing, stomping around in the mud, refitting horse tack.

Of course, as soon as he left Helsingør the Corruption disease got worse again. The worst possible timing. He swore under his breath, spitting out vomit and bile onto the patch of melted snow he'd been gagging at for the last half-hour.

A cool hand landed on his forehead. "Sir, you're very warm," Master Frederik said. The Court Physician could not, it seemed, be shaken off: not by war, not by plague, not by any mortal means. Hamlet's father had ordered him to keep a close eye on him since watching him puke his guts up on the first night. Two days on, Hamlet was beginning to tire of his constant presence.

"It is not too late for you to return to Helsingør," the physician said. He looked to the sky. "After all, your stars do not align with this season, my prince. It is unfortunate for you—"

Hamlet coughed and spat bile into the dirt. "I'm fine," he managed, standing with the support of the tree trunk. "A passing sickness. I'm recovering already."

"Your humours—"

"Are very much in alignment, thank you," he said breezily, and wiped his mouth with the back of his hand. Master Frederik's lips pursed, but he held out a small water flask and watched as Hamlet sipped it and rinsed out his mouth. The water splattered into the snow, alongside his sad pool of vomit.

He walked back to his horse on shaking legs. His father's eyebrows descended a little further over his eyes. Hamlet focused on adjusting his horse's reins until he felt steady enough to swing himself into the saddle, and he kept his gaze straight ahead.

The men were already whispering about him, only days into the march. His ribs ached. In truth, every part of him hurt: he hadn't kept a meal down since leaving Helsingør. Being away from the castle should have helped his magic: the way he'd understood it, Kronborg was a hive of Corruption, and the further he got from it, the better he would feel.

That was clearly not the case. His father thought it was nerves, but Hamlet knew what it truly was. He sat in the saddle, bleary-headed with the taste of his own sick in his mouth. The physician kept looking at him from the ground, those wiry grey eyebrows waggling in condescension.

"Marcellus," he called, finding the one person in the crowd he knew who wasn't his father or an insane astrologer. The guardsman-turned-soldier looked surprised, but he pushed through the swarm of horses and men and came to stand a respectful distance from Hamlet's horse. "Marcellus, how much further to Kolding?"

"A few days, Deres Højhed," Marcellus said, wrapping his cloak a little tighter around his shoulders. "The weather has slowed us, I think, but I am no expert—"

"I don't want an expert," Hamlet said. "Experts lie."

The king made a quiet, approving noise.

"We left Helsingør one week ago now, I think," Marcellus said self-consciously. "We aren't far from Slagelse. Not long in the boats, I should think. We will be there in four days, give or take."

"So a few days yet," Hamlet said. "Thank you, Marcellus. That will be all."

It was not soon enough. He pulled his hood over his head, teeth chattering. Soaked to the bone, aching, and stinking of sweat: this was not, somehow, what he'd thought of when he imagined going to war. And he was *bored*. Bored and terrified for his life in alternating waves. It made no sense.

"We have heard nothing from the men we sent to retake Sejerø," he said.

"Not yet," answered Father. "Give them time."

Hamlet bit the inside of his cheek hard enough to draw blood. He couldn't decide if he wished he was among those men, fighting Arion Fortinbras face-to-face, or if he was glad that he was here instead, where he wouldn't have to see Arion die.

Kolding seemed too far away. He wasn't sure he could bear it. He kept thinking about the letter from Rosencrantz, and the utter opacity of it. There was no hint of what they would do in Kolding. There was no acknowledgement of any of the questions he'd asked, let alone answers. They were going to be there, and so was he. That was all he knew.

A wave of nausea swept him again. He tucked his hands further into his furs, masking the cramps as shivers.

What was it that that woman in the Otherland had said?

Stay far from magic and hope that whatever you have rotting inside you dies, and it does not take you with it.

He felt, certainly, like something inside him was dying. It just seemed determined to take him down with it.

But there had to be something he could do. There had to be some spell, some potion, that could make this go away. Ophelia, he knew, could heal people. It stood to reason that Ophelia wasn't the only person in the Otherland who knew how to do some extremely basic healing. There had to be others, others who'd seen people as unwell as Hamlet. Others who'd seen people like Claudius.

And Ophelia's village was small; it seemed not impossible that they just lacked the knowledge to heal as well as a larger town. Maybe Nordsee would have had exactly what he needed; maybe he just needed to find somewhere like it, somewhere he could treat himself quickly and quietly.

As they rode, his back aching and his stomach clenching, he had the beginnings of an idea. And, with the frustration—the desperation—that was beginning to crawl up his throat at the thought of more days like this, he thought it might even be possible.

He just needed a mirror and a reason to slip away.

⋙ ⋘

His eyes were beginning to close from fatigue before he finally saw an opening. The roadside was lined with ancient trees, each more bent and broken than the next. His magic flared within him, but he tamped it down; if he set it all on fire now, there'd be a witchhunt.

But there had to be a way. If he could take the flames and turn them into something else, like Rosencrantz could… If he could turn the fire into a cool, exacting blade, then maybe he could block the way. But what then? Delay the march, sneak away into the trees, risk his father sending out a search party?

Fire crackled within him, around him, the sound of it as loud in his ears as his own breathing.

Hal's jaw clenched. The snow stuck to his eyelashes clouded his vision and he blinked it away. He focused all his attention on that tree trunk: its curve, the way its roots descended into the snow, the way the branches hung low over the road.

He imagined it snapping, cracking in half as if struck by a bolt of lightning—as if some old god decided they wanted it gone, and so their will was done. He imagined what it would feel like to snap that tree trunk himself, and in his mind he took a spear of heat, fire without flame, and touched it to the cold wood.

The king cleared his throat.

"That was a good bit of strategy, earlier," he said, his voice rough with disuse. "Making the ordinary men feel valued is important."

Have you really been fermenting those words for four hours? Hamlet wanted to scream.

"Yes, Father," Hamlet said, gritting his teeth. "Thank you."

"I just want you to know—"

Crack. The tree fell and carved a hole in the snow, plunging across the road. For a moment, he was frozen—it had worked, he'd made the magic do something other than burn!—but then he gave the horse's reins a clever yank, slipping out of the stirrups as he did so. She reared back, and Hamlet let himself fall.

He rolled to his feet as soon as he'd hit the ground, years of practice kicking in. The only move he added was a quick swat to the horse's rear end. As far as she knew, he wanted her to canter on—and so she did, bolting for the tree line. She'd always been flighty; he was glad of it now, even if it was an annoyance the rest of the time.

"I'll be back!" Hamlet called. His father shouted something, but Hamlet just shook his head, pointing to the trees. "Just a moment!"

Marcellus rode his way. Inwardly, Hamlet cursed.

"I'll escort you," Marcellus said.

"Leave your horse here, then," said Hamlet, thinking fast. "She's easily startled, as you already know."

Marcellus huffed out a laugh as he slid from the back of his far sturdier rouncey.

"Do you know which way she went?" Marcellus asked, as Hamlet led the way into the forest. "I can't hear her. She must have stopped somewhere—can't be far away."

"She's a good horse," Hamlet mused. He led them deeper in, into the murky darkness. The satchel on his back must have looked strange: oddly shaped with sharp corners, bumping up and down with each step. He hoped the tumble had not damaged what was within.

Branches cracked beneath their feet. There was less snow here, the forest so thick it shielded the ground almost entirely, but the soil was frozen solid. It was so cold Hamlet could feel it radiating into his feet through the soles of his shoes. He could hear Marcellus's teeth chattering one step behind him.

Slowly, he reached for his belt and fingered the hilt of his dagger.

SMILE AND BE A VILLAIN

Marcellus stopped walking.

"Where is your horse, Prince Hamlet?" he asked, very calmly.

Hamlet didn't know, but he was pretty sure she'd gone in the opposite direction.

He drew the blade.

"You," Hamlet said, "are going to stay where you are. I am going to keep walking. In a few minutes, I'll come back, we'll find the horse, and we'll return to the march. Is that clear?"

Marcellus very slowly raised his hands. His sword hung at his side, untouched.

"Tell no one," Hamlet said.

He was fairly confident Marcellus wouldn't hurt him, but not confident enough to turn his back.

When the guardsman was out of sight, and only the sound of his heavy, frightened breathing signified that he was still standing where Hamlet had left him, Hamlet took the satchel from his back.

From within, he removed a slim, square mirror and placed it on the ground, where it reflected the thick, woven ceiling of branches above him, a sliver of white sky.

Quickly and without pausing, he stepped into another world.

SCENE THREE
ophelia

Ophelia found the heart again easily enough.

Cocky, arrogant men were also unimaginative; Claudius was all of those things, and had therefore moved the heart to a carved-out hole beneath a loose flagstone in his chambers. This time, she was prepared for the monster. She brought a torch, on Solveig's recommendation, and set it alight. It screamed and writhed until it turned into black strands that dissipated on a non-existent breeze.

An idea crossed her mind; she touched the torch to the cloth bundle, but not even the fabric would burn.

Worth a try, she thought, and scooped up the basket.

Instantly, she felt dizzy. The heart looked, to her, clean of Corruption. That was only because it was so Corrupted that its very fibres were made from Corruption, indistinguishable from it. She looked at the little bundle with distaste, the white linen, the sliver of purple flesh she could see through a small gap.

When she had told Hilga and Solveig what she meant to do, they'd tried to stop her. They said it was too dangerous, too difficult. It was not a task, they seemed to think, for her to do alone.

But do it alone she would. To destroy Claudius, Ophelia needed two things: she needed to destroy this… organ. And then she needed to kill Claudius himself, preferably without him knowing the Corrupted heart was already gone. She felt sick when she thought about murdering him, but it did give her a little thrill of satisfaction to imagine his face changing from gloating to horrified as he realised her blade had wounded him and he was really, truly going to die.

Ophelia replaced the basket with her own. She'd been careful; it was an almost exact copy. A bundle of firm wool wrapped in pale linen looked almost exactly like the heart, and she'd woven the basket herself so that it would be a perfect likeness.

She pulled the flagstone back into place and scooped up her things. She had the heart. She had her plain cloak on underneath the pretty one she normally wore out for walks, so she could change as soon as she reached the water's edge. Claudius was downstairs, eating dinner with her father and some of the council. The queen was there too. Ophelia had done her hair for the occasion, twisting it into an elaborate mound on the top of her head.

The only danger Ophelia was in was of overheating, which was beginning to feel like a very real risk. She wiped a bead of sweat from her forehead, rolled her shoulders twice to shake off the tension, and slipped out into the corridor.

When she entered the apartments, the first thing she noticed was that she was not alone.

It wasn't her father, that was certain. He would have called out; he always did, when he heard the door, because it was 'the genteel thing to do'. And Father would be in his chambers, not in hers.

The person in her room shuffled. Something dropped to the floor with a dull thud. A woman's voice swore in a language Ophelia didn't know and wasn't sure she wanted to.

"Hilga?"

Her aunt emerged, a guilty look darting across her face for one fleeting instant. Then it was gone, replaced by her usual stubbornness.

"I came to help," she said.

Ophelia poked her head into her room, looking at the mess.

"You came," she said, "to go through my things."

"I was looking for a weapon. A woman should always keep a few sharp knives next to her bed, Ophelia. I've told you that a thousand times."

"I have a knife." She patted her belt, the weapon concealed beneath her cloaks. "What are you doing here?"

Hilga at least had the grace to look cowed.

"I knew you would do it, even if we asked you not to," she said. "I couldn't let you, not alone. I want to keep your hands bloodless for as long as I can."

Ophelia went to her desk and crouched, reaching into the gap between it and the wall. She withdrew a soft velvet bag, inside which was an ornate dagger. She handed it to Hilga, who inspected it with a wrinkled nose, as if Ophelia had just handed her a bag full of horse droppings.

"It was from Hamlet," Ophelia explained, the tips of her ears turning red. "I think he thought it would be a funny present."

"Bloody useless," muttered Hilga, weighing the thing in one hand. "Doesn't even have a nice feel to it, but I suppose beggars can't be choosers."

"You could have brought your own."

"Coming here was a spur-of-the-moment decision." Hilga nodded to the basket, still on Ophelia's arm. "Is that the *thing?*"

She nodded. Her aunt sniffed, as if she could smell the rankness of the Corruption coming off it in waves. Ophelia wouldn't even be surprised: sometimes, her aunt seemed more akin to a bloodhound than a woman.

"Come along, then," Hilga said, shoving the dagger into her belt. "No time to waste."

Ophelia almost gave her aunt directions to the nearest exit, but then she remembered Hilga's past, her life in the castle before Ophelia was born. It was strange: she seemed different outside Rúnräd. Maybe it was the fact that she had tied up her long braids into one thick ponytail, or the fact that she had swapped her hand-dyed skirts for a pair of men's trousers; either way, she looked like a threat.

"Give it to me," said Hilga, as soon as they were outside. They crossed the servant's courtyard and hurried down the alleyway that led out onto a narrow street. "You shouldn't carry it for too long. You need to save your strength."

She was right, Ophelia realised. The arm that held the basket felt exhausted already, like the muscle was on the verge of giving out. The tips of her fingers were beginning to go numb.

"There is a secret place," Hilga said, taking the basket and shoving the handle over her broad shoulder, "an old place, where our ancestors used to dispose of Corruption before they fled to Rúnräd. I can take you there, and you'll destroy the heart. Only a Sight Guide can do the spell, or else I'd do it myself."

Her heart thumped out a desperate rhythm in her chest. She kept thinking too far ahead. It was as if, in her mind, the battle with the heart was already won. The hard part was breaking it out; the next step her brain kept coming back to was killing Claudius herself.

Hamlet would never forgive her, of course. And, even if he didn't know it was her, she'd never look him in the eye again, knowing she'd plunged a knife into the chest of his beloved uncle. Knowing she'd felt his blood spill hot over her hands, heard the final gasp of breath escape his twitching lips…

But a man who would perform a spell like he had… A man like that was too dangerous to allow to live. He could not, put simply, be allowed to go on.

Could he?

She wasn't sure when she'd decided she would be the one to kill him. Was there an exact moment? It just seemed like the natural end of things: destroy the heart, destroy the man.

"Do you think… Never mind. It's nothing."

Hilga raised an eyebrow, but said nothing.

The heart sat in its basket, shrouded from the winter sun. It was, once again, unseasonably warm. The snow beneath their feet shone, a hundred thousand tiny crystals in every handful. The trees overhead quivered in a light breeze. One of them dripped icy water down the back of Ophelia's neck, and her entire body gave a shiver in reply.

But the confusing mixture of hot and cold was not enough to distract her from the images flooding her mind. Claudius, laughing snidely; Claudius, smirking; Claudius, bleeding.

"I hope you're prepared for what this ritual involves." Hilga's words cut through the birdsong and the crunch of their feet on the snow. "It won't be pretty."

"I know," Ophelia said. Solveig had explained it to her. She had wanted Ophelia to make an informed decision. Deep down, Ophelia knew the truth: her aunt, like everyone else, saw that she would not retreat from this fight.

"Solveig," Hilga said, as if reading her mind, "knows more than she lets on, at times. I think there is one part of this story that surprises her: that it is you destroying the heart, and not her."

"But she didn't know he had a heart like this," Ophelia said automatically. "And Claudius wasn't married last time he was at court, so he couldn't have had the heart… could he?"

"No, but I think she saw that potential in him." Hilga cast her a sidewards glance. There was something sharper than curiosity in her gaze: a paring knife, peeling back the layers of Ophelia's beliefs. "I suspect she saw someone else sticking a sword through his belly. Not you, child."

Relief felt like plunging into a warm pool. She almost laughed. The burden of choice was gone, evaporated. She knew what she had to do. Claudius had to die. It was written in whatever images her aunt saw behind her pale Seer's eyes, and it was just a terrible twist of fate that Ophelia would be the one doing it.

Hilga took the warm pool and froze it over in an instant.

"Of course, when Claudius's life ends isn't for you to decide. We can destroy this heart, kill whatever near-immortality he has made for himself… but what happens after that isn't your decision to make."

Ophelia's mouth worked soundlessly for a few moments. "But why not?" She felt strangely wounded by Hilga's words and their unexpected retraction. "He's evil! He destroyed my wards, he created some kind of guardian monster that hurt Hal, he's having an affair with the queen… Father wants me to marry him, and you think I should just let him live?"

"I think," Hilga said, "I want you to live a life without blood on your hands. If you kill him, Ophelia, there is no way back. If you're caught, there is no life for you; if you're not, you'll never be the same again."

"Laertes will kill people," she said, knowing this was a fruitless argument. She wasn't even sure she wanted to win. She just wanted not to lose. "Why is it different when it's a man on a battlefield?"

"I never said it was."

Hilga said nothing more on the subject, content to whistle a quiet tune and let the basket dangle dangerously from her fingertips. Ophelia touched the bone-handled knife at her belt. This new impulse felt like something to be afraid of, but when she thought about it, Ophelia felt sure she would rather be a free murderer than a prisoner trapped in a gilded cage.

She drew in a breath, and ignored the long-suffering sigh that followed from somewhere to her right.

"When Claudius finds out the heart is destroyed," she said, "he'll know it was me. There isn't really anyone else."

Hilga hummed, but didn't answer.

"He won't just let me live in peace," said Ophelia, conviction hardening her voice. "He'll want me dead for it. There isn't really a way back to Kronborg for me, not if I don't kill him."

"And the king won't let you go free if you do," Hilga said gently. "You can't stay here. You can't kill him. You'll come to Rúnräd, and you'll build a new life."

"And he finds another woman to steal a heart from." She glared at the wicker basket, the way it swung innocently in her aunt's hand, like it might hold a delicious picnic instead of a cursed magical object. "You knew. You knew I'd have no choice but to leave Helsingør, and you didn't tell me."

"Your actions have always been your own, Ophelia." Hilga sighed. "Don't blame others for failing to remind you of the consequences. Now, be quiet: we're almost there, and preparing the altar will require some very neat spellwork on my part."

With one final look at the basket, Ophelia reached into her bag and withdrew the ingredients for a simple warding spell.

She swallowed the tears that threatened to rise in her throat: she couldn't cry now, not even when she thought about her bedroom standing empty forever, not even when she thought about Father sat in his rickety chair by the fire, two cups on the table and a pot of tea going cold as he sat and waited, waited for a daughter to return who never would.

SCENE FOUR
hamlet

Hamlet landed in a tangle of limbs, still shaking off the feeling of falling through, and lay disoriented for a moment amid the shouts and cheers and clattering together of glasses. It took a moment to register that the cheering was at least partially for him: money was exchanged, drinks were finished, and somewhere someone shouted something about 'the third deserter on the floor in a week', which Hamlet decided was a problem to address another time.

The mirror had tipped him out into the middle of a bar. He was hauled up by his shoulder and a glass was pressed into his hand, filled with a suspiciously thick amber liquid. He immediately put it down on the nearest flat surface, even as someone slung an arm around him and shouted something inaudible into his ear.

"I need a healer!"

His voice hardly carried over the celebration. He looked around, pulling away from his overenthusiastic new friend with the sweaty arm. The barman stood, lazily turning on and off taps with a twitch of his finger, filling several grimy glasses at once.

Hamlet banged a hand on the bar. No one else cared, but the barman at least quirked an eyebrow. He looked at Hamlet from beneath strands of greasy, unkempt hair, as if considering whether or not he was worth notice. His eyes skimmed him: unruly hair, fine clothes, sickly, demanding a healer.

He turned back to polishing, by hand, one shiny glass.

"I need help," Hamlet shouted. He slammed his hand against the bar again, but this time he left a smouldering black mark behind. Someone whistled, long and low. "I need someone to point me in the direction of a healer."

He felt the distinct sensation of a knife pressing against the base of his spine.

"You look expensive," someone said in his ear. They pressed harder. "Little lordling, are we? Running away from the war on the other side?"

"He's off limits," came another, more familiar voice.

The knife withdrew from his back as what sounded like a bag of coins was passed around. The barman, who had lifted his eyes in passing notice of this attempted armed crime in his pub, held out a hand for a share of the prize.

Guildenstern looked almost the same as he had in Wittenberg: same cropped black curls, same quirk to his lips, same warm eyes. Something was different though: he seemed tired, slumped, like someone had taken him and crumpled him up and then tried to smooth him out again. Travel had worn out the colours in his usually bright clothes, and there was a smear of dirt on his cheek that he didn't seem to have noticed.

He didn't pause to say hello, nor did he clap Hamlet on the back or hug him. He guided him outside by the elbow, steering him quickly through the still-cheering crowd and out into the street. It was an odd town, built on a severe slope, and Hamlet had to steady himself as he stepped outside.

"How did you find me?"

"Luck," said Guildenstern. "And, you know, Rosencrantz."

This was delivered with an acid note. Hamlet let himself be led—thankfully downhill—into the darkness. It was night time wherever they were, the thick of it, the sky above like velvet studded with pinprick lights. The air smelled clear, not like the mud and shit and body odour of an army on the march.

"I need to go back as soon as I can," Hamlet said. "I just need this potion, or medicine, or whatever it is... Someone gave it to me to soothe the sickness, like what I mentioned in my letter."

Guildenstern quirked an eyebrow. "Didn't know you'd written."

"Yes," Hamlet said, taken aback. "I wrote to you and Rosencrantz. I got an answer..."

"Must have been Ros, then."

Guildenstern was being uncharacteristically snippy. He walked quickly downhill, and Hamlet practically had to jog to keep up. The little town was silent apart from the now-distant noise of the pub behind them. It appeared to have only one street, this town. Hamlet's heart sank. Surely, there had to be someone with the ingredients to make what seemed like a very simple treatment?

He caught the edge of Guildenstern's sleeve and pulled.

"Listen, I need to get back," he said. "Where are we going?"

Guildenstern whirled to face him. If he was trying, Hamlet supposed Guildenstern could probably look quite intimidating. But he wasn't: his expression was as open as a child's, and he only looked at Hamlet with something like pity.

"Whatever he offers you, just make sure you think hard about it," Guildenstern said. Hamlet realised he hadn't stopped walking for no reason, nor was it just for dramatic effect: Guildenstern opened the door of the house nearest them and stepped inside.

Hamlet froze in the doorway, something icy creeping down his spine. The house was eerily familiar. It was an almost identical copy of the Wittenberg house: same tiny bookcase, same rickety table and chairs, same fireplace. There was the pile of empty wine bottles in the corner, larger now than it had been the last time he saw it; on the mantle was a pile of books Hamlet could have sworn belonged to him and were, at this very moment, sitting gathering dust in Kronborg Castle.

And there, in the little doorway that framed their dusty pantry, was Rosencrantz. His back was to them. Candlelight lit him up with a golden glow—except it wasn't candlelight, Hamlet realised. Rosencrantz's arms were held out to either side. He stood stiffly, like an invisible crucifix was holding him up, and in front of him was an orb of golden light, shimmering like molten metal and rotating slowly in place.

"Your spell can't be that good," said Guildenstern, addressing the sorcerer, "if it can't tell he's standing in our house."

The light dimmed. The orb went from gold to coppery brown and dropped to the floor with a clang. Rosencrantz rolled his head first one way, then the other, dropped his arms, and turned to face them.

"Admittedly, it runs a little behind," he said. "It needs some tweaking."

Hamlet looked first at the orb, which was now emitting small puffs of black smoke, then at Rosencrantz, and then around at the house. The only difference between this house and the one he had left behind in Wittenberg was this pantry: instead of food, it was filled with strange metal contraptions, magnifying glasses, vials of multicoloured viscous liquids, and jars of powders. The one nearest him, holding only a pale yellow sandy substance, was labelled *os infantis antiqua*. He turned away, feeling queasy.

Rosencrantz's pale eyes meant something different now as they bored into him. He recognised them, knew now the look of Ophelia's aunt's eyes, the way Ophelia's own were changing day by day, growing paler and paler.

"You're a Sight Guide," he said. The words felt foreign on his tongue. "You can see the future."

Rosencrantz barked out a laugh. "Not quite." The smile he gave Hamlet then was as sharp as a dagger. "Found yourself on the other side of the mirror a few times since leaving Wittenberg, have you? You've learned *all* the right words. Tell me: how is the war effort going? I've been distracted. Are we any closer to a valiant return to Wittenberg, and the days of our youth?"

Guildenstern said, "I'm going upstairs."

Hamlet caught his sleeve again with a sudden urgency. He wanted Guildenstern to stay, because he had missed him; he wanted him to stay because he wanted to understand those cryptic words: *whatever he offers you, just make sure you think hard about it.*

"Wait," Hamlet said, but Guildenstern extricated himself from his grip for a second time, more gently this time, and said nothing else. His footsteps retreated up the stairs. Hamlet was left alone with Rosencrantz, and he couldn't name what it was that he felt, but he knew there was shame there for feeling anything at all.

"Ignore him," said Ros. "He's just worried about you."

Rosencrantz was his friend. Rosencrantz wanted to help him.

So why did Hamlet feel so much like prey in the den of a predator?

"I've been tracking you," Rosencrantz said, nudging the still-smoking orb with his foot. It rolled away underneath the low workbench: another new addition to the Wittenberg house. "I thought it would be easier to come and meet you that way. I wanted to catch you before Kolding, if possible."

"Well, here we are," said Hamlet, unsure what else to say. "You got my letter."

"I did." Rosencrantz tipped his head. "You weren't ill in Wittenberg, were you?"

Impatience coloured Hamlet's tone when he replied. "No, I wasn't. But if you're a Sight Guide, you should be able to see what's making me sick." He gestured to his heart. "Ophelia saw it as soon as I arrived. She says it's some of the worst Corruption she's ever seen."

Rosencrantz took in Hamlet's chest, his scientific gaze boring into him. Ros stepped forward, the space between them narrowing to almost nothing. The Sight Guide pressed his hand to Hamlet's chest, his fingers spread to cup the ragged splay of his ribs. Beneath the soft, worn fabric of his tunic, Hamlet could feel his heart beating out a thunderous rhythm.

And then the Sight Guide laughed.

Hamlet's cheeks coloured. "What?"

"I thought you knew this," Rosencrantz said. "All those stories about the damage Corruption can do—they're nonsensical, Hamlet. Corruption is a natural thing."

He hardly knew what to say in response. He was sure Rosencrantz was wrong, but he seemed so clearly amused, so utterly bemused by Hamlet's worry, that he clearly believed Corruption was harmless. But Hamlet knew Ophelia's fear for him was real: that sort of terror could not be faked, couldn't be created out of nothing.

"It's not nonsensical," he insisted, although the words felt pointless as they emerged. He knew Rosencrantz could not be convinced: if he could see the Corruption the way Ophelia did, and still believe it was harmless, there was no changing his mind. "It's dangerous. That's why I came here—I need something to treat the sickness so I can stay on the march. If it keeps going like this, I'm going to fall off my horse and be trampled to death before we ever reach a battlefield."

"Oh, I can help you with that," said Rosencrantz glibly, turning to examine his many shelves of implements and ingredients. "Easy. But I'm still doubtful it's the Corruption causing it."

He started to root around amongst the jars and bottles until he found what he was looking for. With a triumphant look, he dropped a tiny glass vial into Hamlet's hand.

"A tincture," he said. "Drink it all in one go. You'll feel much better in the morning."

Hamlet eyed it. It could be water, for all he knew. He gave it an experimental shake, and regretted it when he realised there was a layer of grainy white sediment at the bottom which quickly dispersed itself among the contents of the vial.

"It'll definitely work?" he asked.

"Oh, more than likely. I make no guarantees, but it's never failed before."

Hamlet sighed in relief. "If it doesn't, I suppose you can bring me something else in Kolding."

Rosencrantz's mouth twitched. "Oh, no. We won't be coming to Kolding anymore." At the look on Hamlet's face, Rosencrantz merely shrugged. "A change of plans. I haven't told Guildenstern yet, so let's be quiet about it."

Rosencrantz busied himself tidying the workbench, sweeping imaginary dust from its surface onto the floor. Hamlet slung his satchel back over his shoulder. Everything was wrong, off-kilter: the copycat house, Guildenstern, Rosencrantz. He wanted to call Guildenstern back downstairs, to say goodbye, to ask him what was going on, but his voice didn't want to emerge from his throat.

He coughed. "I should go."

Rosencrantz was unbothered. "Oh, you can use our mirror, if you like." He took it out from a corner and propped it up: it was a full-length one, rimmed with gold. Not the one he'd used in Wittenberg, and that gave Hamlet some comfort. Not everything was disturbingly familiar.

"Ah-ah." Ros held out a hand. "I want that vial back. Take your tincture now, please."

Hamlet wanted to say no, and in fact he almost did. But then Ros leaned back against the counter and swept his hands through his messy hair, looking every part the mad scientist, and he said, very gently, "I really have missed you, you know. It's nice to see you."

The protest died in Hamlet's throat.

"I'm glad to see you too," he said. "It's a shame you're not coming to Kolding."

"But we'll see you again soon, regardless," Rosencrantz said. It was like he was thawing out before Hamlet's eyes: a smile appeared on those thin lips, his eyes warming. Strange that they could warm, despite their frost. "Wittenberg calls. Now, drink up."

Hamlet tipped his head back and poured the potion down his throat. The burn was instantaneous, like a strong drink but building and building, searing through his throat until he was sure it was going to burn a hole in him. He doubled over and coughed, nearly threw up, but Ros clamped a hand over his mouth and yanked his head back.

"Keep it down," he ordered. All softness was gone from him: Ros the lover vanished, replaced by the young man with the sharp limbs and the silver tongue. Hamlet felt frightened by the transformation in him, frightened and ashamed. What had he done to deserve this sudden anger?

"Get up. Go back through the mirror, go to your tent, and say nothing, not to anyone, no matter how bad it gets," Ros ordered. "Good luck on the battlefield, Prince Hamlet."

Futile to say anything. He felt his heart twist, even through the pain: there was a void somewhere inside him, a hole carved out by long, cold nights in Wittenberg, by wine and shared lectures and friendship, and he realised now that Rosencrantz didn't share the same cavernous gap inside him.

He was happy for this to end here, in what felt like a betrayal: happy for Hamlet to march into battle alone, happy to sit in a mockery of the Wittenberg house and craft his spells and go back to the life he had lived before

Guildenstern rescued Prince Hamlet from a dark, rainy street.

There was no sound from upstairs.

Hamlet fell through the mirror, the shadow of Rosencrantz's hand on his back burning a hole in his tunic. He clashed heads with a concerned Marcellus, who had been peering over the rim of the mirror, managed to claw his way onto the snow, and passed out.

SCENE FIVE
ophelia

Goosebumps pricked Ophelia's skin, standing out on her arms. Nothing scuttled or flapped. The air was dead.

They stood in a clearing. In the middle there was a pile of stones in the shape of an altar, with a smooth, flat top that may have had writing carved into it at one point, but it certainly didn't anymore. Ophelia dropped the basket with a dense sound and withdrew her little cloth bundle. It squirmed in her arms. She was, once again, hit with the horrific sensation that it was a child and not a Corrupted organ in her arms.

Carefully, she placed the bundle on the altar and folded back the cloth with shaking hands. The heart lay twitching in the cold. When Ophelia peered closer at the altar, she could see tiny golden threads weaving together, hardly perceptible. They withered and curled in on themselves near the heart, their edges fraying.

Ophelia took the knife from her belt. Solveig had told her the steps of the ritual, and she ran over them in her head. Hilga passed her another bag, a little blue one decorated with stars. A pity it would have to be burned after this, like everything else inside the circle, including their clothes.

She hoped Hilga had left their spare dresses outside the ring.

"I'll turn my back," Hilga murmured. "You'll have to do this part alone, I'm afraid. But I'm here, if you need me."

Ophelia's teeth chattered too hard for her to reply.

She looked at the heart. Steam collected around it in wisps, as if the muscle was still radiating body heat. She felt, suddenly, quite sick.

There was no easy way to dispose of something like this. The Corruption existed deep within the flesh, in a place she could not reach with her bare hands. She would have to carve it out, carve through the real world and the magical one, until she could slice through the very threads of magic that resided in everything.

And she would have to be so careful not to sever her own threads nor those of the altar; to take apart only the heart, in case she might destroy something that could never be put back together.

Ophelia sucked in a breath. The air felt colder here inside the circle, and she was acutely aware that she was now alone. The heart twitched again, pulsating.

With a shaking hand, she raised the knife and made the first cut.

Instantly, the heart revealed itself for what it was. Before, it had seemed to repel Corruption, to remain as innocent as a real human heart lying before her. Now, deep purple liquid emerged in a flood, pouring over the stone altar and onto the ground. It hissed when it touched the snow: it was not, she realised, just visible to her. It was physical, real in every world.

Some of it hit her foot and she cried out as it ate through her boot like acid, burning her skin. Hilga called something, but the words made no sense through the haze of pain and purple mist that surrounded Ophelia.

She positioned herself again, despite the throbbing wound in her foot, and sliced. More Corruption; more rotten, twisted blood flooding out from the organ. The bone-handled knife slipped in her sweaty palm, making the next cut ragged and disjointed. She swallowed hard and blew a strand of stray hair out of her face. She had to focus: when she stopped carving up the physical and started to dissect the magic, she couldn't afford to make mistakes.

Blood spattered her arm. The pain was so immense she fell to her knees in the snow, whimpering. The knife landed beside her, making a soft sound as it sank into the glittering crystals.

"Ophelia!"

It was Hilga, urging her to get up. Ophelia stood on shaky legs. She sliced away another ribbon of muscle, avoiding another wash of blood. She focused her mind.

She made no more mistakes.

When the heart was in pieces, muscle severed from valve, vein, and artery, she laid down the knife. This was the part she was afraid of: taking apart the magic that made up the heart, the spell that bound it to the heart in Claudius's chest and kept it beating, free from Corruption.

She held her hands over the knife. It was made from antler and steel. She touched the bone of the handle: she could see the thin golden threads that ran through it, the mark of natural magic.

She called on it. There was no spell for this, only a sense of what to do that came from somewhere deep in her gut.

The threads twanged, tension holding them straight. Ophelia turned her attention to the heart and placed her hands above it, trying hard to ignore the way the pieces wriggled away from her searching hands and tried to leap off the altar.

"*Relinquatis*," she said. "*Et non revertatur.*"

The heart shone purple again, but this time, the Corruption made more sense to her. Here were threads she could pull and shape; this was familiar, this was something she knew how to do. She took up the knife again, the natural magic warming her skin.

With one hand, she manipulated the threads of Corruption to draw one thick, muscular strand taut, as tight as a bowstring.

With the other, she started sawing.

She was almost finished, sweat dripping from her forehead onto the altar below. She kept the pieces of heart in two piles: one side clear of Corruption, one still to be done. The Corrupt side had only two pieces left now, and one of them was almost clear.

The bits she'd removed the Corruption from had almost ceased their twitching. They were just flesh now. She couldn't help but think ahead: she would burn them and bury the ashes deep in the soil, and then she would burn the clothes and everything else that had come within the circle, and destroy the knife, and bury those too. Then Hilga would help her to scorch the earth, and they would wash in the icy stream nearby, and they would dress and go home.

Hilga said something. Ophelia drew her attention back to the heart: her aunt must have seen her focus slip, because her tone sounded like a warning.

Except it came again, the words more urgent now, even if Ophelia still couldn't make them out.

She waited for Hilga to repeat herself for a third time, keeping the knife still, so that she wouldn't make a mistake with the magic.

But she realised what was wrong very quickly once her ears tuned back into the world around her again.

Hooves.

Someone—many someones, by the sounds of it—was coming.

And she had a horrible feeling she knew who it might be.

SCENE SIX
hamlet

Hamlet had no memory of returning to the march. The only thing he remembered, and this very hazily, was Marcellus explaining to the king that Hamlet had been injured by his own terrified horse, and Marcellus had had to bring him back to consciousness before they could make their way back.

The horse was killed almost immediately, the sinewy meat carved up to be distributed amongst the noblemen. Some of it was served as steaks for their dinner. Hamlet prodded it around his plate for a while in the tent he dined in with his father, before his rumbling stomach finally drove him to start eating. He had to admit that it tasted nice, particularly with a dash of redcurrant jam.

His head pounded as they got back on their horses, leaving some soldiers to deconstruct the tents. He'd been issued a new one, which looked familiar for a reason he couldn't place. Her name was Letty, and it wasn't until the evening that he saw Laertes riding on a stumpy-looking steed and realised Letty was in fact his.

He felt bad, but only for a few moments. Letty seemed to like him: she snuffled at his palm when they stopped for a break and ate berries out of his hand. Laertes' sour face stopped bothering him.

But despite his newfound ally, his day only seemed determined to get worse. Master Frederik rode alongside him to 'monitor his injuries' and whispered to Father everywhere they went, casting sidewards glances of doom in Hamlet's direction. It snowed heavily late into the night, and by the time they finally stopped for the night he felt he would never be warm again.

The cold was in his limbs, his skin, his bones; he felt like his insides had been turned to ice, and no number of furs or wool blankets could improve matters.

And when he slept he dreamt of monsters.

But that was not, in fact, the worst part. Because when he woke, panting in fear, the monsters were there too. They crouched at the corner of his tent, enormous things with eyes out on stalks and fluttering wings and savage teeth and claws. Some were like insects, some like dogs; the worst were the bird-like ones, which flew at his face and did not seem deterred even when he tried to beat them away with his arms.

The world itself seemed to change overnight. Thin ribbons of gold wove through his skin, the floor, the very air around him. Webs of a wet, seething substance seemed to hang from the walls of the tent and drip onto the floor, so purple it was nearly black. The ground looked like it was shifting beneath him when he tried to stand, the mass teeming around his feet.

At first, he fought the monsters silently. He was sure they were just a figment of his imagination: he was dreaming, that was all. He could feel sweat cooling on his skin, leaving him shivering. He was just dreaming, although the cries of a silver-beaked creature in the corner drilled into his brain like nothing ever had before.

The creature bobbed towards him on stunted legs. He waved it away, scrambling into the furthest corner of his bed, holding up the blankets like they would protect him. He was dreaming. It didn't matter.

The beak dug deep into his arm. He screamed, the flesh coming apart, blood and bone bursting open with the force…

Except there was no wound, only pain, and when the guards his father had set outside the tent came in to see what the screaming was about, they found no assassination attempt, no debilitating disease. They found Prince Hamlet curled in on himself in the middle of a pile of blankets, his dark hair stuck to his forehead with sweat, rocking back and forth.

No one spoke of it, not really. Not when the prince rode on with shadows under his eyes the next day. Not when he twitched suddenly, as if shying away from something they couldn't see, confusing his horse. Not when he said nothing to his father about the agreement he had finally come to with King Fortinbras, the place their battle would take place, so they could end these skirmishes (or so they said; no skirmish had come within a mile of the king, so far).

Not when he made no response to the news that Prince Fortinbras' force was rejoining the main Norwegian army, that he would fight on the battlefield alongside his father.

They marched at what felt like a glacial pace. Creatures hunted Hamlet's steps, and while he soon learned to ignore their shadowy shapes at the corner of his attention, he couldn't ignore the pain. It was as if it was inside his body, leaving no mark on the skin itself.

He chewed some mint to keep himself awake: the only positive contribution, he thought, Master Frederik had ever made to the world at large. Letty was untroubled by the snow and the creatures, and she clipped along at an impressive pace.

Hamlet wondered, not for the first time, what the hell it was Rosencrantz had given him.

He tried to see the positive side. Perhaps this was only temporary; perhaps it would give him some power in battle when the magic settled, some kind of strength or fortitude, something he could use to Denmark's advantage. Maybe this was a side effect, and the real power would show itself soon.

But he could not shake the nagging feeling that Rosencrantz, surely, had had no reason to lie about the contents of that vial. He kept replaying the scene in his mind, turning his friend's words over to try to make sense of them. The way his entire demeanour had changed, how his hand had clamped itself over Hamlet's mouth to force the potion down his throat, being shoved back through the mirror…

The betrayal felt hollow. He could believe it; there was no reason not to. Whatever love he'd felt for Rosencrantz and Guildenstern, they'd never reciprocated in quite the same way. It was always the two of them, their heads bowed together in front of the fire, their hands finding one another's skin, their feet touching beneath the kitchen table. And Hamlet, watching on. Hamlet, glad of the warmth of their friendship on his face.

It made him feel sick to think about, but there was little else to do. The monsters flew and crawled and shrieked around him, and the world shuddered apart into thousands of tiny threads, and his father spoke of battlefields and blood.

And Hamlet rode on towards what should have been the most terrifying event of his life. Strangely, he felt nothing. He couldn't imagine, anymore, feeling fear worse than what he already felt. There was nothing more to be afraid of.

Hell was empty, and all the devils were here.

SCENE SEVEN
ophelia

The hooves grew louder and louder. Ophelia let out a whimper when they stopped, boots tramping in the snow, but she carried on. She sliced another thread, and another. Her hands were shaking.

She dared not look at Hilga, who was somewhere to her left. Only the visible withering of the Corrupted heart ensured she could carry on, but her fingers grew stiff with cold and terror, and the hooves grew louder until they sounded like war drums in her ears.

"Don't touch her," Hilga spat. Her voice was distant. Where had she gone? The blur of her had disappeared.

She was on the final incision—one more and she could safely set fire to the heart, and then it would all be over…

Someone was in the clearing, inside the circle, rushing towards her. Ophelia screamed as an arm wrapped around her neck, dragging her backwards. She bit into the hand that held her and the man screamed, releasing her. She fought to reach the heart again, her dagger lurching for the final thread, taut and shivering.

She braced herself on the altar and sliced down, severing it. As she did, the man behind her managed to get a grip on her skirts, dragging her backwards, and the spelled knife slipped and buried its point in the back of her opposite hand.

First, she felt the pain. Then her vision flickered, the world turning temporarily to a sea of black and white, then to glaring technicolour.

And then it reappeared, and suddenly there were no threads of gold. No purple shimmered at the edges of her vision.

Her Sight was gone.

She had no time to consider this, or to feel afraid of what else cutting the thread might have done. The heart lay in pieces on the altar, and as the man behind her tried to drag her to the floor, she screamed, "*Explodere!*" and the flesh burst into orange flames, sputtering out greasy black smoke.

She was dragged to the ground to lie belly-down in the snow. Boots crunched across the circle: tanned leather, gleaming silver buckles, not a mark or a scuff.

She managed to raise her head enough to look Claudius in the eye before she hawked up what little saliva she could and spat right on his perfect boots.

He cast her a look of amusement and turned to look at the altar, observing her handiwork like a parent might look at a child's finger painting. Then, he tenderly covered his own destroyed heart with the cotton blanket once more.

"Transport this back to Kronborg, and be careful with it," he ordered a soldier, who swung up onto his horse. He was dressed in the clothing of a castle guard, but she didn't recognise him. "And tie the girl up. She's clearly mad."

There was a scuffle going on somewhere behind her. Ophelia heard Hilga swear, then the hiss of a man who had just been kicked in a very delicate location.

Claudius looked at Ophelia, a slow smile spreading across his face.

"Kill the other one," he said. "She won't be necessary."

Ophelia screamed, redoubling her efforts to pull away from the guard who had her in his grip. He struck her hard across the back of the head with something more firm than a fist, and she clutched the wound as heat burst from a point on her forehead. Something thick and wet glued down her hair.

Metal screamed as a sword was drawn. Claudius tipped his head, directing with his chin.

"Over here," he said. "Make sure the girl can see."

The last thing Hilga did was mouth look away.

But Ophelia couldn't.

The blade came down. Blood sprayed bright in the frosty air, and something broke deep in Ophelia's magic. She felt her eyes roll back and felt her body go limp, collapsing into the snow.

But she did not pass out. She simply went somewhere else.

Darkness. People spoke as if through a waterfall, a raging rush. It was the same voices as before in the chapel—Hal, furious, and Gertrude afraid. "A rat? Dead for a ducat, dead!"

And then she was there, standing at the corner of the room, watching as Hamlet plunged his sword through the tapestry again and again. The arras shivered with the force of it. Someone was moaning—animalistic sounds, gasps and grunts of desperate pain. No words.

Gertrude's hands were clasped to her mouth but she stood still and frozen as she watched her son—Hal, whose teeth were drawn back like an animal's. Hamlet, her

Hamlet, who kept stabbing and stabbing even as a body slumped to the floor, came rolling underneath the bottom of the arras—

Father's face stared up at her. He made a noise, a single quavering note, and was still. Grey brains slid thickly from a wound on the side of his head. His cheek was punctured too, and his chest and belly were just a mess of blood and viscera and fragments of white bone.

"What have you done?" Ophelia wailed, at the same time as Gertrude. But this Hamlet did not look at Ophelia.

He bent and examined the brains spilling from her father's head and then, with disgust painted across his angelic features, he said, "I thought he was the king, but I was wrong. I suppose this is no worse crime, Mother, than to kill a king and to marry his brother, is it?"

Gertrude sobbed into her hands. Ophelia stepped back and back and back, through the wall like a ghost, and slipped into somewhere else. The world rippled before her as tears streaked down her face. They tasted of salt on her tongue.

The rippling was cloth, and when she turned again she saw she was in a tent. It was illuminated in firelight. The red cloth was trimmed with blue and gold, and when she examined the faces of the men crowded around the fire she saw they were familiar.

King Fortinbras, with his greying hair and his eagle-like eyes, his bent posture, crouched nearest the flames. Ophelia scanned the faces: the king and his favoured advisor, a man she dimly recognised from court.

The queen, dark-haired and pretty, stood to the side with her arm around a boy—Prince Fortinbras, she realised. Stocky and broad-shouldered, with a fine-featured face and coppery hair that glinted in the light. His clothes were worn and crumpled from travel, and his hair was wet with rain, and yet somehow he still looked like a prince from a fairytale.

The only difference: he looked afraid.

One more figure crouched in the tent. A young man. His face was hardly visible, swaddled in a large hood, and his glasses were laid carefully to one side.

The stranger sighed. "We've been working together for long enough," he said, "for you to stop tying me up. I don't cooperate well when I'm uncomfortable."

Ophelia saw that his hands were indeed tied behind his back: bound, like he was there unwillingly. Tied loosely, like they thought he wouldn't really try to escape.

His eyes were a pale shade of blue-white, and she realised with a start that she had seen him before. In her dream, standing in an empty room with another man. He was the Sight Guide she was dreaming about.

King Fortinbras ignored the young man's request. "Tell me what you saw," he said, pinching the bridge of his nose.

"What I have already said: the prince, driven to madness. A pile of bodies, and your son on the Danish throne." The ghost of a smile crossed his pointed face. "I have seen to the first already: Prince Hamlet is mad, or he will be before the sun sets tonight. His weakness will shake Denmark's faith. If you are victorious today, Norway's strength will be secured."

"But the boy must live? It is not enough to kill him in battle, like honest men?"

"Yes, he needs to live," said the young man. Impatient, now. "That is what I have seen. *King* Hamlet dies today; *Prince* Hamlet lives; his uncle takes the throne. Is it so complicated I need to explain it a dozen times?" He sat up as straight as he could, with both his arms tied behind his back. "Honestly. Catholic or not, I'm trying to help you."

"I'm less concerned about your religion and more about your magic, which I cannot trust," King Fortinbras muttered, stroking his goatee.

"I don't want this, Rosencrantz," Prince Fortinbras said quietly. A shock jolted through Ophelia. She knew that name. There was something familiar in it, something she couldn't place.

"I didn't particularly want to drive my former friend to insanity," the seer muttered, getting to his knees and brushing dirt off his robes. "But here I am. We all do things we don't want to, to avoid the end of the world as we know it. Do you have the letter?"

This part was addressed to the king, who squeezed his nose bridge and sighed at the impertinent seer.

"Amnesty," the king said. "And safe passage through any country you please, with my blessing. No one will intercept you, Catholic or not."

They untied Rosencrantz. He rubbed his wrists and turned to the mirror at the end of the tent.

"Oh, I almost forgot," said Rosencrantz, turning to Prince Arion with one foot in the mirror. He smiled. "The only bit I've seen of the battle, Prince Fortinbras: you light up."

And then she was awake, awake and screaming, and Hilga's lifeless corpse was lying in the snow.

"I'll fucking kill you," Ophelia seethed, jerking forward to reach Claudius. The guard holding her clapped a hand over her mouth; she bit his finger and held fast until his blood poured into her mouth like wine. He howled, and Ophelia bared her teeth in a vicious smile. "I'll give you a fate worse than death, you sickening, twisted monster—"

"Do you see any Corruption?" Claudius asked innocently, turning over his palms as if he expected to see them coated in purple webs. "My hands are clean, girl. I am innocent, and you..." He frowned at her, shaking his head. "You are not. You've been nothing but a nuisance since I came to Helsingør."

Ophelia managed to get to her knees despite the hold the guard had on her. She sent her head back, and the satisfying noise that resounded told her that the guard's nose was broken. She wrenched a second knife from her dress, launched herself forward at Claudius's shocked face, and plunged the dagger straight into his chest.

Or she would have, if it wasn't for the hidden chainmail beneath his tunic. She screamed in frustration. There were swords at her throat, her back, everywhere, but she didn't *care*—

"Oh, my dear Ophelia," Claudius said, smiling. "You'll have to do better than that."

Ophelia opened her mouth to speak, but before she could, a wad of cloth was jammed into her mouth. Her screams muffled, two guards lifted her and dumped her over the back of their horse.

"Keep her quiet," Claudius drawled, swinging back into the saddle. And then, to her, "I'll see you at the castle, my dear."

A blunt object hit her on the side of the head, and Ophelia knew nothing more.

SCENE EIGHT
hamlet

Tents rippled in the breeze. Hamlet tugged on his leather greaves as his brand new squire, recently collected from a baron who wanted an excuse not to fight, fussed with the clasps and ties of the prince's gleaming armour. The armour and the squire both would be christened at the Battle of Fredericia, as they were sure to call it later.

Later, as he sat on his mount, his father clapped him hard on the shoulder. In his armour the king looked like a very large steel boulder, and Hamlet tried his hardest to stifle the laugh that tried to emerge. Ridiculous. This entire event, he couldn't help but feel, was a joke, a parody.

Father said, "This is the hardest part, the waiting."

Across the divide, Norway's forces were arrayed. He fancied he could see Prince Fortinbras even from so far away, because the flags were more numerous around him and his armour glinted in the sun.

The king chuckled, taking Hamlet by surprise. "You'll meet him soon enough," he said, mistaking Hal's melancholy for bloodlust. "And when you do, you'll aim for the neck."

The creatures were still there, dancing at the corner of his vision. He knew, with a sinking certainty that felt like a lead weight in his belly, that if he became distracted by them he was going to die. The chaos of the battlefield was enough to deal with without seeing the charcoal shadows of vicious, sharp-beaked birds overhead, the smoky trail of a dragon's tail, the horror of blank-eyed people staring at him, their missing limbs dripping purple, viscous fluid.

Worst of all was the way he could see the webbing of the world beneath his feet: the golden strands of magic that rooted the trees to the ground, that scored ancient stones, that surrounded mountaintops; the cold purple tendrils that shivered and moved, infecting everyone and everything with their Corruption.

When he looked at himself in the mirror, he saw the golden strands in his veins dying. And in their place, Corruption flourished.

His legs trembled wildly, so hard that he thought he might accidentally launch his horse forward too early.

This is what you waited for, whispered the voice at the back of his mind. *A chance to prove yourself. A chance to show them all that you can turn the tide.*

"This is nothing like I imagined," he whispered. The wind whipped the words away from his mouth like crisp autumn leaves.

His father's hand came down on his shoulder, gentler this time.

"A good king," he said, "never loves war. Battle should horrify you, should turn your belly to water and set your legs trembling. That's how you know a man from a boy."

Hamlet swallowed painfully. "Then I must be a man," he said, through chattering teeth. "I think I'm going to vomit."

Then the horn blew, and the armies descended.

Two silver seas rushed against one another, breaking like a wave. Hamlet rode over corpses and avoided arrows. Letty, though slower than some, was sturdy. She galloped into the fray without losing her footing. Hamlet tried to remember what he had been taught in training, in the years of combat trials leading up to this moment, but he couldn't. It was all too fast, too hectic.

The copper tang of blood was thick in his mouth, his nose. He slashed and stabbed. He found himself wondering, as he dealt a fatal blow, why killing these soldiers didn't seem to be registering. He knew he was doing it. He knew they were dying all around him, their horses screaming, their bodies collapsing into the mud. But it was someone else's arm, someone else's body. He was two eyes and nothing else.

A halberd slashed through his horse's neck and he was suddenly wrenched back into his body. The luxury of distance was gone.

Hot blood sprayed over his face. He fell from the screaming creature and onto the churned, muddy ground. A Norwegian sword came for his head. Hamlet raised his shield just in time, but the sheer force of the blow knocked him to his knees.

Desperately, he ripped his knife from his belt and stabbed. It was a blind hit, but a good one; the knight screamed and fell beside him, collapsing in a huddle on the ground. Hamlet crawled backwards, watching the man's limbs shake and twitch, and bumped straight into Letty's corpse.

Two horses in a week, his brain supplied. He nearly laughed, except suddenly he was crying.

A large, black bird swooped down at him with a viciously pointed beak that glistened silver in the light: a crow, only five times the size of an ordinary one and surrounded in a purple aura. Hamlet sobbed and raised his shield over his head.

But then the bird noticed the fresh horse corpse, and began to cheerfully rip out Letty's eyes, except… the bird tore at the horse in the place between worlds. The flesh in Hal's world did not go anywhere—but he could see, so vividly, the bird ripping chunks of wet shadowy purple flesh from Letty's eye sockets.

Hamlet fought to his feet. His sword was gone. He had only his knife and his shield. The corners of his vision were all tainted a deep purple, the colour of a fresh heart. Swords clashed over his head, too loud and too fast. Everything was purple and gold, except for the shadows, which were a deep, charcoal grey. Only their eyes were pure black.

They were people, except they weren't. Even the Danish soldiers no longer resembled humans in his mind: purple seeped from them in a fine spray like an aura, alongside phantom limbs and grisly skeletons.

Some of them had droplets of gold running from their bodies in streams. Some of them, the ones with so much purple trailing from their bodies that it looked like a cloak, had strange, bizarre mutations. It was hard to see with their helmets and their armour, but of the ones with their faces uncovered, almost all of them had half of their skulls exposed.

Except that couldn't be right, because they were up and swinging—but it looked so real, these wounded men with their purple sparks swarming them like plague flies. Slowly, Hamlet turned to look for his father.

There he was, underneath the banners. He was still astride his horse, and his huge axe dealt out a lethal kind of fate wherever it was aimed. Purple liquid streamed from both ears, running out of his eyes and ears like a twisted kind of makeup.

The man next to him had a phantom, purple stump that seemed to hover a few seconds behind his living arm. Then, in a moment, a sword came down: the arm was gone. The Corruption blended with the blood that poured from the wound. The knight fell from Hal's sight.

He was struck with horror, so vivid he didn't know what to do with it. If he saw himself in a looking-glass, would he see his own death wound written on his flesh?

"Fyrste!"

Sir Michael stretched out a hand from his horse, just as an arrow pierced him through the eye. The horse reared, terrified.

Hamlet clutched the reins and swung on, pausing only to take the corpse's sword.

He could still taste the foulness of bile, still felt the salt tears trickling from his eyes. But he needed to end this, end this horror now. Find Rosencrantz and beg him to make it all stop.

Find out how his father was going to die.

Now Hamlet was close enough that he could see Prince Fortinbras's every move. The other prince looked up. He had no death wound, or at least none that Hamlet could see.

They locked eyes. For a moment, Hamlet thought that Fortinbras was going to raise his hand, call for the white flag of retreat. But then Fortinbras looked towards the Danish tents.

Hamlet felt the magic before he saw it, felt the raw power sparking in the air like the sky before a lightning storm. For a moment, it felt like the old stories—like Thor was going to come down from the heavens with his hammer flying and decide the fate of Denmark for himself.

Behind Hal, an orange light flared to life. He looked over his shoulder—the tents were burning, a brutal and beautiful light, like sunrise at midday. He laughed, madly, because he could hardly believe it. Perfect fucking Fortinbras, untouched in a sea of horrors, but really he was a monster like the rest.

Fortinbras was using the Danish distraction as an excuse to cut left and right, savage blows that destroyed men in an instant. Beside him, a Norwegian soldier lowered his sword and pushed up his visor, as if he wanted a better view of the carnage. Horatio's face was smeared with ash and blood—and anger. His raven hair, slicked with sweat, stood out against the silver-grey of the field. He was equally untouched by magic.

There is no glory in this, Hamlet thought, watching Fortinbras cut down his men like they were made of paper. *But there's no glory in the ending of it either. We're too far gone.*

Hamlet opened his mouth. A hoarse battle scream emerged from his throat, assembling the Danish soldiers nearest him, and he charged.

Not at Horatio.

Not at Prince Fortinbras.

But at the King of Norway.

He was an impossible target—or he should have been—but Hamlet massacred the left flank of his retinue with startling efficiency. Prince Fortinbras, separated by a skirmish, screamed something. His voice stood out even in the crowd. It was not the cry of a soldier who was winning, but of a frightened boy who knew that he was about to witness something terrible.

Hamlet watched the king's eyes as he saw him approach. They widened, then narrowed. Dark pools, filled with thoughts and memories. His own father was nearby, scattering skulls across the field. He roared something—perhaps encouragement, perhaps a warning—but Hamlet did not hear. He took his stolen sword, and he plunged it deep into King Fortinbras's gut.

A feral roar—something struck the back of his skull, knocking him to his knees. Hamlet's sword was wrenched from his grasp. The Norwegian king screamed in agony at the blade stuck in his abdomen twisting, then fell to his knees beside Hamlet.

The old man slumped. The same man roared again, and when Hamlet looked blearily up through the haze over his eyes, he saw—amidst the shadows—Prince Fortinbras. There were tears pouring down the other prince's face, mixing with blood and grime and leaving pale tracks like scars on his cheeks.

Arion's mouth moved, but Hamlet couldn't hear him. There was a terrible ringing in his ears, and distantly he noted that something warm was running down the side of his head.

Arion strode over, his sword jabbing straight for Hamlet's neck. The other prince was still crying, his teeth bared in an awful mockery of a wild beast. He looked wild; even his eyes were no longer his, clouded by grief and rage.

"You killed my father," Arion screamed. "He loved you like a son once, and you killed him!"

There was a moment when Hamlet considered getting up and fighting.

Slowly, he tipped his head back and bared his throat.

"Arion, please," he managed. "Please."

His teeth were chattering and, as his throat gave an involuntary shudder, he realised that he was still crying. He felt the cold edge of Fortinbras's sword pressing against the bulb of his neck. Relief poured through him.

It was almost over.

In the sky, three shadowy crows wheeled overhead.

And then Fortinbras let out a furious, terrible roar—of anger, of sadness, of rage—and threw down his sword.

"Retreat!" he shouted, raising his hand. "Norway, retreat!"

Hamlet fell forward, onto the muddy, blood-soaked ground, too exhausted to drag himself out of the way of rushing hooves and fleeing feet.

Even with his eyes closed, the shadows danced.

Prince Hamlet's mind slid into oblivion.

SCENE NINE
ophelia

The visions did not stop, not for a long time. Hours and hours trickled by where Ophelia could not tell reality from... well, realities.

She watched Hamlet stab her father to death seven or eight times. She saw things she had never wanted to see—Claudius and Gertrude entwined in bed, the sheets wrapped around their naked bodies—Laertes sobbing over a filled grave—the two young men from her dreams, a stranger and a Seer, dangling from nooses with their faces swollen and purpled in death, their eyes not yet pecked out by crows.

Days passed in a haze. Ophelia was half-aware of the fact that she was alive, but she was more aware of the fact that Hilga was dead, which made it all seem very pointless. She was in her room, she knew that much.

People came and went, and sometimes there were cold cloths on her forehead. They made her skin feel scratchy and tight and she didn't like them.

The first time Ophelia woke properly, it was because Prince Claudius was jabbing his fingers into her mouth. Efficiently, he wrenched her jaw open, pulled out her tongue, and rested a dagger on it. They were alone in the room apart from a maid, who stood wide-eyed in the corner.

"You've finally stopped drooling, at least," Claudius said. For a moment, he seemed to shimmer in Ophelia's mind. She remembered the man he was when he first came to court. So different to who he was now. "You've certainly made a scene, haven't you? You'll be devastated to know I had to call our engagement to an end. I can't marry a madwoman."

Relief swept over her, followed by a surge of panic. If Claudius wasn't going to marry her… was he going to kill her instead? It made sense. She'd do it, in his position. Ophelia made a sound around the dagger that threatened her tongue. If she swallowed or closed her mouth, she risked the sharp point sliding into her flesh. Claudius knew that as well as she did, because he was smiling genially, as if this was any ordinary exchange.

"But you're good for something," Claudius continued. A chill went down Ophelia's spine. "I noticed those pretty sigils of yours—very clever. I'm sure your witch friend taught you those, didn't she?" He drew a finger across his throat, and tears welled in Ophelia's eyes. "I think we can come to an agreement, Seer."

Ophelia stared, rendered entirely soundless. Claudius did a mocking double-take, then slipped the blade from between her lips.

"My mistake," he said, a smile playing on his lips. "I had quite forgotten that you couldn't speak."

"Just tell me what you want from me," Ophelia snarled.

"Your visions," Claudius said plainly. "Your spells. I want you as my personal witch, for as long as I require your services. And, in exchange, I won't have you killed. Isn't that nice?"

She sneered. "What do you need my visions for?" she asked. "They're useless. They don't make any sense."

"Not to you, perhaps. But to me, they're very useful. You see, we are at a very complicated juncture in Denmark's history." Claudius stepped away from the bed, picking up something and turning it between his fingers. Her mother's comb, she realised with a pang of anger. "My brother is a good ruler—there's no doubt about it. But he lacks the hunger needed to deal with Norway's insolence. And that son of his, I'm afraid to say, is entirely useless."

"Hamlet is twice the man you'll ever be."

"We'll see." Claudius smiled at her. "I think you already know what I want, Ophelia. I want to be king, and I want a queen. At first, you see, I thought the crown was out of my reach. I thought I needed to take a pretty young wife and stay at court and work my way up, until perhaps the council would see his son's useless ways and make me crown prince, not that useless boy." He clicked his tongue. "But time is ticking, and I'm not quite as patient as that. And I see now that the crown is within reach—I only need to *take it*."

He mimed plucking something out of the air, then turned to Ophelia with his arms out wide, like a theatre performer.

"How?" she asked. Her first thought was that Claudius wanted to kill Hal. She felt nauseous, but that didn't… solve the problem. King Hamlet would remain on the throne. "What are you going to do? Challenge the king?"

Claudius tapped his nose. "I can't tell you quite yet," he said. "But, I will say… it would be much easier if my brother died in battle. You haven't seen that in your visions, have you? Be honest."

She gritted her teeth. "No. I haven't seen the king die."

"What a pity." Claudius looked morosely out the window. "Anyway, I doubt you're willing to martyr yourself for this cause, so you'll keep that pretty mouth tightly closed, won't you?"

She wanted to disagree, to say that she would stand up like Hilga and take whatever punishment Claudius had to offer. But instead, she braced herself and nodded.

"This is a far better arrangement than marriage," said Claudius, as if they'd just struck a good business deal. "You're not, I hate to say, particularly attractive to me."

"Queen Gertrude is, apparently," Ophelia said, and this time it was her turn to smile.

Claudius watched her silently for a moment. Then he laughed quietly, put down the comb, and made for the door.

"A spy, to add to it all," he said as he left. "You'll be more useful than I'd anticipated."

Ophelia sat up. She felt her head burning with the exhaustion of her magic.

"Fetch a needle and thread," she said in a hoarse voice to the maid who stood motionless in the corner. "And tea with honey."

The girl did as she was told. While the honey soothed her throat, Ophelia stitched. By the time morning came, she had sewn protection charms into the hems of every one of her garments. She had no idea if they would work, but she needed every chance she could get.

"Bring me the prince's wardrobe," she said absently, pulling her slipping shift up onto her shoulder. "Hamlet, not Claudius."

At the maid's questioning look, Ophelia tutted.

"You should do as I say," she warned. And then she smiled, as widely as she could manage through her cracked lips. "I'm quite mad at the moment. Hadn't you heard?"

※※※ ※※※

Ophelia lay in her bed and focused on her stitching. It was all she could do from Helsingør, while she waited for the news to roll in.

The world was all wrong, or rather, it was all right again. She could no longer see the Corruption, could no longer sense it. Everything felt very quiet without it. There was so much more space in her room without the creeping tendrils of purple hiding in the corners.

"Ophelia, you're awake!"

It was Father. He was beaming beneath his bushy moustache, and when he hugged her she could taste metal in her mouth.

Father had not protected her as he should have. She felt so angry—so furious at all the things she couldn't tell him. All the secrets she had to hide, because Mother and Father never truly knew each other. Ophelia sat still as Father hugged her, and she waited for him to pull away.

"My dear," he said, clasping her hands. "Don't fret. I know it's painful, to have an engagement end at such an advanced stage—"

Ophelia let out a high, cold laugh.

She laughed and she laughed, until it turned into a river of tears.

Father did not hold her. He didn't even raise a hand to comfort her. He just stared at her like she was a stranger, a monster in his daughter's bed.

Ophelia felt her heart shatter.

Elsewhere, a battle came to a shuddering end.

SCENE TEN
hamlet

*B*urning. The air stank of it, the bedclothes, the bandages they wrapped his wounds in. Hamlet couldn't seem to escape it. He tossed and turned in a kind of shadow-land, and he could not seem to force himself to leave it. Hands landed upon his skin; he half-woke sometimes and saw shadows flitting in the corners of his vision, but whether they were human or beast he could not say.

He did not know how long he was in that state. Something drew him from it: a softness of the light, an absence of the smell of smoke. There was a soft cloth dabbing at his forehead, leaving behind the comfortable clamminess of cool water on his skin.

Hamlet opened his eyes, and Horatio looked back. Rivulets of water ran down his wrist from the cloth, dripping into the basin he held in his lap. Hamlet traced the droplets, watching them track their way down bare skin, their leap back into the bowl. Horatio's skin. Horatio's hands. Horatio's eyes, settling on him with that unsettling knowing.

Hamlet swallowed and felt instantly sickened; his mouth, now flooded with saliva, tasted as if something had died in it.

"Am I captured?" he asked, his tongue thick in his mouth.

"It's worse than that," Horatio said with a sardonic twist to his mouth. "I'm a turncoat."

Hamlet laughed so hard he nearly fell from the bed, despite his aches and pains. He laughed until he coughed up a disgusting globule of congealed blood, which splattered over the furs in his lap, wine-red. A faint purple aura shimmered over it, then died.

Hamlet pulled his attention from the grim sight. "Is the king dead?" he asked. "I assume Norway lost. I remember Fortinbras calling for a retreat. Rosencrantz and Guildenstern—"

"King Fortinbras died on the battlefield this morning," Horatio confirmed. "They say it was your father who struck the killing blow, but I saw it with my own eyes. It was you."

Hamlet breathed a sigh, half-relief, half-despair. The old man was dead. He had done it, with his own hand: something he could not seem to comprehend. The gravity of taking a life seemed just out of reach.

"Arion lives, I believe," said Horatio. A shadow passed over his face. "Both sides lost many soldiers, but Norway's losses were certainly greater."

Hamlet nodded. "And Arion?" The name tasted wrong in his mouth, too familiar. Not after what he had done. "Is he King Arion Fortinbras now?"

Horatio pulled a face. "His uncle was elected as soon as the news reached Ánslo." The shadows under Horatio's eyes were smoothed by the daylight, Hamlet noticed. He looked, somehow, more well-rested than he ever had in Wittenberg. "Your father was kind enough to grant me amnesty."

Struggling to his elbows, Hamlet asked, "What will you do now?"

And what am I to do? he wanted to ask. Whatever tension existed between them, whatever rivalry, whatever conflict, it felt suddenly reduced. At the end of it all, here they sat: Hamlet and Horatio. Fortinbras was gone. Rosencrantz and Guildenstern were not by his bedside.

"I thought I might go back to Wittenberg now that the war is over. I have little desire to overstay my welcome."

"I never thought you'd leave his side," Hamlet said. He reached for his water, and was surprised when Horatio instead held the cup to his lips and helped him to drink.

Horatio focused his attention on the cup, not meeting his eyes. "Nor did I."

Hamlet breathed hard, his battered ribs moving in and out from the exertion of swallowing. He watched Horatio, convinced that if he looked at him for long enough, he would be able to see through him to the mechanism of his brain, its complicated alchemy, its automaton cogs and wheels.

"He used magic in battle," said Horatio. "He promised me he wouldn't." Horatio looked at the bedsheets, his forehead wrinkling. "I suppose we're allies now, of a sort."

"I suppose," Hamlet said. "Against Fortinbras, yes."

"And the only thing we have in common is that we were both in love with him." Horatio snorted. "What an alliance we've forged, Prince Hamlet."

Hamlet did not disagree. They sat a while and discussed fruitless things: the layout of the field now that the battle had come to an end, the whereabouts of various lords and knights, when the army might pack up and leave for Denmark.

A light breeze stirred the pale cloth walls of the tent. His stomach growled. The sensations of normal life were coming back to him, bit by bit. He could almost forget about the nightmarish monsters on the battlefield and pretend none of it had ever happened. The result of Rosencrantz's potion must have been temporary, he realised. He was not, in fact, going insane.

Then a servant flitted in with his head down and Hamlet flinched at the sight of his dark purple aura, flickering and pulsing in thick, encrusted patches over his body.

Not gone, then. He turned his eyes to Horatio, who was talking about something to do with Wittenberg masters and their lessons. There was no sign of the Corruption that plagued the rest of the world. Horatio was… clean.

"I'll go to Wittenberg tomorrow, by your leave," said Horatio. He stood up to leave, placing the basin to one side.

"You don't need my leave." Hamlet tried his best to smile. "In fact, I owe you an apology. Perhaps many apologies. I only wish you were staying long enough for me to make them standing up."

Horatio smiled back. "I humbly accept at least one of your apologies," he said. "It feels as if… we were children at Wittenberg. It does not feel like that now."

He was right. Hamlet smiled wider. Something in his chest lightened. He was just about to bid Horatio goodbye and stretch out his hand to shake when the other man's face darkened.

"Before I depart," said Horatio, tweaking his glasses, as if he needed something to do with his hands. "There's something you should know."

He described standing outside a tent at night. He recalled a stranger coming out of the trees, dressed from head to toe in black. He had known that figure at once—the tilt of his head beneath his hood, the glint of his glasses, his unusual eyes.

"Rosencrantz," Horatio said bitterly. "I'm sorry, Prince Hamlet."

Hal's fingers tightened on the sheets. "He wouldn't," he said pointlessly, knowing he was wrong.

"To be entirely fair to Rosencrantz," Horatio murmured, "the offer was a good one. A letter of safe passage, I'm told. It remains valid for as long as he needs it."

"No offer is worth what we had," Hamlet snapped. He pressed a hand to his aching forehead. "I would have *died*—I should have known. I knew, in fact. I'm sorry, Horatio. I—I tire."

Horatio's hand was very cool against his own. He squeezed once and let go, and the blood rushed to heat

Hal's skin where Horatio's fingers had just been. "I understand," he said. "Rest. Perhaps I'll see you again one day."

"You will always be welcome in Helsingør," Hamlet said. "And I will see you in Wittenberg, if I ever return."

Horatio left with a wave and a smile, stepping out into the bright day beyond the tent flaps. Hamlet lay there a while longer, staring up at the canvas ceiling. Rosencrantz and Guildenstern would not leave his mind. All their nights in the Wittenberg house, or stumbling through darkened streets, staring at the sky, felt like a lie.

Hamlet had assumed the best of them without knowing anything of their hearts. Perhaps the consequences were his burden to bear.

He knew without question that Guildenstern had known, had always known, for as long as Rosencrantz was working with the King of Norway. Always he had felt that closeness between Ros and Guild, had reached for it, a flower straining for the sun. He craved the devotion they had to each other and they had given it to him, yes, but only in the tiniest droplets, just enough that he might taste its honeysuckle sweetness and crave it again.

A rival theory crowded Hal's mind, one that ached more, yet felt more true. Maybe Guildenstern had tried to warn him—with his distance, his careful phrasing, his avoidance. Maybe he felt guilty. Maybe he didn't want to get too close, in case he might remember who the three of them were before the war swept them into its embrace.

Hamlet rode at the head of the caravan when they left the battlefield, his head in cloth bandages and his arms covered in cuts and scrapes.

I hope this kills you like it kills me, Hamlet thought. With the last of the magic that fizzled in his veins, he reached for Rosencrantz and Guildenstern. He felt nothing, but he hoped somehow his words might reach them, or at least the feeling behind them. *I hope you know I loved you, truly. And I would never have hurt you as you hurt me.*

When the castle came into view over the hill, he felt his eyes fill with tears. He pulled on the reins and rode fast and hard, and he let out a whoop of wild, frenzied joy. The lords and knights who rode behind him echoed his cry. His father laughed, and Hamlet heard him jolt his own horse into action.

As the horns blew and the flags were raised to signal their victory, as the cheers rose up around him and the gates swung open to welcome him, Hamlet felt something approaching joy.

FINALE
ophelia

Hamlet was different after the war.

He did not seem unhappy, but instead strangely energetic, as if he was constantly waiting on the edge of some unknown moment that might ask him for an immediate response. He flinched often, usually at loud noises, often at children crying. He avoided crowds, and he spent most nights wandering the halls or sitting in his library flipping sightlessly through endless pages.

He also kept secrets.

Ophelia could feel them lying between them, in the place where her own secrets also lingered. She tried her best to keep Claudius' name from her lips, and when Hamlet spoke of suppers with his uncle or long rides through the forest together, she turned her attention to blank spots on the wall and waited for him to finish.

They pretended last winter was wiped clean. They pretended nothing had ever happened, and they told each other very little of any consequence, and slowly they started to become friends again.

They sat by the docks sometimes as they had before the war. They could spend hours sitting there in companionable silence, their little fingers only a millimetre apart, watching the ships being unloaded.

He seemed disinterested in everything, except whatever he was searching for in those old books. Something was bothering him, something he would not share, and until he had it figured out, nothing else would be able to penetrate his thoughts. Ophelia did not like this new, strange tension between them. They weren't enemies, but they were a far cry from friends.

But on this fateful day in the middle of a long, hot, drawn-out summer, there was a dance. Ophelia had managed to coax him as far as one of the gardens, where they stationed two guards so that no one could intrude. Even so, Hamlet kept glancing over.

Between glances he seemed happy. He was even smiling, and it was almost the smile she'd missed so much for so long.

"It's getting cooler again, thank god," he said. His freckles were fainter this year than any year before. "I can't abide this heat any longer."

Ophelia smiled back at him and hoped that her thoughts did not shine through. She was happy, so happy. *And yet here we sit, talking of weather and seasons like strangers.* "I like the warmth," she said. "I'll be sad to see it go."

"Would you like to go inside?" he asked. His gaze drew upwards, towards the sky streaked with the bloody blush of a sunset. "You must be getting chilly. Have my cloak, if you—"

A scream cut through the air, and Ophelia's blood turned to ice in her veins.

"Mother," Hamlet whispered, and gathered himself up off the ground. "Mother!"

Ophelia ran after him, tearing through the gardens. Everywhere they passed people who were turning towards that horrible noise, that ear-splitting sound that stopped once, only for a second, and then carried on and came back, so violent the queen's throat sounded as if it might burst.

The passage to the king's private gardens was open. Two guards stood outside, blocking a crowd. Hamlet ran straight through, but they stopped Ophelia and held her at arm's length.

"You have to stay outside," one of them said, clenching his jaw. In the moment of panic, all the carefully-constructed coldness of a palace guard was chipped away, replaced by panic. "I'm sorry, but you can't—"

From the garden, a wail of sorrow came that broke Ophelia's heart.

And then, worst of all, Claudius emerged from the sun-washed, tree-lined pavilion. He stood in the doorway in front of the crowd, his robes in disarray, his hair wild as if he had been running his hands through it in a frenzy. Hamlet wailed again.

"I'm terribly sorry to be the one to tell you this," Claudius said, and gently he closed the doors to the garden, muffling the sounds of grief that still echoed through the corridor. "But the king is dead."

[Exeunt.]

Acknowledgements

I've dreaded writing my acknowledgements since the day I decided to publish *Smile and Be a Villain*. I dread missing someone, because this book was written across such a long period of time; I feel like I've lived three lives since I started this story in 2021, and even then, it really started in the summer of 2015, when I read Hamlet for the first time and found a lifelong love.

Thank you to everyone who beta read this book in all its various forms, from 2021 to 2024; I couldn't possibly list all of you, but know that your comments, questions, enthusiasm, and love for this book has fuelled this process from beginning to end.

My wonderful cover artist Mia Carnevale (@carnemia on Instagram) brought this book to life in a way I never could have imagined. It's been an honour to have her work on *Smile*.

This book would never have been finished if it wasn't for Sharon Choe and Kamilah Cole, who I look up to as my Author Big Siblings. I've learned so much from you, and your endless support and advice and willingness to accept it when I vanish off the face of the earth for months doesn't go unnoticed. I love you both!

My housemates, Harriet and Lou, have put up with more Hamlet-talk than anyone ever should. Also Hannah, Maggie, and Rob, who have dutifully asked how my book is going many times and politely looked away when I unhinged my jaw to scream. Georgia, thank you for the 200 Degrees writing sessions, without which I would never *ever* have finished my edits.

Lucy, thanks for the drinks and the chats and being my adopted child even though you're only a couple of years younger than me. Nanami, thanks for the character art and making me have fun every once in a while instead of acting like a retiree. Nikita, I love you and am begging you to come back from the US. Thanks for listening to me rant about Hamlet and my dating life, which have sometimes felt like similar levels of tragedy.

I also have to thank my mom, who didn't lose her mind when I insisted on spending every single COVID-walk for months talking about my weird Hamlet book. I think you might have told me to go ahead and put magic in it just to shut me up, but it made the story *much* better.

Thank you for putting up with me (and for the love and support and all that other stuff too).

To the English teachers who encouraged me, and to the lecturers at Trinity College Dublin and the University of York who pushed me to become a better academic: I hope you're happy that this is what years of research training has produced.

Thank you to everyone who ever asked me how my book was going. I'm so grateful for the questions, the jokes, the Hamlet memes, the suggestions, the laughs, the hugs, and the joy.

And finally: I held this book in my heart for so long. Now it belongs to you, Reader. Thanks for sharing this journey with me.

About the Author

Yves Donlon is an Irish writer based in York, England. They've been writing queer, angsty fiction for a long time, but *Smile and Be a Villain* is their first published novel. A medievalist and archaeologist, they spend most of their time thinking about dead people and going on day trips to heritage sites, where they *always* rate the scones.

Milton Keynes UK
Ingram Content Group UK Ltd.
UKHW010900080424
440801UK00001B/27

9 798223 548１